Light, Which Impresses

Other Books by Dorothy P. Ward

Organizing for Student Success: The University College Model

A Novel

by Dorothy P. Ward

Fort Worth, Texas

Library of Congress Cataloging-in-Publication Data

Names: Ward, Dorothy P. author
Title: Light, which impresses : a novel / Dorothy P. Ward.
Description: Fort Worth, Texas : TCU Press, [2025] | Includes
    bibliographical references. | Summary: ""She was extraordinary," Sarah
    Delaney says of the young soldadera-a female revolutionary soldier-who
    stares confidently from a framed black and white photo that hangs in
    Sarah's home. Sarah, known as a "bit of a recluse," is famed for her
    photographs of the 1910-1920 Mexican Revolution. At ninety-one, she
    suddenly reached out to Kayla Carlson and Abel Castellano from the Oral
    History Program at The University of Texas at El Paso, inviting them to
    her home to interview her and learn about her life in the border city of
    El Paso, Texas, during the Mexican Revolution"-- Provided by publisher.
Identifiers: LCCN 2025016907 (print) | LCCN 2025016908 (ebook) | ISBN
    9780875659398 paperback | ISBN 9780875659299 ebook
Subjects: LCSH: El Paso (Tex.)--History--20th century--Fiction |
    Mexican-American Border Region--History--20th century--Fiction |
    Mexico--History--Revolution, 1910-1920--Social aspects--Fiction | LCGFT:
    Historical fiction | Novels
Classification: LCC PS3623.A73175 L54 2025 (print) | LCC PS3623.A73175
    (ebook) | DDC 813/.6--dc23/eng/20250507
LC record available at https://lccn.loc.gov/2025016907
LC ebook record available at https://lccn.loc.gov/2025016908

Illustrations by LadadikArt, Adobe Stock.

TCU Box 298300
Fort Worth, Texas 76129
www.tcupress.com

For my parents,
Jim and Jo Ward,
whose love remains a force in my life

The first thing to remember is that the light which impresses the photographic image upon the sensitive film in a fraction of a second when it comes through the lens, can destroy the film as quickly as it makes the picture.

—*Picture taking with the No. 3A Autographic Kodak*

CONTENTS

Part Four

Part Five

PART
ONE

AUGUST 16, 1983

Kayla

"She was extraordinary."

Startled by the voice, Kayla turned from studying the framed black-and-white photograph of a young female warrior, a soldadera of the Mexican Revolution.

"I'm Sarah Delaney." The elderly woman who had entered the room extended her hand in greeting. She looked from Kayla to the photograph and repeated, "She was extraordinary."

The strength of the old woman's handshake surprised Kayla. "I'm Kayla Carlson. It's a pleasure to meet you in person, Ms. Delaney. This is my colleague, Abel Castellano." Kayla directed her attention to a young, bearded man who stepped forward to shake the hand extended to him.

"Honored to meet you, ma'am."

"I hope you don't mind that your housekeeper let us in," Kayla said.

"Not at all. Welcome to my home," Sarah replied graciously.

Tilting her head toward the photograph, Kayla said, "I'm very familiar with your photography from the Mexican Revolution, but I don't recall ever seeing this powerful picture."

The old woman quietly studied the image of the young soldadera. Then, releasing a sigh, she turned to Kayla. "You are correct. You have never seen this photo. It's a personal photograph. She's a personal history."

The woman's reply piqued Kayla's curiosity, but before she could question further, Sarah said, "Please come into the living room and have a seat."

Kayla followed the elderly woman into a sunlit room decorated with bouquets of large, colorful crepe-paper flowers. She settled into an armchair across from the renowned photographer.

"Ms. Delaney . . ."

"Call me Sarah."

"Okay, thank you. I must tell you, Sarah, that Abel and I were thrilled when you called the Institute of Oral History at The University of Texas at El Paso and invited us to interview you about your life in El Paso during the Mexican Revolution. We have long admired your photography from that period, but even in our wildest imaginings, we never expected a phone call from you! When you identified yourself, we were shocked."

"Because you thought I was long dead!"

Sarah's rich guttural laugh surprised Kayla, and though she stammered to dismiss the accusation, it was, in fact, true. Kayla knew of Sarah's reputation as a bit of a recluse. Sarah's years of refusing to grant interviews or attend openings of photographic exhibits featuring her work had long fueled rumors among historians and critics alike of her failing health. The vigor of the elderly woman seated in front of Kayla countered all such speculations about Sarah's exit through death's door.

"At ninety-one, I probably should be in the grave," Sarah chuckled, "which is why we better start recording today."

"Wonderful! Abel will set up the video camera and lights, and we'll get started." Kayla nodded for Abel to collect the equipment from the entryway. "Just out of curiosity," Kayla returned her attention to Sarah, "what made you contact us for an interview?"

"Because my history isn't limited to the past." Without further explanation, Sarah pushed to a stand, and walked over to watch Abel work.

Kayla studied her. Sarah did not look her ninety-one years. Still a handsome woman, she wore a red-and-white striped shirt with the collar turned up at the back, creating a sporty look. Her short hair, though largely gray, still bore strands of brown. Petite, she stood without the stooped shoulders that years often awarded people her age, though Kayla did notice a stiffness to Sarah's step when she returned to the chair.

Once Abel adjusted the position of the lights, he nodded to Kayla. "I think we're ready."

"Before we begin filming, let me say again, Sarah, that it is such a privilege to interview you. Your firsthand account of El Paso during the Mexican Revolution will be an invaluable addition to our oral history library."

"Well," Sarah replied, "then we both have something to gain from reopening the past."

"Good," Kayla answered, choosing not to delve deeper. "Then we'll begin." Leaning forward in the chair, she explained, "The way this interview will work is that I'll ask a question to initiate the session. We want you to share your experiences during the period of the Mexican Revolution."

Sarah nodded.

"I may occasionally ask additional questions for clarification or to further mine a topic, but your life experiences will guide the interview." She paused, then smiled at Sarah. "Ready to begin?"

Sarah gripped the arms of the chair. "I'm ready." She hesitated before adding, "You know, of course, that my memories are only part of the story. My life is like unforwarded film, with the images of one photograph superimposed upon another."

"Of course. We understand," Kayla answered. "Are you ready to begin *your* story?"

"I'm ready." She then added, "I'm ready to return to the past."

"Okay, Abel."

Abel raised his left hand and pointed to indicate the start of filming.

Speaking in a businesslike tone, Kayla stated, "Sarah Delaney interview, El Paso, Texas, 10:15 a.m., August 16, 1983." Smiling, she turned her attention to Sarah and, in what she hoped was a warm, conversational manner, asked, "Sarah, how did you first become interested in photography?"

Without pause, Sarah answered, "Samuel. Captain Samuel Clendenin."

APRIL 1911

Sarah

As Sarah entered the boardinghouse, her landlady, Mrs. Warren, greeted her. "A delivery man left a package for you." Mrs. Warren stood holding a box wrapped in paper and ribbon. "He was quite insistent that you receive this package today."

"Thank you, Mrs. Warren." Sarah took the box and prepared to mount the stairs to her room.

"He made me promise I would give it to you personally. Wonder what it could be," the landlady called after her.

"I don't know. Thank you, again, Mrs. Warren," Sarah answered as she climbed the stairs. At her room, she shifted the parcel to one arm, freeing a hand to unlock the door. Entering the small space, she set the box on the center of the bed, then removed her hat and placed it on the bureau. The bed springs squeaked with her weight as she sat to examine the package wrapped in lavender-colored paper and secured with purple ribbon. She paused for a moment to admire the rich colors, then removed the gift wrap to disclose a red box with gold lettering that identified the contents: No. 3A Folding Pocket Kodak. An envelope rested on top of the box. Sarah opened it and removed a card picturing a sprig of lavender and the sentiment "Birthday Joy." The back of the card read, *12:30 tomorrow in front of the Angelus Café. Bring your camera. Samuel.*

❊❊❊

"Ready for an adventure?" Samuel asked as they exited the café.

"Yes!" Sarah placed her hand on the crook of his arm, wondering what he had planned.

Samuel positioned the brown Stetson on his head, covering thick red hair combed straight back.

Sarah felt Samuel briefly touch the small of her back to guide her across the street. He stopped beside a black Model T and motioned with his outstretched hand. "Your ride, Miss Delaney."

Sarah looked at Samuel to see if he was jesting. He responded by reaching into the cab of the auto to switch a lever on the dash. Sarah watched as he adjusted something under the vehicle's hood before moving to the front of the car to crank-start it.

Once they were both seated, Sarah asked, "Where did you get the automobile, Captain Clendenin?"

"I hired it for the afternoon." He glanced at the road, then steered smoothly onto Mesa Avenue, adding, "After all, you only have one nineteenth birthday."

"And where are you taking me?"

"To Madero's camp." He turned to grin at her. "You've been wanting to see the camp, so today's the day, while peace negotiations continue. You can see the glamorous life I've been living."

Unable to conceal her excitement, Sarah clapped her hands and raised them to her lips. The Mexican Revolution had been the talk in El Paso for months. Daily, the newspapers were full of stories about battles in nearby locations, and the city was full of reporters from across the US covering the revolution.

Sarah knew that Samuel had come to El Paso from San Francisco at the start of the year to join Madero's rebellion against the Mexican dictator Porfirio Díaz. She met Samuel soon after he had enlisted into La Falange de los Extranjeros, or the Foreign Legion, a company in Madero's army consisting of soldiers of fortune as well as men who, like Samuel, sought adventure, a change of lifestyle, and, as Samuel would say, "a good cause for which to fight."

Sarah had moved to El Paso a few months prior to meeting Samuel, relocating from a small farming community southeast of El Paso soon after her father drank himself to death, inconsolable over the passing of her mother the previous year. It was just after Sarah moved to the city in November that she fully understood how only a narrow, shallow river physically separated El Paso from Juárez, and how brief international bridges connected the two cities and two countries. At the time of her arrival, El Paso was already abuzz with anticipation of revolutionary battles and intrigue.

Samuel shared news of the battles through occasional letters he sent her from the field and stories he told upon his return to the El Paso–Juárez area, but he relayed little about the actual fighting and said almost nothing about his role. Sarah followed news of the skirmishes through the local newspapers. But unlike many in El Paso who viewed the potential fight for control of Juárez as great theater, she dreaded it, fearing for Samuel's safety. Still, visiting Madero's camp today held considerable excitement. She had read in the newspaper about the insurrecto encampment that stretched along the Rio Grande, read about the small adobe house that served as Madero's headquarters, and about the grove of cottonwood trees the newspapers referred to as "Peace Grove" because of the negotiations taking place there. She looked forward to seeing these sites.

The warm wind felt good against her face, and Sarah reached to replace a strand of hair that escaped from under her hat. Suddenly, she had a thought that made her uncomfortable. "Samuel, what if fighting breaks out while we're in the camp?"

"Well, grab a rifle and start shooting." Samuel did not take his eyes from the road. After a moment of feigned seriousness, he laughed, took her hand, and placed it to his lips. "There is an armistice. No fighting. You're safe. I promise." He smiled his reassurance.

As they traveled along the road toward the brick plant, Sarah could see people on both sides of the river. Newspaper articles had described crowds gathering to watch and cheer the insurrectos as the rebels went about their daily business, but she was surprised by the large number of spectators on the US side, which only increased the closer they got to the footbridge at the brick plant.

"Are there always spectators?"

"Yes, some days more than others." Samuel turned the steering wheel, carefully maneuvering the car to the side of the road, stopping within a short distance of the suspension bridge. "Today the crowd is particularly large."

Samuel and Sarah exited the vehicle. Cupping her elbow, he asked, "Ready?"

"Wait. I want the first photograph I take to be of you."

Samuel protested, but Sarah insisted. "Stand beside the automobile." She backed a short distance away and removed the camera from the leather case slung over her left shoulder. She depressed the button to release the bed of the camera and used the metal tab to lower and lock the bed into place. Squeezing the release on either side of the lens, she extended the red leather bellows and raised the viewfinder. She set the speed, stop, and distance, stabilized the camera against her body, and peered down into the viewfinder, just as the camera's manual had instructed.

"You look like a professional photographer."

"Be quiet and still," she ordered. Once she centered Samuel and the automobile in the viewfinder, she depressed the exposure lever. "My first photograph!"

"You could have selected a better subject," Samuel grumbled. "You ready now?"

She forwarded the film, folded and returned the camera to its case, then took Samuel's arm, announcing, "Ready."

They crossed the road, joining the throng of people moving toward the suspension bridge or to the riverbank. The crowd was a mix of men, women, and children, with many of the men carrying jackets they had removed due to the heat of the day and women holding parasols for protection from the sun. The visitors' excitement seemed incongruous with the reality of an armed camp poised at the edge of Juárez and on the verge of a potential battle for the leadership of a nation. Many in the crowd called encouragement across the river to the insurrectos, shouting, "Viva Madero! Viva México!" The Americans tossed apples, oranges, and coins to the rebel soldiers, who waded into the river to catch the offerings. Others in the crowd passed field glasses back and forth, in hopes of glimpsing Madero, Orozco, or one of the other revolutionary leaders.

At the base of the suspension bridge, Samuel took Sarah's arm to assist her as she mounted the steps. She felt the footbridge sway slightly with her weight.

Sarah alternated between monitoring her foot placement on the rough bridge and looking at the camp that spread across the desert landscape before her. The size of the encampment and the amount of activity amazed her. At the end of the bridge, Samuel took her elbow as she descended the steep wooden steps.

"Oh, Samuel," she spoke softly, "this is so exciting."

He guided her into the camp, into the midst of insurrectos, many who wore bandoliers crisscrossing their chests, ammunition belts encircling their waists, or both. Some carried rifles, and some carried canteens to the river; some were on foot, and some were on horseback. Many wore sombreros of various brim widths and crown heights; others wore Stetsons with brims flat or upturned. The rebel troops had no uniform and no consistency in their dress.

Moving deeper into camp, Sarah saw clusters of women. Most were preparing food around a fire, some had babies nestled in a rebozo, or shawl, tied to the mother's body; others had small children playing in the sand at their feet. Some of the women wore bandoliers across their chests and ammunition belts around their waists, similar to the men. These were the camp followers, the soldaderas Samuel spoke of with respect. Samuel had told her how the women followed their men from battle to battle, gathering and preparing food, caring for the wounded, providing "marital comfort," birthing and raising children, and picking up a rifle to fight, as needed.

Sarah also noted that visitors from El Paso crowded the camp. Reporters recorded information on slim pocket notebooks, and professional as well as amateur photographers snapped pictures of posed and of natural camp scenes. Sarah studied a stylishly dressed woman wearing elbow-length gloves and an oversized straw boater with a large bow at the back; the woman sat sidesaddle atop a horse. She wore a borrowed bandolier across her chest, a pistol strapped to her hip; she gripped a rifle waist high as though ready to raise it to a fighting position if necessary. Staged at the head and rear of the horse stood an insurrecto soldier, wearing a large sombrero and holding a rifle. A photographer counted aloud, "One, two, three," then depressed the pushpin of the cable release. "Got it," he declared. "Beautiful!"

The woman looked at Sarah and smiled her excitement. "This is great fun. You should be next."

Sarah smiled and shook her head to decline the offer. When she indicated to Samuel she was ready to move on, she heard the photographer announce, "A quarter for a photo postcard to commemorate your visit to the Madero camp. Just a quarter and you'll have a photograph that will make you the envy of all your friends."

As they began to walk away, a voice called, "Captain Clendenin!" They turned toward a man Sarah immediately recognized from newspaper descriptions and photos; he wore his distinctive green velour hat with the downturned brim.

"Colonel Garibaldi," Samuel greeted.

As the man strode toward them, he said, "Well, introduce me to this lovely young lady." He spoke in a formal English tinged by an Italian accent. The unbuttoned jacket and knotted tie he wore blew loosely about as he walked briskly to them, kicking up dust around his knee-high leather boots laced to secure tucked pant legs.

"Colonel Garibaldi," Samuel responded proudly, "this is my sweetheart, Miss Sarah Delaney. Sarah, this is my commander, Colonel Giuseppe Garibaldi II."

"It is my pleasure to meet you." Garibaldi bowed, took Sarah's hand, and with great formality, raised it to his lips.

"Samuel speaks often of you, Colonel Garibaldi."

"I'm sure not nearly as often as he speaks to me of you, and please, call me Peppino." He smiled, his white teeth peeking beneath a carefully trimmed moustache. "And explain to me what such a lovely girl sees in such an ugly lout." He struck Samuel's arm playfully with the back of his hand.

"Well," Sarah hesitated.

"Don't answer that question, Miss Delaney. I'm sure Samuel is a wonderful beau," he smiled at Samuel before continuing, "if you like tall, lanky red-haired men. In fact, Miss Delaney, may I borrow Samuel for a moment? I promise I won't keep him from you for long."

"Of course."

"Will you be okay?" Samuel asked.

"Yes, of course."

"I won't be long. Don't stray far."

The men walked just out of earshot. Sarah noticed that Samuel positioned himself to keep an eye on her, but soon the two men leaned toward one another in private conversation. Sarah removed her camera from its case and photographed them.

Sarah scouted her surroundings. An extended family sharing a meal caught her eye. There were four men, one appearing to be the father; the others ranged in age from late teens to early twenties. Two females served the men, handing them food from a comal, or griddle, that rested on two large stones in the fire pit. The older of the two was pregnant and moved about with an unhappy exhaustion. Near her, a child about two years old played in the sand. The other girl seemed sixteen or seventeen years of age. She engaged in animated banter with one of the younger men, resulting in outbursts of laughter from them all. Sarah studied the girl. She wore a light-colored blouse tucked into a long billowing skirt decorated with a vertical pattern of darts and, wrapped around her shoulders, a dark blue rebozo. Tall and slender, the girl wore her hair in an unruly knot at the nape of her neck. Sarah felt drawn to the energy of that campsite, so she walked toward the gathering. The men turned to face Sarah.

"Buenas tardes, good afternoon," Sarah greeted.

"Buenas tardes," the older man replied.

Sarah noticed the girl had moved to squat beside the fire.

Aware that all eyes were on her, Sarah raised the camera. "Me da permiso?"

The older man nodded his approval.

Sarah nervously stepped back to center the campsite in her viewfinder. Just as she depressed the exposure lever, the girl moved her hand, as if shooing a fly from her face.

Sarah lowered the camera. "Gracias."

"De nada," replied the older man.

Sarah turned from the campsite, spying an odd-looking mesquite. She walked closer and shuddered. Skewered to thorns, more than two dozen headless rattlesnakes decorated branches of the stunted tree.

Sarah startled at Samuel's voice behind her. "They'll be skinned and cooked for food."

"Ugh," Sarah replied.

"You'd be surprised. Snake meat is really quite tasty."

"No thank you," she answered, positioning the camera to photograph the grisly sight.

"Come."

Samuel took Sarah's arm after she finished taking the photograph, guiding her farther into the camp. He pointed to a group of about eight men who stood atop a small hill watching the activity before them. All had long, untucked shirts, and while most wore pants, some wore only a loincloth. They all wore huaraches, leather sandals. A few held rifles; the rest of the men carried bows and arrows.

"These are Tarahumara Indians who serve under Garibaldi's command," Samuel explained. "They're fierce fighters and tremendous runners. They often serve as messengers because they can race tirelessly for miles." Samuel raised his hand in greeting.

"Do you think they'd let me photograph them?"

"I'll ask."

Sarah stayed back while Samuel climbed the hill to communicate with the men. He waved her forward, moving to assist her up the hill. When she neared the group, the Tarahumara displayed their armaments by notching arrows on bowstrings or kneeling on one knee to sight shouldered rifles. They maintained gravely serious stares until Sarah called out "Gracias" after taking the photograph.

Samuel patted the arm of one man to signal his appreciation, then rejoined Sarah.

"You have quite an interesting mix of soldiers in this camp."

"We also have Yaqui Indians. Under Díaz's rule, the Indians have lost their lands and have been enslaved to work in mines and on plantations."

Suddenly, the sound of a band playing the Mexican national anthem interrupted their conversation.

"Let's see what this is all about," Samuel said.

Inhabitants and visitors of the camp began moving toward the river, drawn by the music. Sarah held Samuel's arm through the thickening crowd. When they reached the outskirts of their destination, Samuel inserted himself to move them to the front of the gathering.

Sarah recognized Concha's Mexican Concert Band. She also recognized La Casita Gris, the small adobe house that served as Madero's headquarters. She knew the structure from newspaper photographs, which dubbed the building "the provisional capital of México." At the front of the little house stood a small wooden shade festooned with green, white, and red banners—the colors of the Mexican flag. Positioned along the edge of the covering, smaller flags waved in the breeze. Beside the door, a Tri-State Bell Telephone sign was affixed to the adobe structure. Sarah smiled, remembering reading in the newspaper that Madero received free telephone service in exchange for the advertisement. Sarah took a photo of the structure with its decorations, telephone advertisement, and men milling about in front.

"The gentleman standing at the edge of the covering to the right by the post," Samuel leaned to her ear so that she could hear him over the music. "See him? That's Francisco Madero."

Sarah studied the leader, who stood at stiff attention. Initially surprised by his short stature, she remembered reading that he stood only five foot two. Coming from a wealthy family, he appeared dressed more for a leisurely horseback ride in a park than for leading a revolution. He wore a tan, whipcord suit, his riding breeches tucked into knee-high leather boots, the collar of his shirt neatly secured by a knotted tie tucked beneath a buttoned Norfolk jacket. His dress included a flat-brimmed campaign hat with a wide green, white, and red band around the base of the pinched crown. Sarah adjusted the distance on her camera to bring him into better focus, then took the photo as he looked in her direction, studying the crowd.

When the band concluded the anthem, Madero stepped from under the shade, applauded the musicians, and then, with a raised right hand, signaled for silence. The crowd responded almost immediately.

Madero's voice had a high-pitched quality as he spoke loudly to be heard by the gathering. His arms behind his back, he presented a commanding presence, captivating his audience.

"He's thanking the band. He's thanking the supporters from the United States." Sarah turned to see Garibaldi, who had positioned himself behind them. Garibaldi smiled and continued his loose translation. "He's thanking the revolutionary forces fighting for their country, for democratic elections, for a one-term presidency, for a better life for themselves and their children." Garibaldi paused to listen, then continued, "He says we must end the tyranny of Díaz's thirty-one years in office, a period that has seen México's wealth stolen from the many to enrich the few." He paused once more. "Madero is encouraged by the peace negotiations and believes they will result in Porfirio Díaz resigning the presidency because the revolution will accept nothing less, the people of Mexíco will accept nothing less."

Madero concluded with a raised fist and a shout of "Viva México!"

The crowd roared in response: "Viva México! Viva Madero!"

Madero waved in reply before returning to the adobe house. The band struck up a rousing military march.

"Viva la Revolución," Garibaldi added in a conversational tone. "Captain Clendenin, Miss Delaney," he bowed, "I will return for the honor of a dance should the music selection become less militaristic." He tipped his hat and walked to the front of the adobe building to join a tall, power-fully-built man dressed in a dark suit and tie. The two immediately engaged in conversation while looking out at the crowd.

"That's General Pascual Orozco," Samuel informed Sarah.

Orozco, wearing a black high-crowned Stetson, stood a head taller than Garibaldi.

Sarah watched a third man join the two.

"That's Colonel Francisco 'Pancho' Villa," Samuel identified. "He doesn't smoke, and he doesn't drink, but I bet he has a bag of peanut brittle tucked in a pocket."

Sarah studied the man to whom Samuel referred. He measured the same height as Garibaldi, but he was thickly built. He wore a khaki suit without the tie worn by the other two men, and his flat-brimmed Stetson, positioned at the back of his head, exposed wiry black hair. Slightly bow-legged and slightly pigeon-toed, Villa stood as if rooted to the ground when he threw back his head in laughter at something Garibaldi said.

Sarah raised her camera to capture a photograph of the three insurrec-to leaders engaged in conversation.

Samuel leaned to Sarah's ear and shared, "Orozco and Villa came to Madero's army with troops they recruited. Their soldiers are loyal to Madero, but their first loyalties are to their commanders. In fact, they iden-tify themselves as gente de Villa, Villa's people, or gente de Orozco."

Sarah nodded her understanding, continuing to study the three leaders as she folded the camera and returned it to the case.

The band concluded the military march and launched into a waltz that drew an appreciative murmur from the audience. A few couples moved from the fringes of the crowd to dance. Sarah glanced furtively in the direction of the adobe house and glimpsed Garibaldi striding in her direction. Sarah tugged Samuel's arm.

"What?"

"Let's dance."

"Sarah, I'm no dancer."

"Please, Samuel, before Garibaldi reaches us."

Samuel demonstrated his understanding of her plea by taking her right hand in his left, placing his other hand above her waist, then moving away from the crowd and to the music.

They were awkward in their waltz, having never danced together. They moved stiffly in each other's arms. Samuel looking about uncomfortably—his eyes glancing anywhere but at hers. When he stepped solidly on her foot, he stopped, red-faced, stammering his apology.

Sarah laughed. "Samuel," she tried to soothe him, "we had to get that first misstep out of the way. Now we can relax." She smiled encouragingly.

"Well, I fear I have many more where that came from."

Sarah chuckled. She felt Samuel relax when they moved again with the music. Their feet kicked up puffs of desert sand as they waltzed among the other couples, both El Pasoans and insurrectos. When her gaze met Samuel's, she realized, with a sudden awareness, that she loved him.

Catalina

Catalina squatted next to the small cooking fire to receive from Marta plates heavy with tortillas, beef, and beans. The food weighed warm in her hands, but it wasn't the food that made Catalina flush with heat. Though she tried, she could not calm her heart, which raced knowing that Mayo sat with her family, that she would serve him, that she would raise her eyes to his when she handed him the food. Turning from the fire, she took a deep breath before stepping toward the men who sat in a semicircle of talk.

"Papá," she offered, and he took the tin plate from her without a glance.

She moved to Mayo. When she saw that he watched her, she looked to the ground. "Señor," she invited, extending the food.

"Gracias, Cata." He reached with both hands, his fingers trailing lightly against her skin as he took the plate.

The warmth thickened deep in her belly, and she raised her eyes to his. She stepped back, awkward with emotion. Embarrassed, she returned quickly to the fire to focus on her duties.

Catalina trained her eyes, if not her thoughts, on her brothers, whom she now served. Miguel took the proffered food without looking beyond the hand that presented it. Diego, however, took the plate with a gravity quickly betrayed by a knowing smile when he thanked her.

"De nada," she answered, tugging a lock of his hair.

Catalina examined the expansive camp teeming with fellow insurrectos and with Americans who visited for amusement. Catalina had little experience with Americans. She knew some of them served in Madero's army, even camped nearby. She had heard from others that Americans fought bravely in battle, that some died alongside the insurrectos. But she knew these men did not fight for reasons that sparked her family's fight.

At the time Pancho Villa came to their mountain village to recruit soldiers for the revolution, Catalina and her family had only lived there briefly. Her family had recently escaped from a hacienda after rurales, the hated federal police, killed her brother Felipe when he sought justice for the rape of Fátima, their youngest sister. People joined the revolution for different reasons, but Catalina and her family fought for Felipe and Fátima.

Catalina remembered when her family had fled the hacienda; their trek into the mountains had been arduous. They traveled quickly, with little rest and less food. They knew the hacendado, Don Arias, would have rurales pursuing them because they had taken what he felt belonged to him: themselves.

They fled the hacienda the same night they buried Felipe, taking the few possessions they could strap quickly to the horses. Catalina rode holding twelve-year-old Fátima, who remained mute since the brutal attack. Seated behind Fátima in the saddle, Catalina spoke softly to her sister, telling her how life would be different when they reached the mountains. Though she became weary with the weight of her sister resting limply against her, Catalina neither complained nor asked for help. She just continued talking softly to Fátima, hoping her words would bring her sister back.

They traveled quickly at night, avoiding roads. During the day, they hid to rest. When they stopped, they fought exhaustion only long enough to care for the horses; then they lay down for a brief, troubled sleep. Fátima, however, never seemed to sleep. While Catalina and her family rested, Fátima sat, sometimes motionless, sometimes rocking, staring into the distance as if watching for someone or something. Though Catalina thought her sister must have slept a little in her arms as they rode, Fátima never breathed the deep breath that accompanies sleep. And when the family woke to eat, Fátima refused food, ignoring Catalina's coaxing and her father's commands. The only water she drank was that which Catalina managed to dribble between her clenched teeth. By the third night of travel, Fátima developed a fever. As they rode, Catalina felt her little sister grow so hot that though the night's cold numbed Catalina's fingers and toes, her clothes grew damp from Fátima's fire. Catalina rode forward and whispered to her father of Fátima's illness.

Her father paused the family amid an outcropping of rock. He lifted his youngest child from the saddle, carried her a short distance, then knelt, cradling Fátima. He whispered for Catalina to bring water. He loosened the blanket in which Catalina had wrapped Fátima. He tilted back his daughter's head, parting her lips with his thumb and forefinger. "Give her a little water. Only a little," he cautioned. He brushed the hair from Fátima's face with his calloused hand and encouraged, "Swallow, mijita, little daughter."

"A little more water, Cata."

Catalina poured a thin stream between her sister's parted lips. She watched Fátima struggle to swallow, as if she were choking down sand.

When their horses responded to a distant whinny, Catalina's father said, "We must go." He held Fátima while Catalina mounted, then lifted her onto the saddle. "Hold her tightly," he instructed. "Remember what I told you. If the rurales catch up to us, your brothers and I will fight. You ride to safety with Fátima. Don't hesitate, Cata. Don't look back."

Leaving Miguel behind to scout, they nudged their horses into a lope. Catalina held Fátima tightly to keep her from sliding off the saddle. She feared at times that the passive weight of her sister would pull them both from the horse, but Catalina gripped the animal with her legs and managed to keep both of them astride. She fought exhaustion that quivered in the muscles of her arms and thighs and the fear that formed a fist in her belly.

When Miguel rejoined the family from his reconnaissance, Catalina could tell that something was wrong by the anxiousness with which he spoke to their father. Miguel dropped back to speak with Diego and Marta while Catalina's father motioned her beside him.

"Rurales," he said just loud enough for her to hear. "Follow closely. If the time comes, do as I've instructed."

"Yes, Papá."

He placed his hand on Fátima's forehead then cheek. "We cannot rest," he said as much to himself as to Catalina.

For the remainder of the night, they rode hard, trying to distance themselves from the rurales. Though at times they feared the rurales were almost upon them, they felt an exhausted relief when early morning light revealed a land empty of other riders. But Catalina dreaded the toll the night had taken; she knew her sister's strength seeped from her.

Following her father's lead, Catalina leaned back to balance the horse's momentum as she guided the animal into a deep arroyo. They rode along the narrow opening to a sudden bend where, from the dirt wall of the arroyo, a single juniper stretched its roots toward a small pool of water. Her father dismounted, handed his horse's reins to Diego, and stepped back to lift Fátima from Catalina's arms.

When Catalina dismounted, her knees buckled from exhaustion, and she hit the ground hard before her mind even registered she was falling. Using the stirrup for support, she struggled to stand on legs that seemed too heavy to be her own. She moved clumsily to where Fátima lay. Kneeling beside her sister, Catalina took Fátima's hand in hers. Already, warmth was leaving the body; already, color was leaving the skin. Fátima breathed in such shallow draughts that the weak rasp in her throat was the only evidence she was breathing at all.

Catalina moistened a cloth and placed it to Fátima's mouth, trying to ease the dryness that cracked her lips. Catalina knew her sister was dying. She lay beside her, cradling her as she had all those nights on their pallet at home.

Catalina closed her eyes to avoid the agonized look on her father's face. "Fátima," she whispered as they used to each night until sleep forced them to quiet. "Fátima, remember last summer when we waded into the river to escape the heat. Remember how cool the river sand felt between our toes. Remember, Fátima, how hard the river tried to coax you from me while you floated, and how hard I had to pull to keep you from the river's tow. Remember, Fátima? Remember?" But Fátima did not acknowledge her. Though Catalina still hugged her little sister tightly, she knew that Fátima had drifted from her grasp.

"Cata," Marta called, holding out another tortilla with meat and beans, motioning with her head toward the men. Catalina had moved so completely into her memories that it took a moment to return to the present.

Catalina accepted the tortilla, pausing while Marta prepared a second. Then, with the food balanced in both hands, she crossed from the fire to the men. She concentrated on concealing emotions stirred by Mayo's presence. She served her father silently, careful to avoid any interruption of conversation. Then she stepped to Mayo and extended her hand to offer the second tortilla. When he reached to take what she offered, he did not look at the food; he looked into her eyes. She returned his gaze, and suddenly, Catalina felt a hunger she had never known. And she stood unmoving, having forgotten all around her until Diego called to bring her back to reality.

"Cata," Diego said, "Marta has prepared my food, and if you do not serve me soon, I will be too weak to fight the federales." He continued, attracting the family's attention to himself, "And I will need a lovely señorita, no, two lovely señoritas to care for me and help me regain my strength."

"Please eat, my brother," Catalina spoke as she returned to him from the fire. "If you grow weak, I fear for your health. You're too ugly to win the care of a señorita."

Diego laughed with his family, then demonstrated his hunger by taking an exaggerated bite, spilling food onto his shirt.

"And too messy," his father added, shaking his head at his son. "All you will attract are flies."

Diego laughed louder than the rest as he lifted the food from his shirt to his mouth.

"Buenas tardes," a woman's voice caught Catalina's attention.

"Buenas tardes," Catalina's father replied.

Catalina moved back to squat beside Marta at the fire, surprised that an American woman would approach their campsite alone. Catalina wondered at first if the petite young woman might have gotten separated from her group of sightseeing Americans, but then she raised a camera to indicate her desire to photograph them, asking, "Me da permiso?" Catalina understood that they were a novelty for the American. Her father's nod of approval surprised Catalina. Determined not to be a model for someone's amusement, Catalina watched the young woman step back to capture their camp scene; when she saw the movement of the American's finger, Catalina waved her hand before her face as if shooing a fly.

"Gracias," the photographer said.

"De nada," Catalina's father replied.

"Why do you think the Americans cross into our camp, Cata?" Marta asked in a whisper. "Do you think they are scouting our strength and our positions?"

"No, Marta," Catalina answered honestly. "I think they come to our camp because we amuse them. You've seen them watching us each day across the river. They hope to be entertained by our battle." She paused for a moment, thinking further. "But maybe there are so many Americans in camp today because they know peace is near. Maybe they know the outcome of the peace talks, and that there won't be a battle."

Marta appeared to consider Catalina's explanation, but she still looked warily at the Americans.

Some who roamed through the encampment looked more Mexican than American. Catalina watched an old man bent by the weight of his years walk in front of a slight, white-haired abuela, and a short, wide-hipped woman with three boys and a baby. Catalina listened when the small group stopped at a nearby campfire to ask for Orozco's soldiers. She wondered if these were some of the Mexicans who had crossed into the United States seeking refuge from the fighting. What did it mean if they now crossed back to their homeland, even if only to visit a loved one serving in the insurrecto army? Perhaps peace truly was at hand.

When the men finished the meal and sat smoking cigarettes, Marta and Catalina took the respite from work to eat. Marta alternated between taking a bite of the food and feeding little Pablo, who continued to play, pausing only to take another bite at his mother's urging. Otherwise, they ate in silence. Then Catalina and Marta began cleaning their campsite from the meal.

While she worked, Catalina stole a glance at Mayo, who uttered his thanks before departing. She thought of when he first rode into Villa's camp in December. He'd arrived alongside Catalina's father, brothers, and a few other men, driving a small herd of horses taken from the large rancho where he had been a vaquero, a cowboy. Catalina's father took a great liking to Mayo and invited him to share their family's campfire. Catalina paid him little attention, and he to her. He was not unattractive, built with the lean strength of one whose life is in the saddle. But to Catalina, he was simply another man for whom to cook, wash, and serve. She did not begrudge his sharing their campfire; to her, he was little more than an additional chore.

Then two weeks ago, after the battle at Bauche, Catalina's eyes suddenly focused on the man. After the battle, after the beaten federales retreated to Ciudad Juárez, the insurrectos gathered at night to celebrate their victory, taking turns describing their prowess in combat. When stories of the fighting began, Catalina noticed that Mayo withdrew. She realized he never participated in any boastings of battle. She suddenly felt a curiosity about the man who for months had shared her family's campfire.

The next morning, while Marta and she prepared breakfast, Mayo arrived. When she served him his food, Catalina commented, "You disappeared last night."

"On the night of a victory, I prefer the company of horses," Mayo replied.

As she stood, surprised by his remark, Catalina knew he studied her. She felt no discomfort at his gaze. Unlike the eyes of so many men, his look did not violate. And for the first time in her seventeen years, Catalina felt drawn to a man.

Catalina forgot her memories when "Mexicanos, al grito de guerra," the Mexican national anthem, began to play. Diego called excitedly to his family, "Come, let's see what the music is about. Come, Cata," and he tugged at her arm.

"I'll stay in camp with little Pablo." Their father encouraged, "The rest of you go on."

"Are you sure, Papá?" Catalina questioned. "I can stay."

"No. Go with your brothers."

"Papá's just hoping the attractive photographer will return," Diego teased.

"Go on, hijo, before I find work for you," their father warned.

Walking toward the music with her brothers and Marta, Catalina saw the area had lost any semblance of the battle-ready encampment with which she was familiar. Vendors, carrying trays of candy and tobacco, hawked their wares to the crowd. Groups of insurrectos worked in teams to butcher some of the cattle and goats that had been taken from ranches or corralled as strays. One soldier, his blood-smeared arms shoved elbow-deep into the carcass of a steer, shouted to passersby that there would be meat for all, courtesy of President Porfirio Díaz and his supporters. And Americans wandered everywhere.

Catalina and her family arrived at the edge of the gathering as chants of "Viva Madero! Viva México!" erupted. They joined in the cheers. Then the band struck up a military march, quelling the chants, and Diego guided the family through the crowd for a better view. When the band played a waltz, a few couples separated from the throng of onlookers to dance.

"Look," Diego spoke to Catalina, pointing to a couple dancing. "Our photographer."

Catalina smiled her recognition of the young woman with the camera. "Perhaps I should offer to take their picture."

At the conclusion of the waltz, the band broke into a lively schottische, and more couples joined the dancers.

Swaying with the music, Catalina watched the couples. From behind, a man said, "This is music for dancing, not for listening."

Catalina turned to see Mayo. He leaned forward to ask Miguel in a formal manner, "May I have your permission to seek a dance with your sister?"

Before Miguel could answer, Diego interrupted, "Yes! I will find a partner and join you." Then he pushed his way into the crowd.

Miguel glanced disapprovingly in Diego's direction. Answering with the authority of his position in the family, Miguel said, "You may ask my sister for a dance."

Though Catalina heard her brother's answer, she kept her eyes averted, pretending the music gripped her attention.

"Catalina," Mayo spoke formally, "will you dance with me?"

Catalina answered "yes" in a voice just louder than a whisper.

They joined the circle of dancers. Self-conscious at first, Catalina soon relaxed. When Diego and his partner slipped in beside them, Catalina smiled at her brother.

At the song's conclusion, Mayo stepped close to Catalina and whispered, "We must find time to be alone. I wish to talk with you."

"Yes," she replied. She would risk her family's disapproval.

"We should dance another," Diego volunteered enthusiastically.

"Let's dance another," Mayo agreed.

The music began as if cued.

During the song, Catalina and Mayo became separated from Diego and his partner. Though she looked for Miguel and Marta, Catalina didn't see them among those dancing or watching. At the conclusion of the tune, realizing the crowd shielded her from her family's view, she said to Mayo, "I'm very thirsty. Let's get some water to drink."

Mayo led the way around couples who danced when the band played anew. Once they moved beyond the crowd of onlookers, the air became cooler and free of the dust the dancers stirred.

Catalina walked with Mayo, happy to be alone with him even though they were in the middle of a camp swarming with insurrectos and visitors.

"May I buy you something to drink?" Mayo motioned in the direction of one of the makeshift stands.

At the stand, Mayo paid for two cups of horchata. Catalina drank deeply at first. Once she satisfied her thirst, she drank smaller draughts, enjoying the sweetness of the rice drink.

"May we walk a little, or should we return to your family?"

"Let's walk."

They balanced their cups on the stand and moved toward the edge of camp, anxious to be free from the swell of people. They walked into the desert hills until far enough from camp to feel comfortably hidden.

"Let's stop here for a while," Mayo suggested.

Mayo removed his jacket and spread it on the ground for Catalina to sit. He sat beside her, shifting uncomfortably.

Catalina turned to Mayo, but before she could speak, he took a deep breath and said, "I think, Cata, the fighting will end soon. I think the revolution will be victorious."

Catalina studied the broad straight length of his nose, the moustache that formed a thick arc above his lips.

"Soon we must find new lives." He paused and took a deep breath. "Cata," he spoke more softly, "I want you to be my wife."

Cata took his hand and without hesitation said, "Mayo, I want you for my husband."

Mayo leaned to kiss her lips. He was not shy in his kiss, nor was she in returning it. And when he kissed her again, Catalina lay gently back to the ground, her arms around his neck, pulling him to her.

"I will talk with your father," he whispered.

"Yes," Catalina agreed, knowing she would be Mayo's wife with or without her family's consent.

He kissed her again and again. The hunger that once burned deep in her belly now consumed her. His hands moved over her body, caressing those parts never touched by another man. And each touch excited an ache of desire. She wanted to feel their bodies joined.

Abruptly, his caresses ended, and Mayo lifted his weight from her. "Forgive my behavior, Catalina. I should wait."

Catalina answered by pulling his body to hers.

MAY 1911

Sarah

Sarah paced inside the Otis Photo Studio, waiting anxiously for the proprietor to return to the front with her developed pictures. After her visit to Madero's camp, Sarah could hardly wait to drop off the roll of film for printing, so first thing Monday morning on her walk to work at the Popular Department Store, she stopped at this studio advertising "Kodak films finishing." Now Saturday, she returned, excited to see what she had captured with her camera.

The curtain separating the store from the studio suddenly parted, and the proprietor returned carrying an envelope. Rather than handing the envelope to Sarah, he removed the contents and placed the photographs on the counter for her review.

"Who is the photographer?" he asked.

Sarah picked up the first photograph to examine it. "I am."

He seemed surprised. "You took all of these photographs?"

"Yes. Why do you ask?"

"They're quite good."

His reply surprised Sarah. She stammered, "Thank you."

"Nice composition, interesting subject matter." He looked at the stack of photographs.

Sarah felt her face burn red.

"There's great interest in the Mexican Revolution. I'm not just talking interest here on the border but interest throughout the US and the world."

Sarah nodded, not understanding what this had to do with her photographs.

"Let me introduce myself. I'm A. J. Otis. I own this studio." He glanced at her name printed on the envelope. "Sarah Delaney, I'd like to use some of your photographs' negatives to print picture postcards. Like this photo," and he held up the picture of the Tarahumara Indians. "And this one." He pulled the photograph of Garibaldi, Orozco, and Villa from the stack. "And this one." He pointed to the photograph of Francisco Madero. "And this one." He pulled out the photo showing the mesquite adorned with rattlesnakes.

Sarah didn't know how to respond to the man, whose face did not convey the excitement in his voice.

"What I'm proposing is that I use certain of your negatives to create photo postcards. I'll print the postcards at my expense, and I'll handle the marketing of them. I will pay you a portion of the profits—twenty percent. Your name will be credited on the picture, but so will Otis Photo Studio." He paused again, gauging her response. "You're not going to get rich from the sale of photo postcards, but you will earn pin money."

Sarah briefly studied the slight man. He stood eye-to-eye with her, his face gaunt and his look intense.

"Talk with your husband about my offer. Better yet, bring him to the studio, and I'll work out the details with him."

Sarah did her best to mask both her irritation at his last remark and her excitement over his business proposition. "It's Miss Delaney." Though she felt a bit like an imposter since she was at best a novice photographer, the offer interested her, so she countered, "I will accept the business offer but only if you agree to teach me how to finish film."

Otis cocked his head in surprise. After a moment's thought, he replied, "You have a deal."

He removed the negatives from the envelope, replacing them with the stack of photographs, and handed the envelope to her. "Come back on

Monday to see the postcards."

Sarah gripped the envelope to her chest. The small bell positioned on the doorframe tinkled when she opened the door to depart.

"And take more photographs of the revolution, Miss Delaney," Otis called out as she exited the establishment.

Once Sarah passed the studio's window, she paused to catch her breath and whispered to herself, "What just happened?" She couldn't refrain from smiling. She hurried to San Jacinto Plaza, oblivious of passersby, to find a vacant park bench. She removed the photos from the envelope to study each one. Their clarity and sharpness made her recall the heat, energy, and crush of humanity that day. She smiled when she reached the photo of Samuel standing beside the Model T. He looked so serious for his twenty-nine years, and to her, so handsome. She held the photo briefly to her chest before placing it at the back of the stack. Next was the picture of the insurrecto campsite. She lifted the photograph to view it more closely, the men staring sternly at her, the child playing in the sand, one woman looking at the comal on the fire, and the younger woman squatting, the pattern of her skirt crisp, her face a smear of movement. Sarah returned to this photograph after reviewing each of the others. Something in the picture captured her attention in a way the other photographs didn't. One woman chose to stare at the cooking fire, but the position of the younger woman, squatting to stare at the camera while rendering her face a blur, made Sarah wonder if the photo captured an error of movement or proud defiance. Sarah carefully returned the pictures to the envelope. She couldn't wait to tell Samuel about her business deal.

When Sarah arrived at the boardinghouse, she found Samuel in the parlor. He called to her, standing as she entered the foyer.

"Oh, Samuel!" she exclaimed. "What a nice surprise! I have so much to tell you."

"Let's go for a walk," he responded with a seriousness that concerned Sarah.

"Is everything okay?"

"Yes, of course," he answered, but his demeanor contradicted his reply.

Sarah noted that he dressed in the khaki suit and brown shirt he wore in camp. His tall leather boots laced over the lower legs of his trousers, and the pocket of his jacket bulged with what Sarah suspected was a pistol.

Sarah decided to leave the photographs in her room before departing with Samuel. She would show them to him another time. When she descended the stairs, she found Samuel at the front door waiting for her. He opened the door when she reached him, and they exited into the warm May morning.

Samuel guided her away from downtown. They walked in silence. After several minutes, Sarah had to break the tension. "Samuel, what is it?"

"Let's cross the road to some shade, and we'll talk."

Sarah followed him to an empty lot with several large mulberry trees; they halted in the shade of the branches. Samuel looked in the direction of Juárez, then began to speak. "Sarah, what I am going to tell you is for your ears only." Samuel placed his hands on her shoulders and looked into her eyes.

Sarah nodded. "I understand."

"The peace negotiations have failed."

"Oh no!"

"Porfirio Díaz has refused to resign the presidency."

"So there will be a battle for control of Juárez?"

"Well, Madero wants to call off the attack on the city and take the fight away from the border. He knows a battle in Juárez will result in bullets and possibly shells firing into El Paso. He fears the US will use any such occurrence as justification for sending American troops into Juárez."

"Would the US really send troops into Mexico?"

He shrugged his shoulders. "It could happen."

"If you leave the border, where will you go?"

Samuel looked intently at her, then looked away. "I think Orozco, Villa, and Garibaldi will disobey Madero's orders."

"What does that mean, Samuel?"

He looked at her anew. "The troops are becoming demoralized. Insurrectos have camped in that desert sand awaiting orders to attack for more than two weeks. Madero is a gentleman, an intellectual, a visionary—he's a lot of things, but he's not a soldier."

Sarah placed her hand over Samuel's balled fist. "What will happen?"

"If the officers are unable to convince Madero to attack, they will take matters into their own hands."

"So, with or without Madero's orders, there will be fighting for control of Juárez?"

"Yes."

"Oh, Samuel!" Sarah felt a heaviness in her heart and tears well in her eyes.

"I have to get back to camp, Sarah, but I wanted to see you." He pulled her to him, held her tightly. "I couldn't bear to think of you believing peace is at hand. It's not, at least not without a fight for control of Ciudad Juárez."

Sarah lifted her head from his chest, and he leaned down to kiss her. Sarah returned the kiss with a passion previously restrained.

Samuel whispered, "I love you, Sarah Delaney."

"I love you, too, Samuel." She flushed hot with emotions at their first time expressing love for one another.

"Let me walk you back to your place. I have to return to camp." He raised her chin with his forefinger. "No more tears."

They walked slowly back to the boardinghouse, Sarah's arm in his, neither of them in a hurry to reach their destination.

At the front door, Sarah halted. "Samuel, be safe," she urged.

"I will. Now, go inside. Don't watch me leave."

❂❂❂

Sarah stood at the mirror, already dressed for work though it was only 6:00 a.m. She wanted to depart from the boardinghouse before breakfast; she couldn't bear to listen to table talk about the revolution.

After Samuel had left her on Saturday, she spent the remainder of the day locked in her room. On Sunday, she read local newspapers, searching for clues about the coming battle. No hint existed, only an article about the failure of the peace commission. The article described how Madero addressed his troops, informing them that the peace negotiations had foundered, that Porfirio Díaz would not agree to an immediate resignation of the presidency, and that the revolution continued. Madero told the troops he would leave a three-man peace commission to keep the door open for a diplomatic resolution, but there would be no battle for Ciudad Juárez.

Sarah had a fitful night, waking to every sound in anticipation of the fighting. By 4:30 a.m., she gave up any attempt at sleep. She rose to ready herself for work and depart prior to breakfast. She would get coffee and pastry at a downtown bakery on her way to the department store. Sarah lifted the strap of the camera case onto her shoulder, positioned her hat on her head, and took one final glance in the mirror.

At the Popular Department Store, Sarah busied herself with straightening a table display of embroidered handkerchiefs.

"You're very busy this morning."

Sarah turned to see Paola, who joined her after helping a client with a purchase.

"Did you have a good weekend?" Paola asked as she assisted Sarah. "Did you see Samuel?"

Sarah halted for a moment, caught off guard by the innocent question. "I did on Saturday, but only briefly."

"What does he think about Madero's decision to withdraw from the border without a fight?"

"We didn't discuss it. Madero didn't announce his plan to the troops until Sunday." Sarah felt bad about lying to Paola. They had known each other since December when Sarah started employment at the Popular. Paola trained her as a saleswoman, and they became fast friends. Paola had been beside her at the five-and-dime lunch counter on that afternoon in February when Samuel sat on the stool next to hers and struck up a conversation over a bowl of chili.

"My father and brothers were furious when they heard about Madero's plan to withdraw. My father said Madero is a fool. Juárez is key to freeing México from the dictatorship of the old goat. Well, he used a more colorful word in Spanish." Paola chuckled.

When an elderly woman entered the women's department, Sarah seized the opportunity to absent herself from the conversation.

After Sarah completed the sale, she noticed Paola was occupied with a customer. Sarah felt relieved to be alone with her thoughts. She wondered why she had experienced such anxiety ever since Samuel shared news of the ensuing battle. After all, Samuel had fought in many battles. While she always worried for his safety, she never felt the level of unease she now experienced. Perhaps the proximity of the anticipated conflict made its danger more real.

Sarah startled at the first sharp *pop, pop, pop*. When the gunfire continued, she looked across the room to meet Paola's wide-eyed gaze. They crossed the floor to one another.

"Do you think they're fighting?" Paola asked incredulously, taking Sarah's hands in hers.

"I don't know."

They stood together, listening. During the past two weeks, El Pasoans had become accustomed to occasional gunshots ringing out, but the fierceness of the present exchange suggested something far more intense. When the shooting did not abate, people began moving to the store's exits with a sense of excitement.

"Go see," Paola urged. "I'll keep an eye on our department."

Sarah hesitated only a moment before hurrying to the street. She followed the stream of men rushing toward the border to try to view the fighting. The gunfire intensified, spurring the crowd, seemingly afraid the battle might conclude before they caught a glimpse. The men passing her on the sidewalk talked and laughed excitedly as if they headed to a sporting event and not a life and death struggle for the soul of a nation.

As she walked toward the Union Train Depot, Sarah noted that businesses had quickly posted sandwich boards outside their doors and fliers on their windows selling rooftop viewing of the combat. Some establishments even offered a refund if the fighting petered out before materializing into a full-blown battle.

Sarah reached the Union Depot in fifteen minutes, and already a throng of people gathered along the tracks. Many crowded atop train cars and flatbeds loaded with railroad ties. Some stood inside boxcars watching the fighting through open doors and gaps between wooden slats. A few who had field glasses called out the action they viewed. Standing on the tracks, Sarah could make out movement of men along the river, and she could see puffs of smoke rising into the air, but little else. Suddenly jostled by the growing crowd, Sarah lost her footing. Two strong hands gripped her waist, preventing her from falling. She turned to see a red-faced man in a business suit grinning at her.

"You were almost a casualty of war."

"Thank you for your help."

"My pleasure, ma'am. Happy to lend a hand," he said, nudging the grinning man next to him. "Or two."

Sarah suddenly realized that the crowd consisted entirely of males. She did not see another woman among those gathered. Her discomfort at this discovery overrode her desire to remain. Sarah glanced again at the scene across the border, said a prayer for Samuel's safety, and turned to walk against the stream of men continuing to arrive to view the fighting.

When Sarah returned to the Popular and entered the women's department, Paola met her. "I've been worried about you." And without pause, she asked, "What did you learn?"

Sarah shared with Paola news about the sea of onlookers, the carnival atmosphere, and the movement and gunfire she could detect across the river in Mexico.

As the day wore on, the sound of fighting intensified. No customers entered the women's department. In fact, very few customers entered the Popular at all, as El Pasoans focused on viewing what they could of the fighting. Without customers, the salesclerks collected in small groups to discuss what they heard, saw, and imagined.

Midafternoon, Tomás, one of the clerks from the men's department, brought in an extra edition of the *El Paso Morning Times*. According to Tomás, the *Times* reported the fighting began without Madero's approval. Madero quickly phoned General Navarro, the federal officer in command of the Juárez garrison, to negotiate a ceasefire, promising to halt the fighting by the insurrecto forces if Navarro would stop the federal fire. The two leaders agreed, but when Madero sent a soldier carrying a white flag to return the troops to camp, someone shot the messenger's horse out from under him. No ceasefire occurred. Tomás emphasized the final statement from the article—"fighting is intensifying."

While Tomás regaled the gathered salesclerks with his synopsis of the *Times'* reporting, the store's assistant manager interrupted the group to inform them that due to the absence of customers, he was sending half the employees home. With the assumption that the fighting would continue the next day, the Popular would operate Tuesday with half its staff. He allowed the clerks to determine among themselves who would work.

Paola pulled Sarah aside and said, "I'll work. Go learn what you can about Samuel."

"Thank you, Paola." Sarah hurried to the counter to collect her things.

Once outside, Sarah hesitated, trying to decide what to do and which way to go. She knew she shouldn't reenter the crowd of men without an escort. Her desire to view the battle, to make even a visual connection with what Samuel must be experiencing, drove her to the Otis Photo Studio. When she reached the studio, she pushed forcefully against the door, only to discover it locked. Stepping back, she saw the sign taped to the glass: "Closed. Gone to photograph a revolution!"

Sarah fought back tears of frustration. She stood staring at the sign, trying to identify her next move, when a voice interrupted her thoughts.

"Why aren't you putting your camera to use?"

Mr. Otis leaned in front of her to insert a key into the lock. "Come in," he said, holding the door open for her.

Sarah noted that he looked disheveled, his hat pushed back from his forehead, his tie loosened at the collar, and perspiration beaded along his brow. He took a handkerchief from his pocket and wiped his face. "Are you here to see the photo postcards?" Before she could respond, he asked, "Can it wait for another day? I just came back to get more film."

"I want to go with you, Mr. Otis," Sarah blurted.

He paused behind the counter to look at her. "No, it's too dangerous." Without further discussion, he returned his attention to retrieving rolls of film and placing them in his pockets.

"Please, Mr. Otis." Sarah lifted her camera case to show him. "I can take photos for picture postcards. I won't be a bother, I promise."

Without hesitating to look at her, he answered, "It's no place for a lady."

"Mr. Otis," Sarah spoke firmly, losing the plea in her voice, "my beau is in the fight. I have to see the battle."

He stood to study her, appearing to consider her request. Sarah had a glimmer of hope before he responded, "Then, I really don't want to be responsible for you." He walked to the door, pulled it open, and said, "You'll excuse me, Miss Delaney." He motioned for her to exit the studio.

Sarah waited on the sidewalk while he locked the door. The intensity of the gunfire held her attention.

He nodded to her, raising his hat slightly from his head. "Good day, Miss Delaney."

Sarah didn't respond; she simply assumed his pace. And when he began to walk faster, Sarah matched his stride. After walking briskly for two blocks, Otis stopped, doubling over, his hands on his thighs as he strained to breathe.

Sarah waited beside him while people streamed around them.

Finally, he spoke. "You're going to be the death of me, Miss Delaney." He stood to address her, his breath slowly regaining a more natural rhythm. "I'm a lunger."

"I'm—I'm sorry," Sarah stammered. "I didn't know."

"Of course not," he responded with irritation. "Don't worry, the tuberculosis is dormant," then added, "for now." He pulled out his handkerchief and wiped his face. "But it's damaged my lungs." He started walking at a slower pace than before. "If you're going to shadow me against my will, know that I bear no responsibility for your safety."

"I understand, Mr. Otis," Sarah responded, relieved at his grudging acquiescence.

"And if you've reduced yourself to stalking me, then 'Mr. Otis' is a bit too respectful. Call me A. J., and I will call you Sarah. Agreed?"

"Agreed."

Sarah followed A. J. down South Santa Fe Street, which bordered the Chihuahuita neighborhood where many Mexicans who fled the revolution had settled. She could see a mix of adobe, brick, and wooden buildings, some with chickens and goats in the yards. She noticed a small bodega, its outdoor stands displaying an array of fruits and vegetables. The aproned proprietor leaned against an open door, talking excitedly with two other men, all of whom gestured toward Juárez. As Sarah continued with A. J. in the direction of the international bridge, the sound of fighting intensified. She felt a nervousness in the pit of her stomach.

A. J. climbed the steps to the door of the El Paso Laundry and asked the man standing guard inside the entrance to the two-story brick building, "How much?"

"One quarter."

A. J. turned to Sarah, who was already reaching into her small cloth purse to locate a coin. "You have to pay your own way."

Sarah nodded and placed the coin onto the extended palm of the man regulating entrance into the building. A loud explosion made Sarah duck, and she shuddered, realizing how close they stood to the fighting. She felt relieved to enter the building, but soon they climbed stairs that led onto the flat rooftop, where they joined a crowd of men already watching the battle across the river.

"Stay close," A. J. warned, pushing forward through those gathered.

Sarah followed tightly behind A. J., surprised by how his slight build managed to cut through the crowd. Then she heard his request: "Please, let the lady through." He repeated, "Please, let the lady through."

This tactic served to move them to the front of those gathered watching the life and death theater before them. From the rooftop, Sarah looked into Juárez, seeing men fighting in the streets, smoke billowing from shattered windows, and buildings ravaged with gaping holes. Then she heard the rattle of machine gun fire and watched soldiers scatter, flattening against walls and dashing into buildings. Sarah felt some safety afforded by the roof's brick parapet; still, she felt very exposed.

A. J. struck up a conversation with a group of men, who exchanged stories with him about what they had seen throughout the afternoon. Instead of listening to the talk, Sarah focused on the embattled city.

Sarah removed her camera from its case. Though she knew the camera could not capture details of the battle, she hoped to secure a general sense of conflict through the smoke and scattered wreckage. Next, Sarah turned the camera to the crowd of men watching from the rooftop. She photographed the fixed intensity of their collective gaze as they stared, mesmerized by the fighting before them. Sarah stepped onto the seat of a recently vacated chair. From this elevated position, she framed the sea of fedoras and boaters in the foreground against a backdrop of smoke rising from the battle. She snapped the photo. As she stepped from the chair, she caught a glimpse of A. J. watching her, smiling approvingly.

"Miss, would you like to look through these?"

Sarah turned to a jacketless man who politely extended his field glasses to her.

"Yes, thank you." Sarah folded her camera and slipped it into the case. She took the proffered binoculars from the young man, who smiled his pleasure at her acceptance of the offer.

"You turn this wheel here," he said, directing her attention to the dial centered between the two telescopic tubes, "to focus the lenses. Give it a try."

When Sarah placed the binoculars to her eyes, the buildings and streets suddenly loomed before her, as if she could touch bullet holes that pockmarked walls. It took her a moment to navigate the direction and angle needed to view the struggle she had seen in miniature. Sarah gasped at the sight of bodies—federal and insurrecto—sprawled in unnatural poses of death. She spied wounded among the dead. One man lay on his back, both hands capturing the intestines bulging from his belly, his left leg twitching in disbelief. Another soldier inched forward, face down in the dirt, struggling to reach shelter. Sarah watched two of his comrades race in a crouch to his side, grab the wounded man at the armpits, and drag him limp into a building, leaving a trail of blood in the dirt. Sarah had seen enough. She returned the field glasses to the owner, thanking him in a voice that didn't sound like her own.

She placed her hands on the parapet to steady herself and closed her eyes, but the images of the dead and wounded remained. A *thud* refocused her attention, and before she could respond, a second *thud* sent a spray of pulverized brick, stinging her face and neck. Two hands grabbed her shoulders, turning her, guiding her from the parapet. "It's time to go." A. J. pushed her ahead of him, shielding her back with his. "Those are stray bullets."

They exited down the stairs and from the building along with fellow onlookers. Once outside, they stayed close to the buildings along Santa Fe Street, making their way back toward the center of town. At the plaza, A. J. hailed a taxi. "I'll see you home."

"I can walk. It's just a few blocks."

A. J. opened the door to the cab. "I insist." He moved to the opposite side and entered the cab beside her. "Tell the driver your address."

Sarah paid little attention to the banter A. J. and the taxi driver shared about the day's events. She closed her eyes and thought of Samuel. "Stay safe," she repeated in her head.

When the driver stopped in front of the boardinghouse, Sarah reached into her purse to pay for the taxi ride. A. J. said, "I've got this."

He stifled her protest with a raised hand, and said, "Now, what time can I expect you at the studio tomorrow?"

Sarah looked askance at his question.

He replied, "We have a revolution to photograph."

Catalina

The cannons' boom broke against them in a wave. Catalina placed her hand reassuringly on Marta's arm, then returned her attention to the men who waited patiently at their cooking fire. Catalina and Marta had been working alongside other women of the camp, with little rest since the previous afternoon, to feed an endless line of battle-wearied soldiers. As Catalina served each man, she asked about the fighting. "How is the battle progressing?" she would inquire of men she did not know. But to each familiar face, she questioned, "My father, my brothers, Mayo—have you seen them? Are they unharmed?" And though she knew that in battle, all but now is old news, Catalina held hopefully to every reported sighting of her family.

"They are unharmed," she would whisper to Marta after each new report. Her message remained the same but for the name of the messenger: "'Braulio' or 'Julio' or 'Erasmo' has seen them, and they are unharmed." Though she sought to shore up Marta with her reassurances, Catalina saw that her news offered little comfort to her brother's wife, who responded with wide-eyed silence.

Catalina listened to the sounds of battle, trying to discern the flow of fighting, but the great cacophony of explosions and gunshots informed her only that the fighting remained intense. Then the concussion of cannons began anew. Catalina focused on the soldiers who waited to be fed.

"Señoras," a man's voice commanded their attention.

Catalina looked up to see Coronel Pancho Villa astride a sweat-streaked bay.

"I need two of you to follow the men into the city, closer to the fighting, to care for the wounded until we can transport them to camp or to a hospital."

"I will go, Coronel." Catalina stepped forward, anxious to move closer to Mayo and her family.

"And I," a voice quickly seconded.

Catalina turned to see Chita walking forward.

"Gather supplies." Villa turned his horse to depart. "I'll send soldiers to take you into the city." He pressed his horse to a trot.

Catalina squatted by Marta at the fire. "You'll be here if the men return to eat and rest. I'll be closer to the battle. Now we have two places where our men can find us."

Marta nodded but kept her eyes focused on the tortillas layered on the comal.

Catalina knew her brother's wife would be all right regardless of the battle's outcome because Marta had resigned herself to the winds of fate, her will reduced to acceptance. Catalina placed her arm briefly around Marta's waist, feeling the swell of the child she carried. "Rest when you can," Catalina whispered, then stood.

Catalina and Chita collected supplies they could carry from camp, placing what they assembled into two sacks they secured to their backs with their rebozos. When a pair of soldiers arrived in camp to guide them, they were ready.

Catalina recognized the younger of the two men, who wore a bloodied bandage peeking from under his sombrero. "Ignacio," she spoke, "you're hurt."

He tipped the sombrero lower on his forehead. "Only a cut."

The older man grinned at his comrade's discomfort. "He will still be pretty."

"Eat," Catalina spoke, seeking to end Ignacio's discomfort at the attention. "Then we'll go with you into the city."

"Gracias, señoras," the older man half-bowed. "We'll take tortillas to eat as we walk. We have many wounded soldiers who need care."

His readiness to leave pleased Catalina, who was anxious to find her family. She watched Ignacio and the one who seemed her father's age each fold tortillas into a pocket. Then the older man returned his attention to Chita and Catalina. "I'm Mateo," he said, adding, "We'll leave now. Follow closely and remain cautious."

Catalina and Chita nodded.

"Do you have guns?" Mateo looked at the women.

"No, señor," Chita replied, "but I have a knife." She pulled a long, thin skinning knife from a fold of her rebozo. "For gutting rabbits," she smiled, returning the knife to its place, "or larger animals."

"I have a pistol," Catalina answered, "but only a few bullets."

"Okay. Follow cautiously." He led the way, one hand gripping his rifle, and the other fishing in his pocket for a tortilla.

Catalina walked beside Chita and behind the two men, whom Catalina studied. Mateo was short with a thick body and bowed legs. Ignacio, only slightly taller than his comrade, had the narrow build of a man whose only abundance in life was work. Their pace remained purposeful.

As they moved along the riverbank toward the city, Catalina saw Americans crowding the river's edge in El Paso, watching the fighting. She marveled at the confidence these Americans had that bullets and shells exchanged in battle would not harm them. They must believe their status as Americans on their own soil provided them immunity from injury or death. Catalina felt no such immunity; she remained alert, noting the smoke and dust of battle that hung above Juárez like silt suspended in a river.

Mateo signaled a pause, then squatted and waited for the three of them to do the same. He rubbed his hand over the stubble of a beard, turning his head to gauge the sounds of battle. "We're going to an area taken by our troops. There are snipers, though, so remain alert. Stay low and look for cover." Mateo scanned the area again. "Let's go," and he motioned them forward.

They trotted in a crouch toward a small adobe building. As they moved across open terrain, Catalina had to fight the urge to dash past the others to safety behind a wall. The rattle of machine guns and boom of mortars all seemed to be aimed at their small party. She followed with the coiled tension of a horse tightly reined from bolting.

When they reached the building, Catalina flattened as close to the adobe wall as the supplies tied to her back permitted. The heat emanating from the brick felt uncomfortably warm, but she pressed against the adobe, preferring discomfort to danger. She traced the butt of her pistol through the sash tied at her waist. Though it offered little protection except at close range, she still felt satisfaction knowing she had a weapon. This act did little to quiet her breathing, which continued in short anxious puffs, but the feel of her finger against the trigger gave her enough confidence to lean from the wall to look around Chita and Ignacio to Mateo, who, hatless, peered carefully around the corner of the building.

Mateo's message passed from Ignacio to Chita to Catalina. Mateo would cross the street first. If he drew no fire, they were to follow quickly, one at a time.

Unable to see Mateo's dash to the opposite side of the street, she listened intently. The gunfire remained several blocks away. She moved along the wall, closer to the edge as Ignacio departed.

"They're waving for me to follow," Chita whispered.

"Go with speed and with God," Catalina encouraged her.

Chita raced across the dirt road, her skirt swirling as she ran. In an instant, Chita squatted safely with the others, motioning for Catalina to follow.

Before Catalina could overthink it, she was running, removed from all protection. She raced across what now seemed more of an open field than a narrow dirt street. When she neared the point of safety, a few steps from the wall, she heard the cannon's boom and knew in her heart that the shell careened toward her. Catalina dove for the protection of the building, landing heavily in the dirt.

"She flies," Mateo spoke as if astounded by what he'd seen. "More the skill of a chicken than a hawk, but she flies."

Catalina felt foolish when the shell exploded a great distance from their position. She stood, emptied sand from the barrel of her pistol, and avoided looking at the grins she knew the men shared. She felt relieved when Mateo directed their small band forward.

They moved as a group, trotting in a half-crouch along buildings. In the street and in the alleys between buildings, Catalina spied bodies of federales and insurrectos alike, bloated in death, feeding clouds of flies.

Mateo waited, leaning against a wooden door, his hand gripping the handle. Once they all joined him, he shouldered it open and led them into the cool darkness of the adobe building. Inside, Catalina glanced about the room, trying to orient herself. A bed frame looted of its mattress, a table without chairs, and a wooden closet gutted of its contents informed Catalina that she stood in what had been someone's home. She waited stiffly, not wishing to intrude farther.

"Come, Little Hen," Mateo beckoned to Catalina from a large hole gouged through the apartment's inner wall. "It's too soon to roost." He chuckled in appreciation of his own joke as he ducked through the opening. Next, Ignacio stepped through the hole, his sombrero knocking dirt loose from the rough edge of the adobe. When Catalina followed Chita into the connecting apartment, she heard Mateo's chatter, encouraging them onward, and she glimpsed him disappearing into another cavity. They continued moving quickly from apartment to apartment through the openings previously cut by their comrades. They traversed an entire block without leaving the safety of adobe walls.

Mateo waited at the door, opening it only enough to permit a cursory scouting of the area; then he opened it wider and exited.

By the time Catalina stepped through the doorway, Mateo had already rounded the corner of the building with Ignacio close behind. They moved through a portion of the town that had recently seen fighting. They passed the bodies of two federal soldiers and one insurrecto, all three weaponless and all with pockets torn or turned out as if declaring they had sacrificed everything for their causes and had nothing more to give. Glancing quickly, only long enough to assure herself that each waxen face belonged to a stranger, Catalina continued scouting rooftops and windows for snipers.

Mateo guided them to a single-story building with a front wall gaily painted to depict two doves flying toward one another; the notes issuing from their beaks spelled out the pulqueria's name: "Canción de las Palomas," Song of the Doves.

Before entering the bar, Mateo paused at the doorway to call, "Gabino! Andrés!"

A voice answered from inside. "Have you brought our angels of mercy?"

"Well," Mateo chuckled, looking back at Catalina, "I cannot say if they're angels, but one does fly." He continued laughing at his joke as he led them into the bar.

Inside sat two men, their backs to the counter, facing the doorway. Both cradled rifles and sat with bloody bandages wrapped about wounds.

"We have guarded the liquor and guarded each other from the liquor." The speaker smiled, his large white teeth in sharp contrast to his face blackened with the soot of battle.

"You and Andrés deserve a drink." Mateo spoke, sweeping his hand before him to indicate the makeshift pallets placed across the floor of the room. "Return to camp to eat, rest, and mend."

"We'll stay," Gabino spoke, and Andrés nodded his head in agreement. "The women may need our help."

"As you wish." Mateo turned to Ignacio and placed a hand on the young man's shoulder. "It's time to go."

Catalina and Chita began taking inventory of supplies, cutting bandages from clothing they brought, and pumping water.

Mateo and Ignacio soon returned supporting a wounded man between them. Red-faced and winded, they lowered their charge gently onto a pallet.

Catalina and Chita squatted beside the soldier. Speaking softly to the man, Catalina held his hands as Chita cut away his blood-soaked shirt.

"What's your name, señor?"

He struggled to free his hands from Catalina's grip but lacked the strength.

"Your name, señor, what should I call you?" Catalina persisted, trying to distract him from the work Chita performed.

"José," he rasped.

"José, I'm Catalina, and this is Chita. We need to clean your wound and stop the bleeding. Then you can rest." Catalina glanced at the torn flesh of the man's shoulder and shuddered. "You're going to be fine." She tried to sound convincing as the blood streamed from the wound.

Before they completed the bandaging, another wounded soldier stumbled in, helped by a comrade, and then another, dangling limply between two men who staggered from his weight.

Gabino and Andrés assisted Catalina and Chita. They worked quickly and without pause, but they could not keep up with the number of wounded who walked assisted or were carried into their makeshift infirmary. Injured soldiers filled the pallets, and new arrivals lay in the narrow dirt spaces between pallets, often in the blood and gore of their neighbors. And when those spaces filled, the wounded slumped listlessly against the bar.

Moans, cries, and calls for water issued from the sea of injured surrounding Catalina. She provided the little medical attention she could, using liquor to disinfect wounds and ease pain. She could do little more than clean and bind wounds. For those whose injuries meant certain death, she provided momentary comfort through prayer or touch before moving to help someone who might be saved by her attention.

Catalina finished wrapping the wound of one soldier, tucking the edge of the bandage through a fold in the cloth to secure it to his thigh. She tested her work, ensuring the wrap didn't restrict circulation. Satisfied, she moved to the next patient, pausing momentarily to stretch the tension from her back. The sound of fighting had lessened. Catalina noticed the dimming light filtering through the doorway of the pulqueria. She hoped the diminishing din of battle signaled a temporary truce, as it had the previous night, so the wounded could be transported to hospitals. For now, the women's care served as the gossamer thread tethering many of the men to life.

Andrés had already removed the clothing from a soldier bleeding profusely from deep lacerations shredding the left side of his body. Shards of glass protruded from some of the jagged wounds. Catalina carefully removed the glass, cleaning and bandaging the cuts the best she could. Many of the lacerations needed stitches, but she could not afford the time that would take. As she bandaged the wounds, a familiar voice announced, "You have all done well. You're indeed angels of mercy." Catalina recognized Mateo's voice. "Now, it's time for you to rest. The doctor will take over. Ignacio and I will return you women to camp."

A middle-aged man in a suit took control with authority, examining each of the wounded before giving directions to his four aides for the patients' placement, designating "hospital" or "camp" based on the severity of injury.

Catalina and Andrés continued to bind the worst of the lacerations until the doctor reached their patient. The doctor spoke Spanish colored with an American accent. "You have slowed his bleeding, but he's lost a dangerous amount of blood." The physician spoke without looking at Andrés or Catalina. "Let's transport this man to the hospital." He moved on to examine the next patient.

As the aides responded to the doctor's orders, Catalina stepped toward the doorway, anxious to speak with Ignacio. Tugging his sleeve, she asked, "Do you know of my family? Are they unharmed? Have they returned to camp, or are they still in the city?" She knew she needed to let him respond, but she had so many questions that she could not stop herself. "Can you direct me to them?"

Ignacio hesitated, thinking, and then answered, "They are still in the city." He paused, as if sorting her questions. "They are with troops near the church." He smiled, pleased with his recall, but then his smile disappeared, and his face went ashen.

"What, Ignacio?" Catalina insisted. "Tell me."

Ignacio turned to Mateo for help. "Cata asks about her family."

Mateo, whose attention had been focused on sorting the wounded, responded to Ignacio's plea. "They are brave soldiers. Ignacio introduced me. I told your brothers of your work." He spoke reassuringly. "They're proud of you but anxious for your safe return to camp. I promised I'd escort you."

"And Mayo? What of Mayo?"

"He is with your brothers. He wants me to return you safely to camp."

"And my father?"

Mateo hesitated.

"I'll go to him." Catalina started toward the door, but Mateo caught her arm.

"Wait, Little Hen."

Catalina turned to face Mateo. He no longer smiled. "Your father fought bravely. He is dead."

The finality of the words stunned Catalina like a sharp blow, and she took an involuntary step backward. She didn't cry. She removed Mateo's hand from her arm. "I'm going to my family." She turned and walked through the doorway.

"Cata," Mateo called, "I promised your family I would escort you to camp."

Catalina did not pause. She would go to her family.

"Come," Mateo spoke as he trotted to join her. "I'll take you to your brothers, but they won't be pleased with either of us."

They moved silently, Catalina walking without knowing how she remained erect. The news of her father's death had torn her soul. Somehow, though, she continued forward through the nightmare landscape of broken glass, crumbled buildings, and shattered men. Mateo halted their progress, only long enough to remove a rifle and bandolero from the body of an insurrecto.

"Here." Mateo draped the belt of ammunition over her head and thrust the rifle into her hands.

The rifle weighed heavily, but Catalina was pleased to hold onto something.

They continued into the city, passing fellow insurrectos returning to camp, many bearing spoils of war. One soldier gleefully plucked the two remaining strings on the full-bodied guitarrón mexicano he carried, creating bass sounds that bore little resemblance to music. Another carried a hand-cranked sewing machine under one arm. When he passed them, he exclaimed proudly, "For my woman."

Mateo shook his head with disgust.

They pushed on, destruction surrounding them. Catalina's eyes and throat burned from the smoke of buildings smoldering a few blocks away. She wiped tears and strained to focus on bodies littering the street until Mateo said, "Your father is not among these dead."

He guided Catalina past a bombed-out building with bodies hanging from its windows like garish decorations. On another block they passed a dry goods store filled with insurrectos rewarding themselves with leather boots and linen shirts. In the doorway of the next building, an insurrecto stood with one hand fishing for the contents of a large jar balanced on his hip. He thrust out his catch, offering,

"Pickled pig's foot?"

"No gracias, señor." Catalina held up the flat of her palm for emphasis. She struggled with the sense that she had been bewitched because nothing in the surrounding landscape seemed real.

They continued into the darkening night until Mateo paused. "We're nearing the front. Though the fighting has halted, if you make yourself a target, no sniper will resist. Move carefully."

They turned down an alley, trotting in a crouch, traversing a couple of blocks in this manner. Mateo halted at the corner of a building. "Stay close. We don't want to be shot by our own troops."

Catalina nodded her understanding.

Mateo motioned for her to follow, then disappeared around the corner. When Catalina rounded the building, she saw rubble blocking the street. It took a moment for her to realize the debris formed a barricade behind which soldiers moved. When they neared a group of soldiers, Mateo announced, "Gente de Villa." His identification of them as Villa's people satisfied the soldiers, and they allowed the two of them to continue forward.

Nearing the barricade, Catalina searched for Mayo, Diego, or Miguel, but she didn't see any of them among the rebel soldiers. She feared that her family may have returned to camp. As she began to question her decision to seek them, she caught a glimpse of a man who turned in her direction. Her heart pounded with the knowledge that she found Mayo.

Catalina hurried past Mateo to Mayo, who now sat with his back to the rubble of the barrier. When Mayo saw her, his face registered horror.

"Mayo," she whispered, leaning her rifle against the barricade and squatting to him. He shied away at first, his hands touching her arms hesitantly, but then he pulled her to him, holding her tightly, kissing her face. He released her only to look at her; then again, he pulled her into an embrace.

"I thought you were a ghost," he whispered. "I didn't think you were real."

She cupped his face in her hands.

Mayo gripped her shoulders and examined her. "Are you wounded?"

Catalina glanced down at herself and realized her clothes were stiff with blood of others. "No, Mayo," she reassured him. Catalina now understood his fear upon first seeing her; someone covered with so much blood should not be walking or breathing. "This blood is from the wounded I cared for."

Relieved, he pulled her to him again. "Cata," he spoke softly, and Catalina knew from his tone what he would say even before he uttered the words "your father."

"I know." Catalina leaned back from Mayo. "When did he die?"

"This afternoon, fighting to take this barricade from the federales. It happened so quickly. He didn't suffer, Cata."

"Where is he?"

"We moved his body into a building. Diego and Miguel are there now."

"Take me to him."

Mayo nodded. Before they stood, Mayo warned, "Stay low and alert, Cata."

Catalina collected her rifle and followed Mayo. He turned onto a side street, pausing at an entrance. "Diego, Miguel," he called before pushing open the door.

Catalina entered the room behind Mayo and, in the thin candle-light that diluted the darkness, saw her two brothers standing beside a bed where her father lay. She rushed past Mayo and her brothers to her father, leaning to kiss his forehead, only half aware of Miguel's reprimand, "You shouldn't be here, Cata," and Diego's gentle touch against her hand. Death had cooled her father's skin. She studied his face, his jaw slack, grizzled with days' growth. Blood soaked the blanket that hid where bullets had ripped her father's body. She slipped her hand into his and felt his fingers already stiff. She knelt beside the bed and lay her head on his shoulder. She wanted to pray, but no prayer would come.

"Cata," Miguel spoke sharply, "there's nothing you can do here. You need to return to camp."

Catalina did not move. The grief translated to such a weariness in her limbs that she could not command her muscles to respond.

"Cata!" Miguel repeated. "You don't belong here. You are to return to camp. I'll find someone to take you."

She didn't respond.

"Cata!"

Catalina felt two pairs of hands lifting her to her feet.

"Stand, sister," Diego gently coaxed.

"Cata," Mayo spoke softly, "Miguel is right. You aren't safe this close to the fighting. There is nothing you can do for your father."

"No, I will stay." She answered firmly. She turned to Mayo. "I won't leave you."

"Cata!" Miguel interrupted. "You will do as you're told."

Catalina faced Miguel. "I will stay with Mayo," she answered calmly.

"Mayo?" Miguel asked with angry confusion, looking at the two of them. "You will obey me," he said, raising his hand to strike her.

Mayo gripped Miguel's raised wrist. "She is my woman, Miguel. Cata is my wife."

A confused silence followed; then Miguel hissed, "I should kill you. I should kill both of you for shaming the family."

"There is no shame, Miguel. I love Mayo. We are husband and wife."

Miguel looked past her to Mayo. "Then make your wife obey." Miguel walked from the room.

Miguel's exit left an uncomfortable silence, but Diego stepped forward. "I am pleased for both of you." Diego kissed Catalina on the cheek and gave Mayo an abrazo, slapping his back throughout the hug.

"Gracias, hermano, brother," Catalina reached to squeeze Diego's hand.

"I'll leave you alone with Papá."

After Diego left the room, Catalina moved into Mayo's arms and whispered, "Now they know we're together. We've told my brothers in the presence of my father."

"I'll try to make things right with Miguel," Mayo promised. "We're family now. There shouldn't be bad blood within a family."

"When Miguel sees how much I love you, he won't remain angry." Catalina knew she spoke the truth.

Catalina returned to kneel at her father's bedside. She wished they had talked about so many things; she had so much she wanted to tell him, but she uttered only, "Oh, Papá," as she lay her head onto his shoulder.

"Cata," Mayo coaxed, and helped her stand.

Suddenly, Catalina felt so tired she doubted she could remain standing without Mayo's support. "Let's sit, Mayo. Let's rest just a bit."

They sat on the floor—Mayo with his back to the wall, Catalina resting in his arms, her forehead nestled against his neck. She felt herself sinking almost immediately into the dark velvet of sleep.

Catalina didn't know if she had slept for minutes or hours when she awoke to Diego's voice. Diego offered them a tin of meat, a can of peaches, and a canteen of water to share.

Diego waited for them to finish the food before he spoke. "We're going to use the darkness of night to move closer to the mission church. We've got dynamite, and we're going to try to take the church at daybreak." He spoke directly to Mayo, no longer including Catalina in the conversation. "My sister needs to return to camp. It isn't safe for her this close to the fighting."

Catalina did not wait for Mayo to speak. "I will not leave Mayo. I will fight alongside him."

Diego did not acknowledge Catalina; instead, he looked at Mayo for an answer.

Mayo looked from Diego to Catalina. She met his gaze. Mayo turned back to Diego. "Cata remains with me."

Diego did not argue. He stood and said, "Then it's time to return to the barricade."

Cata went once more to her father's bedside, leaned down to kiss his cheek and place her hand over his heart. "I love you, Papá." That said, she collected her rifle and waited with Mayo for Diego to speak his goodbye to their father. When Diego finished, he blew out the candle.

Walking in the night air, Catalina struggled to keep her nervousness from breaking the surface of her confident exterior. She had been on the fringe of battles before, but she had never been involved in the actual fighting. Now she felt anxious. She didn't want any carelessness on her part to endanger her loved ones.

They returned to the barricade single file, with Diego leading and Mayo at the rear. Miguel waited apart from the other soldiers. When they joined him, he looked hard at Catalina and said, "Our father would not approve of your being here." Then he turned his back to her.

Catalina knew Miguel was right. She struggled to ignore the gnawing sense of her father's disapproval.

The revolutionaries began to push forward one at a time. They would use the cover of darkness to move into buildings near the mission church and prepare to take out the guns at the church's base and atop its roof. The troops needed to be in position and ready to attack at daybreak. Mayo placed his hand on the small of Catalina's back to motion her forward into the line of departing insurrectos.

Crossing an open space, Catalina peered down a connecting street and saw the shadowy figures of fellow insurrectos mirroring her group's progress into the city's heart.

They continued forward until they reached the row of buildings lining the street near the church. Then, the rebel soldiers formed into smaller units, each group entering a building along the alley. Catalina followed Miguel and Diego through the door at the rear of a corner building. When she paused inside the door to shoulder the strap of her rifle, she heard a whisper: "Move along the wall to the front."

Catalina recognized the voice; it was Mateo who spoke.

"So, you've decided to stay for the fight, Little Hen." He grinned as he whispered, "Don't forget how to fly. This time when you hear a gun's boom, it *will* be aimed at you. Now move forward along the wall and stay away from windows."

Catalina's face warmed at Mateo's reminder of her fear. As she scooted forward, following Diego, she told herself she would be brave.

When they reached the front of the room, Diego signaled for her to squat. "Keep your head down, little sister," he whispered in her ear. "There's broken glass on the floor, so move carefully."

They crawled along the front wall of the building, staying below the ledges of two large windows. They placed their hands and knees deliberately, testing the debris on the floor before transferring weight onto their limbs. By the time Catalina crossed the room to sit beside her brothers, rivulets of sweat trickled down the back of her neck and between her breasts.

Mayo sat beside her with his back to the wall. He whispered, "Now we wait."

Catalina felt satisfied to wait alongside her family for what morning would bring. She watched several other men position themselves along the walls of the room. She knew five of the seven who joined her family to take up positions in this building.

Catalina glanced around to familiarize herself with her surroundings. Deeper than wide, the room housed an office. She could make out a desk and cabinets with shelves of ledgers. A kerosene lamp, the only glass object that hadn't been shattered, resided atop one of the cabinets. Next to the cabinets, what appeared to be bundles of papers lined one wall in neat stacks. On the floor, Catalina noticed a small shape that made her breath catch in her throat. She focused through the darkness and realized that what first appeared to be the body of an infant was actually that of a small dog. Catalina restrained herself from voicing her relief. She could not have remained in a room with a dead baby.

Catalina detected movement and turned to see Miguel and Ángel, a fellow insurrecto, positioning themselves at the windows. Catalina noticed three sticks of dynamite protruding from Ángel's waistband at the small of his back. She hoped he would use the dynamite quickly once the fighting started because if a bullet were to strike the explosives, no one in the room would be spared. Catalina wondered who else among their small troop carried dynamite. She hoped the explosives the insurrectos brought didn't pose greater danger to their own troops than to the enemy's guns.

Mayo gently squeezed Catalina's hand to get her attention. He whispered, "You should try to rest before the fighting begins."

Catalina nodded and closed her eyes, but she saw the lifeless figure of her father and the mangled bodies of the men she had treated the previous day, so she opened her eyes, preferring to stare into the gray of the room. She sat waiting, both anxious for the fighting to begin and wishing it would never start. She looked at the men poised with dynamite and guns. She looked down at herself—a rifle resting in her hands, a bandolero across her chest—her life on the hacienda seemed eight years instead of eight months ago.

When daylight began eroding dark, Mateo positioned himself to peer over Ángel's shoulder. Catalina's heart pounded knowing the fighting would soon begin.

Mateo motioned for the men to take their places at the windows. Catalina tucked her feet beneath her to crawl forward when Mayo gripped her arm to stop her. "You need to stay at the back of the room."

Catalina started to protest, but Mayo spoke firmly, preventing further discussion. "Get behind the desk for protection. You'll need to help with any wounded."

Catalina would do as Mayo wished if it meant she could remain with him.

Mayo gave her arm a gentle squeeze. She watched him take a position at the window next to Diego. She looked at Miguel standing, Diego squatting, Mayo kneeling and silently prayed, "Keep them from harm."

Mateo stood between the two windows but clear of the door. He gripped the barrel of his rifle with his left hand; in his right, he held a watch, and he alternated between staring out the window and monitoring the time. He slipped the watch into his pocket only long enough to hold up five fingers for all the men to see. Then he retrieved the timepiece and began his routine anew.

Catalina had been so caught up with observing the preparations for battle that she forgot to follow Mayo's instructions until he turned and motioned her toward the back of the room. She began a slow, deliberate crawl toward the desk. She glanced momentarily at the body of the dog, then quickly looked away. The mutt, more puppy than dog, had been gut shot, entrails and blood spilled from its belly. Catalina continued her painstaking crawl to hide behind the large wooden desk. She placed her rifle within easy reach and positioned herself to keep an eye on Mayo and her brothers.

Mateo held up three fingers.

The remaining three minutes passed sluggishly. Then Mateo raised his hand into the air with five fingers extended. Catalina held her breath as Mateo, with the curl of a finger, ticked off each second until his arm dropped forcefully to his side.

Catalina's ears rang from the explosions of gunshots as the men fired furiously from their positions at the windows. The insurrectos succeeded in their surprise, but the federales quickly regrouped, responding with their own gunfire. Soon bullets splintered window frames, thudded into adobe walls, and ricocheted unpredictably about the room.

Ángel was hit first. Catalina saw him reel from the window and collapse. She crawled quickly toward him, oblivious to the glass fragments that sliced her knees and pierced her palms. When she reached Ángel, she had to fight revulsion, swallowing hard against the bile in her throat. The bullet had ripped off his jaw, smashing through his cheek to leave an eyeball dangling from the shattered socket. He breathed great bubbles of blood through what remained of a nasal passage. Catalina could do nothing. She removed her rebozo, placing it in a ball under his head to comfort him in his death throes.

Soon, another fighter staggered from the window, his mouth agape in a silent scream. A bullet had sliced through his throat; he gripped the wound with both hands, trying desperately to stop the fountain of blood spurting between his fingers. A second bullet spun him to face the window, and he crashed to the floor in death.

Catalina looked to Mayo and her brothers. Uninjured, they fired from their window with little pause.

"Sangre de Cristo!" Mateo cried out when the bullet pierced his side. He dropped to one knee, clawing the air for something to break his fall. From his knees, he fell face down. Catalina reached him as he struggled to raise onto his hands. "They shot me, Little Hen." He tried to grin as he told her the obvious.

"Can you help me scoot you toward the wall, Mateo?"

He nodded. But when Catalina tugged at his arm, he collapsed forward, and she fell backward with his weight.

"Help me turn onto my back." He spoke through gritted teeth.

Catalina placed one hand at his hip and the other at his shoulder. With their combined strength, Mateo managed to roll onto his back, but the effort exhausted him. He closed his eyes and held up a hand, cautioning her to wait. Catalina rested his head on her lap. Blood soaked his shirt and pants, and when he exhaled deeply without taking another breath, she feared he had died in her arms. Finally, his chest rose, and he opened his eyes. "I'm ready."

Catalina placed both hands beneath his shoulders, grabbing him at his armpits. While she pulled, he placed the heels of his boots to the floor and pushed. Slowly, they scooted across to the wall and maneuvered so that he sat upright. Catalina's breath came in gasps as she opened his shirt to expose the wound. The bullet had passed through his right side below his ribcage. The wound bled profusely.

"If you can slow the bleeding, I think I'll be all right."

Catalina lifted a knife from a sheath Mateo wore at his waist. She used the knife to remove Mateo's shirt; then, she cut a long strip from the hem of her own skirt. With the strip of cloth, she secured two balls of material to the the bullet's entrance and exit wounds and hoped the pressure would slow the bleeding. Before she could secure the end of the wrap, the room came alive with a spray of bullets. Without thinking, Catalina pushed Mateo to the floor and shielded him with her body.

When the rattling of the machine gun stilled, Catalina looked to see Mayo and her brothers staring anxiously in her direction. She acknowledged with a nod. Mayo motioned with his hand for her to stay low.

"You need to get the dynamite from Ángel," Mateo whispered.

Catalina saw that two more bullets had ripped Ángel's body. She crawled to him. Though he was considerably lighter than Mateo, Ángel's dead weight made maneuvering him difficult, but finally Catalina managed to free the dynamite. As she removed the last stick, the machine-gun fire again strafed the room. Catalina dove into a corner, curling into a fetal position, cradling the dynamite to her breasts.

"Chinga!" The curse accompanied a spray of blood that splattered Catalina's face. She raised her head to see a soldier writhing on the floor, holding his right foot, the toe of his boot removed by a bullet. Catalina could not attempt to assist him while the federales focused their machine gun on them, so she tucked her head and waited.

Finally, a lull in machine-gun fire. Catalina raised her head to assess the damage. She looked first for Mayo. Once they acknowledged each other, Mayo returned to the fighting, and Catalina sought her brothers, who no longer fought at Mayo's side. Instead, Miguel lay on the floor, the heels of his hands pressed to his eyes. Diego knelt beside him, attempting to pull his brother's hands from his face.

"Diego!" Catalina called loudly to be heard over the gunfire.

Diego turned to find her. Pointing to the adobe wall and then to his eyes, he informed her of Miguel's injury: a bullet striking the wall peppered his eyes with debris. Diego held up a canteen to show he intended to flood Miguel's eyes. Catalina nodded her understanding.

Realizing she still clutched the dynamite to her chest, Catalina looked for the safest place to deposit it. The wall against which Mateo rested seemed the best protected, so she crawled quickly across the room. Mateo motioned for her to place the dynamite behind him so his body could shield the sticks. She did as he directed.

Catalina started her return to the soldier whose toes had been shot off, but a burst from the machine gun forced her to retreat. She lay on the floor, her back pressed against the wall. She looked to Diego, who struggled to guide Miguel into a sitting position out of the line of fire.

Mayo remained at the window, rising up enough to shoot several rounds when the machine-gun momentarily diverted across the front door to the other window. Catalina watched fearfully when he rose to shoot, then ducked beneath the window ledge as the federal fire concentrated in his direction. Catalina held her breath each time he left his cover to shoot. But his instincts seemed correct. Catalina, too, thought she discerned a pattern in the machine gun fire. Mayo rose to shoot. "One, two, three, four," she mentally counted before Mayo ducked beneath the ledge, and the gun again strafed his position. Then as the gun swung away from Mayo, he rose above the ledge to shoot. "One, two, three, four." Then, again he ducked for cover, waited, then rose to shoot. "One, two, three, four," and he sank below the ledge. Catalina watched the dangerous dance. "One, two," Catalina counted when Diego shouted, "Fire," and pointed to smoke issuing from the back of the room. "Three, four," Catalina counted, but Diego's shout had distracted Mayo, and he remained upright a second longer than he should have. Catalina screamed her warning as a bullet hurled Mayo back from the window.

Catalina crawled quickly to Mayo, tucked her hands beneath his shoulders, and found the strength to pull him to slightly better protection afforded by the solid wall. The bullet had struck him in the right arm below the shoulder, exploding the flesh and shattering the bone, leaving the arm tethered by a thin cord of muscle and skin. Catalina wanted to hold Mayo and weep, but she understood that if she didn't control the bleeding, Mayo would die.

Diego crawled to her side. "How badly hit?"

"I need your knife, Diego, and the sheath. I've got to try to stop the bleeding."

Diego handed her the knife. "I can't help you, Cata. We've got to put out the fire, or we'll all die."

Catalina looked through the fog of smoke filling the room to see the flames spreading from the stacks of paper to the furniture. A bullet had shattered the lamp and ignited its kerosene. Coughing from the smoke, she turned her attention to Mayo; she could not worry about the flames. With the knife, she cut another strip of cloth from her skirt. Though unconscious, Mayo moaned with pain when she wrapped the cloth tightly about the stub of arm above the wound. She tied the bandage once, pulling the ends as tightly as she could, then placed the sheathed knife against the tie and knotted the ends around the leather, forming a tourniquet. She made several turns with the knife, tightening the bandage with all her strength. Mayo issued a guttural groan as the tourniquet choked the blood flow from the wound.

Catalina wiped the beads of perspiration from his forehead and whispered, "Mi amor, mi vida! My love, my life!" Mayo desperately needed a doctor.

She coughed, clenching her eyes tightly shut against the sting of smoke. She looked from Mayo to Diego, who, along with another rebel soldier, stomped and slapped at the flames that sought to engulf the building. She looked at the bodies of her dead and wounded comrades. Their troop was reduced to two firing at the windows and two fighting desperately to stop the flames. The blaze prevented them from retreating through the rear of the building, and the federal troops would mow them down if they attempted to escape through the front.

Catalina briefly touched Mayo's face with the palm of her hand. She crawled to Ángel, lifting his head to remove her bloody rebozo. She crawled toward the back of the room toward the fire's intensity. She felt a sense of panic when she could not find the body of the dog; then she spied it under the desk where it had been kicked during the efforts to put out the blaze. She opened her rebozo and placed the stiff body of the dog into its folds. Gagging, she grabbed the guts that trailed from the corpse and tucked them in the shawl with the dog. Holding the bundle in one arm, Catalina crawled to Mateo.

"What are you doing, Little Hen?"

"I need the dynamite," she answered, reaching behind him as she spoke.

He leaned back, trapping her hand against the wall with his body. "Don't be foolish."

Catalina placed the bundle on the floor, reached into her sash, and pulled out her pistol. Placing the barrel to Mateo's temple, she hissed, "We're all going to die if we stay here. Give me the dynamite."

"Put away the gun," Mateo spoke as he leaned away from the wall, freeing her hand.

Catalina tucked the pistol back into her sash, then collected the three sticks of dynamite from behind Mateo. She placed the explosives in the rebozo beside the body of the dog, then wrapped the carcass in the folds of her shawl, leaving several inches of the dog's bloody intestine dangling from the bundle. She removed her bandolier and placed it beside Mateo.

"I don't know your scheme, Cata, but may God be with you."

"May God be with us all," she replied.

Cradling the bundle, Catalina crawled to the nearest window. She quickly explained to the fighter stationed there that she would try to place the bundle with the dynamite against the fortification shielding the federales; the insurrectos were to target the bundle, exploding the dynamite. Watching as one man communicated her strategy to the other, Catalina waited for a pause from the machine gun. She held the bundle tightly, feeling the dynamite against her breasts. She listened intently to the sounds of battle, waiting for the right moment. The rattle of the machine gun stopped.

Without delay, Catalina stepped through the door screaming, "My baby! You've killed my baby! You've killed my child!"

Aware of bullets whistling past her, she walked down the street as if insanity made her oblivious to all but grief. She walked weeping, pulling at her hair with one hand, screaming all the while, "My baby! My baby! Look at what you've done to my baby! Mary, Mother of God, look what you have done to my son!" Continuing toward the church, she became aware the shooting had stopped. Both sides seemed mesmerized by the woman insane with grief.

Catalina could see the barrel of the machine gun positioned behind a fortification at the base of the church. She could see the eyes of the federales who watched her from the barricade; she could see their blue uniforms, their closely cropped heads, and caught sight of the red bandanas and cummerbunds of federal rurales. Catalina felt such hatred. She walked directly to the fortification. She stood before it, looking hard into the eyes of the soldiers, and screamed for Fátima, Felipe, and her father, "Look at what you've done!" She held out the bundle with the intestines dangling from it, and she saw fear in the soldiers' eyes when they looked into the face of a woman driven mad. Catalina placed the bundle at the base of the fortification, shouting, "Here is what your bullets have done. Look at what you've killed."

When she rose to stand, she looked into the face of a rurale whose eyes had lost their fear. He pointed a pistol at her chest and said calmly, "Join your child, mother."

Catalina sprang for cover, but the bullet slammed into her body above her right breast. She landed hard and lay still, awash in a wave of darkness. She did not want to die—her mind struggled to form the thought. She fought the darkness seeking to swallow her. Catalina dragged herself, inching through the dirt to take cover behind stacked sandbags. The effort proved too great. Catalina slipped into unconsciousness, a tremendous explosion the last sound she heard.

"Cata."

The voice called to her from a great distance.

"Cata."

The voice sounded familiar, though she could not identify who spoke.

"Cata, I know you hear me."

The voice seemed closer.

Catalina felt her body lift into the air, and she thought her spirit was ascending.

"Cata."

She recognized the voice, and she struggled to answer. "Papá," she tried to cry out, but her lips would not form the word.

"Cata. Por favor, Cata, please. Open your eyes, little sister. We have won, Cata. Open your eyes and see our victory."

Catalina strained to do as told.

"Open your eyes, Cata, and see the federales defeated."

"Diego," Catalina uttered.

"Yes, Cata." He laughed as he spoke. "Yes, little sister. Miguel is here too."

Catalina opened her eyes, then shut them against the bright sunlight. She became aware that she sat upright, leaning on Diego's chest, Miguel squatting beside her.

Catalina opened her eyes again. She looked at Diego and saw he both smiled and wept. She felt such pain and weakness, but she fought to recall. "Mayo?"

"Mayo has been taken to a hospital. Now it's your turn, little sister. We're going to load you onto a wagon. You're going to a hospital to heal."

"I need to find Mayo."

"We'll look after Mayo, Cata," Diego assured her.

"First, though," Miguel interrupted, "we must look after you. Quiet now. We're going to put you into the wagon."

Catalina gritted her teeth against the pain that seared through her body when Diego and Miguel lifted her. Again, darkness sought to overtake her. She struggled to remain conscious. She tried to brace herself, but a moan escaped from her lips when they placed her on the hard wood of the wagon bed.

"I'm sorry to hurt you, Cata, but it couldn't be helped."

"You're strong; you'll heal quickly." Miguel tried to sound encouraging.

Catalina saw lines of worry on her brothers' faces.

"We must help with the other wounded, Cata."

Diego interrupted his brother, "But we'll be with you soon."

Catalina nodded.

Diego kissed her forehead. "Vaya con Dios, go with God, my brave little sister."

Miguel squeezed her hand. "We will look after Mayo, Cata." Then he left without further word.

Catalina lay on the wooden slats of the wagon bed, anxious for the journey to the hospital to begin. She had to find Mayo. Thinking of Mayo, Catalina failed to notice she shared the wagon with another injured insurrecto until she heard his familiar voice call out, "Halcón!" She turned to see Mateo lying next to her.

He looked at her, the mocking humor gone from his eyes. "Halcón," he repeated with gravity. "You are no little hen, Cata; you're the hawk. Halcón!"

Catalina reached to squeeze Mateo's hand, and the wagon jolted into motion.

Sarah

Sarah listened intently to the eerie quiet, hearing only the occasional gunshot. She glanced at the department store wall clock—1:35 p.m. She turned to Paola for affirmation of what she heard or what she didn't hear. Paola stood holding a blouse, staring toward the window, listening.

Sarah joined her friend and questioned, "You hear it, too? Right? The quiet, right?"

"Yes."

"It may be just a lull in the fighting," Sarah said warily.

"After three days of battle, this quiet is jarring."

"And not knowing what it means?"

They stood listening to the absence of gunfire, neither one wanting to suggest the possibility of peace.

Sarah had grown accustomed to the barrage of explosive sounds after spending a day and a half with A. J. photographing scenes of the El Paso community's response to the Battle of Juárez. They photographed Fort Bliss soldiers cordoning off streets. They used the *Times*' headlines, announcing the number of El Pasoans wounded and killed by stray bullets, as background to photos of men, women, and children gathered along the riverbank and standing on top of trains and buildings to watch the fighting. Only the dark of night silenced the torrents of explosions and gunfire, so the current quiet unsettled her.

Sarah looked again at the clock—it was 2:24. She thought of Samuel and offered a brief prayer for his safety. She couldn't allow herself to hope that the quiet signaled peace. Sarah tried to keep herself busy with menial chores since, again, the normal stream of customers did not materialize in the department store.

"Sarah," a voice rasped from across the room. "Sarah!"

Sarah saw A. J. striding toward her. Surprised, she hurried to him.

Wheezing from exertion and excitement, A. J. held up his hand for a moment to catch his breath.

She stood, barely able to contain her anxiousness.

A. J. swallowed hard, then began. "General Navarro surrendered to Garibaldi."

Sarah couldn't fully form the thought; she looked at him questioningly.

"Sarah, the insurrectos have won; they've taken Juárez."

Sarah let out a squeal of excitement, and without thinking, hugged A. J. He backed away, flustered by her show of emotion.

Paola joined them, attracted to the commotion.

"The federales have surrendered Juárez, Paola. That quiet we're hearing is the sound of peace," Sarah shared.

A. J. stood aside while the two women hugged in their excitement.

Then, in a voice tinged with irritation, A. J. interrupted the celebration. "Sarah," he called to regain her attention. "Sarah!" He continued, "Timothy Tompkins, a *Times* reporter, has secured a pass to cross the border. He's invited me along to take photographs. If you want to join us, you'll have to come now."

Sarah looked to Paola.

"Go," her friend encouraged. "I'll cover for you. If the manager asks, I tell him you became ill. I'll hint it's a woman's issue; he won't ask further."

A. J. shifted uncomfortably. "I'll meet you outside on the corner."

Sarah chuckled at A. J.'s discomfort as she hugged Paola. "Thank you."

"Just be safe," Paola called to her.

Sarah retrieved her camera case, secured her hat on her head, and hurried out to the street to join A. J.

They met the reporter at an agreed-upon location near the international bridge. Tompkins, a tall slender man, dressed in a rumpled jacket, work-creased pants tucked into knee-high boots, and a narrow-brimmed fedora atop his head, greeted them. Clearly keen to cross into Juárez, he began walking before A. J. completed introductions.

"So, you're Captain Clendenin's sweetheart?" Timothy asked as they neared the start of the international bridge.

"Yes. Do you know him?"

"I do. In fact, I've lost many a hand of cards to him." He grinned as if he were sharing a fact better kept secret from a sweetheart. "Would Samuel approve of your crossing into Juárez on the heel of battle?"

"I don't require his approval."

"Oh, a modern woman." Timothy nodded knowingly to A. J.

A. J. held up his hand to avoid being drawn into the conversation. "All I know is that she's a damn good photographer who doesn't take 'no' for an answer."

Sarah's face reddened at the half compliment. "Do you know if Samuel is okay?"

A brief spurt of gunfire in the distance made them all instinctively move closer to the buildings, the walls showing deep scars of war.

"I don't." Seeming to rethink his short response, he added, "But Samuel is a sly fox. If anyone can stay out of harm's way, it's Samuel."

Even though the reporter had no real knowledge of Samuel's well-being, Sarah felt somewhat comforted by his assessment.

Sarah examined the devastation surrounding them. She had viewed the destruction from various vantage points in El Paso, but to be in the midst of it made the fierceness of battle more real. The city looked as if a tornado had ravaged it. Adobe bricks tumbled from gaping holes of bombed-out buildings, shards of glass blasted from windows glittered in the afternoon sunlight, wires dangled limply from shell-shattered poles. And bodies. Though Sarah knew there would be bodies, she wasn't prepared for the number of corpses or the grotesqueness of their wounds. She swallowed hard.

"Let's get some photos of street scenes," A. J. directed.

Amid this destruction, Sarah had forgotten the reason A. J. had invited her. She uncased her camera, focusing it on war-savaged buildings while A. J. captured street scenes that included sprawled bodies of federales and insurrectos.

They kept their cameras out as they journeyed deeper into the city. Timothy guided them to the jefatura de armas, which showed evidence of a hard-fought battle. Bodies of federales in their blue uniforms and sandals littered the grounds around the federal headquarters. A dead horse lay in the street, legs stretched as if in mid-stride, a cloud of flies gorging on the blood from a yawning wound in its side.

Timothy directed them onto Calle Comercio toward the mission church, where, he explained, heavy fighting had recently taken place. As they walked past stores and saloons lining the street, Sarah saw insurrectos rewarding themselves for their victory. From one shop, a soldier exited wearing several Stetsons stacked on his head. Out of the neighboring store, two soldiers burst onto the street dressed in colorful shirts that replaced their battle-grimed clothes.

Sarah noticed that A. J. quietly repositioned himself to walk on the inside next to the buildings. She smiled at his protective gesture.

"You know what helped the insurrectos win," Timothy began as he glanced into a saloon loud with laughter, "is their approach to fighting." He spoke, largely addressing Sarah. "While the federal pelones . . ."

"Pelones?" Sarah interrupted.

"Bald," he pointed to the top of his head, "because of their close-cropped hair. Anyway," he continued as they passed another shop teeming with insurrectos, "the federal pelones fight with little respite, their officers at their backs threatening and berating them. The insurrectos fight more independently, leaving the battle when they're weary, returning to camp for food and rest, then rejoining the fighting once they're rested." Timothy concluded, "A much more civilized way to conduct a revolution."

Suddenly, a burst of gunfire issued from a side street. Sarah crouched in response, then felt herself propelled forward by A. J. and Timothy, who grabbed her at the elbows and began a dash for cover behind a wrecked wagon. They flattened themselves breathlessly against the wagon's wooden bed, which tilted drunkenly from a broken axle. Sarah knew their cover afforded minimal protection against the bullets whistling past. She ventured a glance between the bed's wooden planks to see insurrectos spilling out from doorways of stores and saloons, rifles at the ready, scooting along walls in the direction of the gunfire. A. J. tugged at her sleeve, motioning with his hand for her to lie flat, which he demonstrated himself, lying face down in the dirt. Sarah carefully placed her camera on the ground, then followed suit, her cheek resting on the backs of her hands as she peered in A. J.'s direction. The three of them lay still for what seemed an eternity, not moving even after the gunfire abruptly halted.

"Let's wait," Timothy whispered.

They continued lying prone behind the wagon, even when they heard voices of men returning from the skirmish to resume their celebration. Sarah marveled at the men's laughter and song so quickly following a gunfight that had surely resulted in injuries and loss of life.

Finally, the discomfort of lying face down in the dirt combined with the absence of gunfire spurred them to lift their heads and acknowledge one another. Timothy cautiously rose to a stand, then motioned for them to follow. Sarah stood, blowing a puff of air to remove any dust from her camera lens. She folded the camera and returned it to its case before turning away from the men to brush dirt from her clothes.

"Periodistas!" Timothy called out.

Sarah turned to see Timothy holding up both hands to signal surrender as two insurrectos approached them, rifles raised threateningly.

"Periodistas!" Timothy called again, declaring their status as reporters. He turned anxiously to A. J. and Sarah. "Show them your cameras."

A. J. lifted his camera in one hand while holding his second hand aloft. Sarah slowly extended the case, carefully unclasping the lid to expose her camera.

The two insurrectos kept their rifles trained on them while Timothy used two fingers to gingerly lift a folded piece of paper from his pocket and extend it toward the fighters. "Salvo conducto," he stated, identifying the safe conduct pass.

The older insurrecto took the paper from Timothy while the second one kept a rifle trained on them. Holding the pass upside down, the rebel soldier pretended to read it. He carefully refolded the paper, seemingly satisfied with its content, but rather than returning the pass to Timothy's outstretched hand, the insurrecto slowly tore the paper in half then proceeded to tear it into smaller strips, releasing the pieces to flutter to the ground.

Sarah's heart pounded when the insurrecto raised his rifle anew.

"Timothy!" a voice called from across the street. "Timothy!"

They all looked toward a portly middle-aged man, who, along with three rebel soldiers, hurried across the street, his hand raised in greeting.

"General Viljoen," Timothy responded, clearly relieved.

Sarah recovered her breath, as the two insurrectos lowered their rifles in response to the general's timely arrival and departed in reaction to an order from one of the fighters accompanying him.

"I am very pleased to see you, General." Timothy extended his hand to the man who joined them.

The general accepted the proffered hand, shaking it vigorously. He motioned toward the departing insurrectos. "Forgive our soldiers' indiscretion. Peace is so new that there remain federal enclaves that don't know of the surrender; they continue fighting. Soldiers accept they may be killed in battle, but to be killed in peace is like a cosmic practical joke, so our men may be overly vigilant. Ja?" He concluded with a bow toward A. J. and Sarah.

"Let me introduce General Benjamin Johannis Viljoen, the famous Boer general currently serving as military adviser to Madero." Timothy extended his left hand in the direction of the general, then extended his right hand toward A. J. and Sarah. "General, allow me to introduce my companions, two intrepid photographers, Mr. A. J. Otis and Miss Sarah Delaney."

"My pleasure," the general grasped A. J.'s hand, gripping his elbow in a forceful greeting. He turned to Sarah, accepted her offered hand, and bowed to press his lips lightly to it. "An honor and a surprise to see one so lovely in the midst of such ugliness," and he motioned to the bombed-out buildings.

"We appreciate the timing of your arrival," A. J. responded.

"My distinct pleasure."

"General," Timothy shifted to his role of reporter, "what can you tell us about the last few hours of battle and the surrender?" Timothy pulled a small pad and pencil from his jacket pocket.

"Always the journalist, my friend," the general chuckled.

"Well, not every reporter gets to interview a triumphant general on the day of victory."

Sarah listened, anxious to hear any word of Samuel.

While the three rebel soldiers stood guard, General Viljoen discussed details of the battle. He explained that the fight for control of the mission church had been vicious. Viljoen shared that General Navarro and the remainder of his federal garrison made their last stand in the barracks where a lucky insurrecto cannon shot had destroyed their water tower. The general pulled a large handkerchief from his back pocket, removing his hat to wipe perspiration from his brow. "Imagine, no water in this heat."

"I heard Garibaldi accepted Navarro's surrender?"

Sarah perked up at the mention of Garibaldi.

"Yes, he accepted Navarro's surrender in Madero's name."

Sarah interrupted. "Do you know Captain Clendenin? He serves with Colonel Garibaldi."

"I do know Captain Clendenin. A fine officer."

"Is he with Garibaldi at the federal cuartel?" Timothy asked.

"Yes, I believe he is."

The general's response made Sarah anxious to depart, but she removed her camera from its case to fulfill her role as photographer. "Let me take a photograph of General Viljoen."

"Yes," A. J. added, stepping beside Sarah to capture the photo from a slightly different angle.

"Timothy," A. J. directed, "let's get one with you interviewing the general."

Timothy posed with his pad and pencil at the ready and asked, "Where is Madero, General?"

Sarah took a few steps back to capture A. J. photographing Timothy and Viljoen.

"Madero should be at the cuartel shortly to meet Navarro, if he is not there already."

"Then we best make our way to the barracks." Timothy extended his hand to General Viljoen. "Thank you, sir, for the rescue and the interview."

"My pleasure."

"And our good fortune." A. J. extended his hand.

General Viljoen doffed his hat to Sarah. "Say 'hello' to Captain Clendenin for me." He smiled. "Tell him I said he's a lucky man."

"Thank you, General," Sarah responded, lowering her eyes.

Sarah felt relieved when they resumed their journey.

As they neared the church, bodies scattered about evidenced the fierceness of the fight. The church itself stood badly pockmarked from bullets that had battered its white facade. The smell of gunpowder still weighed heavily in the air. On the street alongside the church, Sarah watched insurrectos retrieve their wounded, placing them carefully into wagons. She wondered aloud where the injured would be taken.

"Well, Madero paid Dr. Ira Bush to set up a hospital for wounded insurrectos in El Paso," Timothy responded, "but Madero can now use military and city hospitals in Juárez."

Sarah removed her camera from its case, unfolded it, and sighted the bullet-scarred church along with insurrectos loading the wounded onto a wagon, then depressed the exposure lever.

Anxious to continue toward to the federal barracks where she might find Samuel, Sarah suggested, "Shall we continue?"

They walked for numerous blocks, surrounded by death and destruction. Finally, Timothy pointed to a brick facade. "That's the federal cuartel, the federales' last stand."

Sarah had to restrain herself from rushing past Timothy to the barracks to find Samuel, so she felt pleased when Timothy and A. J. increased their pace.

The cuartel gates stood open and inside grew a large pile of pistols and rifles with a line of federal soldiers waiting to deposit theirs on the stack. Sarah saw a bearded, gray-haired man standing with a military bearing, almost at attention. His distinguished appearance led her to ask, "General Navarro?"

"Yes, General Juan Navarro in the flesh," Timothy answered.

Sarah observed the air of sadness with which the elderly officer watched the disarming of his troops.

Sarah looked past the ceremony of disarmament, scouting the area for any sign of Samuel; she did not find him. A. J. nudged her, raising his camera. She interrupted her search to position herself near A. J. They photographed the line of soldiers depositing weapons, and General Navarro speaking with insurrecto officers. Then Francisco Madero and his wife stepped from the inner building into view to speak with General Navarro. Sarah captured a photograph of the three together.

"Well, what a pleasant surprise."

Sarah turned to see Colonel Garibaldi, looking dapper, though battle-grimed, in his fighting attire and green velour hat, now with a tricolor hatband. "One does not expect to find a rose on the field of battle." He reached to take her hand and raise it to his lips.

A. J. and Timothy moved closer to redirect Garibaldi's attention. Before they could interrupt, Sarah replied, "I'm glad that you are well, Colonel Garibaldi. Is Samuel here at the barracks?"

"No. I am afraid he is with troops scouting for outliers who don't know of the surrender."

Sarah felt disappointed. That meant Samuel was still engaged in a dangerous activity. She thought of General Viljoen's reference to a "cosmic practical joke" and hoped Samuel remained unharmed.

Timothy quickly gained Garibaldi's attention by stating, "I understand you were the one who accepted General Navarro's surrender."

"Yes, that is true." Garibaldi seized the opportunity to regale them with his role in the surrender.

"We had the barracks surrounded. General Navarro and his troops fought bravely, but we had them trapped, our gunfire blasting from buildings surrounding the cuartel. Our troops lobbed bombs over the wall into the interior of the barracks." Garibaldi paused to ensure he had the attention of all three, visibly pleased to see Timothy taking notes. "From the grocery store across the street, I watched General Navarro attempt to run up a white flag of surrender, but my men refused to accept this action; they redirected their fire to the flagpole, cutting the rope with their bullets and bringing down the flag. The fighting continued. That is when I took control of the situation. I issued the command of 'cease fire' to my troops. On a piece of grocery store paper, I wrote, 'General Navarro, I am giving you ten minutes to surrender' and sent an officer to the gate of the barracks to deliver it."

Garibaldi paused for dramatic intensity. "The doors to the barracks opened, and again, the white flag was raised. General Navarro and his officers exited the cuartel unarmed. I ordered my troops to form a line in front of the barracks, and I stepped forward to accept his surrender. That's when I shook the old man's hand, congratulating him on fighting a brave battle."

With less flair, Garibaldi added, "Of course, I sent word immediately to Madero."

"A photograph, Colonel Garibaldi?" A. J. asked.

"Of course." Garibaldi took a moment to smooth his moustache and reposition his hat to allow for a fuller view of his face. He stared forward, as if looking deep into history, and announced, "Ready."

The church bells began to ring, signaling the newly achieved peace to all within hearing. Timothy leaned between A. J. and Sarah, speaking loud enough to be heard over the clang of bells. "I think this is a good time for us to take our leave. Madero is too occupied with details of the surrender to grant an interview, and the bells will bring tourists and souvenir hunters from El Paso." He turned to Sarah, who found it hard to hide her disappointment. "I'm sorry we didn't find Samuel, Sarah."

She nodded, not trusting herself to speak.

Timothy returned his attention to Garibaldi. "Congratulations on your victory," and he extended his hand.

"Are you departing?" Garibaldi asked, accepting the handshake.

"Yes, I have a story to write." Timothy raised his pad to signal the notes from Garibaldi.

Colonel Garibaldi looked at Sarah. "I know Samuel will sorely regret he missed you. I will tell him I attempted to amuse you in his stead."

As they started to leave, Garibaldi called out incredulously, "Are you on foot?"

Timothy answered, "Yes."

"No, no," Garibaldi insisted, seeming truly aghast. "I will secure a car to transport you." Though he maintained eye contact with the men, he tilted his head in Sarah's direction. "It is far too dangerous still." He stepped aside to speak to one of his soldiers, who nodded before departing. Garibaldi returned, assuring, "It will be just a moment."

Sarah had to admit she would gladly accept the ride. The emotion and disappointment of the day, compounded by the unrelenting heat, had sapped her energy. While they waited for the arrival of the car, Sarah searched the crowd again for Samuel, to no avail. Soon Garibaldi ushered them outside of the cuartel gates to a black Model T. He took her hand, cupping her elbow to assist her onto the front seat of the vehicle. "I hope to see you again soon under more pleasant circumstances, Miss Delaney." He bowed before turning his attention to Timothy and A. J., who had already entered the backseat of the vehicle. "Gentlemen," he dipped his head in salutation, then tapped his hand against the car's fender to signal the driver to depart.

The warm wind blowing through the car felt refreshing. Sarah closed her eyes, turning her face to the breeze. She opened them to see the driver carefully maneuvering around potholes and debris. They passed alleyways lined with buildings scarred from combat and hiding bodies of people and animals alike. And then she saw him, caught a glimpse of Samuel from the corner of her eye. "Stop! Stop!" she insisted to the driver, who responded immediately to her urgent command.

"What, Sarah?" A. J. asked from the backseat.

Without waiting to explain, Sarah leapt from the automobile, calling loudly, "Samuel! Samuel!" and rushing toward him.

And in a single fluid movement, Samuel whirled around, lowering onto one knee, and sighting his rifle on Sarah.

Sarah halted abruptly. "Samuel," she repeated softly, suddenly aware of the danger.

Samuel hesitated, then lowered the rifle to the ground, his forehead sinking into his hands.

They both remained frozen for a moment; then Sarah walked to Samuel, crouching down to hold him, feeling him tremble. "Sarah," he spoke, his voice heavy with emotion, "I could have killed you."

She pushed back his hat, kissed his forehead, kissed his eyes.

He stood, raising her with him. "What are you doing here?"

"I had to see you, to know that you're okay."

"Sarah, it's dangerous. You shouldn't be here."

Several of Samuel's men came cautiously around the building, their rifles at the ready. "You okay, Cap?" one called.

When Samuel turned to respond, the lead soldier met Sarah's eyes, and said in an amused voice, "Yep, Cap's doing just fine." The men disappeared back around the building.

"I've got to go, Sarah. You need to return to El Paso." He peered toward the car. "Who is with you?"

"Hey, Samuel," Timothy waved from the backseat of the car. A. J. leaned forward and tipped his hat.

Samuel picked up his rifle, then put his arm around Sarah's waist to walk her back to the automobile. He acknowledged each of the men before he removed his hat to embrace Sarah. He assisted her onto the running board then the front seat. "I'll see you soon."

"Gentlemen," Samuel addressed the men in the car, "see her safely home." He then focused his attention on Timothy. "We'll talk later," he said curtly without a smile and departed in the direction of his men.

The driver released the brake, engaged the throttle, and edged the vehicle forward.

"Well," Timothy broke the silence, "I guess he's not happy with the quality of company you're keeping. Can't say I blame him."

They all laughed, the uncomfortable quiet broken.

Sarah continued to smile, relieved at seeing Samuel, even if they shared only minutes. She would make Samuel understand why she had to find him and why Timothy and A. J. were not to blame for her choices, even if Samuel thought those choices were ill advised.

Their journey back to the international bridge proved a surprisingly short one given the time it took them to wander through the ruins of the city on foot. They heartily thanked the rebel soldier who returned them safely to the border crossing. He departed with their good wishes and a pack of cigarettes as a thank you.

When they reached the foot of the international bridge, Timothy stopped and produced a flask from his jacket pocket. He unscrewed the top, turned toward the city of Juárez, and raised the flask into the air. "To our sister city. May this victory spell an end to fighting and the beginning of revolutionary change." He offered the flask to A. J., who tilted it briefly to his lips. Timothy took a long drink then started to replace the top. Suddenly he halted, looked to Sarah, and extended the flask. "Forgive my thoughtlessness, Sarah; I should have offered you the first drink. I wasn't thinking."

Sarah hesitated, then took the flask from Timothy. She raised it in a toast to the city, and placed it to her lips, allowing only a taste of the fiery liquid to enter her mouth. It burned against her throat and settled like a warm ember in her stomach. She handed the flask to Timothy, who offered a second round to all, and then, before returning the flask to his pocket, took one more long drink when there were no takers. "Onward," he announced, "I have a story to write, and A. J., you have film to develop."

When they crossed the bridge, A. J. hailed a cab and assisted Sarah into the backseat.

"Come on, Timothy, we'll drop you off," A. J. encouraged.

"No, it's just a few blocks to the *Times* office. I'll walk, get my creative juices flowing."

"I'll get you something for the paper," A. J. announced, joining Sarah in the backseat.

Timothy tipped his hat. "Sarah, A. J., it's been an adventure and a pleasure."

A. J. leaned forward and told the driver Sarah's address.

"I can go to the studio and help you in the darkroom, A. J."

"No, Sarah, not today. I don't have time to teach you. We've got too short of a turnaround. But you can give me your film, and I will select what I think are the best photographs for the paper."

Sarah did as requested, then settled back for the short ride to the boardinghouse. She thought about the contrast between the calm normalcy of El Paso versus the death and destruction in Ciudad Juárez. It seemed inconceivable that the two cities were only a river apart.

When the cab stopped in front of the boardinghouse, Sarah wished A. J. goodnight. She wanted a bath and bed. After a good night's sleep, she could sort through all she had seen and experienced that day.

❈❈❈

Sarah couldn't believe her eyes. She read again at the bottom left corner of the montage, "Photos by A. J. Otis and S. Delaney." Standing beside the newsstand, she wanted to scream her delight, to show all those who passed by that the *El Paso Morning Times* had published her work. Sarah again studied the photos A. J. had skillfully pieced together to form one. The top portion of the photo showed General Navarro standing near the line of his men surrendering their weapons onto the piles of firearms; the bottom half captured the pockmarked mission church with the insurrectos retrieving their wounded. Superimposed over the left side of the two photos, outlined in white, stood the lone figure of Colonel Garibaldi. Next to each of the three sections of the montage, a caption identified the subject. Sarah could not stop her eyes from returning to "Photos by A. J. Otis and S. Delaney."

Sarah purchased a second copy of the newspaper, carefully folding both and placing them under her arm. She stopped at the bakery to drink a cup of coffee and read Timothy's article before she hurried to the Popular to share the photos with Paola.

"How exciting!" Paola hugged Sarah. "I'm so proud of you!" Paola took a step back and held out her hands to feign a stage introduction: "My friend, Miss Sarah Delaney, photographer."

Sarah laughed, pleased to have Paola share her excitement.

❈❈❈

The bell over the studio door tinkled to announce Sarah's entrance. When A. J. appeared from behind the curtain, Sarah began speaking. "Oh, A. J., you performed magic with the photographs. I never imagined my name would appear in print and connected with such amazing work. How can I ever thank you?"

"Well, for starters, take a breath," he replied dryly.

"I'm sorry, A. J., but I'm just so excited. I can't wait to learn how to finish film and produce the quality work you create."

"I can only create quality pictures if I have quality negatives to work with, so you deserve the credit you received in the *Times*."

"Thank you, A. J."

"Let me get your two photos used for the newspaper," and he disappeared into the next room. When he returned, he placed two 8.5 x 12-inch photos onto the counter.

Sarah picked them up to review. Colonel Giuseppe Garibaldi stood proudly, his image crisp, the details of his hat, his hatband, his moustache, and his fighting attire all visible in sharp detail.

A. J. pointed with his little finger to the figure and said, "See, you captured the essence of this man, his self-assuredness, self-satisfaction, and, if one were to look closely at the set of his lips, his arrogance."

Sarah placed the photo on the counter to examine the second, which focused on the mission church with the rescue of the wounded.

A. J. pointed again with his finger to direct her attention. "Look at how the photograph captures bullet holes that riddle the walls of this old church."

As instructed, Sarah studied the small craters embedded across the church's white facade.

"The bullet holes are like wounds to this structure." He moved his finger to hover just above the wagon into which soldiers carefully hoisted their injured. "Now look at the wounded being removed from the church grounds. It's as though the old church and the injured soldiers shared a common fate in the struggle."

Sarah focused her attention on the wagon and the insurrectos lifting one of their injured onto its bed. Then she saw it, a detail she had not noticed when she'd sighted the scene in her viewfinder and took the photograph: decorative darts running in a vertical pattern down the length of a skirt. Sarah gasped in realization; the injured person the insurrectos lifted wore the distinctly patterned skirt of the girl who had hidden her face in a smear of motion when Sarah attempted to capture the campfire scene in Madero's camp. Sarah could not look away from the figure in the picture. Sarah now knew the smear in the photograph at the campfire was no accident; it was an act of defiance by this soldadera.

AUGUST 16, 1983

Kayla

"**Let's** stop now." The elderly woman held up her hand to Kayla.

"Yes, of course," Kayla replied.

Abel turned off the camera and switched off the bright production lights.

"I'm sorry, but I've grown weary." Sarah rubbed her brow with her fingertips.

"No apology needed, Sarah. You have been more than generous with your time and your memories."

"And there is so much more to tell," Sarah added.

"Sarah," Kayla leaned forward in the chair, "this information is wonderful and is an important addition to our library. Is it possible for us to continue our interview another day?"

"Yes. Yes, you must return," Sarah said with an urgency, "but give me a few days. Call later in the week, and we'll schedule another visit."

Kayla studied Sarah as she spoke. She looked visibly older, her eyes lacking the focus they showed at the start of the interview. Kayla wondered how much weariness resulted from the exertion of speaking for so long and how much from the emotion of remembering.

"All packed," Abel announced.

When Sarah scooted to the edge of her seat to stand, Kayla extended a hand to stop her. "Please, Sarah, stay where you are. We can see ourselves out."

Sarah seemed relieved to remain seated.

Kayla reached out to shake Sarah's hand. "Thanks again. We'll be in touch soon."

Abel followed behind Kayla to take Sarah's hand in his. "It has been a pleasure, ma'am." Then he leaned slightly forward, as if engaging Sarah in a private conversation. "Will you be all right?"

"Memories, Abel. The majority of my life is now memories."

PART

TWO

AUGUST 25, 1983

Kayla

"**El** Paso reveled in the Mexican Revolution." Sarah added, almost as an afterthought, "At least initially." She flattened the palms of both hands against the chair's leather armrests. "Two short weeks after the fall of Juárez, Porfirio Díaz resigned the presidency of Mexico and left for Paris to live his remaining years in exile."

It had been a little over a week since Kayla and Abel first filmed the elderly woman. After their first meeting, Kayla worried that the interview had proven too taxing for Sarah and feared she might not agree to a second session. But Sarah called the Oral History office just minutes after 8:00 a.m. the very next day, anxious to schedule their second interview, stating, "We still have history to address."

When Sarah answered the door at their appointed time, Kayla was pleased that the older woman again looked fresh and energetic. The researchers followed Sarah into her living room. Sarah wore a pair of fitted jeans, a red blouse with three-quarter-length sleeves, cuffs and collar turned up, not the style Kayla expected for a woman in her nineties.

Sarah welcomed them warmly into her home, providing a glass of iced tea she said she'd prepared to combat the heat of the production lights. Kayla noted that small talk held little interest for Sarah, so they quickly resumed the interview at the previous point of departure.

"El Paso greatly appreciated benefits the Mexican Revolution provided, as though the struggle of the Mexican people were a gift to the city. The revolution brought journalists who shined a national and international spotlight on El Paso and delivered an infusion of cash into the economy with all the war matériel both sides purchased. It also offered the people of El Paso daily excitement and, eventually, front-row entertainment. And the city showed its appreciation." Sarah smiled, shaking her head in disbelief. "The El Paso Chamber of Commerce held a banquet for all journalists and correspondents. If that weren't enough, the El Paso elite held a lavish event for Madero and key officers, with El Paso's mayor serving as toastmaster. The victorious Madero occupied the seat to the mayor's left while the defeated General Juan Navarro occupied a comparable seat of honor to the mayor's right. These were, indeed, crazy times." Sarah again laughed.

Kayla loved seeing Sarah's pleasure at recalling the absurdities of those days in El Paso.

"We thought Madero's victory would bring peace and positive change to the people of Mexico." Sarah sighed and shook her head. "We were naive." Sarah traced a drop of condensation down the side of her tea glass. "Uprisings against Madero began almost immediately and fighting again erupted."

"Sarah," Kayla interjected, "what role did Samuel play in this renewed fighting?"

"None." Sarah paused, then corrected herself. "Well, none that I know of. After Madero's victory following the 1911 Battle of Juárez, Samuel focused on refashioning himself into a businessman and husband. We married and assumed a normal life, well, a normal life for us. Samuel became part owner and operator of the Crown Saloon, and I went to work for A. J. in his studio. Samuel chose not to engage in the flurry of underground activities in El Paso related to the Mexican Revolution." Sarah looked away, peering into the distance. "But all that changed in 1913."

FEBRUARY 1913

Sarah

"Mmm," Samuel nuzzled Sarah's neck, pulling her closer to him. "Stay in bed a little longer," he encouraged.

"You're going to make me late for work." Sarah half-heartedly struggled against his hold.

"It's cold out from under these blankets," and he ran his hand from her waist to caress her breasts, kissing her neck. "Let me help brace you for the cold," he whispered, his lips against her ear; then he touched his tongue's tip to the base of her lobe.

A pleasant heat spread from Sarah's belly to her loins. She turned to face Samuel. "I'll tell A. J. you waylaid me." She ran her fingertips over the red stubble of beard along Samuel's jawline and pressed her lips to his, tasting smoke and whiskey from his previous night at the Crown.

Samuel slid his hand slowly up her inner thigh. "Hmm, 'waylaid' is it?"

Sarah arched her hips to his. "Shh, stop talking."

They made love with a hunger, until the final shudder of pleasure. When Samuel rose to roll from Sarah, she held him briefly. "Just a few seconds more," she whispered. They lay quietly in the warmth they created; then satisfied, Sarah kissed his rough cheek. "You stay in bed; I have to go." Once Samuel moved from her, Sarah lifted the covers and stepped into the chill of morning.

Sarah left the bedroom, rushing to ready herself for the day. When she returned to the bedside to tell Samuel goodbye, his deep snores greeted her. She didn't wake him; instead, she left the apartment quietly.

The morning air had a bite. Sarah thrust both hands deep into the pockets of her coat and hugged it tightly to her body. She walked quickly because of her lateness and the February chill. As she hurried down the sidewalk, she thought of the morning's lovemaking with Samuel and smiled.

They had married a little over a year and a half ago in June following Madero's victory.

Sarah quickly learned that Samuel enjoyed the nightlife—drinking, smoking, and gambling into early morning with others who shared a similar penchant. Soon into their married life, the opportunity arose for Samuel to go into business with Hugo Constanza as co-owner of the Crown Saloon. It seemed the perfect commercial venture for Samuel, providing both employment and entertainment. And Sarah didn't mind his late nights because Samuel didn't object to her working the hours needed with A. J., even if those hours sometimes extended into the evening and weekend. Sarah and Samuel made sure their schedules allowed ample time to share as husband and wife.

Samuel purchased his half of the Crown with money he'd earned through lucrative—or lucky, as Samuel described them—investments in stocks and bonds when he worked as an accountant years ago. "But that was in a previous life," Samuel would say when Sarah asked him about details of his past.

Sarah breathed deeply, exhaling a visible cloud into the day's chill. She thought again about their morning lovemaking. Sarah felt disappointed each month when the knot of cramps began and the flow of red appeared, but Samuel never complained. Each month when she shared the news, he would hold her and whisper, "That just means I have you all to myself for a little longer."

Seeing a lull in the traffic, Sarah hurried across the street onto San Jacinto Plaza. As she crossed the plaza, her eye caught the figure of a man squatting quietly to feed pigeons gathered around him. She removed her camera from its case and snapped a photo at the moment the man lifted his head to look with delight at a pigeon, wings outstretched, landing on his forearm. She forwarded the film, capturing another photo after two additional pigeons alighted on his shoulder and arm. When her viewfinder caught the man standing abruptly, suddenly aware of her attention, Sarah startled. She lowered her camera to see the hard glare that had replaced the joy on his face.

"Excuse me," Sarah stammered. Then she felt a flash of recognition. "Perdón," she offered, turning to hurry from the plaza. She sensed the man's stare following her. Even after she crossed the street, she felt him watching her, but when she glanced back at the plaza, only pigeons remained, pecking the ground where the man had stood.

Sarah hurried into the studio, bursting through the front door, rattling the bell with her entrance. A. J. stood at the counter. "You're late."

"A. J.," she said breathlessly, "I just photographed Pancho Villa."

"I heard he returned to El Paso last month after escaping from prison in Mexico City," A. J. answered calmly, this news having supplanted the topic of Sarah's late arrival to work.

"Samuel has seen him." Sarah paused, placing her hands on the counter to steady her nerves before continuing. "Villa is a friend of Constanza and regularly stops by the Crown to chat and drink strawberry soda." She placed her camera on the counter then stepped behind the doorway curtain to hang her coat and hat on a wooden hall tree.

A. J. waited for her to return to the front of the studio. "So, how did you get him to pose for a photograph?"

"I didn't. I mean I didn't ask."

"Oh?" A. J. responded with concerned interest.

"I saw a man feeding pigeons on the plaza and thought it would make an intriguing picture. It wasn't until he became aware of me that I realized I photographed Pancho Villa." She shuddered. "He glared at me with such intensity."

"Well, consider his situation. He's a man who recently escaped from a federal prison and the wrath of General Victoriano Huerta, who imprisoned him. The federal troops control Juárez, and I'm sure Huerta has plenty of operatives in El Paso. So, Villa sees a stranger taking photographs of him." A. J. extended the palm of his hand for her to draw the conclusion.

"I understand."

"Come on. Let's develop the film to see what you got." A. J. held open the curtain for her. "If we're lucky, we may have another postcard to sell."

"He wants to see the photographs," Samuel said, sitting on the edge of the bed to unlace and remove his boots. "And he wants to meet the photographer." Samuel turned toward Sarah, who rose onto her elbow. "I assume you are the photographer?"

"Yes," Sarah answered. "I didn't realize whom I was photographing."

Samuel stood from the bed to remove and fold his pants. "Well, Villa came to the Crown tonight and told Constanza about the incident. Constanza told him my wife is a photographer who matched the description." Samuel removed and draped his shirt on the valet stand, then raised the blankets to slide into bed beside Sarah.

"Is he angry? Should I be concerned?"

"No." Samuel leaned forward to kiss her cheek. "He's just cautious." Samuel lay on his back and pulled her toward him to rest her head on his shoulder. "Have you printed the photographs?"

"Yes." Sarah lifted her head to look at Samuel. "They're wonderful."

"Well, I told him we'd meet tomorrow at noon and you would share the photographs with him." Samuel brushed back a loose strand of hair from her face. "Okay?"

"Okay."

"Now, put your head back on my shoulder, and let's sleep. I'm beat."

Sarah slept fitfully, anxious about meeting Pancho Villa. In her mind, she alternated between presenting the photographs in an unapologetic manner or approaching him contritely for invading his privacy.

When morning came, Sarah readily left the bed and dressed for work in a preoccupied fashion. Before exiting the apartment, she returned to the bedroom to tell Samuel goodbye and saw he had already risen. She stepped into his arms, asking, "Where do I meet you, Samuel?"

He kissed the top of her head. "I'll come by the studio to pick you up at 11:45. We're meeting Villa at the Elite Confectionary, so it's a short walk from the studio." Samuel kissed her lips. "Don't worry," he said.

Sarah hurried from the apartment, anxious to get to the studio and reassure herself of the photos' quality. When she crossed the plaza, she glanced at the location where Villa stood yesterday feeding the pigeons. She felt relieved to see it vacant of all but a few birds pecking the ground.

"Why should I feel so uncomfortable," she said aloud before realizing she vocalized her thoughts. But she knew the answer. She knew that prior to the revolution, Villa had been an outlaw in Mexico. While she had heard different justifications for his path into crime, one constant story was his lightning-quick temper. Timothy Tompkins had shared an incident that occurred following the victory in Juárez when Villa marched armed into the Sheldon Hotel, intent on killing Garibaldi for some perceived slight, and had to be escorted back across the border by El Paso authorities.

When Sarah entered the studio, A. J. greeted her with, "You're early," followed by, "What's wrong?"

Sarah told A. J. the story about Villa's visit to the Crown and that Villa wanted to see her and the photographs and that Samuel had agreed to meet today at noon.

"You'll be fine," he insisted. "Samuel wouldn't agree to meet if there were reason for concern." A. J. pulled back the doorway curtain, and directed, "Hang up your coat while I get us a cup of coffee—then we'll examine the photos again."

Sarah placed her hat and coat onto the hall tree, then walked back into the darkroom to gather the photographs they had printed yesterday. She collected the prints from the drying rack and brought them to the front counter, spreading them across the top to compare. A. J. returned from his upstairs apartment carrying two ceramic mugs of steaming coffee.

Standing shoulder to shoulder, A. J. and Sarah viewed the prints, selecting the best copy of each photo. As A. J. placed them into an envelope, he attempted to reassure her one last time: "Sarah, I think Villa will see these photographs for what they are versus any effort on your part to spy on him."

Sarah nodded, taking the envelope and placing it under the counter with her camera.

"We have several rolls of film to process." A. J. said, clearly finished with the topic of Villa. "I'll work in the darkroom. You staff the front."

Sarah occupied herself through the morning with cleaning and organizing the storefront, busy but necessary work that, thankfully, required little focus. The morning hours dragged. Finally, Samuel appeared, ready to escort her.

Sarah stepped back to knock on the darkroom door for A. J. By the time he exited, Sarah had secured her hat and buttoned her coat.

"Samuel," A. J. acknowledged, his hand extended in greeting.

Sarah bent to collect the envelope containing the photographs, then stood, initially leaving her camera under the counter. Then, in a show of confidence, she retrieved the camera and placed the strap of the case over her shoulder. "I'm ready."

A. J. nodded his encouragement when she passed him to exit through the door Samuel held for her. Once outside, Sarah took Samuel's arm.

"Ready to meet the infamous Pancho Villa?" he teased.

"Don't, Samuel."

Samuel chuckled. "I'm sorry, sweetheart." Then he encouraged, "Let's have a pleasant meeting." He jostled her lightly. "Hey, how often do you get to eat dessert for lunch?"

In three short blocks, they stood at the entrance to the Elite Confectionary. Samuel removed his hat as he opened the door for

Sarah to enter. She glanced quickly around the room, past the large soda fountain in the center. Samuel pointed with the brim of his hat toward a small round table where Constanza sat beside a man she recognized as Pancho Villa. Constanza waved and both men stood, hats in hand, to greet them.

"Hello, Sarah," Constanza welcomed.

"Ella es mi esposa," Samuel introduced Sarah as his wife to Villa.

"Mucho gusto, señora," Villa greeted her politely.

"El gusto es mío, señor," Sarah returned the respectful greeting.

Samuel pulled out the chair next to Constanza for Sarah, but Sarah shook her head to indicate she wished to sit beside Villa. Once Sarah was seated, the three men joined her at the table, resting their hats on their knees. A brief awkward silence followed, so Sarah turned immediately to Constanza. "Please express to General Villa my sincerest apologies for intruding on his privacy yesterday." Sarah paused to allow Constanza to translate; then she continued, looking between Constanza and Villa. "I was simply captivated by a man feeding pigeons on the plaza. I did not recognize him as General Villa." Sarah was aware that Villa unsmilingly studied her as she spoke.

Villa responded to Constanza's translation. Then Constanza turned to Sarah. "He wants to know if you have the photographs."

"Sí," she responded directly to Villa. Sarah opened the envelope and handed the two pictures to him. She watched his steely stare melt and a deep laugh escape his lips. He looked again from one photograph to the other, this time leaning back in the chair to release a great belly laugh. He showed the photographs to Constanza without releasing them, then turned his attention again to Sarah. Setting the photos carefully on the table, he spoke with warmth and passion, taking one of her hands in both of his, then motioning with his head for Constanza to translate.

"He says he has never had such photographs taken of him. People always want photos of him on horseback or commanding troops."

Constanza paused for Villa to continue, then translated. "These photographs with the pigeons are now his favorites, and he thanks you."

Villa released Sarah's hand and signaled for the waiter. He spoke again to Constanza, who translated, "He would like to treat us all to his favorite dessert, the Elite Baseball. It's a generous scoop of rich vanilla ice cream covered in chocolate."

"Sounds perfect," Samuel responded, reaching under the table to squeeze Sarah's hand.

❖❖❖

"They killed him."

Samuel's presence in the apartment surprised Sarah as she entered. Samuel sat at the kitchen table, his head resting in one hand while the other gripped a glass with what Sarah knew was whiskey.

"They killed him, Sarah," Samuel repeated, then moaned his pain.

Sarah hurried to Samuel. Cradling his head, she asked, "Killed who, my love?"

"Madero. They killed President Madero, shot him like a dog," and he sobbed for a moment, holding her, before he grew still. He lifted his head, wiping the back of his hand across his nose and eyes, then raised the glass to drain the remainder of alcohol. While he poured another drink, Sarah positioned a chair to face him. She stroked Samuel's cheek and sat back to allow him time to regain control of his emotions.

Local newspapers had been filled with stories about fighting that began on February 9th in the streets of Mexico City. President Madero had trusted General Victoriano Huerta to lead federal troops against the rebel forces, but Huerta proved to be a scorpion, conspiring with rebel leaders. Just a few days ago, the *Times* reported that rebel forces arrested Madero and his vice president, forcing them to resign from office. Huerta then telegraphed the governors of all the Mexican states, informing them that the Senate had directed him "to assume charge of the government."

News of the coup was a hard blow to El Pasoans, many of whom had either fought for Madero or cheered for his success. And now, to hear from Samuel of Madero's assassination.

"Huerta claims he had nothing to do with the killing of Madero and his vice president." Samuel's voice was raw with emotion. "He wants us to believe their supporters accidentally shot them during an attempted rescue." Samuel almost spat the last statement, his voice showing complete contempt.

"Oh, Samuel." Sarah reached to take his hand. "What do you think will happen next?"

"Revolution," Samuel announced angrily, "revolution!"

❖❖❖

Samuel was right, Sarah thought as she folded the newspaper, saddened by the stories of turmoil in Mexico. Revolution had quickly exploded following the assassination. Two weeks after Madero's murder, Villa stopped by the Crown to say goodbye. He would return to Mexico and raise an army to fight Huerta's federal forces. And there were many others who opposed Huerta's blood-stained presidency. Venustiano Carranza, governor of the state of Coahuila and former minister of war in Madero's cabinet, refused to recognize Huerta's legitimacy and called on other governors to refuse as well. By late March, Carranza declared himself the Primer Jefe de Ejército Constitucionalista de México, First Chief of the Constitutionalist Army of Mexico. Soon, fighting spread throughout Mexico, reports of battles appearing daily in the local newspapers.

Sarah read about the influx of Mexican refugees to El Paso as the revolution spread. The wealthier refugees moved into Sunset Heights, while the poorer found living quarters in Chihuahuita, Duranguito, and the Segundo Barrio. Juárez remained under control of Huerta's federal army, and El Pasoans expressed conflicted emotions of worry and excitement over the likelihood that their sister city would again be torn by battle.

Sarah stood from the kitchen table and walked to the sitting room window to peer into the darkness of the street below. She knew not to expect Samuel for several more hours, but she couldn't help hoping he might come home early.

They never discussed the night Samuel wept openly for the loss of Madero, though Sarah tried. But after that night, Sarah felt a change in her husband. He seemed restless, as if he couldn't relax in his own home. One day, when she arrived at the apartment early from work, she found him sitting at the kitchen table, cleaning and oiling his pistols and rifle. Samuel put the weapons back into their scabbards and returned them to the closet, saying the guns needed routine care, but Sarah feared their lives would be caught, again, in the fires of revolution now burning across Mexico.

SEPTEMBER 1913

Catalina

Catalina added more chopped serrano chiles and cilantro to the simmering pot of caldo de res, flavoring the beef broth to her satisfaction before scraping in large chunks of carrot, potato, corn, squash, and cabbage. Placing a lid on the caldo, she reached to stir a large pot of menudo she had prepared before daylight fully flooded their small butcher shop. It was now a little after seven in the morning, but Catalina and Mayo had already spent several hours preparing for customers who, God willing, would purchase small cuts of meat, bring pots to transport prepared soup home, or sit at one of the three small tables in the shop to enjoy a bowl.

Mayo entered from a back room, shouldering a quarter side of beef. Though they had owned the butcher shop for almost a year, Catalina was still startled at the fresh smear of blood that marked Mayo's apron each workday and the sleeve folded and pinned, absent an arm.

Catalina thought about her life since the Battle of Juárez. After the battle, Mayo and she were both transported to the El Paso hospital run by Dr. Ira Bush. The seriousness of Mayo's injury required a longer convalescence than did Catalina's wound. Dr. Bush generously allowed Catalina to help care for Mayo and the other injured. During her weeks at the hospital, Catalina worked hard to learn English, studying in the evenings with one of the nurses and practicing during the day with other caregivers. Catalina thought Mayo and she might remain in El Paso once he left the hospital, and they did for a few weeks while he regained his strength. During that time, Catalina continued working with Dr. Bush and with Hotel Dieu Hospital, now in a paid position, assisting with the feeding, bathing, and basic care of patients. The couple occupied a room in a small Chihuahuita home owned by the family of one of Catalina's coworkers, but as Mayo grew stronger, he also grew restless and wanted to return to Mexico. Although Catalina's family had already departed from the region, she and Mayo decided to settle in Juárez and begin a new life. For a while, Catalina crossed the international bridge each day, continuing her work with Dr. Bush and the hospital. The dollars she earned, though not a lot, went further in Juárez when exchanged for pesos, and that money combined with the few pesos they received for their service to the revolution allowed them to rent a space in which to live and operate a carnicería, or butcher shop. While Catalina missed working with Dr. Bush, she knew she belonged beside Mayo.

Catalina was deep in thought when a voice interrupted her focus.

"Do your customers know they are buying beef from warriors?"

Catalina looked toward the man standing in the doorway of the small shop. Sunlight at his back made it difficult for her to see his features clearly.

"Do they know that a halcón is preparing their soup?"

The man stepped into the room, pulling out a chair from one of the tables to sit. Mayo moved around the counter toward the visitor, motioning Catalina to stay back. And in that instant, Catalina recognized the man. She called out, "Mateo, it's Mateo." Quickly wiping her hands on a towel, Catalina hurried to the front of the shop where Mayo and Mateo stood clenched in a backslapping abrazo. Mateo turned to hug her, kissing her cheek. "You look well, Halcón, healed and strong." He turned to Mayo. "You both look well, much stronger than when I last saw you."

"Yes," Catalina agreed. "We're glad to see you healed and healthy, as well, amigo."

"Please sit," Mayo spoke, motioning toward the chair Mateo had pulled from the table. "Cata, please get our visitor some menudo." Mayo pulled out another chair to sit across from Mateo.

Catalina soon returned with a bowl of steaming menudo and a plate with chopped onion, dried oregano, and wedges of lime alongside folded corn tortillas. She placed the dishes in front of an appreciative Mateo, then returned to the counter to collect three mugs of coffee. After she distributed the mugs, she took a seat between Mayo and Mateo.

Mateo blew steam from the spoon holding broth, tripe, and posole before placing it into his mouth. "Delicioso," he announced enthusiastically, scooping a second spoonful.

They made small talk, the three of them catching up on events in each of their lives. When Mateo finished his meal, he vigorously wiped his mouth and thick moustache, returned the napkin to his lap, and pushed away from the table to cross his legs and light a cigarette he had rolled.

"So," he began anew, "what are two warriors doing selling menudo and beef when El Escórpion sits in the Presidential Palace?"

Catalina saw Mayo tense. Mayo turned to finger his empty sleeve in front of Mateo. "And how would you have me load and fire a rifle?"

Mateo leaned forward, speaking calmly to both Mayo and Catalina. "There is much to be done that doesn't require firing a rifle."

"What would you have me do?"

"Not just you. Cata and you."

"How can we support the revolution?" Cata asked.

"You know that General Pancho Villa commands the División del Norte of the Constitutionalist Army, and his division now controls much of Chihuahua state."

They nodded in acknowledgement.

"The División del Norte has several thousand men, but thanks to the United States' arms embargo, it also has a shortage of munitions with which to fight." He paused to make sure he had their attention. "Living in Juárez, you're perfectly positioned to help with purchasing and smuggling weapons and ammunition across the border to Villa and his troops."

"How would that work?" Mayo asked.

"Villa has access to vast herds of cattle from the haciendas of Chihuahua state." Mateo grinned. "He is ready to ship three thousand head of cattle to El Paso for sale to a local cattle company. And this is just the first of many shipments."

"And our role?" Mayo questioned.

"The two of you will be a respectable business couple. You will deposit checks from the sale of cattle into the Two Rivers and Company account, which we've opened with the El Paso Bank and Trust. With money in that account, you'll purchase munitions from a buyer representing the Shelton-Payne Arms Company in El Paso. The arms buyer will provide you the bill for goods ordered, and the bank will issue a check to you for the purchase amount. This buyer will work with railroad employees to ship the matériel to a location along the border; you will, then, collect the goods to smuggle into México. Remember, while it isn't illegal to buy weapons in the United States, it is illegal to transport munitions into México, so your work is not without risks. Huerta and the United States have agents intent on stopping smugglers."

"And what about this carnicería? Do we simply close this butcher shop we've worked hard to establish?" Mayo asked incredulously.

"No. It's a good cover, but you will need to hire help to keep the shop operating while you arrange arms shipments to Villa."

"And we pay the help how? Cata and I work most of our waking hours just to put food in our bellies and a roof over our bed."

Mateo nodded his understanding. He reached into the pocket of his jacket and placed a small stack of bills on the table. "Here are four hundred American dollars." He pushed the stack of bills across the table to Mayo. "This money is for you to hire employees to help run the carnicería. You both need new clothes, American clothes, to look like successful business owners. You also need to spend time in El Paso, to be seen and to make connections, so eat in restaurants, go to the theater, make acquaintances." Mateo traced a whorl in the wood of the table with his index finger, adding, "And you need to purchase weapons to protect yourselves. There is danger in this work."

Catalina steadied the heel of her hand on the desk as she handed the $45,000 cashier's check to the bespectacled bank executive for deposit into the Two Rivers and Company account. She had never imagined this amount of money, much less held such a check. When Mayo and she received the check from the cattle company's broker, Catalina insisted that Mayo place it immediately into his suit pocket and keep his hand firmly upon it for security throughout the duration of their walk to the El Paso Bank and Trust. While they waited in the small lobby for their appointment with the bank administrator, Mr. Karum, Mayo handed Catalina the check. "Here. You speak English, Cata. You handle the transaction."

A clerk soon summoned them into Mr. Karum's office. Upon completion of the financial transaction, Karum offered the use of his office phone to call their contact at the Shelton-Payne Arms Company to arrange a meeting. The portly banker did not need the name or phone number written on the slip of paper Mayo extended. Catalina watched Karum pick up the black candlestick phone from his desk, place the receiver to his ear and the mouthpiece within inches of his lips. He asked the operator to connect him with Abraham Montoya at 2040. When Karum extended the phone to Mayo, Catalina held the receiver to Mayo's ear as he raised the phone to speak into its mouthpiece. Once they made the arrangements, Mayo and Catalina bid their farewell to the bank executive. They waited until they were in the bank lobby to meet one another's gaze, smiling a shared pride at completing the first phase of their assignment.

Cata placed her hand at the crook of Mayo's arm as they departed the bank and trust. Once outside, they stopped in the shade of an awning so Mayo could quietly share the details of his conversation with their Shelton-Payne connection.

"Señor Montoya wishes us to meet in one hour across the street in the Hotel Paso del Norte lobby. He said the Shelton-Payne offices are closely watched twenty-four hours a day by American and Mexican operatives, so we will meet at the hotel instead for lunch and arrange our order and shipment at that time."

"Then, Mayo, let's walk for a while. It's such a beautiful day."

The luxury of a leisurely stroll on city streets felt completely foreign to Catalina. Their lives had always consisted of work, and while in essence they were working now, the time just to enjoy the sights and sounds of El Paso made Catalina feel both giddy and guilty. They stopped briefly in front of a shop window to admire the displays of men's suits and women's dresses. The individual hat stands scattered across the bottom of the window beneath the clothing reminded Catalina of a garden with colorful flowers blooming in unusual shapes and sizes. She pointed to a large hat, its crown wrapped by a pleated, red-striped ribbon that gathered at the front in an intricate bow, two large pink flowers positioned on the back left side of the brim that dipped in a graceful arc.

"We can buy it," Mayo told her. "You would look elegant wearing it to serve bowls of menudo to our customers." He grinned at her. "Perhaps we can even charge a little more for the sophistication you will add to the carnicería."

Catalina had to laugh imagining the picture Mayo painted of her wearing that large hat while balancing bowls of steaming menudo. She looked again at the window, this time seeing Mayo and her reflection in a mirror behind the displays, and it took her a moment to recognize that they were the attractive couple who smilingly returned her gaze. Mayo stood dressed in his three-piece dark pinstriped suit, the empty sleeve carefully tacked inside the jacket's side pocket, a gray Stetson angled on his head. She rested gently against him, slender and tall in a narrow navy blue skirt, a baby blue blouse, the collar of which was buttoned just below her chin, and a navy blue hat with a brim arched upward, a narrow blue ribbon gracing the crown. Catalina found it hard to look away from their handsome reflection, but Mayo urged her to resume their stroll.

They walked across the street to the San Jacinto Plaza. Mayo directed their path toward the alligator pond. Leaning on the concrete fencing, they studied three alligators sunning themselves, two on the grassy lawn, one partially submerged in the shallow pool. Catalina didn't understand why a desert city caged alligators on its plaza, but there were many things she found curious about her northern neighbors. They sat briefly on one of the nearby benches to watch the mix of automobiles and horse-drawn wagons drive the streets surrounding the plaza. Catalina opened her parasol to shade herself from the late September sun, which still proved searing at midday. Catalina felt at peace.

After they had sat quietly for a brief period, Mayo stood and reached out his hand to her. "Come, we better start toward the hotel so we aren't late for our meeting."

Catalina took his proffered hand to stand from the bench.

They walked together from the plaza to Hotel Paso del Norte, which stood ten stories. After stepping through the front door held open by a uniformed doorman and walking into the two-story lobby, they stopped, amazed at the ornate beauty before them. The ceiling rose to an explosion of color created by a large stained-glass dome. Golden bowls of light hung from the ceiling and salmon-colored columns stretched upward from the floor. Catalina felt as though they had stepped into a palace. They froze, neither comfortable with moving farther into the hotel. When Catalina saw a well-groomed man approaching them, she braced herself, fearing he would ask them to leave since, clearly, they didn't belong inside such a grand structure.

"Señor y Señora Vasquez?"

"Sí," Mayo responded tentatively.

"I am Abraham Montoya," he said in Spanish. He extended his hand to Mayo, then dipped his head to Catalina.

"Please," he directed, "let's go into the dining room for lunch and conversation."

Catalina and Mayo glanced at each other and followed Abraham to the entrance of the dining area, where they were greeted by a formally attired host who led them to a small table at the edge of the room away from other occupied tables, as requested by Abraham. The host pulled out a cushioned chair, motioning for Catalina to sit, then assisted her with scooting the chair closer to the table draped by a flowing white cloth. Catalina glanced around the room, at the columns rising two stories to conclude in ornate capitals, and at the windows, arching almost to the ceiling, bathing the room in sunlight.

A young man dressed in black pants, a white shirt with a collar and tie, and a black waist-length jacket handed a menu to each of them. Catalina looked at the menu, then at Mayo, whose eyes exhibited the same discomfort she felt.

"If you will do me the honor," Abraham spoke, "allow me to recommend one of my favorite meals on a warm day. Paso del Norte serves thick slices of cold beef tongue, which I like with a cucumber salad, asparagus tips, and julienne potatoes. If that sounds pleasing to you, I will order three plates."

Catalina saw Mayo exhale his relief. "Yes, please."

"And perhaps a bottle of wine to share, maybe a white Bordeaux?"

"Señor," Mayo interrupted, "no wine for my wife or me, not when we have business to discuss."

"Then, I recommend the lemon soda. It's very refreshing."

"Yes, please," Mayo answered, looking to Catalina for agreement.

When the waiter returned to the table, Abraham placed the order. Once the waiter departed, Abraham glanced around the room to ensure their privacy then returned his attention to Mayo and Catalina. "You are interested in making a large purchase of equipment?"

"Sí," Mayo answered, passing him the order for .30-.30 Winchester rifles, .30-.30 cartridges, a Colt machine gun, and machine gun cartridges.

Abraham removed a pen from his pocket, jotted down figures, then slid the paper back across the table. He said quietly, "$36,750, which includes the freight."

Mayo looked to Catalina, who nodded; the quoted amount was within the anticipated range.

"Sí," Mayo answered.

"We will transport the cargo on the El Paso & Southwestern Railroad. At Mastodon, New Mexico, sixteen miles west of El Paso, there's a rarely patrolled blind siding where the train's crew will detach the car with your shipment. You will meet the train at Mastodon, unload the equipment onto your wagons—four should be sufficient if you also have a few pack mules—and cross the border."

Mayo looked to Catalina for confirmation, then nodded to Abraham. "Muy bueno, very good."

"The waiter is on his way with our food," Abraham directed their attention to the young man entering the dining room with a large tray balanced aloft. "Let's enjoy our lunch, and then we'll pay a visit to Mr. Karum to finalize the order."

OCTOBER 1913

Catalina

Catalina saw Abraham standing outside the arched doorway of the El Paso & Southwestern Railroad and Freight Depot, waving to catch their attention. It had been a little over two weeks since the three met to arrange the purchase and shipment of munitions. When Mayo phoned yesterday to check on the status of the order, Abraham informed him of the matériel's arrival to the warehouse the previous afternoon. Abraham explained he was having the munitions repackaged—the cartridges in barrels marked "LIME" and kegs marked "NAILS." The guns would be placed in crates labeled "MINING MACHINERY." Abraham said they would ship the order to the Mastodon destination in two days, which would allow Mayo and Catalina time to position wagons and pack mules for transportation of the goods into México. At Mayo's insistence, Abraham agreed to meet this afternoon at the freight depot to review their purchase before it shipped.

"Welcome," Abraham stated enthusiastically, extending his hand in greeting. "I trust you have both been well since our last meeting."

"Sí," Mayo answered cursorily.

"Isn't this weather a nice break from the scorching heat?" Abraham motioned toward the overcast sky.

"Sí," Mayo again responded.

Neither Mayo nor Catalina wished to engage in what they viewed as useless small talk. They were anxious to see the munitions, both to know they received what they had purchased and to ensure they had secured a sufficient number of wagons and mules to transport the matériel into México.

"Where are the goods we ordered?" Mayo asked directly.

"Right this way." Abraham opened the door and guided them into the building. Once inside, he led them down a brief hallway to an interior door on which he rapped a tattoo, pausing before inserting a key into the lock. He cracked open the door and called out, "Just me, boys, with the señor y señora." Then he swung the door open wide enough to permit the three of them to enter.

Catalina glanced around the room filled with wooden barrels, kegs, and crates, acknowledging the two workmen standing in their midst.

"I instructed the men to seal all containers save one of each so that you can see the munitions enclosed within." Abraham guided them to a large barrel without quarter and head hoops. "José," Abraham called. Catalina looked at the man Abraham summoned and noted that he seemed to be studying her, as if trying to place someone who looked familiar. "Remove the barrel head so señor y señora can view the barrel's contents."

Mayo and Catalina watched the man carefully insert a short metal tool and work it around the croze of the barrel to loosen then raise the wooden head. He removed cotton packing, exposing boxes of .30-.30 cartridges tightly arranged in the barrel. Abraham labored to remove one of the closely stacked boxes then opened it to expose the bullets for Mayo and Catalina to see. "There are three barrels and thirteen kegs containing a total of fifty thousand cartridges."

Mayo nodded his approval.

Catalina looked from Mayo and Abraham to José, who quickly

averted his eyes from hers.

"José, remove the head from the keg." Abraham turned his attention to the second workman in the room. "Raúl, let's seal this barrel," he directed, pointing to the recently reviewed container.

Catalina and Mayo watched José repeat the process of loosening then raising the wooden head to expose unboxed cartridges.

"The cartridges in the kegs are loose so those containers have the sound and feel of the nails they are supposed to hold," Abraham explained.

They followed the same process to examine sample crates of the .30-.30 Winchester rifles, the Colt machine gun, and the metal ammo boxes containing cartridge belts for the machine gun.

Once they completed the guided review of the munitions, Mayo looked to Catalina for her approval. She nodded her confirmation.

"The shipment is scheduled to go out tomorrow afternoon. You can expect it in Mastodon no later than 4:00 p.m. That allows you several hours of daylight to transfer the load from the detached boxcar. Then you can cross the border at night."

"Muy bien," Mayo said.

"Now that our business transaction is complete, may I suggest we finalize our deal with a drink at the Crown Saloon? It will be my treat."

"No, gracias, señor. Cata and I need to return home to complete arrangements for transporting the munitions into México."

Catalina turned to thank the two workmen only to see José staring at her with what she thought was a sudden look of recognition.

"Well, if you change your mind about the drink, you know where to find me," Abraham spoke as he opened the door for them and then escorted them to the building's exit. Once outside, he extended his hand to Mayo. "I hope all goes well tomorrow, and you are soon safely returned to México." He dipped his head in Catalina's direction, saying, "señora."

Parting ways outside of the depot, they watched Abraham jog to the street and whistle down a cab. Mayo observed, "He must have a strong thirst." They both laughed, feeling good about their progress toward getting munitions to Villa and the revolution.

"Let's ride the streetcar back to Juárez," Catalina suggested.

"Yes," Mayo agreed, and they turned in the direction of the closest streetcar stop. They walked a couple of blocks, enjoying the cooler temperature provided by the overcast sky. When they rounded a corner, they heard a voice call out, "Señor, señora!" They turned to see the workman Abraham had referred to as José hurrying in their direction. When he reached them, he encouraged, "Please, let's step into this alleyway."

They followed him around the corner, stopping when they had progressed to the middle of the alley. "Can you return to the depot at dark?"

"Por qué? Why?" Mayo asked suspiciously.

"I need you to see something."

"See what?" Mayo asked, his voice barely masking his irritation.

"Please, just meet me. I can't explain now. I have to get back to the depot." José turned immediately to hurry from the alleyway, pausing only to call back, "At dark."

❊❊❊

When Catalina leaned against Mayo, she felt the hard metal of the Colt 1911 resting in his jacket pocket. After their encounter with José, Mayo determined they should not go to the meeting unarmed, so they caught the streetcar downtown to purchase the pistol.

They wandered the city, too anxious to eat or drink anything, wondering aloud about the purpose of the meeting with José. Finally, the sun began to set, so they made their way back to the depot. When they reached the concrete deck surrounding the building, José materialized from the shadows. "I was afraid you might not return. Please," he urged, "follow me."

Catalina held lightly to Mayo's arm. She felt him shift his hand into his pocket concealing the pistol. They followed José through the dark hallway, back to the room that housed their munitions.

"Quickly, please," José urged them through the open door into the dark room, then closed and locked the door behind them. Only then did he switch on a battery-operated lantern, raising it aloft to illuminate their path to the barrels. He extended the lantern to Mayo. "Please hold this while I open the barrel."

Catalina took the lantern from Mayo in case he needed to reach for the pistol. She looked about the room to ensure they were alone. Using a hammer and hoop driver, José removed the head hoop and next the quarter hoop, relaxing the barrel staves' grip on the lid. When he lifted the wooden head and removed the cotton packing, he revealed a barrel filled with bricks.

"Chinga!" Mayo cursed. "What kind of a game is this?" he asked angrily. "Do bricks fill the other barrel?"

"Sí," José answered. "Even the barrel you examined this afternoon is only half filled with boxes of bullets; the other half is filled with bricks. The kegs marked 'NAILS' contain nails; the crates for the rifles are weighted with wood and bricks instead of guns. Would you like me to show you?"

"Sí!" Mayo answered.

Catalina and Mayo watched José remove the hoops and lid from a keg and gather a handful of nails.

"Chinga!" Mayo repeated. "Enough, that is enough. You don't need to show more."

Still holding the lantern to illuminate the deception, Catalina asked, "Why are you risking your safety to show us this dishonesty? What do you expect in return?"

"Nada, señora," he answered as if slightly offended. "I expect nothing in return."

When José quickly raised his hands to his chest, Catalina saw Mayo's hand again slide smoothly into his pocket.

José unbuttoned his shirt as he spoke. "You don't remember me, señora, but I remember you." He pulled open his shirt, exposing the puckered, purple skin of his shoulder. "You cared for me during the fighting in Juárez; I will not betray your kindness." He rebuttoned his shirt and spoke to Mayo. "What will you do now that you know of this deception?"

"We will get our money returned," Mayo hissed.

"He is leaving town," José warned. "Abraham sold your munitions to a Mexican federal operative and bragged that he would be on his way to another city long before you discovered his trickery."

"We must go now," Mayo directed Catalina.

"Gracias, José," Catalina extended the lantern.

"Let me lead you back to the exit."

When they reached the outer door, Mayo, clearly anxious to depart, quickly extended his hand to José in thanks. "Gracias."

They exited into the warm night air, and Mayo began walking at a fast pace, causing Catalina to jog a few steps to catch up with him.

"Where are we going, Mayo?"

"That hijo de puta said he would be drinking at the Crown, so I will find that son of a bitch and make him return our money. You need to go home, Cata."

Catalina didn't answer. She would not return home without Mayo, but he marched forward in such a blind rage that she did not wish to engage him in an argument. She followed beside him, sometimes having to trot a few steps to stay up with him. By the time they reached the streetcar stop, Catalina's side burned from exertion.

Once on the streetcar, Mayo refused to sit beside Catalina on the wooden bench, choosing instead to stand holding the rail next to the exit, ready to spring onto the street once they reached downtown. Catalina studied his face, his jaws clenched tightly in anger. When they reached their destination, Mayo turned to Catalina and said, "Go home," before he bolted from the streetcar. Catalina stood quickly and followed, staying a measured distance behind him as he strode with determination and paused briefly to speak to a passing man, who pointed across the street to a two-story building with a large sign illuminated by a streetlamp. When Mayo crossed the street and disappeared through the doorway of the saloon, Catalina positioned herself in front of the Trailblazer Café, on the other side of an alley separating it from the Crown. She did not have to wait long before Mayo exited the saloon behind Abraham. Catalina quickly turned her back to them, hoping neither saw her as they walked into the alley. Almost immediately, she heard a scuffle followed by a cry of pain. She entered the alley to see Abraham clutching a knife, standing over Mayo. Without pausing to think, Catalina rushed to kneel beside Mayo, slipping her hand into his pocket.

"He attacked me," Abraham stammered. "It was self—"

Before he completed his sentence, Catalina stood, emptying the gun's magazine into Abraham. The initial impact slammed his body against the café wall, each subsequent shot causing his body to jerk as he slid down the side of the building, crumpling to the ground.

Catalina dropped the gun and knelt to Mayo. "Mayo, mi amor, Mayo." She could feel the blood pumping in a thick stream through her fingers that pressed against the wound in his breast.

Mayo rasped, "Cata, he has killed me." He then fell quiet and still.

Catalina felt hands pin her arms and pull her backward, away from Mayo. She struggled to break free from the grasp, but the hands gripping her were too strong.

"Let me help you," said the man who held her. "Let me get you away from this scene." Only then did she see a crowd gathering at the entrance to the dark alley. Someone in the group shouted, "Call the police!"

The hands that held her pulled her forcefully down the unlit alleyway to the back of a building. "Quick, down the stairs." She went down two steps before stumbling, falling hard against the concrete slab at the bottom. Catalina felt herself lifted and pushed through an open door into a darkened basement storeroom, then heard the door locked behind her.

The man spoke in a hushed voice. "I'm a friend to Pancho Villa." Though Catalina couldn't make out the man's features in the dark, she could tell from his silhouette that he was a large man. "You need to stay here. You'll be safe. Let me return to the alley. There will be police, so you need to remain quietly in this room. I will come back with news as soon as I can."

When Catalina didn't respond, the man lowered his face within inches of hers and said firmly, "I need to hear you say you will remain quietly in this room until I return. Otherwise, I can't leave you."

"Sí," Catalina answered numbly, "I will wait for your return."

"Good," he answered. "It may be a while. There is a cot in the corner. Let me lead you to it."

Catalina tensed when he grasped her arm.

"Trust me," he urged, guiding her to the cot. Once Catalina sat, he released his grip. "I will return as soon as it is safe to do so. Please remain quiet."

Catalina watched through the darkness as the man climbed interior stairs. When he opened the door at the top, noise and light from the saloon flooded the basement only to be quickly extinguished by the door's closure, followed by the click of a lock.

Catalina sat silently in the dark, her arms wrapped tightly to her body. She felt the stickiness of Mayo's blood in the fists she formed, aware that his life had slipped through her grasp to pool in the filth of that alleyway. Catalina didn't cry; she sat too stunned by the day's events. Then, she started to tremble, unable to still her body. She sat in the dark, oblivious to the time that passed. When the door opened at the top of the stairs, Catalina remained quiet, ready to accept her fate.

A single lightbulb dangling from the ceiling dimly illuminated the room. Catalina watched a large man descend the stairs and come immediately to her. She knew by his size that he was the man who had taken her from the alley. When he reached the cot, he squatted.

"Are you all right, señora?" he asked in Spanish.

"What of my husband?" she inquired, though she knew the answer. "Is Mayo alive?"

"No, they are both dead. I'm sorry."

"I want to see him." Catalina stood.

The large man rose to block her. "The police have removed both bodies." He continued, "The police found the pistol beside your husband's body. They concluded the two men killed each other, but they know a woman may have been involved, as a witness if nothing else, so it's best for you to remain here for a while." He paused. "I found this in the alley." He extended his hand to expose a small cloth purse gathered by a pull string at the top. "Is this yours?"

"Sí, gracias." She took the purse from him.

"Is there someone I can call to assist you?"

"No."

"Try to rest a little." He encouraged. "My partner is going to get clothing for you. Then we'll see about getting you home."

Catalina looked down at her blouse and skirt stained with Mayo's blood. "Gracias."

"Rest if you can."

Sarah

"Sarah, Sarah!"

Sarah woke to find Samuel sitting on the edge of the bed, gently shaking her. She sat up quickly. "What's wrong, Samuel?"

"Sarah, I need your help. I need you to get out of bed."

Sarah pushed back the sheet. She took Samuel's offered hand and stood from the bed. "What's the matter, Samuel? What do you need me to do?"

He switched on the bedroom light and said, "Sarah, there's been a double murder outside the Crown."

"Are you all right?" Sarah asked anxiously, looking him over for signs of injury. "Were you involved?"

"No," he assured her. "You're going to have to trust me, Sarah. I need a skirt and blouse or a dress that will not be returned to you."

"Women's clothing?" Sarah asked, having difficulty grasping the request.

"We have a woman hiding in the basement of the Crown."

"Okay, Samuel." Sarah held up her hand to slow the conversation. "What woman? What is going on?"

"There was a man in the bar last night, bragging about bilking a Mexican couple attempting to smuggle arms across the border to Villa. Apparently, the couple learned of the deception and came to the Crown seeking the return of their money, or at least the husband came into the Crown."

"What happened?"

"The two men stepped into the alleyway, and a fight broke out. One man was stabbed and the other shot; both are dead."

"What of the woman, Samuel? How was she involved, and why is she in the basement of the Crown?"

"One of the dead men was her husband. Constanza hid her in the basement to keep her from being picked up by the police."

"Was she involved in the killing?"

"I don't know." Samuel paused, then added, "The police think the two men are responsible for each other's death, but they want to question the woman as a witness." Samuel pressed his thumb and forefinger to his eyes then pinched the bridge of his nose. "Sarah, the woman has just seen her husband murdered. She shouldn't have to spend the rest of the night being questioned by police. Please," he encouraged, "give me clothes for her to wear so we can get her across the border and to her home. Her clothes are stained with her husband's blood. Without a change of clothes for her, we'll be stopped at the bridge."

"Of course." Sarah thought of how she would feel if she saw

Samuel killed. She walked to the closet. "Does she have my build?"

"Taller," Samuel answered. "Old clothing is fine. You won't get it back."

Sarah removed a green skirt she had recently purchased, then lifted a cream-colored blouse. She folded each piece.

"Are you sure?" Samuel asked. "These are very nice; they won't be returned."

"I'm not going to send old clothes to a woman who's just lost her husband." Sarah returned to her closet to remove a chemise. "She probably needs an undergarment, too." Sarah folded the chemise and placed it on top of the stacked clothing. She retrieved a box from the closet shelf, emptied its content, and placed the clothes into it. "Would you like for me to go with you, Samuel, to help?"

"Thank you, Sarah, but no." He placed the box under his arm and leaned to kiss her. "I love you. Please go back to bed and try to sleep."

Sarah followed Samuel to the front door. "I'll be home soon," he called back to her as he exited the apartment.

Catalina

Catalina stared at the bloodstained clothing crumpled in a pile on the basement floor. She retrieved her blouse. Placing a finger at the seam, she tore a strip stained with Mayo's blood and raised it to her lips. "Mayo, my love," she whispered. She folded and placed the strip into the small purse. Then, she removed the American bills she had secured in her purse with a clip.

Catalina heard a knock at the stairway door, followed by a pause. The door opened a crack, and the man who introduced himself as Constanza called out, "Are you dressed? May we enter?"

"Sí," she responded.

Constanza and the red-headed man introduced as Samuel came down the stairs.

"Good. The clothes fit."

"Yes, thank you."

Constanza spoke. "Señora, I've borrowed a car to drive you home."

"Gracias." Catalina looked down at the bloodstained clothing. "Where should I put these?"

"Leave them," Constanza answered. "We'll take care of them."

"Señor," Sarah extended her hand that held the folded bills. "Please, take this money for the clothes, and . . ."

Constanza raised his hands, avoiding the money she offered. "No. No payment is needed."

Catalina pushed the money forward. "Please, I have one more favor to ask of you. I don't want my husband, Mayo, buried in an unmarked grave. Please, señor, use this money to see that he has a proper burial. Please." Catalina placed the bills in Constanza's palm. "Please."

"We will do so, señora," he assured her. "Now, let me see you home."

NOVEMBER 1913

Sarah

Several weeks after the murders at the Crown, Sarah woke with a start. She reached for Samuel, but he had not yet come home. She lay still for a moment, listening to gunshots interrupting the November night. Switching on the table lamp beside the bed, Sarah threw back the covers and slid her feet into slippers. She retrieved her woolen robe and wrapped it about her against the coolness of the room then looked at the clock on the table—it was 2:34 a.m. The firing continued, so she hurried to the apartment window. She looked into the darkness, seeing little. A boom rattled the apartment windows, causing her to take a step back.

Sarah startled at a sudden ringing, and it took her a moment to recognize the sound came from the telephone. She hurried across the room to answer it.

"Sarah," Samuel spoke excitedly, "did I wake you? Do you hear the gunfire?

"Samuel, yes, I hear it. What's happening?"

"There's fighting in Juárez. The rumor is it's Villa."

"Villa?"

"That's the rumor. Listen, I'm going to see what I can find out. I'll head home after I learn more, but don't expect me any time soon."

"Okay," Sarah responded, trying to conceal her disappointment at his delayed return home. "Please, stay safe. Don't do anything foolish."

"I'll be safe, Sarah. Don't worry." Another loud explosion made Samuel exclaim, "Wow, did you hear that!" Sarah noted the excitement in his voice. "I've got to go, Sarah. I'll see you in a few hours."

Sarah started to repeat her wish for him to stay safe, but Samuel had already hung up the phone.

Sarah returned to stare out the window. She thought about the rumor Samuel just shared. Only a few days earlier, on Monday, Huerta's troops in Juárez had participated in celebratory activities to honor the federal victory over Villa's army in Chihuahua city. Cathedral bells rang, a military band played, and soldiers paraded through the streets. Now, she stood listening to sounds of battle in the early hours of Saturday morning, and Samuel said it's Villa.

For a couple hours, the sound of fighting intensified, but around 4:00 a.m., Sarah noticed a distinct lessening of gunshots, and by 8:00 a.m., the noise of battle ceased altogether. Sarah stood at the stove, spooning coffee into the percolator's filter when Samuel rushed through the front door.

"Sarah!" he called excitedly before realizing she stood in the kitchen. He entered, tossing his coat and hat onto a kitchen chair. "Sarah, come sit," he encouraged, taking a seat.

Sarah adjusted the flame under the coffee pot, then joined Samuel. Before she could ask questions, Samuel blurted, "Sarah, you won't believe what happened in Juárez this morning. It *was* Villa who attacked the city." He laughed and slapped his knee with delight. "Villa seized a train carrying coal and cargo between Ciudad Chihuahua and Juárez. He forced the conductor at gunpoint to wire the Juárez headquarters with news that Villa and his troops had destroyed the tracks to Chihuahua city and had been sighted in the train's vicinity; the conductor asked headquarters for guidance. Headquarters instructed the conductor to return the train immediately to Juárez." Samuel paused to laugh, taking great pleasure in the story. "So, Villa loads two thousand soldiers into the boxcars and rides straight into the Juárez train yards. All the while, the federal garrison is completely unaware. Villa's troops disembark from the train and are in the center of Juárez before a shot is fired. What a brilliant maneuver!" Samuel beamed. "A damn Mexican Trojan horse, Sarah, Villa's Trojan horse! Just brilliant!" he exclaimed.

"Juárez is now under Villa's command?"

"Yes, Sarah. Can you believe it?" Samuel shook his head, chuckling to himself, then stood abruptly, pulling Sarah to her feet. "Get dressed; I'm taking you to breakfast." Before she could protest, he added, "I know we both need sleep, but I'm too excited to rest."

❀❀❀

It took several rings of the phone to pull Sarah from her deep well of sleep. When she became fully conscious of the repeated ringing, she pushed back the covers and hurried to lift the receiver before the sound woke Samuel. "Hello," she said, her voice thick from sleep.

"Did I wake you?"

Sarah recognized A. J.'s voice. "No. Well, yes. Samuel and I decided to nap since neither of us got much sleep last night. Hard to ignore the fighting in Juárez. What time is it anyway?"

"It's 1:30 in the afternoon," A. J. answered her question before continuing. "I watched the fighting last night from the Hotel Paso del Norte rooftop. All sorts of excitement, including US troops cordoning off streets and units of American cavalry racing to guard the border. I haven't really slept either, but I'm heading to Juárez. I think there'll be opportunity for some good photographs. Want to come?"

Sarah hesitated, then, glancing toward the darkened bedroom, responded, "I'd better not. Samuel is home; I should stay with him."

"Okay." A. J. sounded disappointed. "I'll do my best to represent our little picture postcard enterprise."

When Sarah hung up the phone, she saw on the table a tented piece of paper with her name written in Samuel's handwriting. She picked it up and read, "*Couldn't sleep. Gone to work. See you tonight. Love you,*

Samuel." Sarah regretted having slept through his departure. Without Samuel at home, Sarah didn't want to remain in the apartment. She returned to the phone and called A. J. "Where do we meet?"

"I've got a car and driver. I'll pick you up in fifteen minutes."

Sarah dressed hurriedly and was waiting outside the apartment building when A. J. pulled up. Sarah got into the back seat with him.

Once they crossed the international bridge, Sarah expressed surprise at the appearance of normalcy in the city. "Look," she pointed to the street before them, "no smoldering ruins, no drunkenness or looting, no random gunfire. Except for a few shattered windows, the city appears largely intact."

A. J. added, "Even the streetcars between the two cities started running again at noon."

The driver continued toward the center of town, as A. J. instructed, turning onto Calle Comercio. There, Sarah saw rebel soldiers guarding a detail of defeated federal troops forced to load bodies onto waiting wagons. A. J. asked the driver to pull over and stop. Sarah followed A. J. out of the car to photograph the macabre procession.

They returned to the car, driving only a short distance before A. J. suddenly called out, "Stop, stop!" He pointed across the street, directing Sarah's attention to a slender man standing at the side of the road, speaking with another. A. J. shouted, "Timothy! Hey, Timothy!"

Timothy Tompkins turned toward their vehicle, then recognizing them, jogged to the car, tossing a cigarette butt to the curb. Leaning into the vehicle, he asked, "Where are you two headed?"

"You tell us," A. J. answered.

Timothy climbed into the passenger seat. "Let's go to the federal barracks. There's military drama happening there."

A. J. directed the driver accordingly.

Timothy turned in his seat to face them. "Well, this seems like old times, the three of us together in Juárez after a battle."

"Much calmer this time, though," Sarah added.

"Yes," Timothy agreed. "Villa has guards at downtown stores and saloons with instructions to shoot anyone who attempts to loot. He's keeping the city and his soldiers orderly and quiet."

"Where is Villa?" A. J. asked. "Have you seen the conquering hero?"

"He's set up headquarters in the customs house. I got a brief interview with him. Said he's bringing up about five thousand infantry and cavalry from Villa Ahumada; they should be in the city in the next day or two."

"I'm sure he's expecting a quick reaction from Huerta," A. J responded, "since Juárez is so important strategically."

Sarah recognized the federal barracks in front of them as the driver slowed to avoid sightseers carelessly consumed in conversation. The driver pulled the car onto a sandy lot near the entrance to the barracks, parking beside two other vehicles.

A. J. and Sarah gathered their cameras. Once outside of the car, A. J. asked Timothy, "What's happening here to draw such a crowd?"

"Executions," Timothy answered, already striding toward the entrance.

"Executions?" A. J. responded, clearly surprised.

Timothy paused for A. J. and Sarah to catch up. "Villa ordered all federal officers executed. I think he's making an afternoon of it." Timothy renewed his quick walk through the outer structure of the cuartel.

They positioned themselves among the crowd gathered to witness the executions. Suddenly, ten rebel soldiers commanded by an officer marched forward five prisoners. The rebel officer in charge directed the prisoners to line up with their backs to the wall. While Timothy threaded through the crowd in search of information, Sarah and A. J. uncased their cameras. Sarah took photos of onlookers, of the firing squad, of prisoners who stood awaiting their fate. She tried not to think of the event about to take place, desperately hoping to avoid the gaze of any man awaiting his death. The prisoners stood stoically, facing their executioners, until one spoke loudly to the officer in charge.

A. J. turned to the man standing beside him and asked, "What did he say?"

The man translated. "He asked the captain to accept a letter the prisoner wrote for his mother."

"Sí," they heard the captain in charge agree.

Sarah watched mesmerized, positioning her camera as the federal prisoner marched forward to hand a folded note to the captain. She snapped a photo of the exchange, with one man reaching to accept a final missive from the extended hand of the other. Without any show of emotion, the federal officer marched back to his position along the wall and turned to face his executioners. Sarah took another photograph of the five prisoners, hoping to capture how each unflinchingly faced his impending death.

Villa's captain raised his pistol; the ten soldiers shouldered their rifles. "Uno," the captain called out. "Dos," he announced, and as he snapped his arm downward calling "Tres," the federal officer who had written his mother a parting letter, shouted, "Viva México!"

Ten rifles fired, piercing the five prisoners, who toppled to the ground. Sarah observed puffs of adobe dust floating above the fallen bodies and smoke from the gun powder wafting in front of the rifles. At the captain's order, the soldiers of the firing squad shouldered their rifles, performed an about-face, and marched from the execution site.

"I'm sorry, A. J., but I can't stay here to watch any more executions." Sarah struggled to contain her emotions.

"Nor I," A. J. responded quietly. He leaned forward to Timothy, who had rejoined them, and said, "We're leaving. Are you coming with us?"

Timothy turned toward them, his notepad and pen in hand. "No. I'm going to hang around, see if I can get an interview with the officer in charge."

A. J. gripped Sarah's arm.

"I'm okay," she responded.

"I'm not," he replied, maintaining his grip until they had exited the barracks and returned to the car. Once they were seated, A. J. directed the driver to return to El Paso.

Sarah and A. J. sat silently, staring in opposite directions. They passed a sightseeing bus filled with enthusiastic passengers on their way to the barracks. They drove past a wagon, the mules straining to pull their gruesome load of bodies. They passed stores guarded by armed soldiers. Near an intersection, they passed a small group of Villa's soldiers sharing cigarettes and conversation. Looking at the gathering of men, Sarah startled in recognition. She turned in her seat to see Samuel standing among the soldiers, engaged in animated discussion. Sarah wanted to call to him, catch his attention and ask him to return to El Paso with her, but she didn't. She remained silent as the car got in line to cross the international bridge.

❋❋❋

"What's wrong?" Sarah asked upon returning home from her Monday workday to find Samuel standing at the sitting room window, staring at the street below.

He turned to face her without speaking.

"Samuel, you're worrying me. What's wrong?" she repeated, placing her coat, hat, and camera on a chair before going to him.

"Nothing is wrong, Sarah."

"But why aren't you at work?"

Samuel pulled Sarah to him, placed a kiss just above her ear, and said softly, "Constanza's covering. I took the night off so we could talk."

Sarah pulled away, trying to control the anxious feeling stealing into her belly. "Talk about what, Samuel?"

"Let's sit," he directed, holding her hand to walk with her to the couch. He sat and said, "Join me," patting the cushion beside him.

Sarah sat instead on the chair next to the sofa. "I'd rather sit here."

Samuel cleared his throat, his discomfort obvious. "Okay."

"Oh, Samuel," Sarah pleaded, "just tell me what you need to share."

He leaned forward, resting his forearms on his knees, his hands clasped between them. "Sarah, you know I love you; you know I love our life together, but you surely must have sensed my restlessness since news of Madero's murder."

Sarah didn't respond. She sat numbly in the chair waiting for him to speak what she already knew he would say.

"Sarah," he continued, "I met with Villa and volunteered to join his forces to fight Huerta." He paused for Sarah to respond, but she sat silently.

Samuel again cleared his throat before continuing. "I will return to service in Villa's Division of the North with the rank of captain."

She nodded her understanding, not trusting herself to speak.

"Sarah, you and I will be all right. It will be like when we courted."

He scooted to the edge of the cushion, moving closer to her. "With Villa in control of Juárez, he'll often be in the city, which means I will often be with you."

Sarah knew Samuel had made his decision; they had nothing to discuss other than details of the arrangement. "When do you report, Samuel?"

"Day after tomorrow?"

The immediacy shook Sarah, but she would not let it show. "And what of the Crown?"

"Constanza has agreed to hire someone to assist in my place." Samuel reached for Sarah's hand. "Sarah, we don't know how long the revolution will last. If Villa continues to be victorious, I may be home before the new year, and you'll be begging me to take on some other adventure that gets me out of your hair." He smiled at her, hoping to lighten the mood.

"Wednesday will come quickly. You have a lot of loose ends to tie together by then." Sarah stood, concluding the conversation.

❀❀❀

Sarah and Paola carried steaming dishes of sweet potatoes, mashed potatoes, green beans, cornbread dressing, pork tamales, cranberries, and giblet gravy to place at the center of the crowded table they set for their Thanksgiving Day meal. Timothy stood at the kitchen worktable, hovering over A. J. to provide unwanted instructions for carving the turkey and ham.

"Timothy," Sarah called, attempting to rescue A. J. "Please pour the wine."

"Yes," A. J. added, clearly pleased, "pouring alcohol is something he's good at."

Sarah and Samuel had invited their friends to join them for Thanksgiving dinner, and Sarah refused to withdraw the invitation just because Samuel chose to rejoin the revolutionary army last week. Besides, her friends provided a much-needed distraction.

Sarah had not seen Samuel since late last Friday when he surprised her at the studio, arriving to inform her of his impending departure from Juárez. A. J. allowed them privacy to embrace and express their love for one another before saying goodbye. That was the last time Sarah spoke to Samuel.

Timothy called her Sunday night to share news of fighting in Tierra Blanca. He told her that in response to word of an impending federal attack, Villa had ordered the destruction of railway lines leading north, forcing the federals to halt their advance at Tierra Blanca, a location of Villa's choosing, about thirty miles south of Juárez.

On the second day of fighting, Timothy drove a hired car to the battle site. Upon his return to El Paso that evening, he called Sarah to report he had seen Samuel, who was weary but unharmed. The battle raged for three days, concluding in victory for Villa's forces.

Sarah returned her thoughts from Samuel and the battle to the Thanksgiving meal she and her friends gathered to share. After Paola removed biscuits from the oven, placing them into a cloth-lined basket and onto the table, Sarah announced, "Let's eat."

A. J. and Timothy pulled out chairs for Sarah and Paola to sit, then took their own seats.

"This all looks delicious, Sarah," A. J. complimented.

"Well, it took a team effort," she replied. "A. J., will you lead us in a prayer?"

After A. J. concluded a brief prayer of thanks for the food and the friends with whom to share it, Timothy raised his wine glass, proposing a toast to Samuel and his safe return. The reference to Samuel caught Sarah off guard, and she had to swallow hard to fight her emotions when they clinked glasses.

They each reached for the closest dish of food, serving themselves, and passing to their right, repeating the process until all dishes had circulated and their plates were full. They ate quietly for a few minutes, the scraping of knives and forks the only sound.

Paola broke the silence. "Sarah, everything is delicious."

A. J. and Timothy, both with mouths full, grunted their agreement.

Timothy put down his fork, swallowed, then asked, "So A. J., what would you be doing if you weren't here enjoying this wonderful spread and charming company?"

"Um," A. J. held up his hand to signal he needed to finish chewing. He dabbed the corners of his mouth with his napkin and answered,

"I believe I'd be warming a can of condensed soup on the stove in my apartment." He waited until the groans ceased before he returned the question to Timothy. "And you? What would you be doing?"

"Well," Timothy answered, holding aloft his fork balancing a bite of turkey and dressing, "I'd probably be at my desk in the newsroom, eating a ham sandwich and swigging a bottle of beer."

"Well, that's a sad sight," A. J. retorted.

"And you, Paola," Timothy asked, "what would you be doing?"

"My family is visiting an elderly relative in Albuquerque. I couldn't join them because of work tomorrow, so were I not here with all of you, I'd be home alone."

"Then it's good we can share this day. Who needs more of anything?" Sarah asked. As she reached to pass the sweet potatoes Timothy requested, she heard a voice behind her. "Any room at the table for one more?"

Sarah recognized Samuel's voice. She stood and rushed into his arms.

After a brief embrace, he held her at arm's length. "Careful, Sarah, I'm pretty grimy."

A. J. and Timothy stood to shake Samuel's hand, and Paola rose from her chair, saying, "It's so good to see you, Samuel. Let me get you a plate."

"Give me a few minutes to clean up, and I'll join the festivities."

Sarah excused herself and followed Samuel into the bedroom. She sat on the bed and spoke with him while he selected clean clothes from the closet and the chest of drawers.

"It's good to be home, Sarah, and I'm pleased you went ahead with Thanksgiving, as planned."

"I'm so happy you're here, Samuel. How long will you be home?"

"Let's talk about that later, Sarah." He collected his clothing, then leaned to her for a kiss. "Why don't you return to our guests. Let me wash up, and I'll join you shortly."

When Sarah returned to the table, A. J. spoke for the group. "We'll finish quickly, Sarah, and get out of your hair so Samuel and you can have time to yourselves." Paola and Timothy nodded in agreement.

"You'll do no such thing," Sarah insisted. "Samuel and I planned to spend Thanksgiving in the company of our friends, and that's what we will do. Timothy," she directed, "will you pour more wine for every-one?" While he stood to retrieve the wine bottle from the worktable, Sarah asked, "Now what can I pass?"

Samuel soon joined them, taking a seat in the chair A. J. had pulled to the table next to Sarah's. "This spread looks great!" he said, placing the cloth napkin onto his lap.

Timothy noted the small piece of bloodied tissue paper stuck to Samuel's chin. "So you return unscathed from battle only to be wounded in an act of personal grooming during your first fifteen min-utes at home?"

"I don't domesticate well," Samuel responded.

Timothy raised his wine glass. "A toast to Samuel's safe return."

Samuel joined them, raising his wine glass, and added, "A toast to sharing Thanksgiving with good friends and my wonderful wife."

They reached across the table to clink glasses.

"Now let me eat." Samuel added, "I'm starved."

They passed each of the serving dishes to Samuel, who filled his plate and began eating with gusto after he topped the meat and dress-ing liberally with gravy.

The conversation around the table remained lively, rich with laughter. Their discussions intentionally steered clear of the battle at Tierra Blanca and the Mexican Revolution. After they concluded the meal with freshly brewed coffee and slices of pumpkin and mincemeat pies topped with whipped cream, Samuel suggested they adjourn to the sitting room for whiskey.

A. J. stood from the table and announced, "I think I've devoured my weight in food and drink. I'll have to take a raincheck on the whiskey."

Timothy stood as well. "While I almost never turn down the offer of whiskey . . ."

"We know," A. J. inserted.

Timothy held up his hand to quiet the laughter. "I think I'm in greater need of a bed and a good night's sleep."

"Let me help you clean the kitchen." Paola rose with her plate in hand. "Then I must get home."

Sarah took the plate from Paola. "Thank you, Paola, but you've helped enough with the meal." When Paola started to object, Sarah placed her hand to her friend's arm. "I won't allow it, though I greatly appreciate your thoughtfulness."

Having called a cab to deliver each of them to their destinations, the friends departed with plates full of food for later. When Samuel closed the front door behind them, Sarah folded into his arms, and they stood quietly. "This is nice," Samuel whispered.

Finally, Sarah pulled away. "Why don't you pour yourself that whiskey and sit with me while I clean the kitchen."

They put the food in the icebox. At Samuel's encouragement, Sarah placed the dishes in soapy water to soak overnight, then retired with him to the sitting room. He poured a glass of whiskey then sat on the couch. Sarah joined him, curling under the arm he placed about her shoulder.

They sat quietly before Samuel spoke. "You asked how long I'll be home. Villa has given me an assignment. I have to depart Saturday for Tucson."

"Tucson?" Sarah lifted her head from his shoulder to look at him.

"Yes. I'm to meet an agent who is arranging an arms shipment into Mexico."

"You're smuggling arms, Samuel?"

"Well," he hesitated, before responding, "yes. Villa needs someone he can trust. He's been double-crossed on several transactions, so he wants me to see the munitions across the border; then someone else will take the pack train through the mountains of Chihuahua to Villa."

"But taking munitions across the border is the illegal part. If you're caught, you'll be arrested."

"Well, the plan is not to get caught." Samuel took a sip of whiskey.

"I'll travel with you to Tucson."

"No, Sarah."

"Samuel, listen to me. A husband and wife taking a trip looks far more innocuous than a lone man traveling, especially one who is an officer in Villa's army."

"Sarah, this isn't a vacation."

"No, but it could appear to be. I'll take my camera; we'll look like tourists."

"Be reasonable."

"All I ask is that you consider my suggestion."

Sarah awoke to see Samuel sitting in a chair by the bed, watching her.

"Good morning, Sleeping Beauty," he said when she sat up and brushed the loose strands of hair from her face.

"Mmm," she stretched, "good morning, Samuel."

"You need to get out of bed and start making preparations if you're traveling with me to Tucson tomorrow."

"Oh, Samuel!" She pushed back the covers and went to him, sitting on his lap. "Are you serious?"

"I'm serious," Samuel assured her. "I got to thinking about what you said, and you're right about attracting less attention as husband and wife. Besides," he smiled at her, "after I introduce you to the criminal side of life, you may decide arms smuggling is your new calling."

They spent the day running errands in preparation for their trip. Sarah arranged with A. J. for a few days off from work. Together, they purchased train tickets for Tucson and reserved a room for two nights at the Santa Rita Hotel. They shopped to purchase a traveling outfit for Sarah, complete with a stylish wide-brimmed felt hat, and concluded their day with supper at the Hotel Paso del Norte.

Sarah slept fitfully, excited about traveling with Samuel but worried about the purpose of the trip. She had finally fallen into a deep sleep when the alarm clock sounded. They both rose with a purpose, and while Samuel got dressed, Sarah made breakfast. After eating the meal and cleaning the kitchen, Sarah bathed. Dressed in her new suit, she studied herself in the mirror, admiring the matching black-and-white pen-striped woolen skirt and jacket. Sarah positioned the black felt hat at a slight angle on her head, admiring the way the large brim arched upward to expose her face.

Samuel called out, "Sarah, we need to be leaving."

Satisfied with her appearance, Sarah slipped on a pair of black gloves that buttoned at the wrist then stepped into the sitting room where Samuel stood waiting beside their shared suitcase.

"My gosh, you're lovely," Samuel expressed, rushing to take her in his arms. He kissed her lips, then her neck. "Perhaps we can catch a later train."

Sarah laughed, pushing him back. "You have a mission to accomplish, Captain Clendenin."

Samuel kissed her again before stepping away to phone for a cab.

They arrived at the Union Depot twenty minutes prior to their scheduled departure, and it seemed only minutes before they boarded the train and settled into their seats. When the train pulled from the station, Sarah watched out her window as buildings and street scenes of Juárez slipped past, slowly at first, but then at an increased speed while the train moved along tracks skirting the two countries.

❈❈❈

Sarah woke with a start at the squeal of brakes. She had not intended to sleep, but the gentle sway of the train rocked her into a deep, satisfying slumber.

"Welcome to Tucson," Samuel said.

When the train slowly rolled to a stop at the station, Samuel stood, stretching his legs, then reached for Sarah's hand to help her rise from the seat. He lifted their suitcase from the overhead rack. Once on the platform, he set down the suitcase to offer his hand to Sarah as she descended the three steps. Sarah took Samuel's arm, following the crowd to the exit where he hailed a cab to the Santa Rita Hotel.

After Samuel paid the cab driver, they entered the hotel's courtyard rich with palm trees and decorative plants. They checked in, then took an elevator to the fourth floor and located their room along the front hallway. While Sarah freshened up in their bathroom, the phone rang. Sarah heard Samuel conclude the brief conversation with, "I'll be downstairs directly."

Samuel had shared he was to meet the American arms agent in the lobby of the Santa Rita Hotel, so Sarah was not surprised when he knocked on the bathroom door to inform her he was leaving for the meeting.

Sarah paced nervously from their door to the window and back, anxious for Samuel's return. When he finally reentered the room, she hurried to him, asking, "What is the plan, Samuel?"

He lifted the suitcase onto the bed to remove a dark brown suit of clothing and his tall riding boots; then he told her of the arrangement. "The matériel is at Calabasas Station, about eleven miles north of

Nogales and the US-Mexico border. The agent has arranged everything: horses, pack-mules, and vaqueros to cowboy the goods across the border." Samuel continued talking as he changed into clothes suited for horseback riding. "We'll take a train to Calabasas; from there, we'll form a packtrain to transport the munitions into Mexico under the cover of night." He sat on the bed to lace up his boots. "If all goes well, I'll be back here by morning."

"I'll go with you to Calabasas."

"Sarah, I don't want you involved further than you already are. Right now," he explained, "if I'm caught, you can claim a complete lack of knowledge about the arrangement, but if you travel with me and the agent to Calabasas, your presence will implicate you."

"I appreciate your concern, Samuel, but the purpose of my coming on this trip is to create the appearance of a husband and wife traveling for pleasure. My joining you during your travel with the agent lessens suspicions."

"Sarah," Samuel stood, taking his hat from the bed. "I don't have time to argue with you."

"Then don't. I will take the train with you to Calabasas then return to Tucson to wait for you."

"This is ill-advised, Sarah."

Sarah inserted the hatpin to secure her hat, took her gloves from the nightstand, then said, "I've made up my mind, Samuel."

Downstairs in the lobby, Samuel introduced Sarah to the arms agent, Jay Wright, and explained the plan for her to travel with them to Calabasas and then return to Tucson. Though the agent seemed baffled by this development, he simply said, "We need to leave."

Sarah and Samuel delayed for several minutes after the agent departed the hotel before taking a cab to the train depot. While Sarah waited for Samuel to return from the ticket counter, she studied Jay, who stood hat in hand a few people in front of Samuel. Jay was a short, round man with a ridiculous comb forward that started at the crown of his head and ended in bangs across his forehead. Sarah thought he looked even more absurd next to Samuel's lanky strength.

Samuel and Sarah followed Jay's lead, boarding a short outbound train. Though they entered the same car as Jay, they took a seat several rows behind him. Sarah and Samuel rode mostly in silence for the fifty-minute trip. When the train came to a stop, they followed Jay from the car to the platform of a desolate station marked by a worn sign declaring it Calabasas. Jay led them a few hundred yards down a dirt road to a wooden outbuilding with a corral full of mules and horses. He guided them inside the dilapidated barn where men and boxes awaited them. Sarah stood aside watching Samuel identify random boxes to be opened to reveal their content. After he reviewed ten boxes stenciled "FARMING EQUIPMENT," he nodded his approval to the agent and said, "I'm satisfied."

Jay called for a young vaquero to join them. Sarah noted the slight build of the young cowboy who responded to Jay's summons, and when the cowboy extended a hand in greeting to Samuel, Sarah was surprised by the man's attractive, almost feminine facial features. Only when the person Jay introduced as Cata spoke did Sarah realize with a shock that the individual dressed in charro clothing was, in fact, a woman. Sarah couldn't take her gaze from Cata, who wore men's pants, with a decorative trim running along the outer seam, and leather half-chaps buckled around the calves of her legs, extending over her knees. She wore a high-collared blouse under a waist-length gray jacket with sleeves that bore the same decorative trim stitched on her pants. She had a six-shooter and knife scabbard strapped about her hips, and two bandoliers crossing her chest. A thick braid peeked from under a large sombrero. Sarah watched, mesmerized by the young woman's self-assurance when she translated Samuel's requests into orders that spurred twenty men into immediate action.

Sarah followed Samuel outdoors as the barn became a flurry of activity. Some of the men began saddling horses and pack mules while others carried boxes from the barn. Sarah listened when Samuel explained to Cata the plan for transporting the munitions across the border. They were to split into three teams of seven men: four men responsible for leading a string of three pack mules each; three men serving as scouts for the team, with one scout in the lead and two monitoring the team's flanks. The leader of each mule train would assume the rear position to oversee the progress of the team. The three packtrains would take different paths to the designated meeting place across the border to avoid risking loss of the entire shipment should they encounter a US Army patrol from the Nogales garrison.

Samuel spread open a folded map to show Cata the designated drop off point and discuss the three paths to that location.

Cata agreed with the plan, volunteering to serve as a scout for Samuel's group. She told Samuel that, with his permission, she would identify the leaders of the other two packtrains. She proceeded to call two men to her, repeating Samuel's orders in Spanish. Sarah watched, fascinated by the men's respectful attention to Cata.

Sarah turned her focus on the vaqueros tightly wrapping boxes in canvas, then roping each box securely to a sawbuck pack saddle on the standing mules. The men placed an additional top load onto a few of the larger mules before fixing a canvas tarp over the shipment each animal carried.

Sarah watched the dexterity and speed with which the men pig-tailed the mules to each other. Suddenly, a horse's high-pitched squeal and ensuing commotion caught everyone's attention. Sarah followed Samuel, who hurried to see the cause. One of the vaqueros lay on the ground moaning, his hands hovering protectively above his ribcage; a large gray danced its aggression as two men sought to calm and distance the horse from the injured man. Apparently, the horse had kicked the vaquero into a corral post. Cata knelt to examine the injured vaquero, then stood to inform Samuel that the man showed signs of fractured ribs and would not be able to ride. Hearing this news, Sarah stepped forward, announcing to Samuel, "I'll ride in his place."

Samuel looked at her with a surprise that suggested he had forgotten she was even among them. It took only a moment for him to gather his thoughts before saying forcefully, "Absolutely not."

"If I ride, you won't have to redistribute the pack mules. You can proceed as planned."

"No. It's too dangerous."

"Samuel, a person doesn't grow up in a farming community not knowing how to ride a horse and shoot a gun. I can handle myself."

"Sarah, this is a ridiculous idea. Are you planning to ride sidesaddle in that skirt? This isn't a pleasure ride through some park."

"I have pants."

Sarah turned to Cata, who had interrupted the discussion to make the offer. Sarah returned her attention to Samuel. "I will wear the pants Cata offers."

Samuel looked at Sarah first, Cata next, then speaking to Sarah, said resignedly, "Okay. This is a dangerous, crazy idea, but okay," he said throwing up his hands. "Get changed and be ready to ride in ten minutes."

"Go to the barn," Cata told Sarah. "I will join you."

Sarah waited in the barn now empty of boxes and men. Her heart raced and her breath came in short quick draughts. She questioned her rash decision to participate in the gun smuggling, but Cata entered the barn carrying trousers, preventing Sarah from racing to Samuel to retract her offer.

"Here." Cata unfurled the rolled black pants and extended them to Sarah.

"Thank you." Sarah sat on a moldy bale of alfalfa to remove her ankle boots. She placed each foot through a pant leg, then stood, turning her back to Cata, and raised the pants over her chemise and under her skirt. After buttoning the pants, Sarah unfastened and stepped from her skirt. She sat to pull on her boots, then stood, looking down, embarrassed by the sight of her legs encased in such an immodest manner.

Cata knelt to roll up the pant cuffs that hung a little too long on Sarah. Then Cata removed her leather half-chaps. She raised her own pant leg to expose a length of boot leather, then extended the leggings to Sarah. "You wear these. I wear boots."

"Thank you." Sarah sat again, and while she buckled the leather legging around her left calf, Cata knelt to buckle one on Sarah's right. Once finished, Sarah stood. "Gracias, Cata."

"De nada. Vámonos. We must go."

Sarah felt uncomfortable leaving the barn in clothing that exposed the shape of her body in such an immodest fashion. She held her rolled skirt to shield the sight of her hips from others and experienced a sense of gratefulness that dusk had turned to dark. When she found Samuel, she discovered two mule trains had already departed. Samuel looked her up and down, then pulled her aside to instruct, "Listen to me. Hold your reins in your left hand and the string of mules with your right. Keep the lead mule at your horse's hip and keep an eye on your string." He paused to make sure she understood, then continued. "If your lead mule starts lagging or your arm becomes tired, you can do a single dally with your rope around the saddle horn, but don't tie the lead to the horn under any circumstance."

"Yes, Samuel."

"And if you ever feel in danger, release the lead rope. I'd rather lose a load of munitions than lose you."

"I will."

"Okay." He took her arm to guide her to a red roan that stood saddled with a rifle in its scabbard. "I'll take the rear of the packtrain, and you, Sarah, will ride ahead of me, third in line."

As Samuel waited, Sarah secured her skirt and hat behind the saddle, then mounted her gelding. Samuel handed her the lead rope to her string of three mules. "Be careful, Sarah. I'll be behind if you need me."

Samuel called, "Cata, prepare to move out."

Sarah watched Samuel hand the agent two thick wads of bills, the second half of Villa's payment, then mount his own horse. He raised his hand, making a forward motion, signaling to Cata for the packtrain to begin its trek to the rendezvous point.

Sarah waited until the last mule of the second string moved a few yards ahead before she squeezed her horse with both legs, clucking to encourage him forward. The horse responded immediately, with the mules following.

It was several years since Sarah had last ridden a horse, but she found she still enjoyed the rhythm of a brisk walk. With the movement of the ride, she quickly warmed against the chill of the night air and relaxed into the saddle. A quarter moon lit the desert landscape, and the horse and mules moved sure-footedly over the sometimes rocky terrain. Sarah kept a measured distance behind the rider and string of mules before her and caught frequent glimpses of Samuel when she turned to monitor the progress of her string. Occasionally, Samuel would nod to acknowledge her, making Sarah smile. The quiet ride provided ample time for her to think about their lives together, and how hers had been enriched by Samuel. Certainly, she never envisioned herself smuggling arms across the border for a Mexican revolutionary army, but she thrilled at the adventure and prided herself on assisting her husband.

After the third hour on the trail, Sarah felt weariness weighting her body. Her legs grew heavy and her back stiffened. Though she shifted in her saddle to search out a temporary ease, her repositioning provided little relief. She remembered Samuel instructing that the drop off point stood about a mile across the border; they should be just a few miles from their destination. She envisioned herself dismounting in an hour or so. Then she could look forward to their return to Tucson, a warm bath and a soft bed. Sarah kept that image in mind as they continued forward.

Catalina

Catalina kept her gelding at a steady trot, swinging away from the mule train to scout its left flank. So far, all had been quiet, but Mayo's murder taught Catalina always to anticipate trouble.

Immediately following Mayo's death, Catalina left Juárez to rejoin Villa's troops. She determined she would be no other man's woman but would fight as a soldier. Sometimes she prepared food for herself and Mateo, but mostly she ate at the campfire of others and always slept alone.

When Mateo offered her the chance to assist an American captain with bringing munitions across the border, she readily accepted the mission as an opportunity to honor Mayo by successfully smuggling much-needed arms to Villa's troops.

Catalina continued to urge her horse forward, zigzagging a distanced path parallel to the packtrain. The thin air of the desert night allowed sounds and smells to travel easily, so she scoured the landscape, watching for motion or flash of a lit cigarette, listening for horses or conversation, smelling for campfire smoke.

So far all had been uneventful, but now that the packtrain neared the border, Catalina knew their likelihood of encountering a patrol increased. She grew additionally vigilant. When she caught the first glimpse of movement over the rise, she reined her horse around, riding at the same pace. Turning in the saddle, she saw an increase in speed behind her, and she knew she had encountered a patrol. Catalina spurred her horse into a gallop, riding northward to lead the patrol away from the packtrain. The patrol pursued her only a short distance. She didn't know if they stopped chasing a lone rider or suspected she scouted for a larger smuggling effort.

Assuring herself the patrol no longer followed, Catalina turned her horse toward the packtrain and pressed the animal into a gallop, racing up rocky risings and into shallow arroyos. By the time she reached the packtrain, both she and her horse were winded. She rode directly to Samuel, who moved toward her.

"A patrol, less than two kilometers away," Catalina warned, sucking in draughts of air, pointing in the direction she had last seen them.

"Take the rear," he directed. "I'll take the lead."

"Give me your mules," Catalina offered.

"No. I want you free to help with other mule strings in case a rider is injured."

Sarah

Sarah knew from Cata's race to the packtrain that their mission faced danger. Her pulse quickened, and she looked to Samuel, anxious for further instruction. Soon Samuel trotted alongside, motioning for her to follow. Sarah guided her string of mules out from the line of pack animals and encouraged her horse into a brisk trot following Samuel's string. They rode to the head of the line, Samuel setting the pace for the packtrain. They maintained this quickened pace, the weary animals stumbling over rocks and roots, their burdens heavy on their backs. Just when Sarah began to hope they had slipped the patrol, she heard the zip of bullets as the mule train crested a ridge. Samuel urged their riders into a faster gait. Sarah turned to monitor her string as they moved into a lope over the rough terrain. She could see the troopers gaining ground. When she looked again, the patrol had closed the distance, their horses racing without the encumbrance of mules that lumbered forward under the weight of packs.

Sarah followed Samuel's lead as he urged the packtrain into a gallop. She made a quick dally of her rope around the saddle horn to help maintain her grip on the string of mules. The zip of bullets thickened. Sarah heard them thud into sand or zing off rocks surrounding the packtrain. She glanced back to see the troopers had dismounted and knelt in a firing position to steady their rifles and improve their aim. A sharp crack caused her lead mule to kick and dash forward, pinning

Sarah's leg to the gelding. She saw where a bullet struck a box tied to the mule's pack. Sarah didn't have time to be frightened. She loosened the rope from the saddle horn, allowing slack; the mule veered right, then resumed its position at the gelding's hip, as Sarah had hoped.

Samuel led the packtrain behind a ridge. He did not lessen the pace, even though the firing stopped. Sarah worried that the troopers had remounted to continue their pursuit. She wondered how much longer their exhausted mule train could outpace the patrol. When she twisted in her saddle to glance back, she saw no soldiers. Though Samuel continued to press the packtrain forward at a staggering pace, Sarah knew they must have crossed into Mexico, causing the US soldiers to halt their pursuit. Finally, after racing forward for several more minutes, Samuel began to slow the mule train to a walk, animals and riders huffing their exhaustion. They proceeded at the lessened pace for another fifteen minutes, allowing the horses and mules to cool from their exertion. Then, Samuel led the mule train into an arroyo that provided shelter for the riders and their animals. Following Samuel's lead, the riders dismounted.

Sarah swung her right leg over the saddle. Holding onto the horn and cantle, she removed her left foot from the stirrup and lowered herself to the ground. The muscles of her legs quivered their fatigue, so she held briefly to the stirrup.

Cata and one of the other scouts rode forward. Samuel directed the man to care for Sarah's and his horses and mules. While Cata translated the order, Samuel handed a canteen to Sarah, warning, "Drink only a small amount." As Sarah took a sip, Samuel whispered, "You did great." Sarah smiled with pride, returning the canteen to Samuel, who took a brief drink before securing the cap. Samuel requested that Cata and Sarah follow him to take stock of the men, animals, and munitions they carried. As they walked the trail of men, Samuel complimented each with "Bien hecho, good work." Miraculously, they had not lost any animals or men; their injuries amounted to one man with a flesh wound to his arm. As Samuel continued to check the packs, Sarah remained beside Cata to assist with caring for the wounded man.

Sarah watched Cata take a large knife from her scabbard to slit open the man's shirt and expose the oozing wound. Cata examined the injury and announced, "We need to clean and bandage the wound." Sarah retrieved a canteen for Cata, who knelt beside the seated vaquero. "We need bandages," Cata added as she poured water onto the wound. Sarah thought for a moment, then remembered the undergarment she had tucked into her pants. Sarah turned to raise her jacket and pull a large section of the chemise from her waistband. She faced Cata. "Here," Sarah said. "Gracias," Cata replied, standing to expertly cut three long strips of cloth. Cata knelt again, and Sarah followed. Cata folded one strip to form a pad. She again rinsed the wound, then placed the pad against it directing Sarah, "Hold." While Sarah held the makeshift pad in place, Cata wrapped the second strip around the arm, securing the pad. Cata then tied a sling, positioning the injured arm against the man's body. The injured vaquero expressed his gratitude.

They returned to Samuel at the front of the resting packtrain. He asked Cata, "Are we ready to move out?"

"Yes," she replied.

"Let's give the order, then."

Sarah returned to her horse and string of mules. Thanking the vaquero who cared for the animals, she mounted her horse and took the lead rope from the man.

Samuel motioned to Cata, then encouraged his horse forward and up the arroyo's embankment. He turned the packtrain in an easterly direction and set the pace at a brisk walk. Sarah watched Cata trot past her to Samuel. After speaking briefly, Cata spurred her horse into a lope to resume scouting ahead. Samuel kept the packtrain moving through the desert at a constant pace. After fewer than thirty minutes on the trail, Sarah saw a rider trotting in their direction. When the rider gained ground on the packtrain, Sarah recognized her as Cata. She watched Cata slow her horse to walk beside Samuel, then move slightly ahead so that Samuel followed. Sarah thought with relief that they must be nearing the rendezvous point.

Cata guided them behind a small rock-strewn hill, the drop-off point, where one of the other packtrains already rested. Cata directed Samuel to a grizzled, middle-aged man. This must be Villa's agent, Sarah thought to herself when she observed Samuel shake his hand and point in a southernly direction across the desert.

One of the vaqueros relieved Sarah of her horse and string of mules. She immediately found a boulder upon which to rest. Shortly, the third packtrain arrived. Sarah watched Samuel, Cata, and the agent take stock of the animals and supplies. When Samuel turned from them, Sarah knew he sought her, so she stood and walked stiffly to him.

"Our job's finished. A couple of the men will ride with us to Nogales. There's a hotel there where we can rest until morning; then, we'll cross the border and catch a train back to Tucson."

"Sounds wonderful."

Samuel started to walk away, and then paused. "I'm proud of you, Sarah."

"Thank you, Samuel."

"And I think I know the perfect gift to get you for Christmas." He paused for effect, then said, "A horse."

D E C E M B E R   1 9 1 3

Sarah

When Sarah entered the studio, rattling the bell over the door, she saw A. J. step past the curtain to stand behind the counter. "Good morning," he greeted. "How was your trip?"

"Invigorating. How has business been?"

"Busy. Lots of film to finish, Thanksgiving and all," he explained.

Sarah placed the full-length apron over her head and tied it at the back. "Then I better get into the darkroom."

"Wait. I have something for you," A. J. said, opening the cash register and reaching to the back of the drawer. He pulled out an envelope and handed it to her.

Sarah peered into the envelope to discover it filled with $10 bills. "What's this for?"

"It's $100. We were right about the interest stirred by Villa's taking of Juárez. We've had orders for our photo postcards from New York, Boston, Philadelphia, Los Angeles, Chicago. Never underestimate Americans' hunger for the macabre. The wagon loaded with bodies and the federal officers facing the firing squad are favorites."

"But $100, A. J.?"

"That's your share, and we have more orders to fill."

"I'm amazed." Sarah looked at the bills and laughed. "I'm rich," she said carefully placing the envelope into her purse.

"Well, richer than you were." A. J. paused before continuing. "Sarah, it's not my affair, but may I suggest you tuck that money away."

"What do you mean, A. J.?"

"Nothing, really." He hesitated. "It's just that with Samuel's current occupation, you may need quick access to money one day."

"Yes, and . . . ?"

"Just a suggestion. Really, it's none of my business."

Though A. J.'s recommendation perplexed her, she replied, "I appreciate your looking out for me."

He nodded, turning his back to her as if embarrassed. "Let's get busy."

✦✦✦

It was Christmas morning. Sarah lay in bed awake, forcing herself to remain still, fearful of disturbing Samuel's sleep.

Samuel had surprised her several days ago, arriving home unexpectedly. Earlier in the month, General Villa had assumed the provisional governorship of Chihuahua state and was occupied with confiscating property, including large haciendas with expansive herds of cattle, from the state's wealthiest families to support his army and provide meat to the public at a greatly reduced price. Samuel had requested and received a week of leave to return to El Paso for a business concern. Unaware of his intended leave, Sarah was surprised when Samuel met her at the studio earlier in the week at the close of her workday. He had already been to the apartment to bathe, shave, and change clothes. That first evening, he whisked her off to supper at the Hotel Paso del Norte; afterward, they strolled through the San Jacinto Plaza admiring the city's Christmas decorations before heading home.

Sarah could not take time off from work at the studio due to backlogged orders for their photo postcards of the Mexican Revolution. In fact, they even had orders for reprints of postcards from the 1911 Battle of Juárez. Samuel was very understanding about her schedule. She did not ask him how he occupied his days, but every evening he met her at the studio to take her to supper then home. Each night was filled with lovemaking.

Because of Samuel's limited stay in El Paso, they decided to celebrate Christmas Day by themselves, so a couple of nights ago, they had gathered with A. J., Timothy, and Paola at a restaurant to enjoy each other's company, exchange gifts, and raise a glass to Christmas good wishes.

While she continued to lie in bed this Christmas morning, Sarah thought about the Christmas Eve midnight mass she had convinced Samuel to attend. She pictured the festive colors of the altar, the smell of incense, and the sound of voices singing as she now lay against Samuel's warmth. She was content to remain in bed with his arms around her. She didn't want to think of his departure in two days, so she tried to focus on the happiness she felt today.

Samuel kissed her neck. "Merry Christmas, sweetheart," he whispered. She turned over in his arms and buried her head beneath his chin, responding, "Merry Christmas to you, my love." They lay quietly, resting in each other's arms. Then Samuel kissed the top of her head and announced, "I saw a Christmas package with my name on it. I'm getting up to see what Mrs. Clendenin got me," and he threw back the covers.

"I'll make coffee for us," Sarah offered.

"Does that come with a slice of cake?"

"For breakfast?" she asked, tying the sash of her woolen robe.

"It's Christmas."

"Okay," she chuckled.

When Sarah returned from the kitchen with the tray, she saw Samuel standing at the window peering into the street. As soon as he noticed her, he rushed to take the tray and set it on the coffee table.

"What were you looking at?" Sarah asked.

"Just checking the weather. Looks like it's going to be a nice day," he added. "After opening gifts, we'll have to get dressed and take a stroll."

They fixed their coffee before Samuel carried the colorfully wrapped packages from their location under the small ceramic Christmas tree they had purchased their first Christmas as husband and wife. He balanced the gifts on the table next to the tray. Sarah removed the largest of the packages and handed it to Samuel.

"Open this one first," she said.

It took only moments for Samuel to tear the ribbon and paper from the box and remove the lid. He lifted out a fringed woolen poncho richly designed in diagonal gray and black striping overlayed with a southwestern diamond pattern.

"This is very handsome, Sarah."

"Try it on."

Sarah watched him lift the poncho over his head, then let it fall. "You cut a very striking figure, Captain Clendenin." She took him by the hand. "Come look," and she led him into the bedroom to stand before the mirror.

"It's perfect, Sarah."

"There's one more gift for you," and she directed him back into the sitting room to hand him the second package, which he unwrapped with the same rough efficiency as the first. From the box he removed a large Bowie knife cradled in a hand-tooled leather sheath. He admired the detailed work on the sheath, then removed the knife, studying the clip point and fingering the cross guard. He gripped the buckhorn handle.

"This is wonderful, Sarah." He hugged and kissed her. "Thank you." He returned the knife to its sheath before handing Sarah a thin package. "A little something for you from your adoring husband."

Sarah removed the ribbon and wrapping carefully before raising the lid. She lifted a pair of red leather gloves that snapped neatly on top of the wrists. "These are lovely, Samuel."

"Try them on."

Sarah slipped her hands into the gloves. "They're so soft," she said, turning her hands to admire them.

"Deer skin," Samuel explained. "I thought you needed a decent pair of leather gloves if you plan to continue engaging in riding excursions."

"I love the gift, Samuel, but I think I will put them to tamer use."

"Well, I don't know about that. Get dressed. I stabled another gift for you; she awaits your arrival."

Sarah looked at him in disbelief, but she took the hand he extended to raise her to a standing position.

When they entered the bedroom, Samuel asked, "Now where are

those pants you borrowed from Cata?"

"Samuel, I'm not wearing those again, and especially not on Christmas morning."

"Please yourself," he responded to her protestations, "but do dress warmly for our outing."

While Sarah dressed, she worried about caring for the horse it appeared Samuel had bought her. Sarah told herself she would act excited about the gift; she would not hurt his feelings.

"You ready?" he called to her.

"Yes. Let me get my scarf and coat."

"Don't forget your new gloves."

Sarah fixed her hat on her head, then slipped on the pretty red gloves. "Are we walking?"

"It isn't far," he assured her. "Let's go meet the newest addition to our family." Samuel opened the front door, placing his hand at her back to usher her out.

While the morning air had a chill, the cloudless sky rescued the day from uncomfortably cold temperatures. Sarah paused outside the apartment building waiting for Samuel's lead. He guided her around the corner and walked to the center of the block, pausing on the sidewalk.

"Well, Mrs. Clendenin, what do you think of her?" he asked, signaling with an outstretched hand toward a shiny black automobile parked next to the curb.

Sarah hesitated, then looked from the automobile to him. "Samuel?" she questioned.

"Merry Christmas, sweetheart, she's all yours," he responded proudly.

"Oh, it's beautiful, Samuel," she gushed, but after peering through the open window at what seemed a complex combination of pedals, levers, and switches, she voiced her concern: "I don't know how to drive a car."

"Well, you have two days to learn."

They walked around the automobile, which Samuel identified as a 1913 Model T Sport Roadster. The folding convertible top and the body of the car were midnight black, but the front dashboard was a lush mahogany. Samuel pointed out the square kerosene cowl lamps and round acetylene headlamps for night driving. Polished brass accented the radiator and both sets of lamps. A single stuffed leather bench stretched beneath the convertible roof. Samuel walked Sarah to the back of the car and raised the door to a compartment at the car's rear, exposing a leather rumble seat for additional passengers.

Samuel opened the passenger-side door for Sarah to enter the vehicle. Then he returned to the driver's side, leaning into the vehicle to explain the handbrake and the purpose of the three floor pedals, identifying them as clutch, reverse, and brake. He explained the advance lever and throttle on opposite sides of the steering column, then showed her how to move the ignition switch on the dash between choke and battery. Following Samuel's request, Sarah exited to the front of the car. She listened carefully to his warning about gripping the crankshaft with her thumb under the rod before cranking the car. Samuel demonstrated, and on the second lift of the crank, the car started.

"Climb in and let's take her for a drive."

In the car, Sarah studied Samuel's actions while he explained each step he took to steer the car onto the street. Samuel repeated the steps, identifying each, as he accelerated.

"At approximately ten miles an hour, shift from low to high gear by removing your foot from the clutch and using the throttle to provide more gas," and he demonstrated the process.

"I don't think I'll ever drive faster than ten miles an hour," Sarah responded nervously.

Samuel laughed. "Oh, you will, Sarah. I know you far too well. You'll never be content with moving slowly." He looked at her and chuckled. "This baby will go forty-five miles per hour, and I fully expect you'll be asking that of her as soon as you get the hang of driving."

When Samuel accelerated, the rush of wind caused Sarah's hair to whip about her face; she laughed with excitement. Samuel turned to her and grinned, both of them enjoying the feel of hurtling forward.

After they drove beyond the smelter and the brick plant, Samuel began to decelerate, then slowly edged the car from the road, coming to a stop in the sand. He turned to Sarah. "Okay, your turn."

"Not yet," Sarah protested. "I'm not ready." But Samuel had already raised the handbrake. He left the engine idling while he encouraged Sarah from the vehicle to switch positions on the seat.

"Slide behind the steering wheel," he said, ignoring her protests. Once Sarah scooted behind the wheel, Samuel joined her on the seat. He said, "Now, I'm going to talk you through the steps."

Sarah followed Samuel's instructions, laughing nervously when the car moved forward.

"Steer it back onto the road," Samuel guided.

Sarah thrilled at the car's reaction.

"Very good, Sarah," Samuel encouraged. "Okay, hear the sound of the motor? You're ready to shift from low to high gear."

Sarah nodded nervously.

Samuel directed her through each step. When the engine began to sputter, Samuel instructed her to give it more gas till the engine recovered.

Sarah squealed her excitement as the car increased speed.

"You're a natural," Samuel announced proudly. They sped down the road for fifteen minutes, Sarah enjoying the thrill of controlling the car. "Okay, Sarah, now you have to learn to slow down and come to a halt, something that might not come as naturally to you," Samuel chuckled.

Sarah performed the steps Samuel recited. He was correct in his assessment of her having greater difficulty slowing to a stop, and she had to revert to the handbrake to bring the vehicle to a halt.

"A little rough," Samuel assessed, "but you'll get the hang of it."

"Ready to take over?"

"Nope. This is your baby. You're the one who'll drive it. Are you ready to take charge?"

Sarah hesitated for a moment, then gathering her courage, announced, "I am."

They spent the remainder of the day with Sarah practicing starting, braking, backing, and maintaining the car until she gained confidence in her ability to fully operate Samuel's gift to her. When they returned to the apartment at dark, Sarah felt exhausted yet exhilarated.

While Samuel relaxed with a couple glasses of whiskey, Sarah prepared a light supper. After they ate and Sarah finished the dishes, she found Samuel in the sitting room examining the Bowie knife. When he noticed she had entered the room, he said, "Thank you for a wonderful Christmas."

Sarah extended her hands to indicate she wanted him to stand. When he rose to his feet, she said, "It's still Christmas Day," and led him into the bedroom.

✦✦✦

Sarah hated entering the empty apartment. As she walked through the sitting room and into the bedroom, she half expected her footsteps to echo in what now seemed a hollow space; Samuel had departed for Chihuahua city this morning.

They spent their last night together eating dinner at the Sheldon Hotel, driving around the city streets and out to Fort Bliss so that Sarah could practice under Samuel's tutelage one last time. They spent the remainder of the night cradled in one another's arms. When they rose in the morning, Sarah prepared breakfast while Samuel bathed, shaved, and dressed. They ate quietly, taking every opportunity to caress, resting a hand on the other's shoulder when pouring coffee or rubbing a thumb across the other's fingers when passing the sugar.

Samuel insisted that Sarah leave the apartment prior to his departure. "I don't have your strength," he whispered while he held her. "I couldn't bear to leave knowing you're still here."

"Then stay," Sarah sobbed.

"I can't. You know I have to go."

"But I don't know. You could choose to stay."

"Sarah," Samuel pleaded.

They kissed and held tightly to one another. Then Sarah released her hold and stepped back. "I love you, Samuel. Stay safe." She quickly donned her scarf, coat, and hat, then slid her hands into the red gloves, snapping them at the tops of her wrists. She gave Samuel one last kiss before leaving the apartment.

Sarah planned to drive the car to work because she wanted to show Samuel that she had confidence to drive alone. Cranking the engine to a rumbling start, she paused to look up at the apartment window where she knew Samuel stood watching. She threw a kiss, then stepped into the automobile and accelerated onto the road.

At the studio, knowing of her sadness, A. J. left her largely alone in the darkroom. Sarah occupied herself throughout the day with printing several stacks of photo postcards while A. J. prepared previously printed postcards for shipment to fulfill orders they received from train stations, cigar shops, souvenir stores, and newspaper stands in cities across the United States. Since Villa's surprise capture of Juárez, their picture postcard business now brought in more money than their portrait studio or film finishing.

Sarah chose to work late to catch up on backorders, but eventually A. J. insisted she leave for the night. Now she stood alone in her bedroom wishing she were anywhere else. She decided against eating supper; she didn't feel hungry. Sarah determined simply to go to bed. She switched on the lamp and changed into her nightgown. When she pulled back the bedspread, she discovered a folded sheet of paper with her name written in Samuel's handwriting. She opened it to read a single sentence: *You are the love of my life*. Sarah clutched the note to her breast and wept.

JANUARY 1914

Sarah

"**Otis** Photo Studio."

Sarah overheard A. J. answer the telephone while she posed a young mother and her three-year-old daughter who came to the studio dressed for an afternoon photo shoot. The mother had explained when she scheduled the appointment earlier in the week that she wanted to send a photo portrait as a gift to her husband serving with the US Army Corps of Engineers in the Panama Canal Zone.

"Oh, dear God!" Sarah heard A. J. softly exclaim. "Are you sure? Oh, dear God!"

Sarah positioned the child on a tall chair, raising her to a height just below the right shoulder of her mother, who stood beside her. The mother wore a forest green dress, the neckline gracefully completed by white scalloped lace at the throat. Her curly brown hair was gathered in a bun at the back and arranged in wisps about her face beneath a forest green hat. Hazel-green eyes peered intently at the camera as Sarah captured the mother and daughter in the focusing hood then depressed the pushpin of the cable release. "One more," Sarah directed. "Great!"

"Yes," Sarah heard A. J. speaking in undertones, "if possible, that would be best."

"Let's take a couple of photos with the two of you gazing toward one another," Sarah directed. She peered through the focusing hood as the woman gently called to her daughter. The child turned her eyes to her mother's, and loving smiles formed on both faces. "Beautiful!" Sarah exclaimed after depressing the pushpin.

"I will see you soon." Sarah noted A. J.'s conclusion to the call: "Nor I. This is terrible, terrible news, but we always knew it was a possibility."

"I'd like to photograph each of you separately, if I may." When the young mother hesitated, Sarah answered, "You aren't charged for photos you don't wish to purchase."

"Well," the young woman thought briefly. "Okay."

Sarah moved quickly to seat the child in a lower chair angled so the little girl's body turned slightly to the right. Sarah adjusted the lights and directed the mother to stand beside the camera so that the child turned her head to the left, looking from the corner of her eyes at her mother. Sarah depressed the pushpin. "Just perfect, little Annie."

"I would like for you to take a seat on the chair, Mrs. Jenkins." While the young woman positioned herself, Sarah moved the camera nearer, adjusting to capture a headshot. Sarah held the little girl's hand, while instructing the mother, "Tilt your chin slightly downward. Great. Now, look into the lens of the camera as if you were gazing once again into your husband's eyes."

The woman's face softened immediately, and a slight smile graced her lips. Sarah depressed the pushpin. "Wonderful!" Sarah concluded. "I think we have a good selection of photographs from which you may choose, Mrs. Jenkins."

The woman stood to assist her daughter into her coat before donning her own.

"The photos should be ready by the end of next week, so please come by at your convenience." Sarah walked them to the door. "Bye-bye, Annie." She bent to speak at eye-level to the child. "Come back to see me, okay?"

The child shyly nodded her agreement.

"Thank you, Mrs. Jenkins." Sarah waved from the entry as they departed. Closing the door, she folded her arms across her chest. "Brr," she said to A. J., who watched from behind the counter. "It's freezing outside."

"Yes, it's a miserable day," he answered distractedly.

Sarah worried about A. J. and about what appeared to be the ominous content of the phone call. She had noticed him growing thinner, but she attributed it to the additional work to fill orders pouring in for picture postcards. Lately, she noticed he seemed easily winded from minimal exertion. Sarah didn't want to intrude on her friend's privacy, but she decided she would monitor his health more closely and would shoulder a greater load of the work to provide him some relief. Besides, with Samuel away in Mexico, she preferred working in the studio over spending long evenings and weekends alone in the apartment.

Sarah had just moved behind the curtain when she heard the jangling of the bell over the door followed by familiar voices. She stepped back into the front room to discover both Timothy and Paola standing with A. J.

"Well, what a nice surprise," she exclaimed. "What occasion brings you two here?" She walked forward to hug Paola and greet Timothy. Sarah noted a strange awkwardness to her friends' presence, as if they would prefer to be anywhere but facing her. When A. J. said, "Why don't we step into the back room," Sarah knew something was wrong, but what was amiss hadn't fully formed in her heart. When Paola reached to take her arm, she suddenly knew. She backed away, repeating, "No, no, no!"

"Sarah," Timothy said, reaching her first to prevent her slow crumple to the floor. A. J. quickly joined him, and Sarah felt herself guided to another room and placed on a chair with the three of them gathered about her.

"It's Samuel, isn't it? Is he badly wounded?" Sarah wanted to know but dreaded hearing the truth.

"Sarah," Timothy squatted to take her hand in his. "I'm so sorry, but Samuel died at the Battle of Ojinaga, killed yesterday in the fighting."

Sarah tried to absorb what Timothy said, but her mind couldn't fully grasp such news. "How do you know, Timothy? How can you be sure? Witnesses often tell conflicting stories. How can you be sure it's Samuel and that he's dead?" Sarah couldn't stop herself from peppering Timothy with questions, seeking even a splinter of hope.

"Sarah," Timothy answered, "I would never have come to you with such news had I not confirmed the story. The correspondent with whom I spoke knew Samuel personally, and even he went one step further, verifying Samuel's death with his commander. When Samuel was killed, he wore the poncho you gave him."

Sarah felt her body collapse into sorrow, her hands covering her face and her head leaning toward her lap. She wept uncontrollably while her friends sought to comfort her. She cried, her body shaking with the violence of her sobs. Then the convulsion of tears halted as quickly as they began. Sarah raised her head to see the three friends silently crying their own sadness and loss.

"I'll be all right," she said, trying to convince herself as well as reassure her friends. "Thank you all," she looked to each of them. "Thank you for being the ones to bring me this awful news." The tears began anew. She fought to collect her emotions, then asked, "What about his body, Timothy?"

"The correspondent reported that Samuel had been buried with the other dead."

Without saying a word, A. J. handed her his handkerchief.

They all remained quiet, sharing their grief in tearful silence. After a few minutes, Sarah stood. "Thank you all for your caring and support. I know Samuel valued your friendship." She choked back a sob. "But I need to return to work, and so does each of you."

They all protested. "Sarah, why don't you take a couple days for yourself," A. J. encouraged.

"No, A. J., I need to stay busy."

"You need time to think this through, Sarah," Timothy insisted.

Sarah shook her head. "I don't want to go to that empty apartment. Not yet. I'd rather remain here and work."

"I'll stay with you in the apartment," Paola offered.

Sarah took Paola's hands in hers. "I love you for that offer, Paola, and for your friendship, but I prefer to remain busy. Nights will provide an eternity for me to grieve; for now, I just want to keep occupied with work."

They all nodded their understanding.

"Thank you all again, my dear friends." She turned to A. J. "I'm going into the darkroom to develop film from the last photo session." She kissed each of them on the cheek before walking away.

When Sarah arrived at her apartment building that evening, she remained outside in the dark until a bitter cold wind forced her indoors. She stopped at the entryway in front of her mailbox, as she did each day. When she opened her mailbox, she saw a letter with Samuel's handwriting on the envelope. "Oh, Samuel," she moaned, lifting the letter to her breast. She hurried upstairs. Fumbling to fit the key into the lock of her apartment door, Sarah clutched the letter tightly. Once inside the apartment, she switched on the overhead light and hurried to set down her camera and purse. She didn't pause to remove her hat or outer garments; instead, she opened the cutlery drawer and took out a table knife. Trying to still her hands, Sarah inserted the knife blade into the fold of the envelope, carefully tearing it to reveal the letter within. She pulled out a kitchen chair and sat before removing and unfolding the letter dated a week earlier. It read:

January 4, 1914
Ciudad Chihuahua

My Dearest Sarah:
Happy New Year, my love! I wish I could have been in El Paso to welcome 1914 with a kiss from your sweet lips, but what comforts me is knowing we will share a lifetime of New Year's celebrations wrapped in each other's arms.

I am thinking of you as I prepare to depart from Chihuahua city tomorrow morning, bound with reinforcements for Ojinaga. By the time you receive this letter, you will likely have already read a newspaper report about renewed fighting for control of that border city. Villa, himself, will lead the attack to capture Ojinaga from General Salvador Mercado and General Pascual Orozco. Since General Mercado ran from Villa at Tierra Blanca and then abandoned Chihuahua city before Villa's advance, Mercado will likely behave much the same at Ojinaga in the face of Villa's arrival. I don't want you to worry one bit; I don't anticipate much of a fight.

As I write this letter, I am kept warm by the poncho you so thoughtfully gave me. I don't dare take it off because the poncho has attracted attention and compliments of too many men; I fear seeing it worn by another fellow if a window of opportunity were raised. I treasure the poncho because I feel your loving embrace through its folds.

I hope you are enjoying the automobile and finding it useful. I hold in my memory the picture of you behind its steering wheel, your hair blowing about your face, a smile of delight gracing your lips; that vision brings me great pleasure.

I'm sorry to cut this letter short, but I must complete final preparations for tomorrow's departure, and I want to post this letter tonight to ensure you receive some communication from me, even if it is brief. I promise a longer letter soon.

I love you dearly, Sarah, and I love you always. I look forward to the near future when I return to your side and into your arms. For now, I am sending a thousand kisses your way.

All my love and devotion,

Samuel

The letter still in her hand, Sarah lay her face onto the crook of her arm and sobbed.

A U G U S T   2 5 ,   1 9 8 3

Kayla

Kayla could see the strained emotion on the elderly woman's face as she related details of her husband's death at the 1914 Battle of Ojinaga. While Kayla didn't want to interrupt her, she recognized the emotional toll reliving past sorrows had taken on Sarah. In fact, Kayla felt drained herself, having been caught up in the lives Sarah described. She determined to bring the interview to a close after the old woman completed her current thought, not wanting to tax her further.

Sarah dabbed her eyes with a tissue as she continued. "You may not know that five days before the Battle of Ojinaga, Villa's representative met in El Paso with an executive of the Mutual Film Corporation and signed a contract granting the corporation all rights to film Villa's battles. The contract provided Villa five hundred dollars in gold and 20 percent of any revenues earned by films of his skirmishes. Villa delayed his attack on the federal troops at Ojinaga until the film crew could travel from New York City and cross the border." Sarah paused, her forefinger tracing the veins along the back of her left hand. She continued to speak without lifting her eyes. "In less than two hours, the battle concluded in a complete rout. Mercado and almost five thousand of his troops, camp followers, and their children frantically forded the Rio Grande, escaping into the United States only later to be transported and interned at Fort Bliss." Sarah paused in her story, visibly steeling herself. "Twelve days after Villa's victory at Ojinaga, Mutual premiered their newsreel in New York City." Sarah raised her head to look directly into the camera. "The audience complained that the battle lacked drama."

"Sarah, let's conclude today's interview," Kayla suggested.

Sarah nodded her agreement.

PART

THREE

S E P T E M B E R   1 2 ,   1 9 8 3

Kayla

Kayla balanced a glass of lemonade in one hand and a plate holding a wedge of cake in the other as she took her seat across from Sarah. Almost three weeks had passed since Abel and Kayla last met with the elderly woman, the delay a result of Kayla's belief that Abel and she might be getting too emotionally entangled in Sarah's life story. After the last interview, Abel professed a haunting sense of loss and sadness resulting from Samuel's death; Kayla had to admit she, too, carried a burden of sorrow.

It was Sarah who contacted her by phone to inquire about their next meeting, stating, "We need to proceed with our interviews, Kayla; I have too much past and too little future for us to delay our sessions."

Kayla felt embarrassed by what she perceived as her own unprofessional behavior and her failure to maintain an intellectual and emotional distance from the subject of their oral history interviews. She apologized to Sarah for the pause, making excuses about an excess of work, and concluded the call by scheduling their next session for the following week.

As soon as Kayla and Abel arrived at the house in the morning and rang the doorbell, Sarah swung open the door to greet them, guiding them into the living room, where she had positioned two trays—one with a pitcher of lemonade, three glasses, and a small ice bucket; the other with sliced apple cake, plates, forks and napkins. Beside each tray stood a stout ceramic pot filled with large, colorful crepe-paper flowers.

At Sarah's insistence, Kayla and Abel took the offered refreshments while Sarah assumed her seat in the armchair to wait for the start of the interview.

"Take your time and enjoy," Sarah said. "But I'm ready when you are."

"The cake is delicious," Kayla remarked after only one bite, then placed the plate on the table next to her chair. "I'll nibble on it throughout our session, but let's go ahead and begin."

"Abel," she signaled.

"Ready," Abel responded, taking a drink of lemonade to wash down a forkful of cake; he placed the plate and glass aside. Looking through the viewfinder, he signaled the start of filming.

"Sarah Delaney interview, number three, El Paso, Texas, 10:40 a.m., September 12, 1983. Sarah, our last interview concluded with your discussing the filming of the Battle of Ojinaga." Kayla dodged the mention of Samuel's death. Sarah seemed willing to take the direction Kayla offered.

"Yes, the film." Sarah paused briefly, appearing to collect her thoughts. "Well, after the Ojinaga film received a less-than-enthusiastic reception," Sarah picked up the story's thread, "another studio executive came to Juárez in February to renegotiate the contract with General Villa. They agreed upon a fictionalized biography that would integrate actual battle footage with scripted studio film.

"The studio replaced the sweater and slouch hat Villa often wore in battle, attiring him in the Hollywood version of a military uniform, which Villa then wore into combat." Sarah shook her head with amused disbelief.

"Mutual released *The Life of General Villa* to theaters across the US, and its fictionalized depiction of the revolutionary leader achieved a level of success the Battle of Ojinaga film footage did not." Sarah paused quietly, her eyes staring unfocused at the polished wooden slats of the floor.

Kayla sought to regain the momentum of the interview. "But El Paso inherited the Mexican federal troops and families routed in the Battle of Ojinaga."

Sarah raised her head to refocus on Kayla. "Yes, El Paso, more specifically Fort Bliss, inherited the results of the Ojinaga rout."

JANUARY 1914

Sarah

Sarah shifted the car into high gear. Beside her sat Timothy, who turned to peer out the back window at A. J., perched on the rumble seat.

"Does he look cold?" Sarah voiced her concern.

"A. J.'s pretty well bundled. His hat is pulled low on his forehead and his coat collar turned up around his neck and mouth; only his eyes are exposed to the weather." Timothy chuckled. "Besides, we're almost to Fort Bliss."

Sarah nodded. Just fifteen days had passed since she received news of Samuel's death, and on each of those days, she had worked to the point of exhaustion hoping night would bring mind-calming slumber. But even when she managed to find sleep, she always woke abruptly in the night feeling the absence of Samuel's warmth; night after night, she lay in the darkness with a hollowness yawning deep into her soul.

When Timothy invited A. J. to tour the Fort Bliss internment camp imprisoning Mexican federal troops from the Ojinaga rout, Sarah insisted she join them. Both Timothy and A. J. tried to convince her not to come, but Sarah wanted to see for herself the caging of those responsible for Samuel's death; she wanted to look into the faces of the persons who took Samuel's life in their effort to keep the usurper Huerta ensconced in the presidential palace.

The *El Paso Morning Times* provided details of the refugees' plight following the Battle of Ojinaga. Sarah felt no sympathy when she read about the thousands of people corralled without shelter outside of Presidio, Texas, the town across the river from Ojinaga. Nor did she experience any concern for the hardships the refugees endured during the bitter cold of January when the Fifteenth US Cavalry marched them four days across sixty-seven miles of rough terrain from Presidio to the railhead at Marfa, Texas, only to transport them by train to a makeshift prison at Fort Bliss. When an article identified the forced trek as the "March of Sorrow," Sarah felt it was her grief not the refugees' to which the newspaper gave name. Sarah hoped her soul would find some peace at the sight of Mexican federal troops caged behind strands of barbed wire.

"Turn right here," Timothy pointed to a road that veered ahead.

Sarah guided the car in the direction Timothy designated, driving past the sign announcing they had entered the military reservation. Sarah soon brought the automobile to a halt near an entrance to the guarded compound.

Sarah and Timothy exited the vehicle to take the various pieces of camera equipment from A. J. so that he could extract himself from the rumble seat.

A. J. removed the woolen rug from his lap, then stood, positioning his hand atop the car, and leapt to the ground.

"All set?" Timothy questioned.

"Yes," Sarah answered, placing the strap to the camera case over her shoulder. She knew her presence worried A. J. and Timothy, so she tried to sound as nonchalant as possible, though her heart pounded with anxiety. She wondered if she would sense the killer, if her body would tingle like an alarm that's been tripped should she come across the person who took Samuel's life.

When Timothy reached one of the two armed sentries, he announced, "I'm Timothy Tompkins with the *El Paso Morning Times*. My colleagues and I," he motioned with his left hand toward Sarah and A. J., "are here to meet with the post commander, General Hugh Scott."

As Timothy spoke, Sarah peered past the strands of barbed wire at the tent city alive with men, women, and children, many seeking warmth around a campfire flaming a short distance from the entrance of a tent.

A soldier just inside the compound stepped forward. "Allow them to enter, corporal." He walked in their direction, his hand extended. "I'm Lieutenant Carpenter." Once they completed introductions, the lieutenant stated, "The general is expecting you." He directed them toward a large tent, then had them pause outside the entrance. "One moment, please, while I inform the general of your arrival." The lieutenant disappeared through the flap of the tent only soon to reemerge and stand at attention with the flap raised as a burly bespectacled man with a thick white moustache stepped into the cool sunlight. "General Hugh Scott," the lieutenant announced.

Once outdoors, the older man removed the campaign hat secured beneath his arm and placed it squarely on his bald head, leaving a thick ring of white hair exposed beneath the hat's brim. "Welcome," he said, extending a hand to Timothy then to A. J., and tipping his hat to Sarah. When he slipped on yellow leather gloves against the chill, Sarah noted the absence of his pinky and ring fingers on his left hand. Sarah blushed when the general caught her gaze and held up his gloved hand, sewn with the two fingers absent. "The Indian Wars," he announced.

"I'm sorry," Sarah stammered, apologizing as much for noticing the injury as for the injury itself.

"Don't be," he concluded in an abrupt but not unkind manner. "Shall we begin the tour?" The general motioned them forward. "I'll take you around, answer questions, then leave you with Lieutenant Carpenter so you may take the photos you wish."

"Thank you." Timothy stepped forward to walk beside the general; Sarah and A. J. followed with the lieutenant.

The sheer size of the camp amazed Sarah. Tents erected in neat rows formed roads that stretched into the distance. Around each tent milled men and boys draped in green US Army blankets; women and girls secured rebozos about their heads and shoulders against the cold. Many of the inhabitants had head bandages, arm slings, or crutches.

"How many are interned in this camp?" Timothy asked, pen and pad in hand to take notes.

"Approximately 3,300 troops, 1,067 women, 312 children."

The size of such caged misery astonished Sarah.

The general continued, "Included are General Salvador Mercado, who was the federal commander at Ojinaga, and eight brigadier generals."

General Scott paused the walk to direct their focus toward different areas of the camp. "The far eastern portion of the compound," he pointed, "is officers' row. We have walled tents in that section." With the opposite hand, he guided their focus in a northerly direction. "We've erected bathing facilities with hot and cold running water on the north end of camp."

He renewed their walk down the road formed by rows of tents. "We have medical officers examining prisoners. They treat those with injuries and minor illnesses, and segregate anyone with a contagious infection or disease."

Three young girls with a toddler caught Sarah's eye as she followed the general between the rows of tents. None of them older than ten, their dresses, worn and ill-fitting, hung loosely about their thin bodies. They stood staring at her from their place near a small campfire. One child, her head lowered, peered upward with haunted eyes. The second girl stared with a look of confusion, as if trying to understand the reason for her surroundings and for the visitors' gawking presence. The third and oldest child held a toddler half her size; the girl watched the visitors, her head raised proudly and her eyes glaring with defiance. Sarah suddenly felt ashamed of the satisfaction the refugees' plight had provided her, ashamed of her belief that they deserved to suffer because of the hurt she endured from the loss of Samuel.

"We conduct roll call each morning and again each evening, and we patrol the perimeter with armed guards to ensure no escapes," General Scott explained while guiding them forward.

The general pointed out the metal trash cans beside the tents. "The occupants of each tent are responsible for maintaining the cleanliness of their assigned area."

The general paused before one of the tents inhabited by a family. "Buenos días," he greeted them.

They responded in kind.

General Scott pointed to a beehive-shaped adobe oven created from mud and a scrap of sheet metal. "I am constantly amazed by the ingenuity these refugees demonstrate, especially the women. They take rough scraps that most American citizens would toss on the trash heap, and they fashion a stove that draws air properly. The US Army could learn from such creativity."

The general turned to face his entourage. "When the refugees first arrived, we fed them army rations—navy beans, boiled beef, even apple pie—but they grumbled about the food. I decided simply to supply groceries to which they are accustomed and let them prepare their own meals. So now we distribute rations of beef, pinto beans, corn, chili peppers, and they do their own cooking. I no longer receive complaints about their meals."

Sarah focused on a petite mother who squatted at the fire to stir a pot, an infant secured to her chest in the folds of a rebozo. "Is the campfire the only heat the families have?"

General Scott looked in the direction of Sarah's gaze, then returned his attention to her. "For many of them, I'm afraid it is. We distributed all the tent stoves in our inventory. We've ordered additional stoves, but that's small comfort for those with little more than a canvas tent and blankets to protect them from temperatures that dip below freezing in the night."

Sarah watched the general look down the row of tents at the scenes played out around the small cooking fires. "I hate to see women and children living in these conditions, knowing that while I sleep warmly sheltered in the post commander's house, there are mothers and their babies sleeping on cots in canvas tents." He turned to face Sarah, addressing her directly. "The truth, Mrs. Clendenin, is that the families of soldiers are too frequently asked to carry an unfair burden of suffering and pain." He paused as if reflecting on his own past, then continued. "A soldier is often called to a life of deprivation and danger, but it's a life he chooses. A soldier's family is asked to make sacrifices simply because of their love for the soldier." He shook his head. "It's not a just expectation; it's not a fair exchange."

Sarah fought to stop the tears welling in her eyes. She felt A. J. gently touch her arm.

"I'm afraid all of this has upset you, Mrs. Clendenin." General Scott extended a white handkerchief he removed from his uniform pocket.

Sarah wanted to blurt out, "I'm a soldier's widow; it's not 'a fair exchange'"; instead, she uttered, "I didn't expect to feel as I do." Speaking that truth provided Sarah a well of strength. She staunched the tears and addressed the general. "The US government has gone to admirable lengths to meet the needs of these refugees under its care. With its supply of groceries, medical attention, bathing facilities, and shelter, this compound probably provides most of the people better living conditions than those to which they have been accustomed, but," Sarah extended her hand in a sweep across the panorama of the camp, "they are still forced to live corralled behind barbed wire and watched by armed guards who prevent their departure." Sarah concluded, half expecting her statement to be met with an order from the general for Lieutenant Carpenter to escort the three of them from the compound.

General Scott's square-jawed face exhibited no emotion as he looked at the orderly rows of tents across the camp. When he returned his gaze to Sarah, the old soldier calmly responded, "I don't disagree." He then focused his attention on Timothy and A. J. "I'm going to take my leave now. Lieutenant Carpenter will continue as your guide. He will be able to answer additional questions you might have." The general removed one glove to shake hands with Timothy and A. J., then tipped his hat to Sarah, uttering, "Mrs. Clendenin." Returning Lieutenant Carpenter's salute, General Scott exhorted him, "Take good care of our visitors, lieutenant."

"I will, sir."

As they watched the general depart, Lieutenant Carpenter asked, "Do you have additional questions about the camp? Is there an area of the compound you'd like to visit?"

"I'd like to take some photographs that capture the size of the camp," A. J. responded.

"I'll tag along to ask a few additional questions," Timothy stated.

Sarah added, "I wish to remain in this area to take some photographs of family life."

"If you promise not to stray from this row," the lieutenant addressed Sarah, "I'll leave you here while I escort the gentlemen to the perimeter of the compound."

"You have my word, Lieutenant Carpenter."

Sarah noted that A. J. seemed ready to protest leaving her alone, so she quickly addressed him. "We can capture a greater variety of photographs if we separate."

A. J. nodded in agreement.

"Gentlemen, if you will follow me," Lieutenant Carpenter directed.

Sarah hesitated for only a moment, watching the direction the men headed. Then she returned to the mother squatting at the cooking fire, stirring pots before her.

"Me da permiso?" Sarah asked, pointing at the camera and then to the woman to help make her request understood.

"Sí," the woman answered shyly.

Sarah knelt, positioning herself to capture the young mother with a baby strapped securely to her chest as she stirred food in pots blackened by fire. Next, she stood and stepped back a distance to frame the scene to include the tent as a backdrop.

"Niño o niña?" Sarah asked, pointing to the child wrapped in the rebozo.

The young mother smiled proudly, "Niña," and lowered a portion of the rebozo to expose the baby girl's face.

"Qué bonita," Sarah complimented. She indicated she would like to take a photograph with the baby's face exposed. "Me da permiso?"

"Sí," the mother answered.

Sarah captured a photo of the mother peering lovingly at the face of her infant. "Muy bien," Sarah smiled, "Gracias."

"De nada."

Sarah stepped away from the young woman to focus her camera on the line of tents stretched before her. She hoped to capture the various events taking place at each.

Sarah returned to the tent with the adobe oven to photograph the woman squatting in front of it, monitoring the preparation of the family's meal.

In front of another tent, she photographed two men, one seated on an overturned bucket while the other, dressed in the uniform of a Mexican federal officer, served as barber.

Sarah retraced her steps to the shelter with the three young girls and toddler. A mother, not much taller than the oldest girl, stood beside the tent draping recently washed clothing over a rope tied between their tent and the neighboring one. Sarah approached the mother to ask permission to photograph the family. The mother paused in her labor to shyly agree to Sarah's request. Sarah photographed the mother as she finished placing the recently washed clothing on the line to dry. Sarah positioned herself at an angle from the tent to square the Graflex camera on the mother at the clothesline and the children arranged around the fire at the tent's entrance. Still balancing the toddler on her hip, the oldest girl walked boldly from the campfire to Sarah. The girl motioned toward the camera, speaking a level of Spanish Sarah didn't understand. It took her a moment to realize the girl wanted to see the camera. Sarah motioned for the girl to place the toddler on the ground. When the young girl complied, Sarah handed her the camera, then lifted the toddler onto her own hip. The baby girl looked at her with surprise but was soon playing with the tin cup she grasped in her tiny hands. Through a series of gestures, Sarah directed the young girl to look through the focusing hood while she pointed the camera at different areas of her family's quarters. The girl smiled her excitement when she saw her siblings and then her mother through the hood. Satisfied, she handed the camera back to Sarah in exchange for her baby sister.

"Making friends, I see."

Sarah turned to find A.J standing behind her along with Timothy and the lieutenant.

"My young friend here may be a budding photographer," Sarah responded.

"If there is nothing further I can provide," Lieutenant Carpenter moved to conclude their visit, "then I will escort you to the exit."

"You've been most generous with your time and information,

Lieutenant Carpenter," Timothy replied. "I think we have the info and photographs we need." He looked to A. J. and Sarah for their agreement.

"Very good, then, this way." The lieutenant led them down the dirt road formed by rows of tents and back to the entrance guarded by two armed soldiers.

Before departing through the gate, they again expressed their appreciation for the lieutenant's time and asked him to convey their gratitude to General Scott.

Once outside the compound and away from the armed guards, Sarah paused to look back at the internment camp. Just on the other side of the barbed wire fence stood the young girl holding the toddler, her two sisters standing beside her, peering between the merciless wires that hemmed them in. Sarah positioned her camera to capture that cruelly incongruous scene of children imprisoned behind barbed wire. The oldest girl waved to Sarah as she snapped the photo.

Sarah walked to the automobile, where A. J. and Timothy waited. Looking back at the enclosure, Sarah commented, "I know we can't simply allow a foreign army to enter our country at will, but these almost five thousand people are refugees from war."

"Well, there are refugees, and then there are refugees," Timothy responded, studying the people in the guarded internment camp. "In December, five hundred of the more affluent Mexican citizens fled Chihuahua under the protection of General Mercado, traveling with these very troops to Ojinaga," Timothy emphasized, pointing to the guarded enclosure. "When the rich immigrants left the federal army in Ojinaga to cross into the United States, they were met by a committee of El Paso businessmen who went to Presidio, Texas, to assist the well-heeled refugees with getting their belongings through customs, arranging their transportation to El Paso, and finding lodging in our city."

Timothy drew heavily on the cigarette he placed between his lips. Exhaling a stream of smoke, he added, "And among them was the wealthiest man in the state of Chihuahua, the former Chihuahua governor General Luis Terrazas, who managed to transport a share of his vast wealth to El Paso loaded in the back of twenty wagons. He, then, rented the entire top floor of Hotel Paso del Norte for the comfort of his family and their twenty-seven servants."

"And to think of those children caged behind barbed wire and sleeping in an unheated canvas tent in January," Sarah responded, her voice heavy with concern.

"Well," Timothy repeated, "there are refugees, and then there are refugees." He took a final drag from his cigarette before tossing the butt on the ground to extinguish it.

❋❋❋

Sarah placed the recently brewed pot of coffee on a metal trivet and rearranged the plate of cake and cookies on the serving tray as she awaited the arrival of Constanza and the soldier who was joining him. Constanza had called in the morning to request a visit. He explained he wanted to bring a soldier who served with Samuel and who was with him at Ojinaga. The soldier had visited Constanza at the Crown the previous evening and asked him to arrange a meeting with Samuel's wife.

Sarah had planned to spend her Sunday at the studio printing the final photographs from the Fort Bliss internment camp. But once she received Constanza's call, she remained in the apartment busying herself with anything and everything to expend her nervous energy.

Sarah walked again to the window to stare at the street below. Constanza had not said why the soldier wished to meet with her, but Sarah knew why she wished to meet the soldier. She hungered for any information the soldier could provide about Samuel's death.

Sarah retraced her path from the window to the kitchen. Deciding to place the refreshments in the sitting room, she arranged the food and drink on two trays that she positioned on the table in front of the sofa. Stepping back to examine the display, Sarah decided the table looked too crowded, so she lifted one of the trays to return it to the kitchen when a knock at the door caused her to place the tray back on the table.

Rushing to open the door, Sarah felt a jolt of confusion when Constanza stood at the entrance with an attractive young woman rather than the soldier Sarah expected.

"Hello, Sarah," Constanza stepped through the doorway to take Sarah into his arms and lightly kiss her cheek. "How are you, my dear?" he asked, holding her hands in his.

"It's good to see you, Constanza," Sarah answered before turning her attention to the young woman who stood quietly behind Constanza's large bulk. Sarah studied the woman as Constanza stumbled over an introduction.

"I'm so sorry," Constanza stammered. "I've forgotten my manners."

There was something so familiar about the woman, but Sarah couldn't place her.

"Sarah," Constanza stepped beside the woman, "this is Captain Catalina Vasquez."

It took a moment more before Sarah connected the name with the face. "Cata!" Sarah said with a warm surprise. Without thinking, Sarah grasped the woman's hands. "It is so good to see you again."

"It's good to see you, Mrs. Clendenin," Cata answered, smiling nervously.

"Call me Sarah," she replied, releasing her hold. "Please, let me take your coats and hats."

Cata removed the strap of a large leather satchel from her shoulder and lowered the bag to the floor so she could shed her woolen coat; then, she pulled the pin from the back of a fashionable hat she wore. She handed Sarah her coat and hat but held onto the leather satchel.

"Please, take a seat," Sarah directed them into the sitting room, "while I put these away." As Sarah entered the bedroom to place their outer garments across the foot of her bed, she thought about Cata, now dressed in a long black skirt and a white long-sleeved blouse with lace crowning the high neck. Though her attractive face remained the same, Cata appeared so differently from the memory of the warrior fixed in Sarah's mind.

Sarah returned to the sitting room, announcing, "I brewed a fresh pot of coffee to help take away some of the winter chill. Cata?" she offered.

"Yes, please."

"How about you, Constanza?"

"I'd love a cup, Sarah."

Sarah poured three cups of coffee and handed Cata and Constanza each a cup with a spoon balanced on the saucer. "I'll let you prepare the coffee to your liking. Please help yourselves to some pastry."

Sarah sat in the chair beside the sofa shared by Cata and Constanza. Anxious to conclude the niceties, Sarah had to force herself to sit back while the guests prepared their coffee, and Constanza filled a plate with dessert. She placed her own cup on the end table next to her chair. She really didn't want the coffee; she knew her nervous stomach wouldn't tolerate it.

Just when Sarah thought she could not hold back her questions any longer, Cata began to speak. "I didn't know how to find you," Cata said, looking intensely at Sarah.

Sarah sat riveted, more by Cata's gaze than by her statement.

"I went to Constanza to find you," Cata continued, maintaining the strength of her look.

"How do you know Constanza?" Sarah asked, not really concerned with their history, but Cata's statement seemed to require the question.

"Sarah," Constanza interjected, brushing cake crumbs from his upper lip, "remember last October when you gave Samuel clothing for a woman whose husband had been killed in the alley outside the Crown?"

"Yes," Sarah answered Constanza but kept her eyes focused on Cata.

"I am that woman," Cata concluded.

"Did Samuel recognize you at Calabasas?" Sarah asked, trying to fit the pieces together.

"No," Cata replied, setting her cup and saucer back on the tray. "Not then. I assisted as Samuel's translator in Ciudad Chihuahua; I identified myself at that time."

"And you were with Samuel at the Battle of Ojinaga?" Sarah questioned, moving forward to sit at the edge of her chair.

"Yes."

"Did you see him," Sarah halted, choking back tears. Clearing her throat, she started anew, "Did you see Samuel die?"

"No." Cata paused, then answered, "I saw his body."

"How was he killed?" Sarah didn't want to know, but she had to know.

"A gunshot to the head." Cata touched her index finger to the left side of her forehead, indicating the location of the wound. "He was leading a charge, I was told, and looked back to encourage his troops forward. He died," she paused as if searching for the word, then added, "instantly."

"I see," Sarah answered, imagining Samuel's body sprawled on the desert sand. She refocused her look on Cata. "Thank you, Cata. I needed to know how he died."

"Yes, you needed to know," Cata agreed. She lifted the leather satchel onto her lap. "I brought you some of his things." Cata reached into the bag and removed a gun belt holstering two pistols. She handed the leather belt with the weapons to Sarah.

Sarah took the belt from Cata and studied it. She ran her hand across the buckle, then traced the initials "SC" tooled into the leather. "Thank you, Cata," Sarah spoke with a quiet rasp.

"And this." Cata removed from the bag the Bowie knife cradled in its tooled leather sheath and passed it to Sarah.

Sarah gripped the sheathed knife in both of her hands, and wept, sobbing her grief.

Cata stood to console Sarah, removing the weapons from her lap, then gently touching Sarah's hair.

At that kindness, Sarah let herself be guided forward against Cata's legs, and she wept into the folds of the woman's skirt. She held onto Cata until her sobs stilled; then she leaned back. "I'm sorry, Cata," she said, reassuring her guest. "I'm all right."

Cata resumed her seat next to Constanza on the sofa.

The three sat quietly, Sarah not trusting herself to speak. She stared at Samuel's weapons, which Cata had placed on the floor at Sarah's feet. When she felt sure she had control of her emotions, she looked again to the young woman, and said, "Thank you, Cata, for bringing some of Samuel home to me."

"I know loss." She looked toward Constanza then back to Sarah. "You showed kindness to me the night my Mayo died."

"Sarah," Constanza leaned forward, "Cata has more information about Samuel."

Sarah turned from Constanza to Cata.

"I saw Samuel buried. I marked his grave."

"I am so appreciative, Cata. That means a lot to me." Sarah crossed both of her hands over her heart.

"Wait, Sarah," Constanza interrupted, "Cata has more to tell."

Cata continued, "General Villa will bring Samuel's body to Juárez if you wish, but you must get approval to cross his body into El Paso."

FEBRUARY 1914

Sarah

Sarah looked in the mirror, lowering the veil of her hat. She studied her reflection, examining the black woolen suit she wore. Satisfied, she lifted the veil and walked to the window. She knew A. J. and Paola would soon arrive in the car A. J. had rented to take them to the bridge for the funeral procession.

As she waited at the window, Sarah thought about her meeting with General Scott in his office a couple weeks ago. A. J. and Timothy had insisted on going with her to the appointment at the general's headquarters on Fort Bliss, but Sarah stood firm, asserting that while she appreciated their offer, she felt it best to go by herself. Sarah believed she alone could effectively present her request.

When she entered General Scott's headquarters, she was greeted by his adjutant, who announced her arrival, then guided her to a large office. The general met her at the door, welcoming her with a friendly formality. He directed her to a chair positioned in front of a prominent wooden desk, but then surprised Sarah by sitting in the chair next to hers.

Skipping any exchange of pleasantries, Sarah laid out her request. She identified herself as a recently widowed wife of a soldier and observed General Scott's formal military bearing soften. She disclosed that her husband, Captain Samuel Clendenin, had fought with Colonel Giuseppe Garibaldi's Foreign Legion during the Madero Revolution, then enlisted in General Villa's Division of the North to fight against Victoriano Huerta's overthrow of the Madero presidency. When Sarah stated that Samuel had been killed in January at the Battle of Ojinaga, she saw the general's face register surprise.

"And yet you spoke on behalf of the federal refugees who fought at that battle," the general stated more as an observation than a question. "Remarkable!"

Sarah described General Villa's offer to return Samuel's body to El Paso for burial, to which General Scott replied, "Then General Villa must have great respect for Captain Clendenin. How can I help?"

Sarah explained she needed his assistance with getting the necessary approvals to bring Samuel's body across the border into the United States.

When General Scott answered, "Let me look into this request, Mrs. Clendenin," she recognized their meeting had concluded. At the general's direction, she left her contact information with his adjutant.

Two days after their meeting, Sarah received a call from the adjutant informing her of the arrangements for a US Army honor guard to receive Samuel's body on the Santa Fe Street International Bridge.

As she continued to watch from her apartment window, she reviewed the preparations, trying to reassure herself that she had addressed all the necessary steps. She purchased their plot at the Evergreen Cemetery and arranged with Nagley & Kaster Funeral Home for a hearse to transport the casket. Sarah accepted General Scott's offer of a military chaplain to conduct the graveside service. From the Potter Floral Company, she ordered an "open heart" standing funeral spray for the gravesite and a white floral casket cover for Samuel's ride in the hearse. She purchased a granite headstone from Pioneer Granite and Marble Works to be carved and installed marking Samuel's grave within the month.

Sarah wondered who might attend the service. Timothy publicized today's procession in a piece published in yesterday's *El Paso Morning Times*. The article heralded the return of an American hero of the

Mexican Revolution and featured a handsome photograph of Samuel wearing his Stetson, knee-high laced boots, riding breeches, and gun belt holstering two six-shooters. Sarah had been surprised when she read about some of Samuel's exploits depicted in the article; Samuel rarely spoke with her about his battle experiences. Timothy detailed Samuel's fame among the revolutionary army for destroying over 250 miles of railroad track, effectively foiling the plans of federal troops and, among Garibaldi's Foreign Legion, earning Samuel the nickname "Emperor of Explosives." As Sarah thought about the Samuel described in the article, she couldn't help wondering how much she didn't know about the man with whom she shared her life.

A long black car pulled to the curb in front of the apartment building; Sarah took a deep breath to steady herself and headed to the door without waiting for A. J.'s knock. When she met him on the stairs, A. J. offered to assist her with putting on the coat she carried draped over her arm. She thanked him but refused; for now, Sarah wanted to feel the cold to help ground her to this event that otherwise seemed unreal.

A. J. opened the back door for Sarah to slide onto the seat and into Paola's caring embrace.

"Thank you for being here, Paola," Sarah whispered.

Paola kissed her cheek, then held her hand as the car pulled from the curb.

The drive was a short one. Soon they arrived at the bridge, where police and military worked together to block traffic. Once A. J. identified Sarah as Mrs. Clendenin, the policeman directed them to park a few yards ahead of the horse-drawn hearse.

The size of the crowd already gathered along the sidewalks both in El Paso and Juárez surprised Sarah.

After the driver did a U-turn, parking, as directed, A. J. turned in his seat to address Sarah. "Let me notify the military authorities we're here."

She nodded numbly.

When A. J. returned to the automobile, he brought Timothy, who crossed to Sarah's side of the vehicle and leaned in. "You doing all right?"

"Yes," Sarah answered unconvincingly, "thank you."

"It won't be long now," A. J. said, reentering the car. "The procession should begin fairly soon."

"Okay," Sarah responded before turning to Timothy. "Thank you for the article, Timothy," Sarah spoke, shading her eyes from the midday sun. "I think your writing is responsible for the crowd that has gathered."

"Well, Samuel had lots of friends in El Paso and Juárez." Timothy added, "He will soon have even more admirers. I received word this morning that Associated Press has picked up the article and wants me to write a second piece after today's services. So, Samuel will receive the national recognition he deserves."

The sound of a slow steady drumbeat silenced the crowd of onlookers and snapped the Army honor guard to attention. Timothy assisted Sarah from the car while A. J. circled the vehicle to help Paola exit.

"Do you wish for us to stand with you?" A. J. asked as Sarah stared down the bridge toward Juárez.

"Thank you, A. J., but I think I would prefer to receive Samuel by myself."

"Okay, Sarah. We'll be on the sidewalk if you need us."

Paola kissed her lightly on the cheek, whispering, "We're here for you."

"Thank you, Paola," Sarah responded, and waited briefly for her friends to step away. Then Sarah lowered the black veil and walked to the center of the bridge to await Samuel's arrival. She could see the four drummers leading the procession, their drumbeat slow and solemn. Who knew, she thought, that a drum could produce such a mournful sound. As the procession moved closer, Sarah saw two coachmen riding atop an odd-looking horse-drawn carriage bearing Samuel's casket draped with a Mexican flag. Upon a more focused look, Sarah realized Samuel's casket rested atop a gun carriage, the cannon positioned level beneath the funeral bier. Behind the carriage marched two rows of men, each row consisting of six revolutionary soldiers. Alongside, on horseback, rode a line of soldiers in charro dress. Sarah recognized Cata as the lead rider, wearing the type of richly embroidered pants and waist-length jacket she had worn at Calabasas, a large sombrero crowning her braided hair, which she had coiled neatly beneath it.

When the procession reached the center of the bridge where Sarah stood, it halted in step with the final drumbeat. Sarah walked to the carriage, her heart pounding. She first placed her hand on the flag-draped coffin; then she leaned forward to rest her forehead against its hardness. "Oh, Samuel," she whispered. She remained in that position for a few seconds, the soldiers and the crowd quietly respecting her final reunion with her husband. Sarah raised her head, kissed her gloved hand, then placed the hand on the coffin before stepping back so the transfer of his body could continue.

The revolutionary soldiers who walked behind the carriage formed two rows of three men on each side. Then six men who formed the inner rows stepped forward to grasp the casket handles, and at an order from Cata, the six men of the outer rows presented arms. Facing the carriage, the soldiers on horseback saluted their fallen comrade. Sarah watched as the men removed the casket from the gun carriage, then marched it with solemn deliberateness to six US Army soldiers who made up the honor guard. The revolutionary soldiers continued presenting arms and saluting until the transfer of the casket to American soldiers was complete.

Sarah watched the honor guard place the casket into the back of the hearse and close the glass-paneled doors. She then turned to find Cata as the revolutionary soldiers maintained a respectful military stillness. Looking at Cata, Sarah raised her right hand, patting it twice over her heart.

Cata dipped her head slightly, acknowledging Sarah's gesture of gratitude.

Sarah walked slowly back to meet Timothy, A. J., and Paola at the car, its engine already running.

"A beautiful ceremony," Paola expressed as she hugged Sarah to her.

"Yes," A. J. agreed, "a great show of respect for Samuel." A. J. took Sarah's arm to assist her into the car while Timothy helped Paola. "I'll see you at the cemetery," Timothy announced before jogging across the street.

Once A. J. settled onto the front seat, he looked back and announced, "the hearse has started forward." Then he directed the driver to "pull behind the hearse and follow it to Evergreen Cemetery."

When the auto eased from the curb, Sarah could see Samuel's coffin through the large glass windows that surrounded it. She closed her eyes and thought, "You're home, Samuel. You've come back to me." Sarah opened her eyes to see A. J. turned in the seat, staring past her.

"Sarah, look," A. J. directed, motioning with his chin toward the back window.

Sarah turned to see a combination of cars and wagons forming a civilian procession following behind their car and the horse-drawn hearse.

❂❂❂

Sarah woke, surprised by the sunlight streaming through the curtained windows. She fumbled for the clock next to the bed and saw it was past 7:00 a.m. This was the first she had slept through the night since learning of Samuel's death. She threw back the covers, anxious to begin her day, and rose to wrap in the warmth of her robe.

In the bathroom, she washed the sleep from her eyes. Looking in the mirror, Sarah studied the young face that returned her gaze. She felt as though the last two months had aged her greatly; the reflection in the glass showed otherwise.

Sarah went into the kitchen to brew a pot of coffee. She took out a mug and spoon, then stood watching the pot until it percolated. Gripping the steaming mug, she sat at the kitchen table to reflect on yesterday's events.

This morning, her recall of the funeral proved much more vivid than what she registered at the time of the service when she watched it as though from somewhere outside her own body.

A couple hundred people gathered at the gravesite to pay their respects to Samuel. Men and women—some dressed in funeral finery, others wearing street clothes—stood listening to the chaplain's words as he read from Scripture, spoke of a soldier's selfless sacrifice "to lay down his life for others," and led the gathering in an enthusiastic, off-key rendition of "The Old Rugged Cross." Following the conclusion of the hymn came a plaintive, soul piercing performance of "Taps," played by a single military bugler who stood at a distance from the funeral attendees. Sarah recalled the honor guard's ceremonial folding and presentation of the Mexican flag to her; she remembered standing in a kind of befogged dullness after receiving the flag.

At the service's conclusion, Timothy, A. J., and Paola ushered Sarah through the crowd, people expressing their condolences as she passed. Her friends guided her into the backseat of the waiting car before Timothy took his leave.

Sarah knew she should remain at the gravesite to receive sympathies and remembrances of Samuel from those who wished to share, but she felt so wearied by grief that she simply wanted to lie down alone in her apartment before the burden of sadness crushed her.

"Please," Sarah pleaded, "take me home."

On the drive to her apartment, A. J. shared that Constanza spread word through the funeral crowd of his plan to tap a barrel of beer at the Crown for all who wished to raise a glass in Samuel's honor.

Sarah smiled. "Samuel would like such a celebration."

By the time they arrived at Sarah's apartment, she had convinced Paola and A. J. that while she appreciated their offer to stay with her, she needed to be alone. They both walked her to the apartment door, leaving only after she promised to eat some of the food Paola had prepared and delivered to her apartment the previous evening.

Once Paola and A. J. departed, Sarah closed the front door and walked into her bedroom. Removing her hat and shoes, she lay on the bed, not even bothering to undress or turn down the covers. She remained in that position, focused on memories of Samuel, reviewing scenes of their life together even after night's darkness replaced the light of day. Sometime during the night, she settled wearily into sleep, waking only long enough to remove her clothes and burrow naked beneath the blankets.

Now, Sarah sat in the kitchen ready to begin the new day. She stood to pour a second cup of coffee. After taking a sip, she set the cup on the tabletop and moved to the icebox to retrieve the ham Paola had prepared for her and two eggs. Sarah had not eaten since yesterday morning, and now, suddenly, she felt ravenous. She prepared a large breakfast of ham, eggs, and toast.

She felt renewed by last night's sleep and this morning's meal. As she washed the sticky yolk and smear of grease from her plate before placing it on the drying rack, Sarah thought about the day that lay ahead. She would return to the cemetery to spend time alone with Samuel, but then she had the remainder of the day unplanned.

Sarah dressed for the cool drive. She enjoyed the chill of the wind against her face and the car's response to her throttling for increased speed. She drove faster than she should on the city streets until she reached the main entrance of the cemetery; there, she slowed the vehicle, driving respectfully along the dirt roads dividing Evergreen into neighborhoods of the dead. She parked under the shade of the lone tree near Samuel's plot.

Flowers blanketed Samuel's grave in a quilt of color. Though the flowers had wilted from the cold of night, most of them retained some of their hue. At the head of the grave stood her open-heart spray.

"Good morning, my love," Sarah spoke as though she had just entered a room where Samuel sat waiting. "I'm so happy you came home to me." Then Sarah broke into tears. She allowed herself to weep with abandon, knowing no one watched; she permitted her soul to moan its grief, knowing no one listened. She wept until her body hiccupped in spasms of sadness.

Sarah wiped her eyes and nose with a handkerchief. "I know you don't like to see me cry, Samuel, and there will come a day when I visit without tears. But this is all very fresh, so you have to allow me time to mourn." She paused, looking to move away from discussing her grief. "I'm sure you know Constanza tapped a barrel of beer in your honor. I fully expect to hear reports of strange noises and odd occurrences at the Crown, all attributed to your joining in the toasts. Knowing how you loved the nightlife, I will believe all those stories," Sarah chuckled.

"Samuel, I try to think you are working late at the Crown or that you have reported for duty and are camped safely in a rebel-controlled city. I know these are silly thoughts, but it helps me imagine your absence is temporary." Sarah released a sigh.

"But you're home now, my love. You're with me."

Sarah busied herself with refreshing Samuel's gravesite. Talking to him as she worked, she removed flowers that had browned and peeled dead petals from flowers that retained even a little color. Satisfied with her work, Sarah scanned the cemetery for a bin to dispose of the debris she held in her hands. She spied a container next to a small stone building that housed equipment for the groundskeeper. As Sarah walked in the direction of the building, she noticed a woman standing at a plot adjacent to the stone structure. The woman peered down at a gravesite, her hand resting on the headstone. Sarah swung wide, not wanting to invade the woman's privacy.

At the metal bin, Sarah released her handful of flowers and petals. When she turned to retrace her steps, she noticed the young woman had raised her head to look in Sarah's direction. "Cata!" Sarah spoke her surprise.

The two women walked toward one another, each smiling her plea-sure at seeing the other. When they came together, they felt a brief awk-wardness; then, Sarah reached for Cata's hands.

"Cata," Sarah said, "I can't find words to thank you sufficiently for bringing Samuel back to me."

The young woman smiled shyly. "Samuel belongs home." Cata turned to point toward the grave where she previously stood. "I come to visit my husband, Mayo." She returned her gaze to Sarah. She placed the palm of her hand over her heart. "He lives here." She pointed to the gravesite. "But I can honor him there."

Sarah nodded her understanding.

"May I see where Samuel is buried?" Cata asked.

"Yes, of course." Sarah placed her arm through Cata's and guided her down the road to Samuel's plot.

At the grave, the two women stood quietly, looking at the carpet of flowers, until Cata broke the silence. "He was a brave man, a good soldier."

Sarah thought for a moment before responding. "You know Samuel so differently from how I know him. He will always be a soldier and com-rade to you, but he remains a husband and lover to me." Then she added, "I guess we each know just a part of another person."

"We remember him differently, but we remember him; that's most important," Cata concluded.

Sarah nodded, repeating, "We remember him."

They stood quietly, each focused on her own thoughts. Then Cata stated, "I will go now."

Sarah experienced a shock of panic. She didn't want Cata to leave. She didn't fully know why. Maybe she just didn't want to be alone. Sarah blurted, "How did you get here?"

"Taxi," Cata answered, appearing surprised by the urgency of the question.

"I have an automobile. I can drive you."

Cata studied Sarah briefly before answering, "Okay. That would be good."

"Great," Sarah felt an odd relief.

"I want to say goodbye to Mayo first."

Sarah pointed to her auto parked beneath the tree. "I will meet you at the car."

Sarah waited until Cata had walked some distance away before she spoke again to Samuel. "I like her, Samuel. Cata seems a good person. She's been a good friend to us. Keep a protective eye on her in battle, if you can." Sarah looked skyward at the bright blue day, then returned her gaze to the gravesite. "I miss you so much, Samuel, my love. I hope I made you as happy in life as you made me." Sarah wiped away tears. "I will visit again soon, but you and I both know that wherever I am, I carry you with me." Sarah kissed the fingertips of her right hand, then placed the hand beneath the bed of flowers to touch the dirt of Samuel's grave. "I love you, Samuel."

When Sarah got to the car, she glanced in the direction of Mayo's gravesite and saw Cata walking toward her, Cata's full skirt swaying with each step. Once she reached the vehicle, Sarah asked, "Ready?"

"Yes," Cata opened the car door.

Sarah cranked the vehicle before entering the auto. She drove to the entrance of the cemetery, then braked. Turning to face Cata, she asked, "Do you have to return right away? If not, would you like to go for a drive? Maybe find a place to eat?" Before Cata had a chance to answer, Sarah explained, "I just don't want to go back to that empty apartment, Cata. Not yet."

"Yes," Cata smiled, "let's drive."

Sarah turned left onto Alameda Avenue, heading away from town. After a very short distance, they entered a rural area with a scattering of dairy farms among fields awaiting the spring plow. They drove along irrigation ditches, past large cottonwood trees growing beside the road. Sarah throttled to increase speed, enjoying the motion. She saw Cata remove her hat to allow the wind to tug and tousle strands of hair loose from the braid coiled at the nape of her neck. Sarah did the same, steering with one hand on the wheel as she removed her hat.

Cata spoke loud enough to be heard over the wind passing through the car. "The farms remind me of my home."

"I came from a farming community, too, but my parents ran a small mercantile store." Sarah spoke, maintaining her eyes on the road.

Cata shared, "We worked on a hacienda. We raised goats, chickens, and cattle. We paid the hacendado in goods and in work."

"What we call sharecroppers in America."

"Sharecroppers?" Cata repeated.

"Yes. You pay a share of your crop, a share of your labor."

"Yes, then, 'sharecroppers,'" Cata agreed.

The vacant fields, lonely livestock, and adobe homes they passed reminded them of their earlier years, and they exchanged stories of their families and lives before the revolution.

When they entered the small farming community of San Elizario, Cata pointed to the white church. "Let's stop," she suggested.

Sarah parked the car next to the modest plaza across from the adobe mission.

"Let's go inside the church," Cata said.

Once they exited the automobile, they stood beside the car, each attempting to tidy her hair. Finally, Sarah said, "Well, this will have to do," and she positioned her hat on her head to hide the disarray.

They climbed the few steps to the mission's entrance; then Sarah pulled open the heavy wooden doors. A musky odor greeted them. Genuflecting while making the sign of the cross against their bodies, they sat on wooden pews across the aisle from one another.

Sarah closed her eyes in prayer, but Samuel did not occupy all her thoughts. She offered thanks for Cata's entrance into her life. Studying the vigas of the ceiling, Sarah considered Cata riding to alert them of the US troops outside of Nogales, Cata bringing Samuel's body home, and now Cata sharing her day to lessen the dark grief Sarah had borne since Samuel's death. She prayed her gratitude before turning to look at Cata, who nodded her readiness to leave the church.

Sarah followed Cata back into the bright sunlight.

"Are you hungry?" Sarah asked.

"Yes," Cata answered emphatically.

"Let's see if there is a café in this community."

As they started around the plaza, Cata stopped a young Latino dressed in overalls to ask in Spanish about a place to eat.

Sarah looked across the plaza in the direction the young man pointed.

After Cata said her thanks, she informed Sarah of the only restaurant in town, adding, "He says it is very good."

"Let's go," Sarah encouraged.

Cata took Sarah's arm, walking with the ease of an established friendship. They crossed the plaza to enter an adobe building into a room with two long tables, each covered with red tablecloths. One table had several men engaged in humor-filled conversation over plates of food.

"It smells wonderful," Sarah expressed.

A heavy-set woman greeted them in Spanish, encouraging them to take a seat.

Sarah and Cata sat across from each other at the closest table. The woman, who introduced herself as Juanita, exchanged a rapid Spanish with Cata. When Juanita departed, Cata explained to Sarah that the restaurant served a comida corrida, a prepared meal that included soup, drink, main dish, dessert and coffee for one price.

"That sounds perfect," Sarah responded.

Juanita returned balancing a tray with two cups of a steaming vegetable soup, a container of warm corn tortillas, and two glasses of jamaica, a hibiscus tea.

Sarah and Cata ate enthusiastically. As soon as they finished their soup, Juanita removed the cups and spoons, soon returning to serve plates filled with rice flaked by cilantro, chunks of roasted beef, cubed potatoes, and pinto beans.

"This is a feast," Sarah announced. After tasting each item on the plate, Sarah accepted the small bowl of salsa from Cata and sprinkled a measured spoonful of the spicy relish over much of the food. They both ate with vigor fueled by their hunger and the rich flavors of the meal.

Upon completion of the main course, Juanita reappeared to take their plates, only to return with two large cups of coffee and two small pumpkin-filled empanadas for dessert.

Sarah laughed when Cata puffed out her cheeks to demonstrate her fullness. Sarah nodded in agreement. Still, both women took a bite of the small tart, widening their eyes to signal their shared appreciation of the dessert.

"What a find this café is," Sarah announced, taking a second bite of the empanada.

When they finished eating, they sat conversing over cups of coffee, enjoying each other's company.

Sarah reached across the table to squeeze Cata's hand. "It has been a long time since I have felt this happy. Thank you, Cata."

"It is a good day," Cata added.

When Juanita returned to offer more coffee, Cata and Sarah declined. Sarah insisted on paying while Cata shared their compliments with the matron.

When they exited into the afternoon light, Cata suggested, "Let's walk around the plaza."

They walked arm-in-arm in front of the buildings that horseshoed the plaza. Sarah felt the sunlight against the back of her neck and thought of Samuel. She experienced a sense of peace.

They circled the plaza twice in a slow stroll, then begrudgingly agreed they needed to return to the automobile to begin the hour's drive back to El Paso.

"Promise we will share such adventures in the future," Sarah encouraged when they reached the car.

"We will," Cata agreed, adding, "God and the revolution permitting."

Sarah entered the studio to see A. J. sitting behind the counter gripping a cup of coffee with both hands. He wore a sweater over his shirt and under a buttoned jacket.

"Did you just come from outdoors?" Sarah asked removing her hat, scarf, and coat to hang them on the rack behind the curtain.

"No, I'm just chilled." Then he added, "Keep your distance. I think I may have caught a cold."

Sarah ignored his warning and kissed his cheek. "Thank you for being with me through Samuel's funeral. Thank you for always being here for me, A. J. You're a good friend."

Embarrassed, A. J. brushed a knuckle against the location of her kiss. "How are you, Sarah?"

"Honestly, I'm better than I've been since Samuel's death." She added, "Bringing him home to people who knew him, gathered to honor him and celebrate his return gives me a sense of peace I haven't felt for weeks." She added, "I miss Samuel terribly; I think of him constantly, but knowing he's home provides me a sense of calm."

"I'm glad."

"And I slept through the night," she added.

"I wish I could say the same." A. J. took a sip of coffee, then turned his head to clear his throat.

"It's a quiet morning, A. J. Why don't you go upstairs and get some rest? I'll keep an eye on things."

He started to protest, but Sarah interrupted. "I'll call you if I need you. Now go rest." Sarah tugged at his arm to pull him from the stool.

"Okay, I'll go upstairs for a short while." He walked through the curtained area, stopping at the foot of the stairs. "Call me if you need me."

"I will, A. J. Now go." Sarah made a shooing motion with her hand. Once A. J. departed, Sarah busied herself, straightening up the studio, dusting the furnishings and the framed photos. As she worked, she thought of her friend. His thinness provided him little reserve to fight illness.

When Sarah finished cleaning and organizing the studio, she went into the darkroom to see what work A. J. had completed and determine what needed her attention. Switching on the safelights before closing the door, Sarah walked to the drying rack. She reached to remove a photo printed on a full sheet of paper, then drew back her hand as if from a flame. Samuel's funeral procession stretched across the photo paper. Sarah quickly turned from the rack. Her sense of peace shattered.

❈❈❈

The ringing of the telephone caught Sarah off-guard, and she glanced at the clock as she rushed from the bedroom to answer the phone. A 7:30 a.m. phone call gave her a sense of foreboding.

"Hello," she spoke into the mouthpiece, trying to disguise the concern in her voice.

"Mrs. Sarah Clendenin?" a man asked.

"Yes," Sarah answered in a tone indicating both confirmation and questioning.

"This is Captain W. D. Green of the El Paso Police Department."

"Yes," Sarah responded, the phone call confusing and disquieting her.

"Ma'am, I'm sorry to call so early in the morning, but I wanted to make sure I reached you today."

"What may I do for you, Captain Green?"

"Mrs. Clendenin, you were married to the recently deceased Captain Samuel C. Clendenin, correct?"

"Yes," she responded, taken aback by the question.

"Well, first, my condolences for your loss."

"Thank you," Sarah responded, anxious for him to get to the purpose of his call. "What may I do for you?"

"Ma'am, I would like for you to come to police headquarters today."

"What is the purpose for my visit?"

"Mrs. Clendenin, we'd like to talk with you about your husband."

"In regard to what?"

"Ma'am, it's a conversation best had in person. Can you meet with me at ten this morning?

"Yes," Sarah answered, her mind racing with questions.

"Just ask for Captain Green at the front desk. I'll see you at ten. Goodbye, Mrs. Clendenin."

Before Sarah could respond, she heard the click disconnecting the caller. Sarah returned the receiver to its hook, set down the telephone, and struggled to steady her hand as she wrote on the pad next to the phone: *"Captain W. D. Green. 10:00 a.m. police headquarters. Samuel?!?"* She knew she didn't require a reminder for any of the information she recorded, but emotionally, she needed to have something concrete to carry from the phone conversation. She tore the page off the pad, folded it, then slipped the note into her purse.

Sarah returned to the bedroom to finish dressing for work. She hated leaving A. J. alone to manage the morning's business, but she knew he would understand that it couldn't be helped. Two days had passed since she returned to the studio to find A. J. ill. While his cold had not improved, it had not worsened.

Grabbing her coat, scarf, and hat, Sarah decided she would drive to work today to shorten her time away from the studio. As she hurried down the stairs to the car, her mind raced with possible reasons for the meeting with Captain Green. Sarah thought of the murders outside the Crown last fall. Had the police discovered more evidence? Had they learned about Constanza and Samuel's role in helping Cata escape to Juárez? But why wouldn't the police question Constanza rather than her? Maybe they had found the clothes she'd given to Cata. But there was nothing to link the clothes to her. Sarah's mind leapt to another possibility. Perhaps the police learned about Samuel's and her munitions smuggling. What if Jay Wright had been arrested and chose to disclose Samuel's and her involvement in the Arizona gunrunning operation, turning them in as collateral for a lesser charge and more lenient sentence? Sarah then mentally jumped to the possibility the police had positive news to share. What if Samuel weren't dead? Sarah had not viewed his remains because she knew the deterioration the desert sands would have wrought on the body; she took Cata's word that the person in the casket was Samuel. Cata said she didn't see Samuel killed but discovered his body. According to Cata, Samuel took a bullet to the temple. Wouldn't that disfigure the dead person's face? Did Cata base her identification of Samuel's body on the gun belt and knife? Maybe he had been wounded, and another soldier took his weapons. Sarah had seen bodies stripped of their belongings after the Battle of Juárez. But if Samuel were hospitalized with a wound, why a call from the El Paso police? Sarah couldn't shake the foreboding wedged deep into her heart.

Sarah parked in front of the studio and hurried inside.

"Good morning," A. J. greeted her hoarsely.

"A. J." she blurted, "I have to meet with Captain Green this morning at police headquarters."

"What? Slow down." A. J. held up his hand to signal the need for calm. "Start again."

"Captain Green from the El Paso Police Department called this morning and requested I meet with him at ten today. He said he wanted to talk with me about Samuel, but he wouldn't share any other details regarding the purpose for the meeting."

"That's odd," A. J. responded, his brow furrowing with concern.

"Captain Green said it would be best if we conversed in person."

"Sarah, why don't you remove your coat and take a deep breath," A. J. encouraged. "It may be nothing more than a few questions related to Samuel's business venture with the Crown. The newspapers are always publishing stories about Green's focus on gambling or liquor violations."

"But why would the police wish to speak with me? Why wouldn't they talk with Constanza?"

"Perhaps they have spoken with Constanza, or perhaps they are going to speak with him after they meet with you." A. J. stood next to Sarah. He extended his hand. "Here, give me your coat and hat."

After Sarah unbuttoned her coat, A. J. held it at the collar so she could remove her arms from the sleeves.

"I don't know why the police might wish to speak with you about

Samuel," he continued as he placed her outer garments on the hall tree, "but it does you no good to speculate. You'll shortly know the purpose of the visit, so try to remain calm until there is reason to feel otherwise."

Sarah appreciated A. J. trying to settle her nerves, but she detected worry in his voice.

"I have an appointment for a photoshoot this morning. I can try to reschedule it if you would like for me to go with you to the meeting," A. J. offered.

"No. I'm just being silly." Sarah tried to sound convincing.

"I can check with Timothy or Paola. One of them may be free."

"No, I'm fine, A. J." Sarah attempted to turn their attention to a different subject. "Now, what takes priority today?" she asked, trying to sound refocused. "Do we need to print additional copies of the bullfight postcards?"

"I'm not sure what we have in stock. Why don't you check?"

Sarah got busy, trying to occupy her thoughts with work. She reviewed current orders they received for photo postcards, separating those requests for which they had existing stock from orders requiring them to make additional prints to fill requisitions. Since the meeting with Captain Green would interrupt her morning, Sarah decided to postpone processing additional picture postcards until the afternoon.

She organized orders with similar postcard requests across a long table, then began counting cards by photo and placing the completed stack with the corresponding order. When she caught her mind wandering to the meeting at police headquarters, Sarah would begin her tally anew, chastising herself for her inattention.

Sarah managed to keep busy until A. J. interrupted, "You'd better get ready to leave, Sarah. You don't want to be late for your meeting."

Sarah looked at the wall clock. It was just nine thirty, and a five-minute drive would get her to the police station. A. J.'s anxiousness fueled her own, so she decided to stop work and prepare to depart. While she put on her outer garments, Sarah was aware of A. J. hovering protectively nearby. He followed her to the door, holding it open for her. "I'm sure all will go well," he offered as parting encouragement. "Call if you need me, Sarah."

The drive to police headquarters was brief, and a single circling of the block revealed a parking space around the corner from the entrance. Though Sarah knew she had arrived early, she entered through the outer door with "El Paso Police Department" painted in bold block letters across the glass. She stopped at the front desk to claim her appointment with Captain Green. The officer in charge directed her to take a seat in one of the wooden chairs lining the wall, but Sarah couldn't relax enough to sit, so she removed her hat and coat, then stood holding them as she waited alongside the row of chairs.

While her wait seemed unnervingly long, when Sarah looked at the wall clock, only seven minutes had passed.

"Mrs. Clendenin?"

Sarah turned to her left to see a middle-aged, paunchy man in a blue uniform striding toward her.

"Yes," Sarah responded, walking in the direction of the police officer.

"I'm Captain Green," he announced. "Thank you for meeting with me today."

"Of course," Sarah replied, adding, "I'm anxious to learn the purpose of the meeting."

"Let's step down the hall to my office," and he extended the palm of his hand to guide Sarah.

"It's here to the right," Captain Green directed, pausing to allow Sarah to enter the office first; then he followed, closing the door. He pulled out one of two chairs in front of his desk. "Please, have a seat." Sarah placed her hat and coat on the second chair and watched Captain Green walk around the meticulously organized desk to take a seat across from her.

Sarah noticed the long panoramic photograph on the wall at his back and assumed the three rows of uniformed men looking into the camera with serious determination represented the officers of the El Paso Police Department.

"Before we get started, can I get you anything? A cup of coffee, perhaps?"

"No, no thank you," Sarah responded, anxious to learn the reason for the meeting.

"Okay." Captain Green took a deep breath. "Mrs. Clendenin, I asked to meet with you in my office today because of a rather sensitive matter." He repositioned himself in his chair "Are you familiar with the name Charles Scott O'Malley?"

"No," Sarah responded, searching her memory for any glint of familiarity. "No, I've never heard that name before. Why do you ask? Should I know the name?"

Rather than answering Sarah's questions, Captain Green asked, "How long were you married to Samuel C. Clendenin?"

"We married in June 1911, so not quite three years," Sarah answered, confused by the line of questioning.

"And how long had you known Captain Clendenin prior to your marriage to him?"

"We met in February of that same year."

"Mrs. Clendenin, what do you know about your husband's life prior to his arrival in El Paso?"

"Well, I know Samuel came to El Paso from San Francisco. I know he once worked as an accountant, that he successfully invested in stocks, which allowed him to afford a change in lifestyle. I know he joined Madero's revolution because he wanted adventure and to fight for what he viewed as a just cause." As Sarah listed what she knew of Samuel's background, she began to realize that neither Samuel nor she shared much with each other about their pasts. Their relationship always existed in the present.

"Was Captain Clendenin born and raised in San Francisco?" The captain looked up from the pad on which he recorded notes.

"No. Samuel said his family is from a small town in Massachusetts, near Boston. He was estranged from his family and refused to say much about them other than they parted ways over conflicting beliefs—I assumed religious beliefs—and Samuel left home at nineteen." Sarah began to feel defensive, realizing she had now shared most of what she knew of Samuel's past. "Why are you asking these questions, Captain Green? What is the reason for this meeting, and how are Samuel and I connected to it?"

"Mrs. Clendenin," Captain Green responded calmly, "the newspaper articles written about the return of Captain Clendenin's body to El Paso have sparked a lot of interest across the country." He opened a manila folder on his desk. "Our office has received communication from several sources regarding Captain Clendenin. The one of most immediate concern is from a Mrs. Mildred O'Malley, wife of Charles Scott O'Malley." Captain Green paused. "Mrs. Clendenin, Mrs. O'Malley claims that Samuel Clendenin is Charles Scott O'Malley."

"No. No! That's impossible," Sarah blurted, her mind grasping to make sense of the information Captain Green shared. "Why would she make such a claim? She must be confusing Samuel with someone else. What evidence does she provide to support such an assertion?"

"Mrs. O'Malley sent several documents, including a copy of her marriage certificate." Captain Green removed items from the file to place on the desk in front of Sarah. "Their wedding photo and a copy of the first page of a will identifying Mrs. O'Malley as sole benefactor of Charles Scott O'Malley's estate."

Sarah gazed blindly at the documents. Finally, she reached for the wedding photo. Beside his bride, a younger Samuel stood looking proudly at the camera, his eyes staring straight through Sarah.

"What if," Sarah stammered, "what if this O'Malley isn't Samuel? What if he just looks like Samuel? There are people, even people who aren't related, who resemble one another, who even appear to be twins."

"There is more, Mrs. Clendenin," he answered patiently. "Several law enforcement officers have contacted the El Paso Police Department regarding Samuel Clendenin." He removed a sheet of paper from the file to place in front of Sarah. "This is a wanted poster from Springhill, Massachusetts, for Charles Scott O'Malley; he's accused of embezzling $14,000 from a manufacturing company where he worked as an accountant."

Sarah looked at the headshot featured on the poster, seeing the small scar that Samuel bore on the outside corner of his left eye. The description beneath the photo described Samuel: red hair, green eyes, 6'1", slender build.

"I'm afraid there's still more." The captain showed her two telegrams from police offices in San Francisco and the Bay Area. "These police departments identified a Scott O'Malley, who matches Samuel Clendenin's description, as a 'person of interest' in a series of bank breakins in and around the San Francisco Bay Area. If you notice the dates of the burglaries," Captain Green held the telegrams forward with one hand and pointed to the dates with the other, "they occurred a few weeks before Captain Clendenin first appeared in El Paso."

Sarah gripped the arms of her chair, anchoring herself from bolting out the door. "Are there any eyewitnesses? Did this O'Malley injure anyone during the robberies?"

"They weren't armed robberies; they were nighttime burglaries. The perpetrator entered the banks after closing and employed various safecracking techniques, including skillfully using a measured amount of explosive material."

The captain's reference to explosives made Sarah recall Samuel's nickname—Emperor of Explosives—among his troops. "Did any witnesses see Samuel, I mean O'Malley, at any of the crime scenes?"

"There are no eyewitnesses to the commission of the crimes, but a man matching O'Malley's—and Clendenin's—description was seen in and around each of the banks prior to the burglaries, which is, in part, why he is a person of interest."

Sarah nodded her understanding.

"Additionally," Captain Green continued, leaning back in his chair, "the burglaries stopped around the time of O'Malley's departure from San Francisco and Clendenin's arrival in El Paso."

Sarah sat silently, stunned by the information laid before her. She struggled to formulate questions or arguments that could widen fissures in the evidence the captain presented, but, instead, her mind kept repeating, "Please, Samuel, don't let this be true."

"Mrs. Clendenin, I know I've shocked you." Captain Green leaned forward, placing his elbows on the desktop. "You can see why I wished to meet with you in person."

"Yes," Sarah answered quietly, staring at the evidence arrayed on the desk before her.

"Mrs. Clendenin," he paused, before continuing, "Mrs. O'Malley has hired a lawyer. She is arriving in El Paso on Wednesday of next week." He then advised, "I strongly recommend you seek legal counsel."

"Yes. Thank you."

"Since Captain Clendenin is deceased and was never actually charged with any crimes related to the embezzlement and bank burglaries, there will be no challenges to his estate other than Mrs. O'Malley's claim."

"I understand." Sarah sat drained of emotion. "Thank you."

"May I call someone to take you home?" the captain offered.

"No, thank you. I have my auto."

"You've had quite a shock," the captain countered. "Perhaps it would be best if you weren't alone right now."

Sarah stood, gathering her coat and hat. "I appreciate your concern, Captain Green, but I will be fine." Sarah wished she believed what she spoke. "If there is nothing else, am I free to leave?"

"Yes, of course." Captain Green moved from behind the desk. "Let me see you out."

"Thank you."

They arrived together at the office door, which Captain Green opened; then he said, "Let me help you with your coat."

After Sarah buttoned her coat and placed her hat on her head, she exited, pausing to say "goodbye," but he extended his hand to direct her forward and walked with her to the entrance.

As he held open the main door, Captain Green concluded by saying, "If I can be of any assistance in the matter we discussed, I hope you will contact me."

"You're most kind," Sarah answered. She walked out the door and away from the entrance to the building; then she stopped in the middle of the sidewalk, people streaming past. Her entire life had been altered in minutes. Who she thought she was, she just learned she wasn't.

Sarah stared forward, her arms limp at her sides, oblivious to the passersby until a young man stopped to ask, "Are you lost, Miss?"

Sarah startled at the knowledge that a stranger could read she was adrift, unmoored from her former self.

"Do you need directions?" the young man asked.

"No," Sarah answered, trying to smile her thanks for his thoughtfulness. "I'm just trying to recall how I got here, what path I took. I think I'll take a different route now. Thank you."

The young man tipped his hat to her before departing.

Remembering she drove to the station, Sarah looked to her left, sighting the car parked against the curb. Instead of returning to the automobile, she turned to her right and crossed the street. She would walk back to the studio.

Sarah wandered familiar streets in a daze, her mind fighting to emerge from the fog preventing her from formulating a complete thought. She struggled for explanations or evidence to prove the accusations against Samuel false, but her mind could do little more than examine the edge of her memories.

As soon as Sarah entered the studio, A. J. met her, clearing his throat to ask, "How'd it go?"

"Not great," Sarah answered, continuing back to hang her hat, scarf, and coat.

"Oh?" A. J. followed her past the curtain. "What did Captain Green discuss? Was the visit about some violation at the Crown?"

"No," Sarah answered. She turned from the hall tree to face A. J., whose eyes showed worry. "No, it had nothing to do with the Crown, at least not directly."

Placing the fingertips of both hands to press her temples, Sarah closed her eyes briefly, then reopened them to address A. J. "I will tell you everything, A. J. You have a right to know as my friend and as my employer. But I'm not ready to talk. I've got to try to make sense of all Captain Green shared. Just give me time."

"Of course, Sarah. And you don't have to tell me anything. I'm just concerned."

"I know you are, A. J. You're such a good friend," she added. "I do have to tell you everything. I just need time."

"You don't have to be here today, Sarah. Why don't you take the rest of the day off to gather your thoughts?" A. J. offered.

"No, I do need to be here," Sarah replied. "I need something constant in my life."

A. J. nodded that he understood though Sarah knew he didn't.

"Besides," Sarah added, "I will need to take time off during this week and next, so let me work now."

Sarah returned to the table where she had been filling orders before she departed for her meeting with Captain Green. She worked quietly, continuing the task until she laid out all the stock to complete the orders and identified the postcards requiring a reprint. She spent the rest of the workday in the darkroom until A. J. knocked, telling her to go home.

Sarah finished rinsing the postcards, then placed them into the cylinders of the dryer. Once she completed the work, she turned off the safelights and stepped from the darkroom, blinking at the studio's harsh incandescent light.

A. J. busied himself in the outer office until Sarah walked around the open curtain to depart. Placing her hat onto her head, she informed A. J. of the status of the postcards, wished him a good evening, and said she would see him tomorrow.

A. J. walked her to the front door, then asked, "Where's your automobile?"

"I left it at police headquarters."

A. J. look quizzically at her. "Did you have mechanical problems?"

"No."

A. J. cocked his head questioningly.

"I didn't want to drive it."

"Let me get my coat, and I'll walk with you back to headquarters to get the vehicle." A. J. started to step into the studio to retrieve his coat.

"No, A. J.," Sarah called to him. "I don't want the car. I'm walking home."

"Okay," A. J.'s response was more question than statement. Then he added, "Well, I guess if you're going to leave your auto parked somewhere overnight, outside the police station is safer than most. Want some company on your walk home?"

"No. I appreciate the offer, but I need to be alone."

Sarah knew A. J. watched her step into the dusk of early evening. She slipped her hands into her pocket against the chill and recoiled at the touch of the soft leather gloves Samuel had given her. Sarah crossed the street and headed toward the plaza. At the nearest trashcan, she discarded the gloves.

Sarah entered her apartment without turning on a light. She sank into the sitting room chair and sat in the dark reviewing the pieces of Samuel's past that Captain Green had presented. After remaining immobile for hours, Sarah curled on the couch, wrapping her coat about her, and slept from exhaustion. When she awoke in the early morning, Sarah went into the bathroom and ran a tubful of water. She undressed, stepped into the bathtub, and sank up to her chin in the warm liquid. She remained in the tub, replenishing it with hot water whenever it cooled. Finally, Sarah submerged beneath the water, staying under until her lungs ached. She burst to the surface gasping for breath.

She soaped a washcloth, scrubbing her skin from head to foot. Next, she released the hair from the knot at her neck and washed it, scrubbing her scalp. After rinsing the suds from her hair and body, Sarah stepped from the tub to dry herself.

Sarah looked into the mirror as she brushed her hair, letting it hang in loose wet strands down her back. She stared at her reflection. Though the face that returned her gaze looked the same, Sarah knew she was changed. Sarah determined during the night that Mrs. Mildred O'Malley could have everything of Samuel's; Sarah would not engage a battle for what she didn't want. All she would fight to keep was the money she had earned. She dressed in her underclothes and robe, then went into the kitchen to make breakfast.

Sarah left early for work, hoping to have some uninterrupted time to speak with A. J. When she arrived to the studio, she found A. J. standing at the counter wearing his overcoat.

"Heading somewhere?"

"No, no," A. J. responded, embarrassed. "Just a little chilled."

"Do you have time to talk?" Sarah asked, removing her own coat against the warmth of the studio.

"Yes, I have time. Want some coffee?" Samuel offered.

"No, but let's sit."

A. J. retrieved a chair from the back for her, then took a seat on the stool.

Sarah told him the entire story Captain Green shared with her. While she spoke, she saw A. J. color with anger, but he remained quiet until she said, "And I don't want my situation to bring scandal to your business, so I understand if you can no longer employ me."

"Nonsense!" A. J. blurted, hammering his fist on the counter. "The only scandal is on Samuel, or whatever his real name is. You bear no guilt in this matter."

"Well, others won't see it as you do," Sarah replied resignedly.

"I don't give a damn what others think. They're fools if they don't see the truth," he replied angrily. A. J. cleared his throat, taking a moment to calm himself before continuing. "You'll need a lawyer. If you don't already have one in mind, I know a good lawyer. We can call him this morning."

"Thank you, A. J.," Sarah responded quietly.

A male law clerk dressed in a well-fitted suit welcomed Sarah and her attorney Peyton Wycliffe to the law office of Knollenberg and Loomis. The young man guided them through the outer office paneled in a rich dark walnut, to an inner door leading into a room with a long table at its center. As Sarah entered the room, two men stood immediately while an attractive young woman only a few years older than Sarah remained seated.

Peyton pulled out a chair for Sarah across the table from a man who bore facial features and red hair similar to Samuel's. The lawyer then reached to shake hands with the older man standing at the head of the table.

"Please, let's all take a seat before we make introductions, shall we?" the older man directed. Once everyone was seated, he began anew. "I am Attorney Otto Knollenberg representing Mrs. Charles Scott O'Malley." As he used his hand to direct their attention to the woman across the table, Sarah made a mental note of the lawyer's reference to her husband's name. "And Mr. Ballard O'Malley, the older brother of Mr. Charles Scott O'Malley. And you've met my law clerk, Mr. Brian Falvey." Smoothing his hand over a well-groomed white beard, Knollenberg nodded to Sarah's lawyer.

"I am Attorney Peyton Wycliffe representing Mrs. Sarah Delaney Clendenin."

"Well, then," Knollenberg took charge, "let's begin. As I'm sure you have all been briefed, Attorney Wycliffe and I have already met on our respective client's behalf, and we wish to review agreements reached for our clients based on the wishes of all involved." The lawyer looked first at the O'Malleys for their nod of agreement, and then turned his attention to Sarah and her attorney.

More than anything else, Sarah wanted these proceedings concluded. She nodded.

Knollenberg placed a pair of oval spectacles low on his nose, then peered at notes scrawled across a yellow legal pad on the table in front of him. "Now Mrs. Clendenin," he spoke, turning his attention to Sarah.

Sarah steeled herself for what she expected to follow.

"Since Charles Scott O'Malley, aka Samuel C. Clendenin, never lawfully executed any divorce proceedings to terminate his legal marriage to Mrs. Mildred O'Malley, his subsequent marriage under the name of Samuel C. Clendenin to Miss Sarah Delaney is considered void by the state and does not stand as a legal union."

Sarah swallowed hard, determined not to cry, not to show any emotional weakness during these proceedings. She looked only at Attorney Knollenberg and her own attorney. She did not glance in the direction of Samuel's relatives.

"Both parties," Knollenberg continued, "have agreed not to contest the will of Mr. Charles Scott O'Malley, which designates Mrs. Mildred O'Malley as sole recipient of his marital estate, which includes his financial interests in the Crown Saloon. However, Mrs. O'Malley has agreed to award Mrs. Clendenin the wages she earned during the thirty-two-month period of her marriage contract with Mr. Samuel Clendenin. Based on the payroll records from the Otis Photo Studio, which employed Mrs. Clendenin during that entire period, the amount is $1,624."

The attorney peered over the top of his glasses to ensure his clients and Sarah voiced no objection. He then continued. "My clients have one more request that we have not previously discussed. They would like to apply to the courts for a disinterment-transit-reinternment permit for the body of Charles S. O'Malley, aka Samuel C. Clendenin."

Sarah turned quickly to her attorney to question the request. She had come to terms with what she learned about Samuel's past, and she did not object to the settlement of the will, but this unexpected turn rocked her in a way she didn't fully understand. It felt like a complete erasure of Samuel Clendenin from her life.

"Now just a minute," Sarah's lawyer protested.

"Peyton," Knollenberg said with studied familiarity, "you know as well as I do that my clients have legal control of O'Malley's body." Then he addressed Sarah directly. "I'm sorry, Mrs. Clendenin. I know this request must come as a shock to you, but the truth is the O'Malleys have the legal authority to request such a permit. Your objection will only prolong the process, but the result will be the same—the permit for reinternment will be granted."

"May I speak?" The question from O'Malley's widow came as a soft interruption, capturing everyone's attention. "I would like to address Mrs. Clendenin directly."

Sarah turned to look at the woman who had married Samuel before Sarah knew he existed, who claimed legal rights not only to his name, to his family, to his estate, but now to his body in death. This is the woman, Sarah thought, whose insertion into her life removed Samuel from any memory Sarah had of a happy marriage.

"Mrs. Clendenin," she began, looking unfaltering at Sarah, "I want to share with you a part of my life with Charlie so that maybe you can understand, at least a little, why I am making such a request."

"All right," Sarah responded, trying to control the icy edge sharpening her tone.

"I have known Charlie since we were children in grammar school. I have loved him for most of my life." She spoke haltingly, carefully measuring each statement. "When he was twenty and I eighteen, we married."

Sarah shifted in her seat but did not interrupt.

"Charlie always had a wild side. He loved gambling, drinking, and staying out at night with the boys, but he began to settle down to home life when our daughter Sula was born a little over a year after we wed."

Sarah felt her chest heave with the news of Samuel's child, a blessing she never shared with him. She listened as Samuel's first wife continued.

"A doting father, Charlie made Sula his priority. He spent nights at home helping care for our daughter—playing with her, bathing her, rocking her to sleep—things most fathers don't do." She paused to collect herself, then continued. "But a cruel fate changed us. Our Sula died of whooping cough at sixteen months. Grief overwhelmed our lives. Instead of turning to one another for comfort, I turned to religion and Charlie chose alcohol. Often, he didn't come home after work until early morning and would return to work still drunk from his night's adventure. I think," Mildred looked down at her lap before returning her gaze to Sarah, "he couldn't bear to be in the house now empty of Sula." Mildred removed a handkerchief from her purse, choosing to grip it rather than dab her eyes. "Then one day, Charlie left for work and never returned."

Mildred glanced toward Ballard, her brother-in-law, who nodded his support. She continued addressing Sarah, speaking to an audience of one. "Charlie's employer accused him of embezzling money, and the rumor spread that Charlie had run up a large gambling debt, which he paid before he left town. We tried to find Charlie. His parents hired a detective to track him. The private detective traced Charlie to Butte, Montana, where he worked in a mine, but Charlie somehow got scent of the detective and disappeared once again. We lost track of Charlie. He clearly didn't want to be found, at least not by me, not by his family." Mildred peered at her hands she placed on the table. "Then the *Boston Globe* printed an article about Mexico's posthumous return of the man regarded as an American hero of the Mexican Revolution, and in the accompanying photograph, Charlie stood smiling from the page as though reaching out to us from the grave."

Mildred leaned forward against clasped hands she rested on the table's edge. "Mrs. Clendenin, Charlie has a six-year-old son he never met. Charlie didn't know—I didn't know—I was with child when he left." Mildred took a deep breath. "I want to bring Charlie home to Springhill, to bury him next to our Sula so that his son Harrison can have some connection with his father." Mildred sat limply against the back of the chair, appearing emotionally spent.

Sarah looked at the woman sitting before her; all sense of animosity toward Mildred washed away. "Of course," Sarah replied, "I won't pose a barrier to your returning the body to Springhill. Charles O'Malley belongs with you. Restore him to his family."

Sarah left the apartment at daybreak. She wanted to visit Samuel's grave at an hour too early for workmen, family, and interested onlookers. She wanted to be alone with him to speak her heart before others arrived for the day's scheduled disinterment of his body.

The car started slowly, requiring four cranks in the cold grey morning. Sarah settled behind the steering wheel. The visit to the cemetery would be her final farewell to Samuel. She had already transferred his clothing and his weapons to the O'Malley family to do with as they wished. While Mildred O'Malley wanted to make a gift of the car to Sarah, Sarah insisted on reimbursing Mrs. O'Malley the $825 Samuel had paid for the automobile. Now Sarah viewed the Model T Roadster as a vehicle she purchased for herself.

Sarah made good time, passing only a few delivery trucks and wagons on the road. She thought of Timothy Tompkins, who had called her again yesterday to see if he could provide any assistance with the transfer of Samuel's estate. Timothy felt such remorse for the fallout resulting from his articles detailing the return of Samuel's body to El Paso. Though Sarah tried to assure him that he bore no responsibility, she knew he ached from the role his articles played in her pain.

Paola, too, reached out, staying in regular contact with Sarah by phone while respecting her request for time alone during this process of transferring Samuel and his property to the O'Malleys. When she first communicated with Sarah after learning of Samuel's betrayal, Paola quickly dismissed Sarah's offered release from any obligations of friendship. Sarah knew her scandal could taint those closest to her, but Samuel's duplicity only seemed to strengthen Paola, Timothy, and A. J.'s ties of loyalty to her.

Sarah turned into the Evergreen Cemetery, parking beneath the tree. She exited her car and walked slowly to Samuel's graveside. She stood quietly, peering down at the dirt beneath which Samuel's body lay. After pausing in silent observation for several minutes, Sarah spoke from her heart.

"I've come to say goodbye, Samuel. Your family will be returning you to Springhill, where you will lie beside your beloved Sula and can be visited by the son you never knew and the wife you chose to abandon."

Sarah took a deep breath before continuing. "I loved you, Samuel. I loved you completely." Sarah thumped her chest with a clenched fist as she spoke. "You have broken my heart, first by your death and then by your betrayal."

Sarah lowered her hand to her side, pausing before continuing to express her thoughts. "I know that Mrs. O'Malley attributes your changed behavior to the death of your little girl, but Samuel, I think you played your pain like a well-dealt hand of cards. You used your hurt to escape from a life you didn't want, to allow a life of adventure you readily sought."

Swallowing hard, Sarah struggled to hold back tears. "And you used me, Samuel. I provided temporary comfort between your adventures, the calm that sharpens the thrill of danger. And you would have left me as easily as you left Mildred, stealing away with cowardly disregard." Sarah felt a burn at the back of her throat as she declared, "I will not shed another tear for you."

Bending to the grave, Sarah grasped a fistful of dirt, then stood, allowing it to filter slowly through her fingers and back to earth. Her fist emptied, she wiped the palms of her hands against one another to rid them of any residue. "Goodbye, Samuel." She turned from the grave to return to her automobile.

Catalina

The activity around Samuel Clendenin's grave caught Catalina's attention. She had come in the morning to visit Mayo and say her farewell since she would be departing Ciudad Juárez in a couple of days as part of Villa's push through central Mexico. She had not intended to stay long at Mayo's gravesite, but she remained once she saw the removal, then loading of Samuel Clendenin's casket into a hearse. During the process, Catalina looked to see if Sarah stood among those gathered to view the disinterment. Catalina saw a woman weeping, being comforted by a red-haired man, but that woman appeared taller and heavier than Sarah.

When the loaded hearse pulled from the gravesite and departed the cemetery, a car followed it, carrying the weeping woman, red-haired man, and older, white-bearded gentleman. When only the two workmen remained, Catalina made her way to the gravesite.

"Buenos días, señores," Catalina greeted them.

"Buenos días," they replied.

"Why has the body of Capitán Clendenin been removed from this grave? Where is it being taken?"

The two men stopped their work. Leaning on the handles of their shovels, they exchanged knowing grins, waiting to determine which of them would respond to her query. Finally, the young workman dressed in overalls answered, barely containing his pleasure at the tale. "The hombre had two wives. Wife number two buried him, not knowing about wife number one. Wife number one, not knowing about wife number two, tracked him down and demanded he come home with her." The two men looked at each other, struggling to contain their laughter.

"And where is the 'home' she is taking him?" Catalina asked, ignoring the men's glee.

"Far away from wife number two is all I know."

"Gracias," Catalina replied, and turned to depart, leaving the two men to chuckle and shove one another in their shared delight at the story.

Catalina's heart weighed heavy for the pain Sarah must feel at this revelation about Samuel's other wife, his other life. Catalina regretted the role she played in returning Samuel's body to El Paso. She had thought bringing Samuel's body to Sarah might provide his wife comfort and help to repay the kindness Samuel and Sarah showed her at the time of Mayo's death. What it brought, she feared, was heartache.

Catalina had not come to El Paso with the intention of visiting anyone but Mayo. Now she knew she could not leave the city without visiting the woman who had become her friend.

Sarah

Lost in thought, Sarah climbed midway up the stairs before noticing the figure sitting on the top step near her apartment door. Sarah stopped in her tracks, pulling her hands defensively to her chest.

"Sarah." The person stood.

Recognizing the soft Spanish pronunciation of her name and the person who uttered it, Sarah bent forward briefly to release a breath of relief before responding with her recognition. "Cata."

"I'm sorry to surprise you, Sarah."

"No," Sarah insisted, "I should be more observant rather than walking blindly about." Sarah continued up the remainder of the steps to hug Cata. "It's good to see you. Is everything all right?"

"Yes, of course. I came to see you."

"Please come in." Sarah unlocked the door and motioned Cata into the apartment. "This is really such a nice surprise. I can use a visit from a friend today."

Cata entered the apartment carrying a canvas sack and paused just inside the entrance.

Sarah reached out her hand. "Let me take your hat and coat."

Before removing her outer garments, Cata extended the sack. "For you. For tonight."

Sarah took the sack and peered inside to discover three bottles of wine. She smiled her appreciation. "Just perfect. Why don't you toss your coat and hat on a chair in the sitting room while I open one of the bottles."

Sarah entered the kitchen to place the bottles on the worktable. She removed her own coat and hat, placing them across one of the kitchen chairs, then reached into the cabinet to collect two wine glasses. By the time she located the corkscrew, Cata had joined her. Sarah poured a generous serving of red wine into the two glasses, then handed one to Cata.

"Shall we go into the sitting room?" Sarah suggested.

"No," Cata replied. "Let's sit here."

"Let's," and she pulled out a chair from the kitchen table.

Once seated, Cata took her glass of wine in hand and raised it, gesturing for Sarah to do the same. "Women warriors," she toasted.

"Women warriors," Sarah repeated and clinked her glass with Cata's before each took a drink of the crisp, dry wine.

"Just what I need," Sarah remarked, taking a second sip.

Sarah noted that Cata seemed to want to speak but hesitated, so Sarah wasn't surprised when Cata finally stated, "I visited Mayo at the cemetery today."

Sarah nodded, understanding the direction of the conversation. "And you saw Samuel's body had been removed from the grave."

"Yes. I am sorry."

"You deserve to know the story, Cata, so I will share it with you, but then I don't want to speak further of Samuel tonight."

"You don't have to tell me, Sarah; I don't have to know."

"You have a right to know, Cata." Sarah drained the wine from her glass, then poured a second before relating Samuel's history: his previous marriage, the death of his child, the abandonment of his young wife, the birth of a son he never knew, and his suspected life of crime. Sarah shared how the wife and family searched years for Samuel, finally locating his body in El Paso through articles in their local newspaper. She explained the family's desire to return him to his home in Springhill, Massachusetts. Sarah spoke as though the tale belonged to a person other than herself.

Cata reached across the table to take Sarah's hand. "I am to blame," she said, her voice thick with emotion. "I should not have interfered with fate."

Sarah squeezed Cata's hand. "Cata, the blame is Samuel's, only Samuel's. He lived for himself alone, without regard for any who loved him or for any who placed their trust in him. Now," Sarah said, releasing Cata's hand, "Samuel's story is finished. I don't want to speak of him again tonight," Sarah said with finality, pouring Cata a second glass of wine.

"Have you eaten?" Sarah asked, followed by, "Are you hungry?"

"I am hungry," Cata answered, appearing almost surprised by this realization.

"I don't have a lot in the icebox," Sarah said, standing from her chair, "but let's see what meal we can fix." She opened the icebox door and announced, "I have eggs; I have bacon."

"Potatoes?"

"Yes, I have potatoes in the vegetable bin," Sarah answered, pointing to a small, curtained pantry.

"Onion?"

"Yes, I believe I have one onion."

"Chile?"

"Let me check." Sarah closed the ice box door, then peered into the vegetable bin. "We're in luck." Facing Cata, Sarah held the stem of a jalapeño between the thumb and forefinger of each hand. "We have the makings of a feast," Sarah declared, beginning to feel the effects of the wine.

The women stood beside one another at the sink, Sarah passing the bar of soap to Cata after lathering her own hands. They shared the hand towel, using opposite ends of the cloth. Sarah handed Cata an apron, then placed her own over her head, tying it in the back.

"Let's work from the kitchen table." Sarah drained the remnants of the wine from the bottle into their glasses, then opened a second bottle to set on the table. She put two wooden cutting boards on the tabletop along with two sharp knives. Sarah gathered and rinsed the vegetables, then positioned them on a plate, which she placed on the table along with two empty plates.

"You have to be the one who chops the onion, Cata."

"Okay," Cata answered, looking at her questioningly. "Why?"

"I promised myself I wouldn't shed any more tears today."

The women burst into laughter, the wine fueling their jocularity.

As they worked side by side at the table—Sarah peeling and slicing potatoes, Cata peeling and chopping the onion—they talked about their pasts, one person's story triggering a memory from the other, laughter erupting after most of their tales.

Cata shared a story about a day when she remained in bed ill, and her brother Diego took over her chore of milking the goats. An older female nanny refused to let him touch her udder, threatening to butt or kick him whenever he tried. Diego resorted to wearing Cata's skirt and blouse to mask his smell so the nanny would permit his milking her. Cata laughed, tears streaming down her face as she described her brother's prancing between their house and the goat pen in her skirt.

Sarah followed with a memory of working as a teenager in her parents' store, and a customer paying her for some goods he had purchased. When she grasped his bills and change, the man let out a yelp, shaking his hand vigorously. Confused, young Sarah looked at what she held in her hand only to discover a bloodied bandage among the cash. Sarah and Cata laughed as Sarah demonstrated the man's pained gestures.

Once they finished preparing the vegetables, they moved to the stove, talking all the while. Sarah placed a lit match to a gas burner, then positioned a cast iron skillet on the flame. She laid thick strips of bacon across the pan. Once the bacon cooked crisp, Sarah removed the slices and spooned some bacon grease into a second skillet. Cata fried the potatoes, adding onion and chopped jalapeño. When the potatoes were almost ready, Sarah cracked four eggs into a frying pan. Their talking and laughter continued throughout their cooking.

While Cata served the potatoes, eggs, and bacon onto two plates, Sarah cut two thick slices of bread from a loaf. Cata refilled both glasses with wine before taking her seat at the table.

"Smells wonderful," Sarah remarked, scooping a forkful of potatoes. "Mmm, delicious," she uttered, shielding her full mouth with her hand.

They ate with enthusiasm, punctuating their eating with sips of wine, until they devoured all the food they prepared.

"Coffee?" Sarah offered.

"No," Cata held up her hand defensively. "I will help clean the kitchen. Then I should go."

Sarah hadn't expected that reply or the suddenness of it. She didn't want Cata to leave. "You can't go. We haven't finished the wine," Sarah responded, motioning toward the unopened bottle on the counter.

"I can't drink that bottle. It will have to wait for my return."

"Well, at least stay until we finish the wine in this bottle," and Sarah lifted the open bottle from the kitchen table to show it still contained a quarter of its wine.

"Okay," Cata agreed. "Let's clean the kitchen. I need to move." Cata placed both hands on her belly to indicate her fullness.

The friends worked side by side, Sarah scrubbing the dishes and Cata rinsing and drying them, talking all the while. After Sarah wiped the oven and the kitchen tabletop, they again took their seats.

They continued their conversation, only occasionally taking a brief sip of wine, nursing what remained in their glasses as though neither wanted the evening to end.

Sarah watched with disappointment when Cata drained the remnants of wine from her glass. "I should go," Cata said as she rested the glass back on the table.

"Stay, Cata." Sarah looked around the room, trying to locate a clock. "It's late." Sarah's eyes settled on the empty bottle. "You've had too much to drink to return to Juárez; I've had too much to drink to drive you home."

Cata didn't object, giving Sarah hope, so she continued with her encouragement. "I have a big bed we can both sleep in comfortably. I have a nightgown you can wear and toilet articles you can use. Tomorrow morning, I will drop you off at the bridge on my way to work." Sarah looked into Cata's eyes. "Stay," Sarah concluded.

Cata thought, then replied, "Okay."

They remained seated at the kitchen table, talking and laughing until they could no longer stifle their yawns. "This has been fun," Sarah said standing, "but we should probably go to bed."

Cata stood as well. "Yes."

Sarah guided Cata to the bedroom. Sarah removed a nightgown from a drawer and handed it to Cata, then directed her into the bathroom to show her the toilet articles and bath linens.

Sarah returned to the kitchen to rinse the wine glasses and pour herself a glass of water. She didn't know why she had asked Cata to stay the night but was relieved at not having to face this night alone.

"I'm ready," Cata stood at the kitchen doorway wearing one of Sarah's floor-length gowns, which rose above Cata's ankles. "I will wait here to give you privacy."

After Sarah finished preparing for bed, she returned to the kitchen for Cata, who followed her into the bedroom. Sarah pointed to the bed with the covers turned down. "Is there a side you prefer?"

"No."

Sarah crossed to the far side of the bed and raised the covers to slide beneath them. Once Cata joined her, Sarah reached to turn off the table lamp. "Good night," she wished Cata.

"Good night," Cata replied.

They lay stiffly in the awkward newness of a shared bed, but then the wine, warmth, and night relaxed them toward sleep. Sarah noted Cata's breathing grow heavier. Sarah turned away to drift into her own rich slumber.

Deep into the night, Sarah woke to find herself spooning tightly against the warmth of Cata's body, her right arm resting across Cata's waist. She knew she should try to extricate herself, but she feared waking Cata. Sarah also regretted losing the comfortable intimacy of their touch.

When, resignedly, Sarah leaned gently back, shifting her weight slightly away from Cata's body, Cata's hand moved to take hers, then raised their clasped hands gently to her chest. Sarah resumed her position pressed against Cata's warmth, and they both returned to sleep.

Sun streamed past the curtains when Sarah awoke, still cradling Cata, their hands remaining clasped. She lay quietly in the surprising comfort. Then a change in Cata's breathing informed Sarah they were both awake. Sarah rolled onto her back and immediately felt the coolness caused by their separation.

"Good morning," Sarah offered.

"Good morning," Cata returned.

They remained briefly in bed, Sarah aware of the awkward shyness they shared. "Why don't you rest a little longer while I make coffee," Sarah suggested, then pushed back the covers to stand.

Sarah wrapped in her robe, then went into the bathroom to relieve herself, wash her face, comb her hair and knot it in a bun. She checked her face in the mirror and thought her eyes looked more rested than they had in recent weeks. Sarah left the bathroom for the kitchen.

After she prepared the coffee pot and placed it on a burner, she glanced into the icebox to see what she might offer for breakfast. While she didn't feel effects from last night's wine, Sarah knew she should get something into her stomach. She took a jar of strawberry jam and a small tub of butter from the icebox before shutting the door. Next, she removed the loaf from the breadbox, cut four slices, and applied butter to each. She lit the oven. When Sarah raised to close the oven door, she saw Cata, dressed and standing in the kitchen doorway.

"I should be leaving," Cata said.

"Wait," Sarah urged. "Eat a quick bite, and I'll drive you to the bridge."

"I don't want to trouble you more. I need to return to my troops to prepare for our departure."

"Watch the bread while I dress," Sarah encouraged, placing the tray in the oven. "I will be just a minute," she called back, racing from the room before Cata could make a case for departing now.

When Sarah entered the bedroom, she saw that Cata had made the bed and placed her gown at its foot. Sarah dressed hurriedly, then jotted some information on a slip of paper before returning to the kitchen to find Cata had poured two cups of coffee and placed the warm bread on two plates. They resumed their seats from last night, each preparing her coffee and spreading jam on her bread. They ate with little conversation and none of the hilarity of the previous night. As they neared the end of breakfast, Sarah spoke. "Cata, please stay safe."

Cata nodded in response.

"When you return to El Paso, look for me. I will no longer live in this apartment once the lease ends. Here," Sarah slid the paper across the table. "I've written the address of the studio where I work; you can find me there."

Cata picked up the note and studied the address.

"When you come back to El Paso, find me."

APRIL 1914

Sarah

Sarah sat in her automobile parked outside the Popular Department Store, waiting for Paola to complete her shift. It had been a little over a month since General Villa's troops resumed their push south, engaging in a string of battles the newspapers repeatedly weighted with the same adjective: "*heavy* fighting," "*heavy* shelling," "*heavy* losses." Ultimately, on the afternoon of April 2, Villa's Division of the North succeeded in wresting a major objective from President Huerta's federal forces—the city of Torreón. Sarah followed the day-to-day reporting, wondering if Cata had fought in the described battles, always hoping, praying for her safety.

Then suddenly, a week after Villa's victory in Torreón, the reporting changed its focus from the Mexican Revolution to a conflict brewing between the United States and Mexico. A series of blunders and overreactions by President Huerta's troops and American naval forces resulted in the United States invading the Mexican port city of Veracruz, thrusting El Paso and other border cities into a frenzy of fear of an impending war with Mexico. Sarah thought about the newspaper accounts describing the misunderstanding that led to Huerta's federal troops briefly arresting nine US sailors at the port of Tampico. Upon learning of the arrests, the commander of the US naval fleet protecting American interests in the area demanded the sailors' release, a formal apology, and a twenty-one-gun salute to the American flag. President Huerta ordered the sailors released, provided a written apology, but refused to offer the twenty-one-gun salute. President Woodrow Wilson, who had never recognized Huerta's presidency, used Huerta's refusal as an opportunity for US forces to invade Veracruz on April 21 and prevent the delivery to that port of weapons bound for Huerta. The United States expected rebel forces fighting against Huerta's regime to remain neutral observers of this conflict. In fact, General Villa did brush off the invasion as a struggle between the Americans and Huerta, dismissing any notion of war between the two nations. However, Venustiano Carranza, first chief of the Constitutionalist forces and Villa's superior, demanded that the US withdraw its troops from Mexico, declaring that the Mexican people would unite in their fight against northern invaders.

Tensions in El Paso intensified daily. By the time US troops invaded Veracruz, many Anglo El Pasoans had become swept up in a wave of fear. They suddenly perceived a threat from Mexican Americans and refugees living among them and anticipated an attack from their Mexican neighbors in the sister city of Juárez. Sarah read newspaper articles about deployment of additional troops to El Paso in response to requests by prominent citizens. General John J. Pershing, the incoming commander of Fort Bliss, rushed to El Paso with three thousand troops. Fort Sam Houston deployed a battery to El Paso. Two more batteries of the Sixth Field Artillery arrived in El Paso from Fort Riley, Kansas. Columbus, New Mexico sent troops from the Thirteenth Cavalry.

In just a few days, El Paso transformed from a peaceful border city into an armed camp. Infantry secured El Paso's gas and electric plants. In the Sunset Heights neighborhood, Battery C, Sixth Field Artillery, posted four three-inch guns directed at Juárez. Troops manned machine-gun placements at the Santa Fe and Stanton Street

International Bridges. The army issued shoot-to-kill orders for any prisoners attempting to escape the Fort Bliss internment camp. The El Paso Police increased its force from 60 to 110 officers to help the military patrol city streets, concentrating in Mexican American and Mexican neighborhoods of South El Paso. The commander of the US Border Patrol established headquarters in city hall, with direct phone lines to Fort Bliss as well as to the gas and electric plants. And El Pasoans armed themselves, purchasing all available guns and ammunition.

As Sarah waited for Paola to exit the Popular, she noticed the scarcity of people on downtown streets. She thought of a recent *El Paso Herald* editorial largely addressed to "Spanish-Americans" in El Paso, stating that some of the "more ignorant" Spanish Americans fear they are in danger if there is a "clash." The editorial sought to reassure "these people" that if they remain "orderly and neutral," they would enjoy the "same protection as the Americans."

The frenzy of suspicion and fear enveloping El Paso convinced Sarah to wait for Paola outside work and transport her safely home. Sarah had not told Paola about this plan, so she watched the main doors of the Popular for her friend to exit. When Paola appeared, Sarah saw that one of Paola's brothers walked beside her. Sarah stepped quickly from her auto to call out "Paola! Sergio!" They both turned in Sarah's direction. Sarah waved, walking toward them.

Paola greeted her with a hug and a kiss on the cheek. Sergio tipped his cap to Sarah. "What are you doing here?" Paola asked, genuinely surprised.

"I came to drive you home. With all the craziness in the city, I didn't want you walking."

Paola responded, "Sergio walks with me to and from work, and Gustavo and my father walk together."

"The city has gotten so crazy," Sarah repeated. "Since I'm already here, let me give you both a lift."

"That's not necessary, Sarah," Paola countered.

"Please. I want to," Sarah insisted.

Paola looked to her brother, who nodded his acquiescence. "Okay," Paola agreed.

Sergio insisted on cranking the car before hopping into the small open-air seat at the back.

"You'll have to give me directions," Sarah said, steering the vehicle onto the street.

"Keep south on Mesa Avenue," Paola directed. "I'll let you know when to take a left."

"Oh, Paola," Sarah briefly turned a concerned eye to her friend. "How are you and your family doing during this stressful time?"

"We're careful. We go to work; we return home. Mostly," Paola added, "we try to be invisible."

Disturbed by the last statement, Sarah glanced at her. "I don't understand how El Pasoans who have lived amicably together can so quickly exchange friendship for fear of one another."

"Sarah," Paola spoke as if addressing a confused child, "I love you, but your whiteness blinds you. Look at the section of town we're entering." Paola swept her hand from left to right. "We're in Segundo Barrio now, the Second Ward. How many Anglos do you think live in my community? How many times have *you* ventured into my neighborhood?"

Sarah looked at one-story adobe homes crowded next to one another, at blocks of brick apartments with their doors opening directly onto sidewalks, at paved streets that quickly gave way to dirt roads. She noticed yards with chickens and goats, fruit trees and gardens; small stores with painted signs in Spanish squatting on street corners and tucked tightly between houses. Sarah knew Paola was right; this was not a neighborhood with which she was familiar. Sarah also noticed heavily armed officers on horseback patrolling the area.

"Turn left on the next street," Paola informed Sarah, pointing ahead. She reached to touch Sarah's arm. "I hope I haven't offended you. In El Paso, people do live together 'amicably,' as you said, but we largely live with our own in neighborhoods that reflect ourselves. When something occurs to shake us as a city, we distrust those who aren't as we are; they become the 'other.'"

"I am naive," Sarah responded, embarrassed by her failure at simple observation. She signaled her turn.

"Naive," Paola agreed, "but a dear, trusted friend. Ours is the third house on the right."

Sarah pulled to a stop in front of a flat-roof, one-story adobe home. A small dog waited at the narrow finger of land between hous-es, dancing in circles, its tail wagging with excitement.

Paola leaned to kiss Sarah on the cheek. "Thank you for the ride, Sarah, and for your concern."

Sergio opened the passenger door and assisted Paola from the vehicle. Paola leaned back into the car. "Be safe going home."

"I will," Sarah assured her. "What time do you work tomorrow?"

"Eight thirty. Why?"

"I'll see you at eight ten," Sarah said, preparing to pull away.

"No, Sarah, that's not necessary," Paola responded, standing back from the automobile.

Sarah repeated, "Eight ten," as she pulled onto the street. She felt proud of having done what she could to protect her friend during this period of unrest in the city. She noticed the pair of troopers eye-ing her U-turn. Glancing back, Sarah saw that Paolo and Sergio had already disappeared behind the closed door of their home.

When morning came, Sarah made sure to leave her apartment early to be outside Paola's house by eight. Waiting for Paola and Sergio, Sarah noticed the quiet of the neighborhood. The few men she witnessed leaving their homes walked hurriedly, heads cast down-ward as they moved past the mounted officers who monitored activity on the street. Sarah watched an aproned shopkeeper step outdoors to sweep his entryway with quick, business-like attention before reenter-ing the building and shutting the door.

"Sarah," Paola called as she opened the car door.

"Good morning, you two," Sarah replied, leaning toward the pas-senger side to view her friends. "Ready for work?"

"Really, Sarah, it isn't necessary for you to drive us," Paola replied, looking about the neighborhood before entering the vehicle. Once seated, Paola leaned over to give Sarah a kiss on the cheek. She placed a small parcel between them, announcing, "A couple of egg burritos for A. J. and you since probably neither of you ate breakfast."

"Thank you, my dear friend." Sarah glanced back to see Sergio safely settled on the rumble seat. She checked street traffic before U-turning and noticed the officers on horseback monitoring her progress.

In fewer than ten minutes, Sarah pulled to the curb next to the

Popular Department Store, dropping off Paola. Though Sarah offered to drive Sergio to his place of employment, he insisted on walking the few additional blocks.

The burritos Paola had prepared were still warm when Sarah carried them into the studio. "Have you eaten breakfast?" Sarah called out to A. J.

"I had a couple cups of coffee," he answered, stepping into the front room to meet her.

"Coffee isn't breakfast," Sarah answered, placing the parcel on the front counter. "Paola prepared egg burritos for us." Sarah hung her hat on the hall tree before returning to the counter. She spread the brown paper and removed one of the burritos wrapped in wax paper. "Mmm, smells wonderful," she said, trying to entice A. J. She flattened the wax paper and lifted the edge of the flour tortilla to peer at its contents. "Egg, chorizo, and cheese," she listed before taking a bite. "Delicious," Sarah announced. "Here," she extended the second burrito to A. J.

"Thanks," he said, taking it from her hand. "I'll eat a little later."

"At least take a couple bites while it's warm, A. J.," Sarah coaxed.

To appease her, A. J. folded back the paper, took a single bite and pronounced it "delicious." He rewrapped the burrito, stating, "I'll save the rest for later." Before Sarah could voice an objection, he continued, "Timothy called. He'd like you to accompany him today to photograph new military installations in the city."

"Okay," Sarah mumbled through a mouthful of food.

"It's a good idea. We can capture some interesting postcard scenes for national sales, and I bet the troops will snap up cards to send home so family and friends can see their soldier's brave efforts to defend our country against foreign invasion," A. J. concluded half-sarcastically.

"Will you be okay alone in the studio?"

"I don't anticipate much business given we're a city under siege." Sarah chuckled. "Okay, I'll go."

"Good," A. J. replied, reaching for the phone. "I'll let Timothy know you'll pick him up at the *Times* office."

"Tell him I'm on my way," Sarah responded, shoving the last of the burrito into her mouth, chewing while she collected her hat, camera, and tripod.

Timothy stood on the corner waiting for Sarah, a half-smoked cigarette dangling between his lips. Tossing the cigarette aside after one final drag, he quickly entered the automobile. "Good morning," he greeted. "Glad you're joining me."

"Good morning," Sarah returned. "Where to?"

"Let's start at Sunset Heights."

"Okay," Sarah responded, directing the vehicle accordingly.

They had to park a couple blocks from the installation because of military vehicles positioned along both sides of Oregon Street. Sarah walked with Timothy up the steep hill, the late April sun causing her to break a sweat. At the installation, a military guard stopped them. Once Timothy showed his reporter's credentials and explained the purpose of their visit, the soldier directed them into camp to meet the officer in charge. The captain, a middle-aged man wearing a drab olive and khaki uniform encircled at the waist by a wide leather gun belt and holstered pistol, greeted them. After introductions, Captain Wagner provided a brief tour of the camp. He explained that the four guns, an ammunition wagon positioned beside each, were "sighted and ready for action." Resting a hand on the barrel of one artillery piece, he spoke with great pride about how the guns' placement on the Heights allowed them to fire shells over the El Paso community and into Juárez. "The fire power of these guns deters any consideration of invasion from Mexico," he stated proudly. He smoothed his grizzled moustache with the knuckle of a forefinger, adding in a seemingly confidential manner, "But our main purpose is to settle the nerves of anxious El Pasoans."

Timothy nodded his understanding, then asked, "Do you mind if Miss Delaney takes some photographs of the camp?"

"I think the boys would like to be featured in your photos."

With that permission, Sarah removed her camera from its case. "May I photograph you beside one of your guns, Captain Wagner?"

Sarah captured him in the focusing hood as he posed, exhibiting pride of command. After the photograph had been taken, Captain Wagner excused himself.

Timothy followed Sarah about the camp, sometimes suggesting subjects for her photos, but mostly jotting notes about what he saw and information he garnered from the troops.

Sarah photographed soldiers caring for their picketed horses and mules that had helped transport equipment from Fort Bliss to Sunset Heights, soldiers conducting general maintenance on the guns, cooks busy with preparation of food for the troops. Securing the camera to the tripod, she captured the guns in the foreground with Juárez in the distance.

"Got what you need?" Timothy asked. "Ready to head to the next site?" he questioned, directing more than inquiring.

From Sunset Heights, they drove first to the Santa Fe and then to the Stanton Street International Bridge for Timothy to gather information and Sarah to photograph the machine guns positioned to sweep an enemy attacking over the bridge. The gunners kept watch, shielded behind temporary adobe walls. Sarah and Timothy drove west to meet with troops of the Thirteenth responsible for patrolling along the river between the cement plant and the stockyard. Then Timothy directed their travel to the temporary camp at Ninth and Florence Streets, where the Second battalion of the Twentieth Infantry kept watch along the Rio Grande and southeast El Paso, which included the Segundo Barrio, where Paola and her family lived. After photographs and interviews, Timothy instructed Sarah to drive to the T&P railroad yards where infantry camped, ready to provide a quick response to any emergency. Next, they traveled to Washington Park to visit the camp of a Thirteenth Cavalry squadron responsible for patrolling county roads. At each installation Sarah and Timothy visited, they found soldiers anxious to pose for photographs and willing to share information about their assignment to protect El Paso and its citizens.

When they returned to the automobile, Timothy cranked the car, then settled on the seat next to Sarah. "Ready to call it a day?" he asked.

"Yes," she responded, throttling the car forward. "I've read articles describing the deployment of troops in and around El Paso, but to actually view the net of military protection cast around the city is jaw dropping."

"An invading force is highly unlikely, but El Paso is a tinderbox poised to explode at even the slightest threat." Timothy pulled his hat farther down on his head to resist the tug of warm wind blowing through the vehicle. "The show of military strength is probably necessary to discourage the striking of that figurative match."

"Do I take you back to the *Times* office?"

Timothy thought briefly before flashing a grin at Sarah. "No. This has been thirsty work. Drop me off at the Sheldon for a beer."

Sarah guided the car through traffic on the downtown streets. When they neared the Sheldon Hotel, she requested, "Will you call A. J. and let him know I'm not returning to the studio? I need to give Paola a ride home from the Popular." Sarah eased the automobile to a stop across from the Sheldon.

"Will do," Timothy responded. Once outside the vehicle, he leaned back in. "Let me know when you've selected photos for the paper."

"I'll call tomorrow morning," she responded.

Timothy knuckled a tattoo on the car door, then trotted in front of Sarah's vehicle and across the street.

In minutes, Sarah eased the car to a stop beside the Popular. When she saw Paola and Sergio exit the building, Sarah called their names, waving to catch their attention. They turned toward her hesitatingly, Paola glancing at her brother before walking to Sarah's car.

"Hop in," Sarah encouraged.

Sergio opened the car door for Paola before climbing onto the rumble seat. Sarah positioned the camera and folded tripod between herself and Paola. "Did you have a good day?" Sarah asked as she pulled onto the street.

"Yes, yes," Paola answered distractedly.

Concerned, Sarah asked, "What's the matter?"

Paola seemed to gather her thoughts. "Sarah, this is awkward, but I have to be honest with you."

"Of course." Sarah glanced briefly from the road to see her friend's worried countenance.

"Please don't take offense. You're such a dear friend," Paola inserted, "but Sergio and I can't continue accepting rides from you."

Sarah didn't know how to respond.

"Sarah, I know you want to look out for me, but," Paola paused.

"But what, Paola?" Sarah asked.

"But you are putting my family at risk."

Sarah felt as though she had been slapped by the enormity of Paola's declaration. She replied honestly, "I don't understand."

"I know you don't, Sarah, and I know you're trying to protect me." Paola reached to touch Sarah's arm. "The problem is you're making us visible."

"I see," Sarah answered quietly, though she didn't fully grasp Paola's meaning.

When Sarah turned onto Paola's street, the import of her friend's statement became dramatically clear. A black patrol wagon followed them, coming to a stop directly behind Sarah's car in front of Paola's home. Two police officers exited from the front and another two policemen climbed from the back of the wagon, their hands resting on pistols worn at their hips.

"Out of the car with your hands visible," a young clean-shaven officer wearing an ill-fitting uniform barked at the driver's side while other officers moved to positions around the vehicle.

"Why are you stopping us?" Sarah demanded. She remained seated though Paola and Sergio exited the automobile.

"Shut off the engine and get out of the car," the officer repeated.

Sarah caught Paola's imploring look and saw the fear on her friend's face. Sarah switched off the engine, then exited the vehicle. The police already had Sergio spread eagle with his hands clasped behind his head. One officer patted him down roughly while a second officer held a gun on him.

The small family dog yapped its concern, protesting loudly from the side of the home.

Sarah asked again, "Why are you stopping us?" as a third officer searched the rumble seat, then moved to examine the inside of the vehicle.

Two soldiers on horseback rode over to lend their support to the police.

"That's my camera," Sarah called out to the beefy officer who emerged from the car dangling the case by its strap.

"I recognize you," one of the mounted troopers exclaimed, pointing at Sarah. "You were at the camp today taking photographs."

This announcement directed all attention to Sarah, and the officer questioned, "Why are you photographing a military camp?"

"I'm a photographer," she answered, trying to control her anger. "I work for the Otis Photography Studio. I accompanied Timothy Tompkins, a reporter for the *El Paso Morning Times*, to the camps to take pictures for an article he's writing." She listed what seemed to her a logical progression of reasons in response to the question.

The dog continued to pepper the air with agitated barks.

"And how are these two Mexicans involved with your photographing military installations? Are they your assistants?" the officer asked sarcastically.

"They aren't involved with my photography. They weren't with me at the camps. They are my friends," Sarah spat her response. She glanced at Paola and Sergio, both standing stiffly with their hands laced behind their heads, a barrel-chested police officer standing behind them with a drawn weapon. Sarah felt anger at the affront of police holding them for questioning, but she also felt fear for her friends' safety.

"You've been observed visiting this house numerous times over the last couple of days," the officer closest to Sarah continued. "What interest does this home have for you?"

"I'm simply giving my friends a ride." Sarah noticed a neighbor peer briefly from behind a curtain, then quickly disappear.

The dog bounced on its front paws with each excited bark.

"Let's search the property," the lead officer ordered.

"What about that damn mongrel?" the officer holding the gun asked.

"Shoot it!"

Paola wailed, "No," suddenly unclasping her hands to lunge toward the pet.

In an instant, the officer closest to Paola grabbed her by her coiled braids, jerking hard, slamming her to the ground.

Sergio shouted, "Paola!" but the officer holding the pistol moved threateningly to block Sergio's path.

The small dog skittered back, barking frantically.

Sarah knelt beside Paola, taking her arm to assist her to her feet, and saw the bloody scrapes reddening angrily across her friend's forehead and cheek, the heel of her right hand torn by the force of the fall.

Turning to face the lead officer, Sarah fought to mask her anger. "Let them secure the dog. You don't want the neighborhood misinterpreting gunshots."

The officer seemed to consider Sarah's suggestion before commanding Paola, "Tie up that damn mutt, or we *will* shoot it."

Paola hurried to scoop the yapping dog into her arms. "I've got a rope in the backyard," Paola informed the officer.

"Go with her," the lead officer ordered Paola's bulky assailant.

Sarah felt uncomfortable with Paola out of sight. She exchanged a worried look with Sergio, and they waited anxiously until Paola finally returned to the front.

"Who else lives in this house?" The officer questioned, looking first at Paola and then to Sergio.

"Our father, mother, and brother," Paola answered.

"Are they in the house now?

Paola and Sergio both shook their heads and answered, "No."

The officer in charge directed two policemen to search the backyard while he and the officer guarding Sergio entered the house with Paola and her brother, leaving Sarah outside under the watch of the mounted troopers.

The younger trooper dismounted, maintaining a hold on the reins, while the second soldier, whom Sarah guessed was a few years older than she, remained in the saddle. The younger man, who had identified Sarah as the photographer at his camp, spoke with a slow east Texas drawl. "Now why do you want to associate yourself with Meskins?" he asked as if genuinely trying to understand what he saw as a lapse in judgment.

Sarah glanced toward the house, worried about what might be happening inside. She turned to the trooper, responding, "These are good people. They are my friends. They've done nothing to deserve this treatment."

Ignoring her last statement, he continued. "Aren't there enough white people in this town to be friends with?" he asked, leaning forward to look directly into her eyes. When Sarah didn't respond, he continued. "Now, don't get me wrong; Meskins can be good workers, so if they're cooking and cleaning for you, okay." He looked up at the mounted soldier. "Don't you agree, Hank?"

The trooper named Hank looked down from his mount and nodded his agreement.

"They're not like us," the young soldier addressed her with the seriousness of a preacher striving to save a soul.

Sarah studied his thin, almost nonexistent lips as he sought to pronounce wisdom he didn't possess. Rather than feeling anger at the stupidity standing before her, she felt fear for what Paola and Sergio might be facing inside their home.

"What you think, Hank?" He turned to look at his partner for support.

Hank glanced down once again, and assessed, "I think she obviously don't care none 'bout her reputation"; then he returned to studying the neighborhood.

"That can't be true." The young trooper looked from his partner to focus his attention on Sarah.

Sarah mentally formed a prayer for the protection of Paola and Sergio.

"That can't be true," the trooper repeated. "You care about your reputation, don't you ma'am?"

Sarah had enough of the inane chatter. She responded with a bluff: "I will share the nature of this conversation with General Pershing when I meet with him tomorrow, so if you'll kindly tell me your names."

The soldier stepped back to remount his horse. Once again in the saddle, he replied, "Just trying to offer some friendly advice, ma'am. Take it or leave it."

Sarah turned to face the house, relieved to hear the dog's continued yapping. She saw the two officers assigned to search the backyard now return to enter through the front door. After what felt to Sarah like hours, all four officers exited the house, leaving Paola and Sergio inside.

Three officers returned to the patrol wagon while the officer in charge walked over to the troopers and Sarah. Addressing the troopers first. "All's clear. We didn't find anything suspicious." Then he turned to Sarah, handing her the camera case with exposed film dangling in a curled strand. "You're free to go, Miss"; he drew out the "Miss," indicating he expected her to fill in the name.

"I'm Sarah Delaney," she provided, moving to crank the vehicle.

"Well, Miss Sarah Delaney," the officer added, "I recommend you stay out of Segundo Barrio until this mess with Mexico blows over."

When the car started, Sarah glanced at the house to see Paola's face flash momentarily at the window. Paola nodded quickly to Sarah before disappearing behind closed curtains.

By the time Sarah prepared to pull from the curb, the police wagon had departed, and the troopers continued their patrol of the street. Sarah wanted desperately to get out of the automobile and knock on Paola's front door to apologize and to check on her friend, but she knew her presence would only bring more trouble. She steered a U-turn, then, at the corner, merged right onto Mesa Avenue, driving the few blocks that distanced her from the Segundo Barrio. Once downtown, Sarah pulled to the curb. She rested her forehead against the steering wheel, her hands shaking uncontrollably.

Sarah sat up, staring out the front windshield without seeing the city before her. Instead, she mentally reviewed the events that had just occurred. Now, she felt schooled in how quickly fear devolves into suspicion, then angry action, and she understood her friends' need to be invisible in the face of such guttural emotions.

Sarah took a deep breath to settle her nerves, then merged the automobile back onto Mesa Avenue to drive the remainder of the distance to her apartment.

MAY 1914

Sarah

The image of Mexican federal prisoners marching in ragged procession from the Fort Bliss internment camp bloomed into view across the photographic paper. Sarah gently captured the paper with tongs to lift it from the tray of developer, allowing the remaining solution to trickle from the photo before placing the sheet into the stop bath and then transferring it into the tray of fixer. After placing the photograph into water to rinse away chemicals, Sarah raised the dripping picture to examine the parade of men, women, and children, most of them bent by their worldly belongings carried in bundles on their backs, balanced on their heads, or gripped in each fist.

Two days ago, Sarah had driven to the military post with Timothy to capture photographs of the first two thousand Mexican federal prisoners departing Fort Bliss for internment at Fort Wingate in northern New Mexico. Today, additional trainloads of prisoners would leave Fort Bliss for the same destination. An officer overseeing the transfer explained to

Timothy that relocation of the prisoners was largely to appease El Paso citizens, who feared having thousands of Mexican federal troops living in their midst and resented the allocation of Fort Bliss troops assigned to guard them. At Fort Wingate, a previously vacated military post, soldiers from Fort Meade, South Dakota, would assume responsibility for guarding the prisoners, relieving troops of the Twentieth to return to Fort Bliss and assist in protecting the border and the citizens of El Paso.

In addition to the removal of the Mexican federal prisoners, the announcement in last Friday's newspaper of President Huerta's willingness to halt expansion of hostilities between Mexico and the United States palpably reduced the fever of fear that had gripped El Paso since the Tampico affair and the US invasion of Veracruz. Sarah hoped the move toward normalcy translated to greater security for Paola and her family.

During the past two weeks, Sarah ached to reach out to her friend, to ensure that Paola and her family remained safe, to apologize for drawing down suspicion on their home, but Sarah feared even sending a note to Paola, afraid that agents still surveilled the family. And Sarah didn't know if Paola would welcome any additional intrusion from her.

After placing the photo onto the drying rack, Sarah returned to the enlarger to remove the negative carrier and reposition the strip of film. Just as she prepared to lift a sheet of photographic paper from its protective packaging, A. J. called to her from outside the darkroom door, announcing she had a visitor.

Sarah secured the package of photographic paper in its box and switched off the safelights before exiting the room to discover Paola standing at the front of the studio. Nearly two weeks since the assault by police, Paola's face still bore a faint watercolor of bruising and redness that evidenced the attack. Sarah forced herself to look fully at her friend's injuries, acknowledging to herself the responsibility she bore for attracting the police.

"Sarah," Paola spoke first, holding open her arms for an embrace. "I've missed you," she whispered, kissing Sarah's cheek.

Sarah gently placed her fingertips to her friend's wounded face. "I am so sorry, Paola, for my ignorance and my part in what happened to Sergio and you." Tears spilled from her eyes as she said quietly, "I'm so ashamed."

Paola reached to thumb tears from Sarah's face. "I worried you would blame yourself." Paola shook her head. "Sarah, what happened isn't your fault."

"I called attention to you. I made you visible."

"What you did was show love and concern," Paola insisted. "What happened to us resulted from others' fears."

Sarah removed a handkerchief tucked in her sleeve to wipe her nose. "I wanted to check on you, but I didn't want to cause your family additional difficulties."

"I know. I understood why you didn't reach out, and I didn't know how to get word to you that we were all right. But there is greater calm in the city now; people are on the streets again." Paola pointed at the pedestrians visible through the studio's display window.

"Thank God for a return to sanity."

"Well, I'd better go back to work. Mr. Schwartz kindly allowed me days off to heal, and I've only returned to the store this week."

"We'll get together soon?" Sarah asked hopefully.

"Yes, of course we will." Then Paola asked, "How about Friday's Army Day parade? We could watch together."

"Oh, Paola," Sarah expressed her disappointment, "I'd love to view the festivities with you, but A. J. and I are photographing the parade for the newspapers."

"Well, look for me in the crowd; I'll be proudly waving my American flag."

Sarah heard the military bands and cheering crowd long before the five-mile-long parade snaked into view. A. J and she arrived at the Orndorff Hotel an hour before the 10:00 a.m. start of the parade to set up their Graflex cameras on separate balconies, prepared to capture the pageantry from different angles as the military marched down Mesa Avenue.

Buntings and flags festooned buildings along the parade route. Crowds of excited people, most waving miniature American flags, overflowed sidewalks, and faces peered from the elevated windows of every structure for blocks. El Pasoans turned out en masse to celebrate the five thousand troops of the recently formed Mexican Border Division, headed by Brigadier General John J. Pershing. Schools, banks, stores, and government offices in the city closed so El Pasoans could celebrate the soldiers who guarded their border and protected the citizenry.

Sarah knew the parade served as another effort to assuage nervous El Pasoans, who feared retaliatory attacks by Mexicans living across the border and refugees living in the city.

When the platoon of mounted El Paso police led the march down Mesa Avenue, the procession had already paraded along several other streets to cheering crowds. Sarah watched through her focusing hood, waiting for the street to fill with soldiers of the Sixth Infantry striding behind regimental colors, their rifles carried at right shoulder arms; she depressed the pushpin of the camera's cable release. Next, she photographed the machine gun platoon that followed its infantry regiment, mules bearing machine guns strapped to their backs. Sarah captured a shot of the hospital corps, its ambulances identified by red crosses.

Sarah marked her parade program to ensure she properly identified each unit in her photographs. As she focused her camera on the artillery battery riding into view atop gray gun carriages and caissons pulled by large, thickly muscled horses, she thought about A. J. She worried about his apparent decline in health and his unwillingness to take the time to recover. Today would be particularly taxing because he had promised to deliver prints of the parade to the engraver by 12:30 p.m. for inclusion in the evening paper. Sarah returned her attention to photographing the display of cannoneers and field guns marching below.

Following the artillery, a mounted regimental band introduced cavalry battalions, each trooper outfitted with rifle, saber, and side arm. Sarah snapped a photo capturing the precision of the equestrians navigating a turn while maintaining their lines, like spokes of a giant wheel. Behind the cavalry paraded the signal corps followed by field transportation, which included canvas covered wagon trains pulled by mules. A train of pack mules loaded with equipment and provisions brought up the rear. Sarah photographed the mules tailing doggedly behind guide riders.

As the last of the parade marched from Mesa onto Mills Street, Sarah secured her camera in its case and folded her tripod. When she reached the hotel lobby, she saw A. J. already at the front door impatiently awaiting her arrival. They had one hour to develop film, make prints, and deliver photographs to the Wilson Brothers International Photo-Engraving Company.

"Ready? Let's go," A. J. directed, holding open the front door for Sarah to exit ahead of him. He took the lead, shouldering through a crowd reluctant to quit the streets while they could hear military airs played by bands marching along the next leg of the parade route. Sarah joined in A. J.'s chorus of, "Excuse us," and "Pardon us" as they pressed a path through the throng of people clogging the sidewalk. Sarah saw A. J. occasionally glance back to make sure she remained close behind.

They struggled through the crush of people for several blocks. When they finally escaped the crowd, entering the calm of the studio, Sarah felt alarmed by the wheeze in A. J.'s breathing and the washed-out pale of his complexion.

"A. J.!" Sarah expressed her concern.

"I'm fine," he held up his hand to deflect her worry. "Just winded," he wheezed, then coughed as if to clear his throat. "Let's get busy."

Sarah hung her hat next to his on the hall tree, then followed A. J. into the dark room. They worked quickly side by side, removing completed rolls of film from the camera cases and forwarding partial rolls still in their cameras. Each of them loaded film onto spools, then inserted the spools into developing tanks. As they processed the film, Sarah remained conscious of A. J.'s repeated bouts of coughing. She watched him turn his head during each spell, covering his mouth with a cloth until the coughing stilled, then return the cloth to his trousers pocket and his attention to his work.

Sarah and A. J. operated quickly as a team, squeegeeing the developed film, selecting the wet negatives to place into the negative carrier for printing, then sliding the prints in the stop bath, fixer, and finally bath. They carefully applied blotter paper to help dry the photographs, then placed fresh blotter sheets before and after each print.

"It's twelve twenty," A. J. announced hoarsely. "We've got to go." A. J. placed the photos into a portfolio, which he secured under his arm. They grabbed their hats as they exited the studio. While A. J. locked the studio door, Sarah cranked the car. Though the streets still bustled with people and vehicles, the crowds had thinned. Sarah merged the car with the stream of traffic and headed toward the engraving office. The drive took only minutes, but once there, they discovered the curb lined with parked cars and wagons. A. J. announced, "Let me out; then circle the block."

Sarah had hardly brought the car to a complete stop before A. J.

leapt from the automobile carrying the portfolio and jogged toward the front door of the building. As she pulled back into traffic, Sarah worried, knowing A. J. would have to climb a flight of stairs to reach the engraving office on the second floor. Sarah had just begun her fourth circling of the block when A. J. exited the building. She came to a stop beside two parked vehicles, pausing long enough for A. J. to enter the auto. He smiled to her, and breathlessly announced, "We did it!" Then he exploded into a fit of coughing before he could cover his mouth, and the blood spattered in bright red speckles across the windshield and dash.

S E P T E M B E R   1 2 ,   1 9 8 3

Kayla

"Tuberculosis?" Kayla asked Sarah, who paused to take a sip of lemonade.

"Yes," Sarah answered, resting the glass back on the coaster. "A. J.'s TB had remained dormant for years, but it became active again. In 1914, the treatment for TB patients primarily consisted of sunshine and fresh air, preferably in a warm, dry climate. TB patients from across the country came to convalesce in El Paso's high desert air, so El Paso established several sanitoriums for tuberculars. A. J. moved into the Hendricks-Laws Sanitorium, the city's newest facility at the time, offering private rooms with sleeping porches." Sarah played with a turquoise ring on her right hand as she spoke. "While A. J. convalesced in the sanitorium, I lived in his apartment above the studio."

Sarah chuckled. "A. J. proposed I move into his place by reasoning, 'If you live in the apartment while I'm away, you're more likely to report to work on time.'" Sarah continued to smile. "He followed by insisting, 'I'm not dying, not now anyway, so don't go frilling up the place.'" She added, "And A. J. called it correctly; his TB eventually retreated to a dormant state again, allowing him to live and work out of his studio for many more years."

Kayla grinned, imagining A. J.'s gruff proposal that the young Sarah move into his apartment during his absence. Kayla also admitted to herself the relief she felt knowing A. J. emerged the victor from that round of TB.

"Shall we stop the interview at this point?" Kayla proposed, wanting to conclude this session with the positive news of A. J.'s recovery.

"Yes," Sarah agreed, slightly rocking in her seat to push to a standing position, then stretching the stiffness from her back. "While you're packing equipment, let me wrap some cake for the two of you."

Before Kayla could respond, Abel accepted the offer. "I'd love a slice for later. Thank you."

"Need some help?" Kayla offered.

"I've got it. Thanks."

Kayla helped Abel pack the equipment. They waited, ready to depart when Sarah returned with two foil-wrapped plates.

Abel caught Kayla off guard when he suddenly hugged Sarah after accepting her offering. He followed his affectionate gesture of thanks by stating, "I'm so pleased A. J. recovered. But I'm so disappointed with Samuel's betrayal. I'm sorry he hurt you, Sarah."

Sarah remained silent, looking intently at Abel.

Kayla feared Abel's stumble from professional to personal offended the elderly woman.

Sarah took one of Abel's hands in hers. "Samuel's betrayal disappointed me as well, Abel, but I've grown less angry with him; the years have schooled me to the fact that we are all capable of committing acts that betray the hearts we love."

PART
FOUR

SEPTEMBER 22, 1983

Kayla

"Sarah Delaney interview, number four, El Paso, Texas, 10:10 a.m., September 22, 1983." Kayla followed her verbal date stamping by reminding Sarah where they concluded the previous session. "Sarah, at our last interview, you described photographing the massive military parade on El Paso's Army Day."

Sarah's recall and her ability to pick up the telling of her history at the slightest mental nudge amazed Kayla. Without further prompting, Sarah resumed the conversation as though they had ended the prior interview ten minutes ago versus ten days.

"Our photographs of the parade appeared in a full-page spread on the second page of the evening paper. The photos' effectiveness in capturing the military might protecting El Paso so pleased General Pershing that he wrote personal notes of appreciation to A. J. and to me, mentioning he would seek our services in the future to photograph other important events."

Kayla marveled at Sarah's matter-of-fact mention of significant historical figures with whom she interacted. Further guiding the direction of Sarah's recall, Kayla asked, "At this time period, Victoriano Huerta remained president of Mexico; Venustiano Carranza served as First Chief of the Constitutionalists, who fought against Huerta's presidency; and Pancho Villa commanded the Division of the North, a major force of the Constitutionalist army, correct?"

"Yes," Sarah agreed, "but Huerta's grip on the presidency became more and more tenuous, as did Carranza's control of Villa. By the time Villa took the city of Torreón in early April 1914, his prestige in Mexico and the United States had grown dramatically. As you know," Sarah chuckled, "there are few greater sins in any profession than receiving more accolades than your superior, and the sin becomes unforgiveable if your leader is politically ambitious. Carranza resented Villa's popularity in Mexico and abroad; he worried that Villa's military victories positioned him to assume leadership of the revolution and eventually the country. The first chief acted on those fears by creating obstacles designed to reduce Villa's visibility. Carranza even ordered him to place five thousand of his troops under another general's command rather than allowing Villa and the Division of the North to march on the city of Zacatecas, which housed a garrison of Huerta's elite forces. After several unsuccessful attempts to reason with Carranza, Villa, in a fit of anger, offered to resign as commander of the Division of the North. Carranza immediately accepted the proffered resignation. Villa's generals, however, would not assent to the loss of their military leader. They telegrammed Carranza, refusing to recognize any commander other than Villa and announcing that the Division of the North would march on Zacatecas. So, ten days after Carranza accepted Villa's resignation," Sarah illustrated by raising ten fingers, "Villa led his Division of the North to victory against Huerta's federal troops in the bloody Battle of Zacatecas."

Sarah lowered her hands to her lap. "Villa achieved victory at Zacatecas in late June. By mid-July, Victoriano Huerta resigned the presidency of Mexico, departing the country aboard a German cruiser, and arriving in Spain three days before the flames of war engulfed Europe."

Sarah crossed her legs, leaning back into the armchair. "After Villa's victory in Zacatecas, Carranza stalled Villa's march into Mexico City by denying him shipments of coal needed to power the Division of the

North's troop trains. So, instead of Villa, it was General Álvaro Obregón, Carranza's commander-in-chief of the Division of the Northwest, who led Constitutionalist forces triumphantly into Mexico City in mid-August."

A deep exhalation prefaced her next statement. "In the months following Obregón's entrance into the capital, Mexico experienced continued unrest, the various revolutionary factions engaging in political machinations, maneuverings, and ultimatums. Before year's end, the Mexican Revolution exploded into its bloodiest phase, pitting revolutionary forces against each other."

"And what of El Paso during this period?" Kayla asked, redirecting the interview. "Did the city remain as militarized as it had become after the invasion of Veracruz, and were El Pasoans still worried about the violence of the Mexican Revolution spilling across the border?"

"Yes." Sarah answered succinctly. Then added, "In fact, eleven days after General Álvaro Obregón marched his Division of the Northwest into Mexico City, he and General Pancho Villa arrived in El Paso at the invitation of General Pershing. At the US State Department's urgings, Pershing met with the rebel generals to express the United States' desire for a positive relationship with the new Constitutionalist government and to demonstrate the strength and capabilities of the US Armed Forces guarding the border." Sarah added, "True to his word, General Pershing reached out to A. J. and me to photograph the ceremonies surrounding their visit to El Paso."

AUGUST 1914

Sarah

Sarah stood beside her camera and tripod on the American side of the Santa Fe Street International Bridge fanning herself against the late August heat. With a handkerchief balled in her left hand, she dabbed perspiration beading on her forehead, cooling herself with a repetitive sweep of the fan she held in her right.

Timothy walked up behind Sarah to share the latest news. "Word is the generals will be arriving within the half-hour."

Fort Bliss officials had notified the newspapers of the delay in today's ceremonies due to the late arrival of the special train transporting Generals Villa and Obregón and their accompanying staffs to Ciudad Juárez.

Sarah and Timothy had arrived at the Santa Fe Street Bridge a little over an hour ago, and she occupied her time with photographing the crowds and the entrance of companies from the Twentieth Infantry and Thirteenth Cavalry, which now arranged themselves in formations to welcome the Mexican military leaders.

"Okay, now things are starting to happen," Timothy spoke, directing Sarah's attention with the lift of his chin toward an arriving US Army staff car. "That's General Pershing in the back."

Sarah watched the automobile come to a stop on the bridge and an officer exit the front seat to open a rear door of the vehicle for General Pershing. Sarah had viewed photographs of the general, but she had never seen him in person. She studied him. General Pershing stood ram-rod straight, his lean, fit figure apparent even in the riding breeches and choke-collar tunic of the khaki uniform. He paused to place a gold-braid-ed campaign hat on his head before striding to speak with other officers. Sarah noted his confident military bearing and the respect he received from the soldiers with whom he interacted.

A sudden change in the tenor of activity on the bridge indicated that the ceremonial welcoming of Generals Villa and Obregón would be underway soon. The US troops snapped to attention. Shouts of "Viva Villa!" burst from the Mexican side as a long red touring car, followed by a string of accompanying automobiles, edged across the international bridge, stopping just opposite the US demarcation line.

Sarah recognized Pancho Villa when he stepped from the touring car. She did not recognize the other man, so she confirmed with Timothy that the paunchy man in military uniform was General Álvaro Obregón.

Sarah turned her attention to General Pershing, who strode briskly toward the Mexican generals, accompanied by some of his staff and the man she recognized as Zach Lamar Cobb, El Paso's Collector of Customs. When the groups met on the US side of the international boundary, Cobb provided introductions, resulting in firm, cordial handshakes between the commanders.

Following introductions, Lieutenant Collins, General Pershing's aide, stepped away from the formalities, walking over to Sarah and Aultman, a photographer for the *Post*. Tall and lanky, the lieutenant towered over them as he informed that there would be an arranged photo opportunity. "Please move closer to the ceremony and position your cameras while we organize the dignitaries for a photograph." Without awaiting a response, Collins performed an about-face and returned to General Pershing's side to assist with arranging the twenty or so people who had exited the line of automobiles behind the red touring car.

The generals formed the front line with Villa standing center. In contrast to the military uniforms of Pershing and Obregón, Villa dressed in a Norfolk jacket stretched tightly at the hips, outlining pistols. He stood with his bowtie slightly askew, his Stetson pushed onto the back of his head, exposing tight curls of hair.

Sarah positioned herself near Aultman, about ten feet in front of the dignitaries, and quickly focused her camera lens on the mustachioed generals. "On three," she announced, holding up three fingers to the nods of her posed subjects. Peering through the focusing hood, she signaled the countdown by raising a finger. Just prior to the lift of Sarah's third finger, Villa spoke quietly, then offered a sly smile. Sarah didn't hear his comment, but Obregón gestured toward Sarah as he turned his gaze to Villa. Pershing broke into a broad grin, dimples emerging on his cheeks. Sarah depressed the shutter release to capture the photo.

Immediately, Lieutenant Collins ushered the generals into the open-air staff car, Pershing seated in the front alongside the driver with Villa and Obregón occupying the back seat. The Thirteenth Cavalry led the procession, troopers riding ahead and alongside the generals' car. The line of automobiles containing the generals' staff and a handful of civilian dignitaries followed.

Sarah could hear the shouts of "Viva Villa!" from the throngs of people gathered on the streets of El Paso.

"Let me help you with the equipment," Timothy offered, extending his hand to take the camera and tripod. They hurried to the side street where they had parked Sarah's automobile for quick access. Sarah secured the equipment while Timothy adjusted the choke and cranked the vehicle to start.

Following Timothy's directions, Sarah drove onto Fort Bliss and parked the car beside the parade field stretching along Sheridan Road in front of General Pershing's house. They arrived prior to the procession of dignitaries, which allowed Sarah time to position her camera to capture the entrance of the generals. While Sarah finished setting up, Timothy mingled, mining potential sources for newsworthy insights.

Soon, the long staff car bearing the generals stopped in front of Pershing's home, followed closely by cars transporting their staff. Once all had exited the line of vehicles, the Army band struck up the Mexican national anthem in honor of the visitors; senior officers of the US Army at Fort Bliss stood stiffly in their formal receiving line, awaiting the completion of the national airs and the start of introductions to Generals Villa and Obregón. Once the anthem concluded, Sarah busied herself with photographing the welcoming ceremony.

Engaged in her work, Sarah startled at Lieutenant Collins's sudden appearance beside her. The lieutenant spoke formally, extending General Pershing's appreciation of her services, "but," he informed her, "the formal reception will be closed to photographers and journalists." Sarah understood she had just been dismissed, so she slid the lens board inward, closed the camera bed, and removed the camera from the tripod. While collapsing the legs of the tripod, Sarah searched the crowd for Timothy and realized she stood the lone woman amid a field of men.

Sarah spied Timothy speaking to a small group of officers. Gripping the camera handle in her left hand and placing the tripod under her right arm, she prepared to retrieve her friend. Before she could make her way over to Timothy, someone called, "Señora Clendenin! Señora!" Sarah faced the direction of the voice.

Grinning broadly, General Villa strode with a slightly pigeon-toed gait toward her. When he reached Sarah, he removed his hat and made a modest bow before returning the Stetson to the back of his head. He glared impatiently toward a man who rushed just short of a trot toward them. Once the slight, bespectacled man stood nervously beside the general, Villa began to speak to Sarah, then paused for the translation of his words.

Lips hidden beneath an enormous black moustache, the translator converted Villa's words into English. "General Villa wants you to know how pleased he is to see you today. Your photographs of him with the pigeons remain his favorites." His statement complete, he turned to Villa for the general's next exchange.

Villa looked intently into Sarah's eyes as he spoke at length. Then nodded for his translator to begin.

"The general wishes to express his condolences for the death of Captain Clendenin. He knows the captain loved you as dearly as General Villa loves his own wife. But," the translator added somewhat hesitantly, as if trying to choose the most appropriate manner of conveying Villa's statement, "we men behave like dogs sometimes and don't deserve the good women who love us in return."

Sarah looked down to gather herself. She wanted to agree enthusiastically with General Villa, wanted to say without hesitation that, yes, some men do behave as dogs, but, instead, she regained emotional control, raised her head, and said, "Please thank General Villa for his kind comments."

While the slight man repeated her words in Spanish to General Villa, General Pershing walked up to stand beside the two men, waiting for a lull in the conversation.

"Forgive me for interrupting." He nodded politely to General Villa and his translator before turning his attention to Sarah. "Though we have not met in person, Miss Delaney, I feel I know you through your work." He pointed toward the camera. "And it appears that General Villa's observation at the bridge that you 'command generals' is accurate since you have two of the three generals abandoning reception guests to stand in your presence." He smiled generously, exposing his dimples. "I'm afraid, though, that I need to steal General Villa back to the reception to meet some far less interesting guests."

General Pershing turned politely from Sarah and, in Spanish, addressed General Villa, who nodded his assent.

As the men started to leave, Sarah spoke quickly, stopping them momentarily. "General Villa, do you have any news of Captain Catalina Vasquez?"

General Villa grinned. "Coronela Catalina Vasquez," he corrected. He added, "Muy inteligente," tapping a forefinger to his forehead, "y muy valiente," thumping a fist against his chest.

"God, I've missed these," A. J. spoke, staring at the pork tamale he held above a plate Sarah provided. Ignoring the fork Sarah extended to him, he took a second large bite, flicking his tongue to capture a crumb from his upper lip.

Pleased that A. J. devoured the food with such vigor, Sarah asked, "So what makes you happier—seeing me or seeing the tamales I brought?"

"Don't make me choose," he answered from the side of his full mouth.

Sarah chuckled, encouraged to see him looking stronger than he had in weeks. When he had exited the building to join her on the sanitorium grounds, she noted he appeared to have put on a little weight. Now sitting next to him on the bench, she thought his face had more color than in previous weeks.

A. J. pushed the last bite of food into his mouth, wiped his hands and lips with a napkin, then folded the top of the sack containing a second tamale. "I'd better save this one." He explained, "You know, too much of a good thing." Then he removed a folded mask from the pocket of his jacket and placed it over his mouth and nose. Stretching his legs before him, he asked, "So what have you brought for me to look at?"

Sarah retrieved the portfolio leaning against the bench and removed a small stack of prints.

A. J. took the stack from Sarah, studying the first. "This photo is really good." He held up the photograph of the three generals on the international bridge. "I saw the picture on the front-page of yesterday's newspaper, but the newsprint didn't capture the quality of your original photograph, which is really an excellent contrast of the three generals. Look at Obregón," he pointed to the figure on the left. "Look at his intelligent intensity as he studies Villa. Then Villa," he spoke, moving his finger to the middle figure, "dressed in civilian clothing but barely concealing weapons within quick grasp of his hands. He's positioned square with the camera, while Obregón and Pershing turn slightly toward him, like Villa affects a kind of magnetic pull." He pointed to the right side of the photograph, and said, "Now, Pershing, he stands several inches taller than the other two generals, looking fit in his starched uniform. He smiles broadly, mouth open in relaxed amusement, exuding a comfortable confidence." He motioned with the photo toward Sarah. "Definitely print photo postcards of this one," he said before moving the photograph to the bottom of the pile. "I think it will sell well."

A. J. lifted the second photo from the stack, then raised the next print from the pile for comparison. "This one," he said, motioning with the picture he held in his right hand. "It shows more complete action: the troops are at attention, the touring car is halted, and Pershing is walking toward Villa and Obregón as they exit the vehicle." He emphasized, "This one will sell." He carefully placed it behind the first photo of the three generals.

As A. J. reached for the next photo on the stack, he started coughing, a restrained cough at first, then a series of body-wracking coughs. He quickly turned from Sarah, spilling the photos onto the grass as his body spasmed with each expulsion. He stood abruptly, facing her. "I'm sorry Sarah, but I must go inside."

Sarah saw specks of blood absorbed by the cloth of the mask. She stood to take his arm. "Let me walk with you."

A. J. pulled away, not angrily but forcibly. "No, I'm better alone."

Sarah noticed that the slight color she'd seen earlier in A. J.'s face had now drained, leaving a ghostly whiteness. She watched his unsteady return into the sanitorium. Alone, Sarah bent to collect the photographs scattered on the lawn.

NOVEMBER 1914

Sarah

Sarah sat at the kitchen table in the apartment above the studio. She had just returned to her seat after placing her supper dishes into the sink and pouring a second cup of coffee. Setting the steaming mug to the side, she opened the evening newspaper to review the headlines. The news on the front page focused solely on events in Mexico and the war in Europe. Sarah sighed when she read the top headline announcing, "American Forces Leave Veracruz," followed by a second headline declaring, "Carranza Troops Occupy Veracruz." Sarah thought of the tension created in El Paso by the American invasion of the Mexican port city and the resulting militarization of the US-Mexico border; she wondered aloud what America had gained by the occupation of Veracruz.

Sarah took a sip of coffee, then placed the mug on the table. Running a finger along the ceramic handle, she stared past the newspaper, settling into thoughts of Cata, wondering where she was and hoping for her safety. Sarah thought about the Mexican Revolution, which seemed to spin like a child's top set into motion by the pumping of a plunger. Eventually the revolution would wobble to a stop, but for now, it continued its vigorous spin.

Since late August, when Sarah photographed the visit of Generals Villa and Obregón, the revolution had evolved, pitting forces that had previously united in their fight to remove Huerta from the presidency. In late September, Villa publicly withdrew his recognition of Carranza as the first chief of the Constitutionalists. In October, military leaders of the revolution convened the Convention of Aguascalientes, at which the majority in attendance approved a resolution requiring the resignations of both Carranza and Villa. Accepting this resolution, Villa suggested that not only should both Carranza and he resign, but both should be shot. Carranza fled Mexico City rather than abide by the Convention's order for his resignation. Then last Thursday, Obregón had joined Carranza, declaring war on Villa. She imagined the plunger of the top pumped vigorously again, setting the top spinning with renewed energy.

Sarah folded the paper and put it aside. She didn't wish to read any more about the Mexican Revolution, and she didn't want to learn of new developments in the war raging throughout Europe—too much sadness and pain. Standing from the table, she walked to empty the remaining coffee from the mug, adding the cup to the small pile of dishes in the sink. She would wash them tomorrow. Tonight, she would go to bed and hope for sleep.

But sleep remained elusive. Sarah rolled from one side to the other, her mind racing with news of strife occurring across the globe. Finally, her weariness outweighed her worry, and she slipped into a fragile slumber. In the morning, Sarah arose from bed feeling more tired than rested.

She put a pot of coffee on the stove to brew while she washed and dressed. A quick breakfast of toast and jam, and she exited the apartment for work in the studio below. A. J.'s prediction that the apartment's proximity to the studio would aid in her timely arrival for the start of the workday proved accurate. Sarah found herself beginning work early and climbing the steps to the apartment late in the evening.

With just two days before Thanksgiving, Sarah didn't expect much business. The public's rush to get rolls of film processed would follow the holiday. The current calm allowed Sarah time to tackle a few duties requiring quiet focus. She inventoried supplies, then placed multiple orders to restock what was needed. After spending the morning completing those tasks, she switched to bookkeeping, a responsibility A. J. usually managed and one she didn't relish.

She had been engaged with the accounting book for almost an hour, her attention fixed on the columns and figures of an income statement, so the jangle of the front bell startled her. Unconsciously placing her hand over her heart, Sarah looked up.

"I am always surprising you."

"Cata!" Sarah called, hurrying from behind the counter to envelope the young woman in a hug.

"I found you," Cata whispered.

"Yes, you found me," Sarah replied, hugging Cata tighter before releasing her. "I'm so glad you're here." Sarah briefly pressed the palm of her hand to Cata's face and guided her friend to a chair behind the curtain. "Please, sit. Let me get the stool." Sarah hurriedly returned to the room, sitting on the stool she placed across from Cata.

"How long are you here?" Sarah asked.

"Today and tomorrow. I leave Thursday morning."

Sarah felt a sinking disappointment at the shortness of Cata's visit. "You must stay with me," Sarah blurted, then explained, "I now live in the apartment above this studio." She glanced upward to demonstrate the location. "I would love for you to stay with me."

"Thank you," Cata replied, "I will stay."

They soon conversed with the familiarity of old friends. Sarah told Cata of A. J.'s illness and her decision to move into his apartment during his time at the sanitorium. "Prior to my moving in, A. J. brought in a team to scrub the studio and apartment. He replaced the bedding, upholstered furniture, and curtains, all out of concern." She paused, then added, "He's a good man, a good friend."

"And his health?" Cata asked.

"He's improving." She qualified, "Slowly, but he appears stronger."

Cata spoke of General Villa's mention of Sarah following his visit to El Paso and shared his pleasure at the photograph on the bridge. While Cata spoke, Sarah studied her face, noting that even when Cata smiled, her eyes expressed a weary sadness. Sarah did not want to know the violence Cata had witnessed.

Sarah and Cata talked of their previous trip to San Elizario and the wonderful food at the small restaurant. Pleased by the happiness that memory seemed to bring Cata, Sarah proposed, "Let's take a drive tomorrow. Since Thursday is a holiday, I'll close the studio at noon as a sort of 'Thanksgiving Eve.' We can have the afternoon to ourselves."

"I would like that," Cata answered, then placed her hand over her mouth to conceal a wide yawn.

"Why don't you go upstairs and rest?"

Cata started to protest, but Sarah quickly responded, "I'll close the studio in a couple of hours, then we can share a good supper. In the meantime, you rest."

Cata nodded reluctantly and retrieved her satchel from the floor.

Sarah locked the front door and taped a sign indicating her reopening at 3:45 p.m. She returned to Cata, taking her hand to raise her to a stand. "Come," Sarah encouraged, "just up the stairs," and she led the way into the apartment. She showed Cata the bathroom, sitting room, kitchen, and bedroom. From the chifforobe, she pulled a nightgown and bathrobe to place on the bed and set out fresh linens in the bathroom. "Make yourself comfortable," Sarah urged. "Lie down for a nap, take a long bath, make a bite to eat—anything you'd like. I'll return in a couple of hours." Sarah started to leave, but then stopped to embrace Cata. "I'm so glad you're here."

Back in the studio, Sarah caught herself watching the clock, anxious for five thirty so she could return to Cata. She attempted bookkeeping but remained too distracted to focus on numbers, so she secured the account book in the safe to address on another day.

Finally, five thirty arrived. After closing the studio for the night, Sarah climbed the steps to the apartment. She entered quietly, glancing about for Cata. When she didn't spy her in the sitting room or kitchen, she tiptoed to the bedroom to find Cata lying on her side, asleep on top of the bedspread, fully dressed with only her shoes removed. Sarah listened briefly to the throaty rasp Cata exhaled. She must be exhausted, Sarah thought, then quietly closed the bedroom door before tiptoeing away.

Once in the kitchen, Sarah placed an apron over her head and opened the icebox to remove a chicken she had purchased for her Thanksgiving Day meal. While the oven warmed, she put the giblets into a saucepan with water and lit the eye of the stove. Placing the chicken in a roasting pan along with vegetables, she sprinkled seasonings and slid the pan into the oven. With their supper cooking, she washed and dried the few dishes used in the preparation.

After pouring a glass of buttermilk, she sat at the kitchen table to read the evening paper, but thoughts of Cata interrupted her reading. Sarah pictured Cata's strong, slender figure lit by sunlight that shone through the door when she entered the studio. Sarah mentally traced the contours of Cata's face, the high, prominent cheekbones, the firm jaw, the full lips. In her mind, she gazed into Cata's brown eyes and saw again the sadness beyond her years. Sarah drained the last of her buttermilk, then stood to rinse the glass. She busied herself with setting the table in preparation for the meal, returning to the oven to gauge the progress of the food.

When she turned, she saw Cata standing in the doorway, watching. A warmth emanated deep in Sarah's belly at viewing Cata's slightly disheveled beauty. Attempting to sound unaffected, Sarah asked, "Did you have a good sleep?" But she knew her voice sounded thin and breathless.

"Yes. Thank you."

Sarah regained her composure and said, "Supper is in the oven and should be ready soon. Would you like something to drink—water, tea, coffee?"

"Coffee. Thank you."

"Please sit," Sarah suggested. "I'll brew a pot."

Instead of sitting, Cata joined Sarah at the stove, asking, "What can I do?"

Sarah felt her heart race at Cata's proximity. As self-defense, Sarah answered, "Just sit at the table and talk with me." When Cata started to protest, Sarah responded, "Today you are my guest. Tomorrow, you can help with the work."

Sarah opened the oven door to remove the roasting pan and place it on the workspace next to the stove. "We're having roasted chicken with vegetables," she spoke as she tilted the pan to ladle out some of the drippings into a bowl.

"Smells good."

Sarah pushed a two-pronged fork deep into the breast of the chicken. When only clear liquid drained from the piercings, Sarah turned off the oven and placed the roasting pan in the warming drawer of the stove. She cut four thick slices of bread, then added that plate to the warmer.

Pausing in the preparation of the meal, Sarah lifted a mug from the cabinet, poured a steaming cup of coffee for Cata, and brought it to her with a spoon and creamer. "I remember you like milk and sugar in your coffee," and she pushed the sugar bowl from the middle of the table toward Cata.

"Thank you."

Sarah returned to the stove to make the giblet gravy.

After preparing her coffee, Cata crossed the kitchen to lean against the pantry doorway, sipping from the mug and watching Sarah cook.

Sarah added the strained chicken drippings into a saucepan, sprinkled in flour, and began whisking. She asked Cata about her English, commenting, "Your English is very good, even better than when we last visited."

"I have to learn English so we can talk."

Even though she knew Cata jested, Sarah smiled her pleasure. "But how?" Sarah asked, her eyes focused on her cooking.

"Two of my officers speak English; one even went to a US university. They teach me."

"I'm impressed."

"Good," Cata concluded, adding nothing more to her statement.

Sarah turned off the flame. "Supper is ready."

While Sarah carved the chicken, Cata placed the vegetables into a bowl. The meal was soon on the table.

They ate quietly at first, then relaxed into conversation. At the meal's conclusion, they discussed plans for tomorrow's drive, deciding on a picnic by the river. That settled, Sarah stood from the table, announcing, "I'd better get the food into the icebox."

"I'll help," Cata responded, pushing back from the table.

"No, you relax."

Cata paused as if considering the suggestion, then said, "I wish to bathe before bed."

"Yes, please enjoy. Let me know if you need anything." Sarah began clearing the table. She could hear bath water running while she carved the remaining chicken from the bones then placed the food into the icebox. She filled the sink with soapy water to wash the supper dishes, thinking about their plans for tomorrow afternoon.

When she finished cleaning the kitchen, Sarah hurried to the bedroom to change the bedsheets. She had just stripped the bed when Cata entered the room dressed in the gown and robe Sarah had offered. Cata's hair curled loosely in long damp strands on her chest and down her back. Sarah had never seen Cata's hair freed from braids and bun. Sarah swallowed hard at what felt like a shared intimacy.

"Let me help." Before Sarah could answer, Cata had tucked a corner of the sheet under the mattress. They worked together to make the bed, smoothing the sheets and blanket and placing the folded bedspread across the foot. When they completed their labor, Sarah announced she would bathe before sleep.

Between Cata's bath and Sarah's dishwashing, only lukewarm water remained in the tank, so Sarah kept her bath brief. She dressed in her nightgown and robe, then brushed her hair, leaving it loose.

Though Sarah had not been long in the bath, when she returned to the bedroom, Cata lay curled in bed, her mouth slightly agape in a sound sleep. Because Cata lay uncovered still wearing the bathrobe, Sarah thought exhaustion had probably overtaken her.

Sarah considered waking her so Cata could remove the robe, but decided, instead, simply to let her sleep. Sarah carefully lifted the sheet and blanket over Cata's resting figure, then switched off the lamp and slid quietly into bed. Comforted by the warmth of Cata's body next to hers, Sarah quickly drifted into a sound sleep.

When Sarah awoke in the morning, Cata's head rested against her shoulder, and her arm and leg draped across Sarah's belly and thighs. Sarah lay still, breathing in the smell of Cata's hair. The level of light in the room informed Sarah she needed to rise from bed and prepare for work, but the warmth of Cata's body next to hers made it difficult to leave the bed. Reluctantly, she stirred, trying to remove herself from Cata's touch without waking her, but when Sarah rose to slide from under Cata's limbs, she found herself slammed back to the bed with a startling ferocity. Saddled with Cata's full weight straddling her hips,

Sarah gasped for breath against the two hands gripping her throat.

"Cata," Sarah rasped. "Cata!" She strained to speak.

And as suddenly as Cata had sprung on top of Sarah, Cata released her grasp, removing her weight from Sarah's body. Cata fell back onto the bed, moaning, "Dios mío! My God!"

Sarah lay coughing, trying to inhale a full breath, her throat burning with the effort.

"Sarah, are you okay?"

Sarah nodded her head as she continued to cough.

"Dios mío!" Cata repeated. "Sarah, I'm sorry. I thought I was in camp. I thought someone was climbing into my bed, was climbing on top of me."

"It's all right," Sarah responded, lying flat, trying to settle her senses.

Cata lay back, releasing a heart-wrenching moan. Placing the heels of her hands to her eyes, she sobbed.

"Cata." Sarah turned to soothe her. "I'm all right. It's all right. I knew you weren't fully awake." Sarah stroked Cata's hair, pulling Cata to her, holding Cata until the quake of her body began to subside. "Shh, shh, shh," Sarah whispered. "Everything is all right. Shh, shh, shh," Sarah shushed in a soft repetition.

Cata lay cradled in Sarah's embrace for several minutes before rolling from her. "I will go."

"No, Cata!" Sarah responded immediately. "There's no reason for you to leave."

"Sarah, I could have hurt you badly," Cata paused before adding, "or worse."

Sarah rose to her elbow. "But you didn't. I'm okay. You woke up." She brushed her hand along Cata's cheek to remove a strand of hair clinging to the moisture on her face. "I want you to stay," Sarah insisted.

When Cata finally nodded in acquiescence, Sarah kissed her cheek. "I'll make a pot of coffee."

Sarah pushed back the bedclothes and stepped onto the cool floor. Wrapping her woolen robe about her, she went into the kitchen. She braced herself against the sink, placing a hand to her throat, and remembered the suddenness and ferocity of the attack. She took a deep breath to steady herself. After preparing the coffee pot, she went into the bathroom to wash her face.

Sarah looked in the mirror at the red marks encircling her throat. She placed a cool washcloth to her neck to reduce bruising. After ten minutes, Sarah removed the cloth. Reentering the bedroom, she found it vacant, and Cata's satchel gone.

Her heart pounding, Sarah rushed into the kitchen. Cata sat quietly at the table, her bag on the floor beside her.

Sarah placed her palm to her chest. "I thought you left."

"I am leaving, Sarah. It's best."

"Cata, don't," Sarah insisted, sliding into the chair next to Cata's. "I'm fine."

"Sarah, it could happen again."

"It could, but I don't think it will. We will both be careful." Sarah reached to take Cata's hand resting on the table. "Stay."

When Cata didn't reply, Sarah added, "At least stay for the day. Let's have our picnic. If you wish to leave before night, okay."

Sarah could see Cata considering the proposal, so she encouraged again, "Stay."

Cata nodded slowly in hesitant agreement. "Okay."

"Good." Sarah stood, not wanting further discussion about Cata's leaving. She removed two mugs from the shelf and poured coffee. She placed one mug in front of Cata. "What would you like for breakfast?"

"Just coffee," Cata responded.

"I think just coffee for me, too," Sarah said, then added, "I'd better get dressed and open the studio."

Cata nodded.

Sarah carried her mug into the bedroom to drink while she dressed for the day. To hide the marks on her neck, she selected a cinnamon-colored blouse with a standing collar, then added a loose chocolate-brown skirt. Next, she brushed her hair before gathering it in a bun. Picking up the mug, she returned to the kitchen.

Cata remained seated at the table. Sarah noted that Cata's mug was full; the weight of the coffee pot when Sarah refilled her own mug informed her that Cata had not poured a second cup.

"I'm going to open the studio," Sarah announced, placing her hand on Cata's shoulder. "This afternoon," she assured, "we'll take our drive and enjoy the day."

"Okay," Cata replied with little emotion.

Sarah closed the door quietly, then descended the stairs. Before opening for business, she tidied the studio, sweeping the floors and straightening the photo display in the window. After setting up the cash register with funds for the day, she unlocked the front door, ready for morning business.

Soon, a customer arrived to purchase film. While Sarah assisted him, Cata entered the studio and started for the front door. Sarah quickly excused herself from the customer to call out, "Back by twelve," as both a reminder and a question. Cata waved her hand in acknowledgement.

As Sarah expected, business remained slow. She worked at the front of the studio to watch for Cata. When the noon hour approached, Sarah grew concerned that Cata would not return.

Finally, a little before twelve, Cata walked through the door carrying a paper bag. "I bought bread and pastries for today."

Sarah tried not to show her relief at Cata's entrance, so she masked her excitement with a simple, "Good." Then added, "Why don't you go up to the apartment to get ready while I close the studio? I'll follow soon."

At noon, Sarah locked the front door and placed the "closed" sign in the window.

In the apartment, Sarah and Cata worked together to pack a basket with food for their excursion. They added the remainder of last night's chicken, a can of baked beans, two boiled eggs, a wedge of cheese, a jar of olives, sliced tomatoes, a jar of spicy pickled vegetables, and the bread and pastries Cata had purchased. In a second basket, Sarah added cups, plates, cutlery, napkins, a thermos of water, and a blanket.

The work of organizing supplies for the picnic seemed to lighten the cloak of worried gloom that had clung to Cata since early morning, though she still maintained an emotionally guarded distance from Sarah. Hoping the drive and picnic would restore Cata's comfort with her, Sarah suggested, "You grab one basket; I'll get the other." Sarah gathered her hat and coat then followed Cata from the apartment.

At the car, Sarah opened the rumble seat to secure the baskets. Once the car was running, Sarah slid behind the steering wheel. She squeezed Cata's hand, encouraging, "Let's enjoy our afternoon. It's a beautiful day for a picnic."

Sarah drove west. Leaving downtown, she throttled the car to a speed that whipped her hair about her face. Sarah glanced at Cata, who sat with her eyes closed, a smile of calm gracing her face as the wind tugged her hair loose from its braided bun. Sarah's heart warmed at the sight.

They drove in comfortable silence along the river, past the ground that had been Madero's camp during the first Battle of Juárez. Sarah continued west, wanting distance from El Paso, Juárez, and reminders of strife caused by the revolution. After driving away from the city for half an hour, Sarah searched along the river for an inviting location. She turned south on a narrow dirt road that led to a grove of trees she saw in the near distance. She stopped the car at a shady, secluded location along the Rio Grande.

"What do you think of this spot for our picnic?" Sarah asked Cata.

"It's beautiful."

Leaving their coats and hats in the automobile, they exited the car to identify a flat location shaded by branches of a large cottonwood tree; then they returned to the vehicle to collect their lunch. Together, they spread the blanket and sat to remove the contents of the baskets.

"I'm hungry," Sarah admitted. "How about you?"

"Yes," Cata agreed.

They worked together to open containers of food, filling their plates with the offerings. Since Cata remained largely quiet, Sarah felt the need to replace the silence with chatter while they ate. She steered clear of any reference to the revolution or events of the morning. She talked instead about the loveliness of the warm day, their beautiful surroundings, and the deliciousness of the bread and pastries Cata purchased.

When they ate their fill, Cata leaned on her side, resting her head in her hand. With a finger, she traced the pattern of the blanket. Without looking at Sarah, she began speaking softly. "A rurale raped my twelve-year-old sister Fátima when my family lived on the hacienda."

Sarah's mind startled at Cata's disclosure, which she relayed in a voice that seemed disconnected from the painful event she revealed. Sarah resisted expressing sympathies or extending a comforting touch, choosing to allow Cata to talk.

"The violation crushed Fátima's soul. No matter how hard I tried, I couldn't make her want to live." Cata paused to gather her emotions. "She died in my arms." Tears rolled from Cata's eyes as she spoke. "I swore to myself that I would kill any man who tried to force himself," she stopped, swallowed hard, then continued, "who ever tried to take by force what is mine to give." Cata picked up a twig, toying absent-mindedly with the thin stick until it snapped. "This morning, in my sleep," Cata said, raising her eyes to look at Sarah, "I thought you were that man." She lowered her eyes.

Sarah placed her hand to Cata's face to wipe the tears. Then leaned forward, pressing her lips gently, briefly to Cata's. Sarah pulled back to look into Cata's eyes, then leaned to her again to kiss her lips fully. Cata reached her hand to cradle the nape of Sarah's neck, returning the kiss.

They separated, both lying on their sides, studying each other's face before again embracing. The sudden sound of a bird lifting in flight from the river interrupted their quiet, causing them to separate and rise in the realization that though they lay in a secluded area, they were still visible.

Together, they packed the remains of their lunch and returned the baskets to the automobile.

"Let's walk a little," Cata encouraged.

They strolled along the river, talking some, but mostly enjoying the warmth of the day, the beauty of their surroundings, and the comfort of their new intimacy. While they followed the riverbank, each found an opportunity to momentarily entwine fingers with the other or remove an errant strand of hair from the other's face or press shoulder against shoulder in a shared stride.

When the afternoon shadows began to lengthen, they returned to the automobile for the drive home. Once sheltered inside the cab of the car, they shared a kiss before Sarah rotated the steering wheel to return to El Paso.

Even though Sarah opened the throttle, the drive home seemed longer than the drive to the river. Finally, though, Sarah pulled the car in front of the studio, and they entered the apartment cradling baskets, coats, and hats. Once they deposited their loads on the kitchen table and across kitchen chairs, they turned immediately to one another to embrace in a kiss.

Cata removed the pins securing Sarah's hair, freeing the strands to spill into Cata's hands. Then Cata released her own braids, loosening the weave till her hair hung in curls over her shoulders.

Sarah took Cata's hand, leading her into the bedroom where they stood to kiss, Sarah running her hands along the soft curves of Cata's breasts. Cata unbuttoned Sarah's blouse, exposing her neck. Cata traced then kissed the tender areas her grasp had bruised. Sarah felt chills of desire from Cata's moist mouth against her throat.

They undressed each other, their lips and hands exploring newly exposed skin until they stood naked. Sarah gently traced the purple pucker of a healed wound on Cata's chest. Then, Sarah took Cata's hand and led her to the bed, tossing back the blankets for them to tumble entangled onto the mattress. She tugged the covers over them, providing additional warmth to their passion.

They pressed against one another, their mouths, tongues, and fingers traveling over each other's bodies, discovering one another's pleasures, goading and guiding until each shuddered and moaned her satisfaction. Then they lay holding, surprised but not surprised by the passionate direction of their relationship. Sarah placed her head on Cata's shoulder, her forehead pressed to Cata's cheek and her arm and leg enveloping her lover in a tight embrace. Cata held her, an arm about her shoulder. Together, they drifted into the rich comfort of sleep.

Sarah felt Cata stir, the slight movement pulling her to wakefulness. Her head still resting on Cata's shoulder, Sarah said softly, "I'm starving."

Cata answered in kind, "I'm starving, too."

Sarah gave a quick kiss to Cata before rolling from the bed. She was aware Cata rose to her elbow to study Sarah as she stepped to the chifforobe to retrieve her robe and secure it about her body with the sash. She removed the hanger from the bathrobe Cata had worn the previous night and tossed the robe onto the bed. "I'm finding food."

Cata threw back the covers to stand. Sarah waited in the doorway, glimpsing Cata's strong body before she concealed it in the wrap of the robe. Sarah held out her hand to Cata, then led her into the kitchen. They rifled through the remnants of the picnic baskets to discover bread, cheese, pickled vegetables, and olives. "Will this do?" Sarah asked.

"It's a feast," Cata replied.

When Sarah walked from the table to retrieve tableware and cutlery, Cata followed, pressing against Sarah as she reached for the shelved plates. Kissing Sarah's neck, Cata slid her hand into Sarah's robe, caressing her breasts. Sarah closed her eyes, enjoying the touch. Then, she said with a thick throatiness, "I thought you were hungry."

"Mmm," Cata whispered, her mouth at Sarah's ear, "starving."

Sarah laughed, turning into Cata's arms. "Then we'd better eat first."

Cata released her hold on Sarah. While Sarah positioned the plates and utensils on the table, Cata poured two glasses of water and joined her.

Sarah placed a roll on each of their plates while Cata cut two thick wedges of cheese. They took turns fishing out olives and pickled vegetables from the jars and onto their plates, then lifted their water glasses in a toast before beginning their meal. And as they ate and talked, they couldn't resist touching: Sarah running the side of her foot along the back of Cata's calf; Cata tracing the length of Sarah's fingers wrapped around her glass.

When they finished supper, they separated long enough for Sarah to tidy the kitchen while Cata stepped into the bathroom to prepare for bed. Once Cata announced she had completed her nighttime preparations, Sarah entered the bathroom for a quick sponge bath before brushing her teeth.

Sarah returned to the bedroom to find Cata sitting on the edge of the bed waiting for her. Cata stood and slid the robe from her body. Sarah sucked in her breath to see Cata standing unclothed, wanting her. She went to Cata, who untied Sarah's sash and removed her bathrobe. They returned to bed to make love then hold while sleep overtook them.

When morning came, they lay, still entangled in one another's embrace. Sarah sensed by Cata's breathing that she was awake, but Sarah did not want to disturb their quiet, knowing that when they left the bed, Cata would prepare for her return to Mexico, to the revolution. Sarah dreaded that moment of departure.

Finally, Cata broke the calm. Kissing Sarah's forehead, Cata whispered, "I have to go, mi amor."

"I know," Sarah quietly acknowledged, though neither made an effort to leave the bed.

After another five minutes of holding, Cata gently whispered, "I must get up."

Sarah rose to kiss Cata, then rolled from her arms and from the bed.

"I'll make breakfast. I want to make a meal for you before you leave."

Cata stood from the bed to dress in the robe she discarded the previous night.

"By the time you finish your preparations to depart, the food should be ready."

Sarah dressed quickly before heading into the kitchen. She lit the oven to warm the rolls, then busied herself with frying potatoes smothered in onions, frying slices of bacon, scrambling eggs with chopped tomatoes, onions, and jalapeño. The activity helped distract her from thinking about Cata's departure.

As Sarah lowered the flame, she felt Cata's arms wrap her in an embrace and her lips warm and moist against her neck. Sarah turned into the hold to share a kiss before Cata released her.

"The food is ready," Sarah informed.

When Cata stepped back, Sarah examined her handsome figure in the fitted black embroidered pants and jacket. "You're beautiful!"

Cata shifted the attention from herself by reaching onto the shelf to collect two plates and mugs, then pouring the coffee while Sarah served the food.

Seated at the table, they ate with a quiet sadness, neither one relishing the meal. Finally, Sarah stopped forcing herself to eat. She spoke her heart. "I know you have to leave, but I want you to stay."

"I wish I could stay with you, Sarah, but you are right, I must go."

"Cata, be safe and come back to me."

Cata reached across the table to take Sarah's hand. "I will do everything I can to return to you, Sarah." Cata leaned forward to kiss Sarah's palm, then stood. "I have to leave now."

"I'll drive you to the train station," Sarah responded, looking for a way to be in Cata's presence a little longer.

"No, Sarah."

"Then I'll drive you to the bridge," she offered hopefully.

Cata considered the offer. "All right."

Sarah remained seated at the table to allow Cata time to collect her things. When Cata returned to the kitchen, she carried the large satchel in one hand and a sombrero in the other.

"It's time, Sarah."

Sarah stood to gather her coat and hat. They paused to hold one another, to kiss before exiting the apartment and descending the stairs into the studio. At the bottom of the steps, Sarah called out, "Wait, Cata, let me photograph you."

When Cata started to protest, Sarah quickly exclaimed, "Leave me with something of you until you return."

"Yes, Sarah," Cata agreed, "but we must hurry."

Sarah directed Cata into the portrait studio, positioning her against a white backdrop. Sarah knew she had little time, so she focused the camera on Cata gripping her sombrero and depressed the lever.

"One more wearing your hat," Sarah directed.

Cata placed the sombrero on her head, then focused on Sarah behind the camera. Sarah depressed the shutter release.

"We must go now, Sarah." Cata stepped from the backdrop.

They exited the studio to Sarah's automobile. As Sarah drove south toward the Santa Fe International Bridge, she repeated silently to herself, "Don't cry." She had so much to say to Cata, but Sarah didn't trust herself to speak, so she drove in silence until they reached the bridge.

Once Sarah stopped the car a few yards from the bridge, she reached toward Cata, who leaned across the seat to embrace her and kiss her cheek. Looking into her eyes, Sarah stated, "I will wait for you, mi amor."

Cata squeezed Sarah's hands, replying, "I will find you, Sarah." Then she exited the car.

Sarah watched Cata walk across the international bridge into Mexico. While she hoped Cata might pause to look back, Cata didn't, and Sarah knew neither of them could bear it if she did.

Catalina

Catalina felt discomfort from the hard wooden bench pressing into her legs and back through worn upholstery. Sitting with her face turned toward the window, she kept her eyes shut to passing scenery. The rough rattle of the train jostled her against Mateo, who shared her seat, further fraying Catalina's already ragged nerves.

They had boarded the Central Mexicano at the Juárez train depot over two hours ago, and with each clacking mile, Catalina's longing for Sarah increased. She had not gone to El Paso with the intention of loving Sarah. Catalina had returned to the border with Mateo following orders to transport partial payment for an arms shipment. But Catalina knew she would now do all within her power to regain her soul's peace she thought she'd lost amid the blood and horror of war, to regain a spiritual calm she hoped she might find anew with Sarah.

JANUARY 1915

Sarah

Sarah and Timothy waited outside the Juárez Customs House where General Pancho Villa, now supreme chief general of the Conventionist forces in Mexico, was meeting with General Hugh Scott, now chief of staff of the US Army. The generals and their staffs were negotiating an agreement to halt fighting between Conventionist forces and Carrancistas along the Arizona-Mexico border in order to stop the deaths, injuries, and damages caused when bullets ignored the international boundary.

The dual line of Villista soldiers snapped to attention, presenting arms at the front entrance of the customs house. Sarah and Timothy knew the exodus of dignitaries would soon follow. First, Generals Villa and Scott exited side by side, Villa dressed in a three-piece civilian suit beside Scott, who strode in full military uniform including spurs secured to his riding boots, an unbuttoned fur-lined coat flapping around his burly figure. The remaining dignitaries filled in the background of Sarah's focusing hood as she captured a photo of the participants departing the building.

Shouts of "Viva Villa!" rang out from the crowd gathered across the street as the generals entered waiting cars without pausing to answer reporters' questions. After the automobiles drove away, an official spokesperson exited the building to stand on the steps of the customs house with the announcement that an agreement had been signed. That proclamation concluded the briefing, and the spokesperson reentered the building. Immediately, the crowd began to disperse at the spectacle's end.

"Well," Timothy sounded disheartened, "I hope your photos can shore up my story. It's a bit thin right now." He assisted Sarah, collapsing the tripod after she removed her camera. They started to leave when someone called out, "Mrs. Clendenin!" She turned to see Villa's slight bespectacled translator from the Pershing reception. He waved as he hurried down the steps of the customs house. "Mrs. Clendenin," he repeated when he reached them, nodding briefly to Timothy, "General Villa asked me to inform you and your colleague that following lunch, General Scott and members of today's signing party will spend a pleasant afternoon at the Juárez Racetrack." He brushed a forefinger against each wing of his massive moustache before continuing. "General Villa wishes me to convey that if you enjoy spending a January afternoon betting on horses, and you choose a good position in the stands, you might be able to capture photographs of the generals and their party watching the races from the center top viewing box."

"Thank you," Sarah answered excitedly, "thank you, Señor. . . ?"

"César Ricardo Villaseñor Maldonado, at your service," and he removed his hat to perform a slight bow.

"Thank you," Sarah concluded.

"Yes," Timothy extended an ungloved hand, "much appreciated."

Villa's messenger departed as quickly as he had arrived.

"Well," Timothy remarked, holding the tripod in one hand while reaching with the other to take the Sarah's camera, "my story may have just gotten more interesting." He smiled. "Come on, I'll buy lunch; then we're off to the races."

Timothy guided Sarah to Flora's Café, a small restaurant located behind the customs house. The café served a comida corrida, so without discussion of the menu, Flora delivered two steaming cups of albondigas, a Mexican meatball soup, soon followed by courses including salad, beef, rice, frijoles, and corn tortillas, concluding with a large cup of coffee and a dessert of stewed fruit.

After Timothy paid the bill, the drive to the racetrack took only ten minutes. Timothy carried the camera, halting prior to entering the grandstand to purchase a racing program. They scoured the stands for the best position to capture photos of the now-vacant center viewing box. Sarah directed Timothy to a section in the middle of the grandstand that she thought provided the best angle for photographs of the upper level.

After they had climbed the steps and secured their seats, Timothy immediately removed the racing program from his coat pocket and began studying it. Sarah had never been to the racetrack even though she knew it was a popular destination for El Pasoans, in fact, so popular it was a main stop on one of the streetcar lines. She studied the large oval track before her and examined the stands that stretched on either side, concluding at two large cupolas, each topped with the Mexican flag. Though the stands were open air, a large roof extended to cover three-quarters of the bench-seating. The chilled January day and the dusky smell of horses made Sarah recall her childhood visiting friends' farms.

When a bugle sounded, Timothy leaned toward Sarah and without taking his eyes from the program, he explained, "That's the 'Call to Post.'"

"And?"

"That call signals the race will start in about ten minutes. Now, the jockeys will parade their horses before the stands."

Sarah turned to glance toward the center viewing box. It remained empty, so she focused her attention on the horses prancing before them.

"Beautiful," Sarah commented. "I like the look of the gray."

"Yes," Timothy concurred, glancing back at his program for supporting information before returning his focus to the horses. "Look at number nine. Not as large as some of the others, but notice the muscle tone, notice the alertness of its ears monitoring surrounding sounds."

Sarah turned again to look at the upper viewing box for Generals Villa and Scott and saw them entering the railed section followed by other members of their party who gathered behind the generals and on the steps leading into their box. Sarah elbowed Timothy. "They've arrived."

Timothy looked, then commented, "Seems to be largely the same group we saw departing the customs house."

Sarah lowered the camera bed to extend the lens in preparation. She hoped to capture a few good photographs without making herself obvious or intrusive.

Timothy excused himself to place a bet. While Sarah sat alone, she photographed the track and the stands, which now hosted a sizeable crowd. Timothy returned carrying a bottle of beer and a bottle of soda, extending the latter to her. In a relatively short while, crew members waiting at the starting barrier led the horses and jockeys into their assigned positions. Soon after the crew lined up the horses, the official starter held his flag aloft. When the starter dropped the flag sharply to signal the beginning of the race, the horses burst from the starting line. Spectators in the stands rose to their feet, cheering their favorites as the horses raced down the straightaway, the shouts growing louder as the horses rounded the curve.

Sarah shifted in her seat to see Villa and Scott standing at the railing of their box, watching the thundering horses, the excitement of the race registered on their faces. Villa cupped his hands around his mouth to shout encouragements to the racing horses. Sarah lifted her camera, peered through the focusing hood, bringing the generals into sharp view, and depressed the lens release. Quickly forwarding the film, she caught a second photo of Villa, his arm extended, directing Scott's attention to the horses pounding across the finish line.

"Well, your gray took it," Timothy observed excitedly, holding up a ticket. Once the official finishing order was posted, he excused himself to collect on his bet.

During Timothy's absence, Sarah looked again into the upper viewing box and saw Villa and Scott now seated in chairs facing each other. Elbows resting on knees, they leaned forward in what appeared to be intense talk. Sarah rose to her feet to capture a photograph of them. Just as she prepared to sit, Timothy returned. "Hold out your hand," he directed.

"Why?"

"Trust me. Hold out your hand," Timothy insisted.

Sarah extended her right hand, into which Timothy placed a nickel and two dimes.

"What's this?"

"Your winnings on the gray."

"I didn't bet."

"I placed a bet for you."

When she started to protest, Timothy held up a hand to stop her. "I pocketed my initial investment; you get the winnings."

Timothy looked toward the box where Villa and Scott sat. "I'm going to see if I can get an interview or at least a quote. Be right back." When he stepped into the aisle, he added, "Wish me luck."

Sarah watched Timothy stride two steps at a time toward the generals' viewing box. One of Villa's men waylaid Timothy at the bottom of the steps leading to the generals. Just when Sarah feared Timothy would be turned away, she saw him catch General Villa's eye. Villa glanced briefly at Sarah, then smiled at Timothy and waved him up to join them. At the sound of the bugled "Call to Post," Sarah returned her attention to the racetrack.

She watched the escort riders lead the racehorses and jockeys onto the track for their parade before the spectators. As Sarah studied the horses, she heard a man's voice ask, "May I join you, Miss Delaney?"

Sarah looked to see General Scott standing at the entrance of her row, smiling.

"Yes, please do," and she scooted over to allow more room.

"I saw you sitting alone and wanted to take the opportunity to visit briefly with you."

"I'm glad you did though I think my colleague had hoped to interview you."

General Scott glanced toward the viewing box, then said with a chuckle, "I think General Villa will be happy to regale the young reporter with news of our meeting along with other tales." He returned his attention to her. "So how have you been, Miss Delaney, since we last met?"

Sarah blushed, remembering that at their last meeting she had requested his assistance with the return of Samuel's body and knowing that General Scott would have learned of Samuel's deception. "I've been doing very well, thank you," she answered, trying to sound nonchalant. "And yourself?"

"I'm well," he replied. "The army keeps me busy, what with the revolution in Mexico and the war in Europe. Lots to do, lots to monitor." He looked at the track and the parade of horses. "Beautiful animals, aren't they?"

"Yes, they are."

"Do you ride, Miss Delaney?"

"I did as a girl," she answered, coloring again from a flashback to her more recent Arizona gun-smuggling adventure. She motioned toward the horses as they moved toward the starting line. "Do you bet on the horses, General Scott?"

He chuckled before answering, "No, no. General Villa and I share a reluctance to bet on horses. After all, what would it do to our reputations as cavalry officers if we can't pick the winning horse?" He chuckled again at the thought.

He looked beyond the racetrack at the Franklin Mountains in the distance. "I love this part of the country—the beauty of the mountains, the serenity of the desert."

"I agree."

"I think fondly of my time at Fort Bliss and of the good people I was blessed to meet." He looked at Sarah. "You among them, Miss Delaney."

Sarah felt surprised by this statement, and she stammered, "Thank you."

"Did I ever tell you that I have a Sarah?"

Sarah shook her head in response.

"She's fourteen, my youngest. You remind me of her, Miss Delaney—spirited and kind."

"Thank you, sir," Sarah uttered.

"Well," he slapped his thigh, "I'd better return to my host." Scott stood, adding, "It's been wonderful to visit with you, Miss Delaney." He tipped his hat before starting up the steps to the viewing box.

Sarah sat quietly reflecting on the conversation even when the crowd erupted at the start of the horse race. She remained seated while those around her jumped to their feet to watch until the horses charged across the finish line.

"Got it," Timothy appeared beside her. "Got my interview and my story," he announced excitedly. "More important," he sat beside her, grinning broadly, "Villa invited me to travel in the press car of one of his trains."

"Wow!" she responded, genuinely impressed. "Can you?"

"I'll have to clear it through the *Times*, but I'm sure they'd love to have a reporter embedded with Villa's army, at least for a short period of time." Timothy stood, extending his hand to take her camera. "Ready to head back to El Paso?"

Sarah closed the camera before handing it to Timothy. When she stood to depart the stands, Sarah glanced toward the viewing box. General Scott sat with his back to the track, speaking with another officer, but General Villa tipped his hat to her with a broad smile. She acknowledged with a wave before starting down the steps.

APRIL 1915

Sarah

"**Enough** about fresh air," A. J. responded grumpily to Sarah's offer to go for a drive so he could enjoy a change of scenery and some fresh air. "I want to work. I want to be back in the darkroom."

"Glad you're feeling so much better," Sarah responded.

"Well, tell me you couldn't use the help at the studio." He stared challengingly over the protective mask covering much of his face.

A. J. was right. The orders for photo postcards came in faster than she could print copies to fill them, even starting early in the morning and working late into the night. Still, she worried about A. J. in the darkroom inhaling chemicals. His health had improved, so she didn't want to risk a setback.

Taking advantage of the pause, A. J. added, "Two hours, just give me two hours in the darkroom. Besides, I need to make sure you haven't frilled up the place."

"Okay," Sarah relented, "two hours, but I take no responsibility should you have a setback with your health."

"Nor should you," he countered.

Though A. J.'s stubborn insistence concerned her, Sarah understood his desire to return to the darkroom.

A. J. maintained his gruff manner as they left the lawn of the sanitorium heading to her automobile, and he insisted on cranking the car even though the exertion winded him.

"So, have you heard from Timothy?" A. J. questioned after they drove from the sanitorium compound.

Sarah directed the vehicle toward downtown. "No," she responded, "I've just seen his stories in the paper, which I'm sure you've read."

"How much longer will he be traveling with Villa's troops?"

"Timothy left in late March. The *Times* gave him two months, so I don't expect him back for at least another month."

"Since my days are largely the same, I lose all track of time," A. J. responded. The conversation concluded, A. J. stared with interest at the passing scenery, despite his previous objection to going for a drive.

Sarah thought about Timothy's departure. The Sunday prior to his leaving to join Villa's troops, Timothy met Sarah and Paola at Hotel Paso del Norte for a late lunch. Sarah smiled remembering how he walked into the hotel attired in the outfit he bought for "field work," as he described it. Upon entering the lobby, he removed the large felt hat with the left side of the brim fastened to the crown and took off a tan overcoat he wore like a cape. Beneath the coat, Timothy dressed in a Norfolk jacket and English riding breeches with leather leggings belted about his calves. He cut quite a figure for a Sunday lunch. An outfit in search of an adventure, Sarah thought at the time, but she complimented rather than teased Timothy, who strutted with sartorial pride. They spent that afternoon enjoying one another's company, discussing with excitement what Timothy might encounter when he traveled deeper into Mexico and, once again, into the midst of the fighting. At the conclusion of lunch, Paola and Sarah each wished Timothy well, planting a parting kiss on his cheek. Sarah added a request for him to keep an eye out for Coronela Catalina Vasquez, and if he were to encounter Cata, tell her, "Sarah holds you warmly in her thoughts and prayers."

Sarah returned her focus to the present, slowing the car to park in front of the studio. A. J. opened the passenger door the moment the vehicle halted. He fished in his pockets for the key to the studio, then, in his excitement, hurried into the building without thought of Sarah, who followed. He looked around like a man verifying he had not imagined his surroundings. He examined the display of photos, ran his hand across the front counter, and placed his fingers on the keys of the cash register. Then, he stepped past the curtain and headed toward the darkroom, calling to Sarah, "What postcards need printing?" A. J. waited at the door of the darkroom for Sarah to bring him the list; then he shooed her away, refusing to allow her to join him even briefly. "Go read a magazine or take a nap. I'll see you in two hours," A. J. said, then closed the door.

Sarah fought the urge to hover about the studio in case A. J. needed her. Forcing herself to climb the stairs to the apartment, she propped the door open to hear if he called for her, though she knew he would not. She poured a glass of water, then sat at the kitchen table, distractedly flipping through the latest issue of *Studio Light*.

After occupying herself for an hour, Sarah crept downstairs to listen at the darkroom door. She asked loudly, "A. J., want a cup of coffee?"

"I've got one more hour," he responded. "Go away and let me work."

Sarah smiled at the response. Clearly, A. J. was fine toiling in his element. She returned upstairs to wait out the second hour. She tried to stay occupied doing minor chores around the apartment. When she glanced at the clock and saw it was time to retrieve A. J. from the darkroom, she felt relieved. She gathered her things and left the apartment to call outside the darkroom door, "A. J., are you ready?"

"Give me a couple minutes to finish," he answered.

Sarah waited for him in the front of the studio. A. J. emerged from the darkroom, squinting at the sunlight shining through the windows. Sarah noted a weariness about A. J. and hoped he hadn't overexerted himself. Still, he also exuded an air of satisfaction.

"I loaded a couple batches of postcards into the print dryer with just the fan blowing, no heat. They should be dry by the time you return. Now," he added, "I'm ready to head back to the sanitorium for a quick nap before supper."

A. J. remained largely quiet during their drive to the sanitorium. When Sarah pulled into the parking area at the edge of the lawn, A. J. turned to her and said, "Thank you, Sarah, for giving me the opportunity to work."

Sarah nodded, saying, "Now take your well-deserved rest. I'll see you again soon."

"Yes," he added, "let's plan on repeating this arrangement next Sunday. I think the darkroom is the best treatment for what ails me." A. J. exited the car, waving goodbye before Sarah could reply.

She watched until A. J. disappeared through the front door; then she steered the car toward home.

After Sarah entered the studio and hung her hat on the hall tree, she went into the darkroom to switch off the dryer fan. She removed the rolled sheets of corrugated board and blotting paper that cradled the postcards A. J. had printed. Placing the roll on a long worktable, she opened it a section at a time to remove rows of newly dried postcards. A. J. had made good progress, and she stacked postcards printed from their 1913 negative of the firing squad. Sarah placed the emptied drying sheets aside, then removed another roll from the dryer's second cylinder. Again, she opened the sheets of corrugated board and muslin-lined blotting paper, retrieving a stack of postcards printed of Villa and Scott at the racetrack. She unrolled the sheets further to reveal the next rows of postcards. Flipping over the first card, Sarah felt a sick jolt in the pit of her stomach. She moaned, "Oh no, no, A. J." Sarah stared at Cata, sombrero positioned on her head, cutting a strong, beautiful figure. Sarah understood why A. J. would print copies of the negative, but Sarah would not sell photos of Cata.

Sarah plucked the postcards from the drying sheets and hurried upstairs to place them on the bed, then returned to the darkroom to retrieve the negatives. Back in the apartment, she held the postcards momentarily over her heart before stacking them along with the negatives in a drawer of the chifforobe under folded handkerchiefs and underclothes. She would not profit from photos of Cata; she would not allow Cata to become a souvenir of the revolution.

❖❖❖

Though it was the fourth Sunday in a row that A. J. worked alone in the darkroom, Sarah still propped open the apartment door to listen for sounds that might indicate he needed help. When loud banging suddenly emanated from the studio, she startled. Hurrying down the stairs, she realized the thumps sounded from the front door. She met A. J. exiting the darkroom to investigate the commotion. Together they walked to the locked front door to see Timothy, his hands cupped around his eyes and pressed to the glass, trying to peer into the darkened studio. Under his arm, he cradled a package in a paper sack.

A. J. unlocked the door. "You're making a lot of racket," A. J. protested, hugging Timothy to him. "When did you get back in town?"

"Friday night," he answered, reaching to embrace Sarah in a bear hug.

Sarah smelled alcohol on Timothy's breath and noted the unsteadiness of his stance when he clasped her to him. She also felt the thinness of his body through his loose suit jacket.

"It's so good to see both of you." Timothy held the paper sack in the air. "A little something for us to toast my return home."

"Come up to the apartment," Sarah directed. "I'll get glasses, and you can tell us about your adventure."

Sarah noticed A. J.'s hesitancy. He remained careful when working in the studio, always wearing his mask, washing his hands, and limiting the areas he accessed. He never ventured beyond the studio entrance and the darkroom.

"It's okay, A. J.," Sarah encouraged. "You can keep your mask on except to take a drink."

"Come on," Timothy urged. "Let's celebrate my survival and return," adding, "both of which were very questionable."

"Always the journalist," A. J. responded, "leading the story with a hook." He looked to Sarah. "If you think it's all right."

"I'm sure, A. J." She took Timothy's arm. "Let's go upstairs." Sarah led the way followed by Timothy, then A. J. She directed them into the kitchen, where Timothy removed a bottle of champagne from the sack.

Sarah retrieved three wine glasses and placed them at the center of the table. "These will have to do."

"They're perfect," Timothy announced, removing the wire cage, twisting the cork back and forth until it exploded from the bottle. Placing the cork on the table, he poured the bubbly liquid into each glass, then handed a wine glass to Sarah and one to A. J. Timothy plopped gracelessly into a chair at the head of the table, raised his glass, motioning for them to follow, and toasted, "To sweet home El Paso."

A. J. added, "To your safe return to El Paso."

They clinked glasses.

From the corner of her eye, Sarah saw A. J. untie his mask to place the glass to his lips before quickly securing the mask once again.

Sarah wanted to ask Timothy for news of Cata, but she refrained. Observing that his tipsy good humor appeared forced, she simply stated, "Tell us about your trip."

"Well," he drained his champagne, then poured half a glass, "first, the accommodations. A converted grain car served as relatively comfortable press lodgings for five of us. We had roughhewn bunks, a toilet, a kitchen with a stove that vented through the roof, and a long table made of wood planks on which we ate our meals and wrote our stories. Villa even provided a Chinese cook named Wong, and though our variety of victuals was usually limited, Wong worked magic with whatever we managed to find in towns and communities along the way." Timothy paused to take a gulp from his glass, then added, "What we lacked in nutrition, we made up for in alcohol." He raised his glass to demonstrate, taking another long drink.

"It took days for us to make any real progress toward our destination of Irapuato. The railway men had orders to take us south, but every time we got underway, our train would soon have to switch from the main rail to allow a troop train to pass, so we moved south at a crawl." Timothy finished the inch of wine remaining in his glass, then reached for the half-empty bottle. "We were a fun-loving lot. Excited, like boys on an outing, as though the revolution existed to provide us adventure and our press credentials to afford us immunity. Often, when we got stuck on a side rail, we'd slide open the door to sit with our legs dangling outside the press car, taking turns regaling one another with stories of past adventures or competing to see who knew the most outlandish verses of 'La Cucaracha' until finally our train returned, however briefly, to the main rail.

"One day, we had a lengthy delay in Torreón. The congestion on the tracks had increased dramatically, with troops being shuttled toward Irapuato to confront Obregón's army that had marched north from Mexico City and established a position in Celaya, south of Irapuato. I took advantage of that wait to wander around Torreón."

Sarah studied Timothy's face while he talked, noting that it lacked the joyous animation usually present when he related a tale.

"Villistas filled the streets, so I gathered what information I could about their upcoming offensive. While I wandered about, I encountered old men and young boys searching through horse manure dropped by Villista mounts. I asked a boy why he combed through horse stools. He looked at me with a quizzical expression, clearly surprised by my lack of knowledge. 'For corn,' he answered, then proudly opened a dirty cloth sack to display a handful of partially digested kernels he had already collected. 'If I find enough corn, my mother can make tortillas for us,' he said."

"Good Lord," Sarah exclaimed, placing her hand over her mouth.

Timothy looked at Sarah as if she had broken his spell. "Yes. Think about it. For the last five years, the Mexican people have participated, willingly or otherwise, in Mexico's ongoing revolution. So, who is planting crops? Who is raising livestock? And who is prioritized when food supplies are available?

"Late that afternoon," Timothy resumed his story, "our patchwork press corps reassembled back at the train car we called home, each bringing bits of news along with whatever else we managed to forage, which amounted to two bottles of tequila, six potatoes, two cans of asparagus, a small sack of beans, an onion, a few dried chiles, and half a side of goat." Timothy finished the wine in his glass; then he raised the bottle in offering to Sarah and A. J. When they refused, Timothy drained the remaining content into his glass. "We feasted that night," Timothy said, taking a drink. "And as I devoured the delicious meal Wong prepared, I thought about that young boy who collected partially-digested corn from piles of horse manure to help feed his family." Timothy stared at the table, adding, "But I ate my fill, nevertheless, and went to bed with a belly full of food and alcohol." He paused, tracing the rim of the glass before continuing. "Sometime just before dawn, I was jolted awake by the spastic start of the train resuming its trek south.

"By the time our train reached Irapuato, the battle between Villa and Obregón had already begun. In the days following the conclusion of the battle, I learned that Obregón had mistakenly believed Villa amassed the bulk of his troops at Irapuato, when in fact Villa had positioned them farther south, about midway between Irapuato and Celaya. Obregón directed fifteen hundred men north to sever rail lines to impede the advance of Villa's troops on Celaya, where Obregón had positioned the majority of his army. Those fifteen hundred troops came close to annihilation when they encountered Villa's vastly superior force. Obregón, learning of the potential disaster, took a troop train to rescue his men.'"

Timothy paused to take a drink before continuing. "Villa underestimated Obregón's skill as a tactician and commander. In fact, Villa frequently called him El Perfumado, suggesting Obregón was a dandy, a sissy." Timothy shook his head in disbelief. "In an interview, Villa even predicted disdainfully that Obregón would withdraw rather than fight Villa's troops. So when Obregón's train retreated toward Celaya with his rescued soldiers, Obregón knew Villa would pursue. Familiar with Villa's penchant for ordering his troops to charge the opponent, Obregón had prepared in the days prior to battle. Using the myriad irrigation ditches that crisscrossed the region, Obregón created a network of fortified trenches similar to the trench warfare fought in the current European conflict. Employing well-placed machine guns, Obregón's troops mowed down the Villistas as they charged over and over and over and over and over again," Timothy repeated, closing his eyes, "their bodies tangling in the barbed wire protecting the trenches."

Tears welled in Sarah's eyes as she thought of Cata. Sarah remained quiet, both wanting Timothy to tell his story but not wanting to hear the details of what Cata lived through . . . God, Sarah hoped Cata had survived it.

Timothy continued. "On the second day of fighting, I borrowed a horse and rode toward the battlefield with about twenty-five Villistas. As we got closer to the struggle, we began passing soldiers, most of them wounded or assisting injured comrades or both. They struggled to make their way from the fighting and toward medical care. Many asked politely for a drink of water. We shared most of what we brought in our canteens while gathering information about the battle from them, but the steady stream of injured warriors threatened to drain our own supply. Stragglers whose requests for water we had to deny received the news with a dignified resignation, resuming their march toward medical care.

"When we neared the fighting, the cloying stench of death hung heavy in the air from corpses bloated and rotting in the day's heat and the fields' mud." Timothy pinched the bridge of his nose between two fingers as if attempting to block the remembered smell. He took another drink before continuing. "I stayed a relatively safe distance from the battle and watched the fighting through field glasses for much of the remaining day. At one point it appeared Villa's troops broke through Obregón's line, but confusion followed, with Villa's soldiers retreating at the sound of a bugler's call. That's when Obregón counterattacked with fresh troops, defeating Villa's war-wearied soldiers, many carrying rifles emptied of ammunition, unable to return fire."

"Initially," Timothy paused to take a drink, "both sides proclaimed victory, with Villa declaring the shortage of ammunition as reason for his troops leaving the battlefield. And, in truth, the lack of ammunition did impact Villa's ability to continue fighting, but it is also true that he failed to adjust to Obregón's trench warfare. Villa lost three thousand soldiers who were killed, wounded, or captured."

Timothy continued. "Villa pulled back to await ammunition and additional troops. Still denying defeat, Villa announced he was allowing his soldiers and horses time to rest before the next offensive.

"Six days after his first loss, Villa attacked Obregón's entrenched troops again, convinced the frontal assault and cavalry charges that had served him well in all but the most recent battle would win the day. For almost forty-eight hours, Villa's troops shelled then charged the enemy, who had reinforced their positions with additional soldiers, barbed wire, and machine guns during the previous week's delay in fighting." Timothy drained his glass. "I, again, watched from a relatively safe distance when, on the third day of fighting, Obregón released a cavalry force of about six thousand that he had held in reserve, sheltered in nearby woods. Villa had neither reconnoitered the region, nor had he held any soldiers in reserve. Obregón's fresh cavalry troops caught Villa completely by surprise. The cavalry routed Villa's exhausted soldiers, who abandoned artillery, rifles, and comrades in a frantic race to flee the battlefield and the enemy.

"I later interviewed an officer who managed to escape Obregón's attack by scrambling up a hill. From that point of elevation, he viewed what he initially thought were battalions of Villistas poised to join the fight, but he soon realized the gathered troops were Villistas whom Obregón had taken prisoner. Of the prisoners Obregón captured, over 120 were officers, whom he promptly had executed."

Sarah gasped. "What of Colonel Catalina Vasquez?" Sarah blurted. "Was Colonel Vasquez among those executed?" she asked with an urgency that exhibited her barely controlled emotions. "Do you know her fate?"

Timothy reached to take Sarah's hand. "I do know, Sarah. Colonel Vasquez is the reason I'm here."

Sarah looked intently at Timothy, trying to decipher that statement. "What do you mean, Timothy? Is she alive?"

"Yes, Sarah. She's very much alive." He squeezed Sarah's hand reassuringly. "And I'm alive and returned to El Paso because of her."

Timothy reached into the inner pocket of his jacket and removed a metal flask. After Sarah and A. J. declined the offered flask, Timothy took a serious slug of alcohol. Rather than returning the flask to his pocket, Timothy stood it on the table, keeping it readily available to assist him through the telling of his tale.

"Two days following Villa's second defeat at Celaya, I rode into Irapuato to file a story. Before the piece could be sent over military wires, Major Samaniego, who served as censor, had to read and approve its filing. I had worked with Samaniego previously and our interactions had always been cordial. But when I entered the telegraph office that morning, I interrupted a heated discussion among Samaniego and two other soldiers, all of whom had been drinking heavily. I greeted everyone in the office and handed Samaniego my dispatch, which he glanced at and, without reading, shredded into pieces that he then threw at me. Shocked, I asked the reason for his actions. He responded by grabbing a newspaper from his desk and shaking it at me, shouting, 'You've allowed the Scorpion into the United States.' I explained that I didn't know what he meant, that I had been with Villa's troops for weeks. Now standing and shaking the paper grasped in his fist, he shouted, 'General Victoriano Huerta left his exile in Spain, and is now in the United States. We die to free our country from President Madero's murderer, and the United States welcomes him so he can scheme his return to México.'"

Timothy paused to take another swig from the flask, wiping his mouth with the back of his hand. "It didn't matter that I swore not to know anything about Huerta's arrival in the US; it didn't matter that I agreed the US should not have allowed Huerta's entrance into the country. Nothing I said made a difference in the minds of these three Villistas; I represented the United States, and they would have their justice."

Sarah saw Timothy swallow hard before he continued. "They sentenced me to die."

"Good Lord, Timothy," A. J. blurted, startled by the turn in the story.

"'Good Lord,' is right, A. J.; I immediately found religion," Timothy responded as if trying to lighten the mood, but his voice lacked even feigned humor. "The three Villistas argued among themselves whether I should be shot in the head and dumped on the street or marched behind the building to be executed against a wall with the three of them serving as my firing squad. Finally, Samaniego determined I should be hanged to preserve ammunition already in short supply. So, with a gun at my back, I was marched from the building while one of the soldiers removed a rope from his saddle, then fashioned a noose, which he placed over my head and tightened." Timothy paused, staring at his two hands outstretched on the table.

Sarah reached to place one of her hands on top of one of Timothy's.

He raised his eyes to look at Sarah. "That is when she appeared," he said, "your Colonel Vasquez. She asked where they were taking me. She asked my offense. She told them she would escort me to prison to await a military hearing, and she ordered them to return to work. When they hesitated to release me into her custody, she responded with an unholstered pistol and a warning that their insubordination and drunkenness would land them in front of a firing squad long before I ever saw one. Begrudgingly, they released me to her charge. She quickly commandeered a passing wagon, had me climb into its bed, then climbed in beside me, her pistol still gripped in her hand. I became hysterical. I immediately began swearing I had nothing to do with Huerta's entrance into the US and begging for her mercy. She replied simply, 'I'm taking you to the train station. You're leaving.' I was in such a state of panic, I had to ask her to repeat her statement. When she said, 'You're returning to El Paso,' I'll admit, I wept. And when I regained some composure, I asked her how she knew I came from El Paso. That's when she identified herself as Coronela Catalina Vasquez and said she recognized me from Samuel's funeral procession, having seen me with you." Timothy gripped Sarah's hand. "Your Colonel Vasquez took me to the train station, arranged to get me onboard a freight train preparing to depart Irapuato, and promised to get word to my fellow journalists left behind."

"Thank God Cata found you," Sarah replied.

"Thank God, indeed," Timothy agreed. "Before I boarded the train, Sarah, I conveyed your message to her."

"Oh, thank you, Timothy." Sarah leaned back in the chair feeling emotionally exhausted from hearing Timothy's tale and from feeling relief knowing Cata lived.

"Colonel Vasquez sent a message to you."

Sarah sat erect, anxious to hear.

"She said to tell you, 'Soon.' That's all she said, 'Soon.'"

Sarah could not contain her tears. That one word said everything.

JUNE 1915

Sarah

Sarah gripped the steering wheel tightly, unfamiliar with the narrow dusty road illuminated by the car's headlights. As she drove toward the train station in Newman, twenty miles northeast of El Paso, she listened to Timothy talk excitedly about the anticipated arrest of General Victoriano Huerta, whom Timothy held responsible for his near-death experience in Mexico last April. "This is personal," he said when he phoned her at 4:00 a.m. to ask her to join him. Sarah readily agreed. She wanted to see the arrest of the man who led a bloody coup, the man against whom Cata fought and whose troops had caused Samuel's death.

El Paso had been abuzz for weeks with rumors of a Huerta-led counterrevolution to retake the reins of government in Mexico. Ever since Huerta entered the United States in mid-April, newspapers reported activities suggesting El Paso might serve as the launch site for this latest movement. In May, General Pascual Orozco—one of

Huerta's chief commanders—relocated to El Paso. Then large numbers of Huerta's former officers and political allies began taking up residence at the Hotel Paso del Norte.

Steadying the car against a gust of wind that blew across the desert, Sarah questioned, "Huerta's been in the US since April, so why arrest him now?"

"I'm sure the government has surveilled Huerta ever since his arrival in this country, but his trek to the border is a big deal. My sources tell me the Bureau of Investigation has evidence of munitions warehoused in El Paso to support a Huerta-led military expedition, with Ciudad Juárez as their first target. I expect we'll see more than just Huerta arrested for violating US neutrality laws.

"There, up ahead." Timothy pointed to a small railway station with an unusual amount of activity.

Sarah steered onto the turnoff, parking alongside other vehicles in the dirt lot. The sky had lightened considerably with sunrise, and Sarah could see that several American soldiers formed a perimeter around shrubs with a tall lanky man standing in the vicinity. Sarah recognized the man as General Pascual Orozco.

"Let me find out what's going on," Timothy said, exiting the automobile.

Sarah watched Timothy jog to a group of men engaged in animated conversation, some pointing toward the station, then gesticulating southward down the track. Sarah recognized Zach Cobb, El Paso's customs collector, as he walked briskly from the group and into the station.

Timothy soon returned to the car. Pushing his hat to the back of his head, he leaned through the window and announced, "Well, this is getting more interesting." He gestured toward the shrubs. "That tall gent in the black suit and black hat, that's . . ."

"Orozco," Sarah inserted.

"Yes, that's Orozco. When he saw the caravan with US soldiers, Orozco hid behind the shrubs to discard several items, which included a holstered pistol and a checkbook."

"Checkbook?"

"Yes. It probably shows financial transactions that will prove of interest to American authorities." Tilting his head in the direction of the group of men, Timothy stated, "Especially the man in the gray suit, who's a special agent with the Department of Justice."

"Why did Cobb hurry into the depot?"

"See the two men armed with rifles standing beside the special agent?" Without waiting for Sarah's acknowledgement, Timothy continued, "They're Texas deputy marshals. They just informed the group that Newman is located in New Mexico, and they don't have authority in that state to make an arrest, which is why Zach Cobb rushed into the station."

"So they aren't going to be able to detain Huerta when he disembarks from the train?" Sarah asked.

"Well, Cobb is frantically wiring the superintendent of the El Paso & Southwestern line to arrange for the train to travel past the station, stopping instead a few hundred yards down the track across the Texas state line, where the deputy marshals do have authority to make arrests."

"Do they anticipate trouble if they detain Huerta?"

"And arrest Orozco," Timothy added. "They're taking Orozco into custody as well." Continuing to monitor the group of men, Timothy explained, "That's why the colonel and his soldiers from the Sixteenth Cavalry are here. Word was that carloads of supporters planned to meet Huerta's train, but apparently Huerta nixed that arrangement, not wanting to attract attention."

Sarah exited the car to watch with Timothy as Cobb returned to the group. Cobb's demeanor suggested he had met with success.

Soon the train arrived, rolling slowly past the Newman Station and across the state line into Texas. Once the train came to rest, a porter directed the US officials to board a Pullman car. In minutes, they reemerged with General Huerta, whom Sarah thought looked more like someone's grandfather than the ruthless general who murdered his president and betrayed his country. Sarah captured a photo of Orozco warmly greeting Huerta.

Sarah and Timothy followed as the deputy marshals escorted both Huerta and Orozco from the train to the automobiles that would transport them to El Paso.

When Huerta saw the string of awaiting vehicles, he made a loud pronouncement that caused Orozco to grin.

"What did he say?" Sarah asked Timothy.

"He said, 'What a great honor! Caramba—I feel like the president of Mexico!'" Timothy excused himself to speak briefly with the special agent.

While Sarah waited, she photographed Huerta, now seated in the backseat of the lead car. Huerta glared at her with a sneer of disdain; Sarah thought of Cata and Samuel as she returned his steely stare.

"They're taking them to Cobb's office in the Federal Building," Timothy reported. "I want to get quotes from the porter and a couple of the troopers before we head there."

By the time they reached the Federal Building, the procession transporting Huerta and Orozco had already arrived, their cars arranged along the building's front, so Sarah parked on the side.

Word of Huerta and Orozco's arrest had trickled into the El Paso and Juárez communities. As Sarah followed Timothy into the building, she heard a few shouts of "Viva Huerta!" from a handful of supporters assembled out in front.

Sarah paused at a vacant desk to commandeer a phone. Since it was Sunday, she needed to call A. J. to inform him of the arrests of Huerta and Orozco and to let him know she would not be picking him up to work in the darkroom.

After the call, Sarah joined Timothy in the hallway outside of Cobb's office. While Timothy sought to garner information from anyone entering or exiting the rooms where officials interrogated Huerta and Orozco, Sarah monitored the angry shouts from what sounded like a growing crowd outside the building. Soon, several additional special agents arrived. Before entering Cobb's office, one agent who knew Timothy paused to inform him that Tom Lea, the recently elected mayor of El Paso, requested the transfer of the two generals to a more secure site at Fort Bliss, fearing violence between Huerta's supporters and opponents.

Sarah and Timothy positioned themselves inside the doorway of the Federal Building and watched El Paso police push the crowd back so that agents could exit safely with the prisoners, whom they placed in one car, bookending them in the front and backseats.

Some in the crowd shouted "Viva Huerta!" Some cried out "Viva Orozco!" Many countered with "Viva México!" Huerta raised his hat to their cheers, while Orozco sat sullenly in the back of the automobile.

Once the car departed, police officers quickly moved in to disperse the vocal crowd, arresting those whose shouting escalated to scuffling. As Sarah and Timothy watched the commotion, Sarah expressed surprise at the level of support for Huerta.

Thrusting his hands into his trouser pockets, Timothy replied, "Well, many of El Paso's well-heeled refugees opposed Madero's desire for democracy; they quickly gave allegiance to Huerta when he returned Mexico to the kind of autocratic rule they had prospered under during Porfirio Díaz's reign."

"And now Huerta, who fueled revolution in Mexico, arrives in El Paso, heightening tensions already straining the city," Sarah added.

"True. And I fear El Paso authorities and citizens alike will respond quickly and harshly to such public displays on American soil," Timothy pointed to the shouting crowd.

Once it appeared safe to venture outside, Timothy offered, "Let me buy you lunch. You've got to be starving; I know I am."

They hadn't eaten all day, and Sarah was hungry, but what she wanted more than food was to be back in her apartment. "I'll take a rain check," she replied as they returned to her vehicle at the side of the building.

"Well, if you don't mind, drop me off at the Sheldon. I need sustenance that includes a couple of cold beers."

When they reached the Sheldon Hotel, Timothy thanked her heartily for accompanying him on the Huerta story. "Now, get some food and rest," he encouraged before hopping from the car.

Sarah pulled from the curb, anxious to return to the apartment and fulfill Timothy's recommendation, mentally adding a long soak in the bathtub to his list. The minimal Sunday traffic allowed her to arrive at the studio in minutes. Collecting her camera, she slid across the leather seat to exit the passenger side. As she closed the car door, her eye caught a figure across the street standing in the shadow of an awning. Sarah turned toward the studio door, but a stir of familiarity, a nagging hint of recognition, caused her to look again at the person now walking toward her.

"Cata!" she called, rushing into the street to embrace her, kissing one cheek, then the other.

"We need to get out of the street, Sarah," Cata said, grinning, taking Sarah's hand to lead her to the sidewalk.

"I can't believe you're here," Sarah said, clasping Cata's hand to her chest.

Cata smiled broadly. "Let's go inside."

"Yes, of course." Sarah did not release Cata's hand. Once inside the studio, Sarah led her past the curtained doorway. Quickly depositing her camera and hat, Sarah hugged Cata, kissing her fully and deeply.

"Let's go to the apartment," Cata whispered.

"Yes," and Sarah hurried up the stairs to open the apartment door.

Cata followed, placing her satchel on the floor and removing her own hat before reaching for Sarah. They kissed, holding tightly to one another.

Sarah leaned back, gently brushing her hand across Cata's gathered hair. "How long are you here?"

"I don't know," she replied, reaching to hold Sarah's hand to her face. "Maybe for a long while."

At that news, Sarah kissed Cata, then tilted back her head as Cata brushed her lips along Sarah's neck. "Wait," Sarah said thickly, pausing Cata. "I'm sweaty and dusty. Let me bathe."

"Let me bathe with you," Cata encouraged.

"Yes," Sarah said, and she led Cata into the bathroom.

After Sarah placed the rubber stopper into the drain and adjusted the mix of water flowing into the tub, she began to undress Cata slowly as Cata freed her hair from the braids. Cata reciprocated, helping to remove Sarah's clothing and releasing her hair from its bun. Soon, they stood nude before one another, both shy in their nakedness.

Sarah entered the tub first. She held out her hand for Cata to follow. Cata joined her, sitting in the water to rest against Sarah's chest.

Sarah kissed Cata's temple, then raised a container with water to pour slowly over Cata's hair. Sarah filled the well of her cupped hand with Crème of Rose Shampoo, lathering it with both hands, then rubbing it into Cata's thick hair, massaging her scalp and working the shampoo into the loose strands.

"Protect your eyes," Sarah instructed before rinsing the suds from Cata's hair.

Sarah soaped a cloth. Resting her cheek against Cata's wet hair, Sarah gently scrubbed Cata's throat and neck, leaning her forward to wash her back, then returning Cata to a reclining position to bathe her arms and torso, lingering at her breasts and along the soft hollow of her stomach. "Stand," Sarah whispered, gently kissing Cata's ear.

With Cata standing above her, Sarah washed each of Cata's muscled legs, then surrendered the cloth to Cata to finish her bath.

Cata changed places with Sarah, washing Sarah's hair, then her body, massaging the various parts she bathed. Sarah tingled with desire. They stood to rinse with clean water Sarah captured in a container at the faucet; then they stepped from the tub to dry themselves.

Sarah took Cata's towel and placed it beside hers on the towel bar. She turned to Cata, their bodies pressing against one another, their hands then their mouths retracing areas they had washed.

Sarah moaned, feeling weak-kneed with passion. She urged, "Let's go into the bedroom." Cata followed Sarah, and they tumbled quickly into bed, giving and taking pleasure until both lay spent.

They turned onto their sides facing each other, their legs entangled beneath the sheet.

"How long will you stay in El Paso?" Sarah asked.

"I don't know," Cata replied. She breathed deeply, then added, "I left Villa, left the revolution."

Sarah rose onto her elbow, surprised but excited by Cata's news.

Cata explained, "Villa no longer listens to his advisors. He refuses to change his tactics to defeat Obregón. He insists that if a battle charge fails today, it will succeed tomorrow, so he sends troops to be slaughtered; then those who survive, he sends again." Cata closed her eyes, shutting them tightly. "I could no longer order soldiers to charge into senseless deaths. Since I couldn't follow such orders, I left."

Sarah reached to finger a strand of Cata's hair that curled at her throat. "What will you do?" Sarah asked. "You can live with me and work in the studio. I can certainly use the help."

"I don't know anything about photography."

"I'll teach you," Sarah quickly countered.

"Thank you, Sarah, for your kindness, but I think I will see if

Dr. Bush or Hotel Dieu Hospital might hire me; I worked with them years ago while Mayo recovered from his wound." She ran her thumb across the back of Sarah's hand, adding, "I have spent so many years in armies focused on killing and maiming one another, I think working to help people heal would bring me peace."

"Then, stay with me," Sarah encouraged.

"Thank you, Sarah. I would like that. I will pay my way."

"Just having you with me is enough."

Cata leaned to kiss Sarah's lips, then looked into her eyes to repeat, "I will pay my way."

JULY 1915

Sarah

Sarah and Cata secured the picnic baskets on the rumble seat before driving to collect Paola at her home for the Fourth of July picnic they planned with A. J. and Timothy. From the front window, Paola waved to indicate she saw them, and soon exited the house with a pie balanced on the palm of each hand. Sarah and Cata stepped from the vehicle to assist with positioning the pies on the floorboard of the rumble seat.

When Sarah made introductions, Paola took Cata's hands in hers, depositing a kiss on each cheek as if they were old friends, and greeted her in Spanish. The three women entered the idling car, sliding snuggly on the seat with Cata in the middle. They filled the short drive to Washington Park with lively chatter.

Upon reaching the park, Sarah drove slowly around the perimeter while Paola searched for the Texas flag Timothy promised to plant signaling the spot he saved. Finally, Paola spied the flag at a picnic table under a large shade tree.

"Timothy saved a good site," Paola commented, pointing to the area. Once Sarah parked the car, Paola exited, waving to Timothy and A. J. while Sarah squeezed the bulb of the car horn to catch their attention. Timothy waved back, trotting toward the car.

"Happy Fourth of July," Timothy greeted. He gave Paola a peck on the cheek and then Sarah.

Sarah placed her hand on Cata's shoulder and said, "Timothy, let me formally introduce . . . "

But he let her go no further, announcing, "My savior, Coronela Catalina Vasquez," and he briefly placed his lips to the back of her hand.

"Just Cata," she replied, "no longer coronela."

"Oh? You'll have to fill me in."

"Later, Timothy." Sarah came to Cata's rescue. "Help us carry the food."

Timothy retrieved the two pies, placing them on Paola's outstretched hands. Then he removed the three baskets, handing one to Sarah. Cata gripped the handle to balance the weight between them.

"You've saved a great spot, Timothy," Sarah commented as they walked toward the picnic table. "This place is packed. How did you manage to secure such prime real estate?"

"I paid two boys to arrive early this morning to hold the table."

"Is Timothy crowing about his use of child labor?" A. J. stepped from the tree where he had been leaning.

"Happy Fourth of July, A. J.," Sarah responded in answer, setting the basket on the table before crossing over to place a kiss on a portion of his cheek not covered by the mask. Paola followed to greet A. J. in the same manner.

"A. J., I want to introduce Cata Vasquez," she held the palm of her hand toward Cata. "Cata, this is A. J. Otis."

"Photographer and curmudgeon extraordinaire," Timothy added as A. J. tipped his hat to Cata.

A. J. rolled his eyes at Timothy, then commanded, "Well, offer the ladies a drink."

While Timothy retrieved bottles of soda for everyone, Sarah, Cata, and Paola spread a tablecloth and placed the food from the baskets across the center of the table. Sarah filled a plate for A. J., carrying it to him at the tree against which he leaned while everyone else sat at the picnic table exchanging the various dishes of food.

Once seated, Sarah asked, "So Timothy, fill us in on the Huerta and Orozco drama."

Timothy held up a finger to pause the conversation while he took a bite from a drumstick. Swallowing, he wiped his mouth. "Well," he began, "I'll start with Orozco. Like Huerta, he was on house arrest having bonded out on the day of his arrest. Though Department of Justice agents and US soldiers guarded his home around the clock, authorities discovered yesterday morning that Orozco was no longer inside; he had escaped. Word is that deep in the night, the guards fell asleep, so Orozco simply climbed out of a window, hopped a fence, and disappeared into the darkness. There are all sorts of rumors regarding where he's headed, but all lead eventually across the border into Mexico." Timothy held up his finger while he took three quick bites from the drumstick.

When he finished chewing, Timothy took a drink of soda, then began to speak. "Now, Huerta is another other story. Yesterday, he was again arrested, along with five other former generals and current advisors, on additional charges of violating US neutrality laws. Huerta is currently residing in the El Paso County Jail, but the old general put up a struggle when the deputies arrived to arrest him at the apartment where he was staying with his daughter and her family. When he was taken before the court, Huerta protested that he was being guarded day and night like 'some ferocious animal.'"

"There's a bit of self-realization," A. J. commented.

"Huerta's not exactly suffering in jail. His daughter has arranged for a local restaurant to prepare and deliver all of his meals," Timothy shared, adding, "though Huerta did complain he's having to do without alcohol for the first time in forty years."

Timothy used his cornbread to secure baked beans onto his fork. "And our illustrious mayor's law firm, which is representing Huerta, is working to have the old Scorpion moved from the jail to more comfortable quarters on Fort Bliss."

"I don't understand this worry about Huerta's comfort," Cata forcefully interjected. "This man betrayed his country, murdered the president and vice president elected by the Mexican people, and fought to hold onto power by sacrificing Mexicans in battle, yet the American government wants to ensure he is comfortable. The United States should return

Huerta to Mexico to be judged by the Mexican people."

Sarah felt pride in Cata's outspokenness, though it caused a momentary pause in conversation. Then A. J. observed, "The obvious logic of your comments leaves us speechless, Cata."

When Timothy continued, enthusiastically sharing, "What hasn't hit the paper yet . . . "

A. J. interrupted, stating, "But our intrepid reporter is never quieted for long."

Timothy chuckled, beginning anew. "What hasn't hit the paper yet is that Mayor Lea called the chief of police to put a stop to the espionage taking place in El Paso among the various Mexican factions. The good citizens of El Paso now can simply phone the police station, report their suspicions of espionage, and the police will arrest the offender for vagrancy and deport said offender to Mexico. How's that for due process." Timothy accented the final statement by taking a bite of cornbread.

Sarah winced at the last bit of news. More tension in the already frayed city.

"And on a cheerier note?" A. J. called out for a change of subject.

"Well, on a cheerier note," Timothy picked up A. J.'s direction, "I want to publicly thank my savior." He raised his bottle of soda in a toast.

Paola looked from Cata to Timothy. "I must be the only one who doesn't know the story, so tell me."

"No," Cata protested, looking away.

"Yes. I want everyone to know about my heroine." Timothy launched into the tale of his rescue by Cata.

While Sarah took pride in hearing Timothy's praise of Cata, Sarah felt Cata shifting uncomfortably on the bench next to her.

"So now I'm completely indebted to Coronela Catalina Vasquez," Timothy concluded.

"Cata," Cata corrected him.

"Completely indebted to Cata," Timothy repeated. "Seriously," he said, looking intently at Cata. "I owe you my life." He broke into a grin. "And I'll be hanging around waiting to repay my debt."

"Keep in mind, Cata," A. J. inserted, "you can now call the El Paso police and have Timothy arrested as a vagrant if he becomes a nuisance."

They all laughed at Timothy's expense.

After everyone finished eating, Sarah insisted that A. J. join them at the table. The friends sat sharing stories and laughter until late afternoon wore into evening. When the music began, Timothy suggested they return the baskets and remaining drinks to Sarah's car, then stroll to the stands to listen to the Fort Bliss US Army Band.

The setting of the sun dulled the day's heat as the women walked arm in arm, the men following. Sarah felt truly happy sharing the holiday with Cata and knowing her friends were now also Cata's friends.

They claimed a spot at the edge of the crowd where they had a good view of the bandstand. Sarah recognized many of the patriotic songs the military band played: "The Invincible Eagle," "The Washington Post," and "The Thunderer." The crowd, which whistled and cheered each march, roared to life when the band began playing "You're a Grand Old Flag."

Sarah felt a tingle of warmth when Cata placed her hand at the crook of Sarah's arm. Seeing Cata relaxed and enjoying herself gave Sarah a sense of satisfaction and peace.

The band moved easily into two other songs that shared the same rousing beat as the previously performed marches. After thunderous applause, the conductor signaled the musicians to begin "The Stars and Stripes Forever." Those in the audience who had been sitting rose immediately to their feet. At the clash of cymbals, fireworks whistled skyward, exploding into a shower of color, followed by another, then another. Sarah felt Cata's grip tighten. Sarah turned to Cata, smiling at what she thought was a shared pleasure, but Cata's face was fixed in a look of horror.

"I must leave," Cata said, her eyes searching for an escape path.

"Cata!" Sarah called, following Cata, who pushed through the crowd. Sarah heard A. J. ask, "What is it?" and she knew her friends followed closely behind.

Sarah pursued Cata, who flinched at each new explosion of sparks that elicited squeals of delight from the audience. Sarah caught up to her just as she broke free of the crowd. Grasping for Cata's arm, Sarah startled, pulling back her hand when Cata spun in a threatening crouch to face her. "Cata!" Sarah called out, attempting to snap Cata to a recognition of her. Cata stood slowly, allowing Sarah to enfold her protectively in an embrace. "It's all right," Sarah whispered as Cata trembled in her arms. "Let's go home."

When Paola, Timothy, and A. J. encircled them, Sarah announced calmly to the friends, "Cata and I are going home, now."

They all nodded knowingly. While Sarah held onto Cata's left arm, Paola looped her arm through Cata's right. A. J. and Timothy walked protectively beside them.

Once they were seated in the car, A. J. shut the door.

Cata quietly addressed A. J. "I'm sorry."

"I never cared much for all that noise and showering of sparks," A. J. replied. "You just happened to escape first. It's a pleasure to make your acquaintance, Cata. I look forward to seeing you again soon."

Timothy cranked the car before stepping to Sarah's side of the vehicle. "Thank you all for the great spread today."

The two men stood illuminated by the car's headlights as Sarah stepped on the reverse pedal to back out of the parking space.

Sarah and Paola tried to engage Cata in conversation, but her one-word replies signaled she did not wish to talk, so they remained quiet the remainder of the drive to Paola's house. Before Paola exited the car, she spoke in Spanish to Cata, then kissed her on the cheek. Sarah waited and watched until Paola safely entered her house, then U-turned to head home.

At the studio, Cata helped collect the baskets from the rear of the automobile. Once inside the apartment, Sarah directed, "Just place them on the kitchen table." Then she asked, "Would you like coffee or tea?"

"No. I want to lie down."

"Good," Sarah replied.

"Sarah," Cata spoke softly, "I won't sleep in the bedroom tonight." When Sarah attempted to protest, Cata said, "The explosions tonight returned me to the battlefield."

"I know," Sarah answered softly without attempting to approach Cata.

"I will make a pallet in another room."

"That isn't necessary," Sarah insisted. "We'll be careful."

Cata raised her eyes to Sarah's, answering with finality: "No. I don't trust myself."

AUGUST 1915

Sarah

Sarah sat at the kitchen table studying the sheet of stationery with a running-rose border. On the paper, she had written *Saturday, August 28, 1915*, and below the date, she had penned *Dear General Pershing*. She had not recorded anything beneath the salutation because she couldn't find words equal to Pershing's painful burden of losing his wife and three of their four young children to fire.

Sarah glanced again at the headline of the article printed in the *El Paso Morning Times*: "Wife and Babes of Gen. Pershing Meet Frightful Death at Burned Home." The article detailed how Pershing's family had planned to leave San Francisco within the week to join him at Fort Bliss. The newspaper described the rescue of his six-year-old son, found lying unconscious on his bedroom floor in the burning house while Pershing's wife and three young daughters lay dead in another room, the mother with her arm protectively around one of the girls.

Sarah stared anew at the blank space of the stationery, then pushed herself to record her thoughts.

I write to express my sincerest condolences for your great loss. While I know no words from me can lessen the pain, I do send a heartfelt wish that memories of happy times spent with your wife and children will provide solace to you and come to lessen the ache of loss.

May thoughts of their love bring you peace.

Sincerely,

Miss Sarah Delaney

Sarah knew the words she wrote were insufficient, but she folded the stationery and sealed the envelope to send her message to the general in the morning mail.

NOVEMBER 1915

Catalina

Catalina scoured the marble cross, pressing the soapy sponge into each letter cut into Mayo's headstone. Pausing to examine her work, she sat back on her heels and wiped her forearm across her brow. Though it was the start of November, the day had already warmed enough to draw perspiration from minimal exertion, but Catalina enjoyed the sun's heat on her neck and back.

"There is so much to tell you, mi esposo, my husband," Catalina spoke, dabbing a crust of dirt she spied.

Satisfied with the results, Catalina placed the sponge and bucket of soapy water aside, then reached into a basket to retrieve the clay pot she had purchased for the occasion. Next, she removed cut marigolds, arranging them in the pot. Once satisfied with the arrangement, she centered it in front of the headstone, adding water to keep the flowers fresh.

"Do you like the marigolds' perfume, mi amor?" Catalina asked, admiring how the mica of the clay pot caught the sunlight.

Catalina retrieved two long candles ornamented with metal ribbons and flourishes of decorative wax. She picked up two small candleholders. After securing each taper in a holder, she set the candles on both sides of the flowers about six inches from the arrangement.

Catalina carefully lifted a paper sack from the basket. Balancing the sack on the palm of her left hand, she withdrew a heart made from a hardened sugary paste. The outer edge of the heart was serrated while decorative scoring formed a border outlining the inner edge. In the center of the off-white heart bloomed a bouquet of five flowers made of sugar paste, each petal carefully crafted. Four red flowers embraced a large white blossom at the center. Green sugar paste formed the bouquet's stems and leaves. Catalina admired the sweet sculpture, then raised it to her lips, gently kissing it before placing the heart to rest against the pot of orange flowers. She lit the two candles, then stood back to admire the gravesite she had caringly cleaned and adorned.

Catalina sat on the blanket spread beside the grave. She reached again into the basket to select a small tin box, the sides and lid embossed with the design of a pierced heart. Lifting the tightly fitted lid, Catalina removed the folded strip of cloth stained dark with Mayo's blood. She placed the cloth to her lips, then wrapped it loosely around the first two fingers of her left hand, caressing it lovingly with her thumb. "I miss you, Mayo," she whispered.

As she sat beside the grave, Catalina thought of family she'd lost over the years, of her mother who had died in childbirth, her sister Fátima, her brother Felipe, her father. She wondered if her brothers Miguel and Diego lived, or if they, too, had died during this revolution that seemed never-ending. She offered a silent prayer for Mayo and for the rest of her family.

"The fighting in México continues," Catalina uttered aloud. "And the United States persists in pulling México's strings, like a vendor of marionettes at the mercado in town." She brushed away sand from the blanket, then continued sharing her news. "Two weeks ago, the US president recognized Carranza as chief executive of México.

"Mayo, this president even permitted Carranza to transport troops, munitions, and animals across US land by train to fight Villa at Agua Prieta," Catalina announced incredulously. "The battle at Agua Prieta still rages, but newspapers report that Villa's troops are short of food, water, and ammunition.

"There is more news, Mayo. The Americans have released Huerta to live in his El Paso home because he is dying. Despite the suffering he brought to the people of México, Huerta's comfort is important to the US authorities." Catalina shook her head in disgust.

"And yet I remain in the United States, in El Paso, Mayo." Catalina paused, taking a deep breath before continuing. She looked at the sugar heart balanced against the pot of flowers, then spoke her truth. "I stay because of Sarah." Catalina glanced down at the strip of cloth wrapped around the fingers of one hand. "I love her, Mayo. I didn't intend to love her, but I love her." She gives me a sense of peace; she fills me with great joy." Catalina smiled at the thought of Sarah, then continued. "My love for Sarah doesn't lessen my love for you." Catalina rose onto her knees, leaning forward to run her fingers across the letters of Mayo's name. "You will always remain in my heart, Mayo." She sat back onto the blanket. Pressing the palm of her hand to her chest, she added, "The place where Sarah resides now, too." Catalina breathed deeply, relieved to have spoken with Mayo about her love for Sarah. Then Catalina quietly added, "So I remain in El Paso to be with Sarah. My heart is full with the two of you."

Sarah

"The flowers are beautiful," Cata declared, leaning to smell the red roses arranged in a clear, cut–glass vase at the center of the kitchen table.

"They are for you," Sarah responded.

"For me?" Cata stood from the flowers to face Sarah. "Why?"

Sarah reached to hold Cata's hands. "A year ago, on this day, we gave ourselves to one another."

Cata lifted Sarah's hands to kiss each before embracing her.

"Sit, my love," Sarah whispered.

Sarah retrieved the anniversary supper she had prepared, bringing plates of breaded veal smothered in mushroom gravy, potato pancakes, lettuce and tomato salad, and freshly baked bolillos she had purchased at the bakery. Sarah poured two glasses of wine before taking her seat at the table.

"This looks delicious," Cata complimented.

Sarah raised her glass of wine, signaling for Cata to do the same, then wished aloud, "To a lifetime of love." Cata repeated, "Por una vida de amor." After clinking glasses, they sealed the toast with a sip then a kiss.

They ate, savoring the food while exchanging memories of their first picnic beside the river. They talked of happy events from their first year.

When Sarah served dishes of lemon sherbet to conclude the meal, she placed a small box wrapped in white paper with a red bow beside Cata's dessert.

Cata looked in surprise at the gift, then at Sarah.

"Open it," Sarah insisted.

Sarah watched Cata untie the bow, remove the wrapping paper, and open the box. "It's beautiful," Cata gasped as she admired the gold heart.

"Let me put it on you," Sarah said, removing the necklace from the box to place the chain around Cata's neck. "There," she said, clasping it in the back. Sarah returned to her seat to examine the necklace on Cata. "It's lovely on you."

"Let me look in the mirror," Cata said, standing.

Sarah followed Cata into the bedroom.

Cata stood before the mirror admiring the heart that fell gracefully between her breasts. Cata placed her fingers to the pendant. "It's beautiful, Sarah," she said, choking back emotion. "But I don't have a gift for you."

Sarah reached to caress Cata's face, then embraced her, whispering, "You are my gift, Cata. I don't need anything else."

JANUARY 1916

Sarah

Sarah knew there would be trouble in the city when she saw the bolded headline printed across the front page of yesterday's *El Paso Morning Times*: "**EIGHTEEN AMERICANS MASSACARED**." The subheading provided details that would further fuel the city's anger: "Victims Dragged from Train and Cruelly Murdered, Report Says, on Direct Order of General Villa; Bodies Enroute to El Paso."

Sarah recalled previous newspaper reports addressing the deteriorating relationship between General Pancho Villa and the United States after America recognized Venustiano Carranza as Mexico's chief executive.

Sarah knew Villa's situation in Mexico had become dire. In December, without a single shot fired, Villista officers surrendered the Juárez garrison and its four thousand troops to Carranza in return for amnesty.

Soon in control of the entire state of Chihuahua, Carranza and General Álvaro Obregón invited the American Smelting and Refining Company, ASARCO, to reopen the mine near Cusihuiriáchic, west of

Chihuahua city. They assured ASARCO personnel of the region's safety now that Carranza's government controlled it. American mining personnel, several from El Paso and many well-known in the city, traveled by train in early January to reopen the Cusi Mine, but, as the newspaper reported, Villa's soldiers stopped the train just outside of the Santa Ysabel Station and forced all "gringos" to disembark, ordering the men to strip, then murdering them. Only one American escaped the massacre by hiding in a lavatory before slipping from the train to find cover in some bushes.

The newspaper announced that in response to news of the killings, Mayor Tom Lea ordered the arrest of known Villista officers on charges of vagrancy, reportedly giving them twenty-four hours to leave the city.

Tension in El Paso mounted when the "death special" arrived in the early morning with bodies of the Americans, and the first funerals for victims of the Santa Ysabel massacre began midafternoon. Timothy had called to warn of scuffles breaking out downtown between American soldiers and Mexicans. He urged Sarah and Cata to be alert, take precautions, and stay off the streets.

Fearing the angry unrest, Sarah tried to convince Cata to call in sick to work and remain in the apartment, but Cata refused, insisting she had an obligation to the patients she bathed and assisted at Hotel Dieu. Sarah finally relented. Clearly, Cata's mind could not be changed, and Sarah concluded that Cata would be almost as safe inside the hospital as in the apartment.

Sarah insisted on driving Cata to work this evening; Sarah also would be waiting outside the hospital to bring Cata home when her shift ended at 6:00 a.m. the following morning. On the drive to and from the hospital, Sarah noticed groups of men gathered in angry discussions and teams of teenage boys swaggering along downtown streets.

Back in the apartment, Sarah warmed the previous night's beef stew before sitting at the kitchen table to read the evening newspaper. While she ate, she skimmed the front-page headlines. Several articles addressed the killing of the American mining personnel and the outrage felt across the United States over their murder. Sarah folded the paper and set it aside; she didn't want to read any more about the deaths, sorrow, and anger. Just when she raised a spoonful of stew to her mouth, the phone rang. She hurried to answer the call.

"Hello," she spoke into the mouthpiece.

"Miss Sarah?" The woman asked, her heavily accented voice speaking in a hushed tone.

"Yes," Sarah replied, not recognizing the voice.

"The police took Cata."

"What?" Though she understood the woman's words, Sarah's mind couldn't grasp the message.

"The police took Cata," the woman repeated in barely more than a whisper. "She asked me to call you."

"When did the police arrest Cata? Why did they arrest her?" Sarah struggled to make sense of the information the caller shared.

"The police took her now. Someone at the hospital told that Cata was an officer in Villa's army."

"Oh no," Sarah moaned in reply. Gathering her senses, she said, "Thank you. What is your name?"

"Josefina."

"Thank you, Josefina."

"Will Cata be all right?"

"Yes," Sarah answered, hoping she spoke the truth. Sarah hung up the phone.

Grabbing her coat, hat, and purse, Sarah dressed as she rushed down the stairs and out to the car. Crowds on the streets had thickened dramatically in the short time she had been in the apartment. To avoid the congestion of men seeking an outlet for their anger, Sarah took a roundabout route to the police station, entering the street at the rear of the main precinct in time to see three police officers remove Cata from a patrol wagon. Sarah gasped when Cata, seeming to catch a shoe in her long skirt, crashed to her knees on the street. Her hands secured behind her back, Cata couldn't cushion her fall. Sarah stomped the brake to rush to Cata's aid, but before she could exit her automobile, two police officers roughly raised Cata to her feet and pushed her toward the back entrance of the station. Sarah stood in the street shouting "Cata!" as the police shoved Cata through an open doorway and into the building.

Sarah parked at the first available space, a block from the precinct. She hurried back to the building, attempting to open the door through which Cata had entered, but found it locked. Sarah thudded the side of her fist against the door until an officer opened it wide enough to ask brusquely her business, then direct her to the building's front entrance.

Sarah hurried through the heavy door at the front, walking to the counter to speak with the policeman on duty.

"How may I help you?" asked a thick-set officer, glancing up from the stack of papers.

"Police officers just brought in Miss Catalina Vasquez. It's a mistake. What are her charges, and whom do I speak with to gain her release?" Sarah spouted breathlessly.

"Who are you, and what is your relationship to this Catalina Vasquez?" He peered at Sarah over a pair of oval glasses.

"I'm Sarah Delaney." She hesitated, trying to form an answer to the relationship question. "Miss Vasquez lives with me."

"She your housekeeper?" The officer questioned, apparently unable to imagine any other reason for their living arrangement that wasn't illegal.

"No," Sarah responded. "She is my friend."

The officer raised his bushy eyebrows at her response. "Have a seat," he directed. "I'll check on her status."

Sarah stepped back from the counter, but rather than taking a seat, she paced the floor, anxious for news of Cata. When she spied the officer slowly returning from another room, Sarah hurried to the counter.

The officer waited to speak until he had again deposited his bulk onto the chair. "Your *friend*," he drew out the one syllable word, imbuing it with suspicion and sarcasm, "was brought in on charges of vagrancy. She's being booked."

"Vagrancy?" Sarah responded with incredulity. "How could she be charged with vagrancy? She has an apartment, is employed at Hotel Dieu Hospital, and hasn't been involved in any criminal activities?"

"She's a Villista," he hissed, returning his attention to the stack of papers on his desk.

"I wish to speak with someone in charge," Sarah insisted, refusing to be dismissed.

Glancing from the papers, he responded, "No one is available to speak with you. We're busy trying to keep peace on the streets." He briefly returned his attention to the papers, then looked again at Sarah, who remained at the counter. "Nobody on this force is interested in listening to your complaints of injustice for a Mexican Villista. What about justice for the murdered Americans and their families?" He held himself in check for a moment, before glaring at her, adding, "You need to examine your skin color and your loyalties."

Restraining her anger, Sarah responded, "I will stay until a supervisor becomes available." She took a seat close to the entrance.

While Sarah waited, her mind filled with worry. She feared that most police bore the same grudge against Mexicans as the front desk officer. She worried they would treat Cata as though she were guilty of the murders at Santa Ysabel. Sarah resolved to do whatever she needed to help Cata fight this arrest. While Sarah pondered possible strategies, she noticed a light in the vicinity of Captain Green's office.

Sarah bided her time, closely monitoring both the light that knifed into the hallway and the policeman at the front counter. When the officer turned to rifle through a file cabinet drawer, Sarah grasped the opportunity. Quietly standing from her chair, she hurried toward the light, balancing on the balls of her feet to avoid the clack of heels against the tile. Captain Green's office door stood slightly ajar. She knocked, calling, "Captain Green" quietly at first, but when she saw the desk officer lumbering toward her, Sarah called again, loudly and with urgency, "Captain Green!"

The door swung open as the desk officer barked, "Hey you!" Captain Green stepped from the doorway. He looked at Sarah and then at the officer charging toward her.

"I'm sorry, Captain Green," the winded officer sputtered. "I told her you weren't available to see her."

"Captain Green," Sarah called to redirect his attention. "I'm Sarah Delaney, formerly Sarah Clendenin. I don't know if you remember me."

"Yes, of course, Miss Delaney," he responded. "Please step into my office."

As Sarah walked into Captain Green's office, she heard him say, "Thank you, Officer Burrows. I'll take it from here."

"Please have a seat, Miss Delaney," Captain Green instructed, motioning toward one of the chairs in front of his precisely arranged desk. Sitting behind the desk, he asked, "Now, what can I do for you?"

"Captain Green, there has been a terrible mistake," Sarah blurted. "A friend of mine, Miss Catalina Vasquez, has been arrested on the wrongful charge of vagrancy."

"Hmm," he responded, leaning back in his chair. "Why do you think our officers leveled the charge of vagrancy?"

Sarah answered truthfully. "Because she served as a colonel in General Pancho Villa's army."

"Ahh," he replied, nodding knowingly.

"Miss Vasquez left Mexico and the revolution in June. She's been sharing an apartment with me and working at Hotel Dieu Hospital since then." Sarah leaned forward in her chair, placing her clasped hands on the desktop. "Captain Green, Miss Catalina Vasquez is a good, honorable woman. She isn't guilty of a crime. Her arrest is a result of the angry hysteria in El Paso; her arrest is nothing more than revenge for the murdered Americans."

Captain Green sat for a moment without responding, and Sarah feared that the truth sealed Cata's fate. Then he stood from his chair. "Let me look into her case. Wait here, Miss Delaney. Best for you to avoid the front desk officer." He smiled.

Sarah stared at the panoramic photo of El Paso police on the wall behind the desk. Three rows of uniformed men glowered at her from the framed photograph as if they all held the same disapproving opinion. Sarah returned their glare. When she could sit no longer, she paced the floor, resuming her seat at the sound of heavy footsteps down the hallway.

"Well, you are correct," Captain Green spoke as he entered the office. "Miss Vasquez has been charged with vagrancy." He returned to his chair behind the desk. "She's been booked on the charge already and must go before a judge. Her arraignment is scheduled for nine thirty tomorrow morning. Miss Vasquez will be held in the county jail until then."

"Is there nothing I can do?" Sarah asked, fighting back tears. "I can't bear the thought of her spending the night in a jail cell."

"You would have to pay a cash bond to secure her release."

"Cash bond? What's that?" Sarah asked, hopeful there might be a way to gain Cata's freedom for the night.

"It means you would have to pay the full amount of her bail in cash." He shook his head as if trying to discourage Sarah's optimism. "Frankly, Miss Delaney, bail is set at a very steep rate for Villista officers charged with vagrancy. It's three hundred dollars."

"Three hundred dollars!" Sarah repeated in disbelief. "Does it have to be cash?"

"I'm afraid it does."

"Captain Green, I will pay the three hundred dollars to get Miss Vasquez released from jail, but I can't get that amount of cash tonight. May I write a check for the amount and bring cash tomorrow after the bank opens?"

"That's not standard procedure. You're asking me to make an allowance for you that isn't made for others."

Detecting a slight possibility in his tone, Sarah replied, "I am."

"That is a large sum of money."

"Yes, it is," Sarah agreed.

"You understand you will lose all of that money if Miss Vasquez fails to show for the arraignment?"

"I do."

Captain Green seemed to consider the proposed arrangement.

Sarah leaned forward, placing her hands on the desk. "If you allow me to write a check for three hundred dollars, I will have the cash for you by noon tomorrow, and Miss Vasquez will report for her nine-thirty arraignment, I promise."

He looked hard at her before responding. "Okay, Miss Delaney. I will trust your word though I think you are taking a costly risk."

"Thank you, Captain Green!"

"Thank me by having Miss Vasquez appear for her arraignment tomorrow."

"She will be there," Sarah assured.

"Come with me, then."

Sarah followed the captain to a small office in the building's basement. He explained their agreed-upon arrangement to the clerk, who sat at a desk surrounded by file cabinets and ledgers.

The clerk repeated Captain Green's words. "Accept a check?"

"Yes," Captain Green responded with authority, "accept a check for the full amount of the bail."

"Yes sir, Captain Green."

"I will leave you to complete the necessary paperwork, Miss Delaney, while I secure Miss Vasquez's release from the holding cell."

The entire process of filling out the required forms and providing a check took about fifteen minutes though to Sarah the time crept. After the clerk handed Sarah the receipt and cautioned her against misplacing it, Captain Green reentered the room with Cata beside him.

"Miss Vasquez is free to leave with you," Captain Green announced.

Cata stood stoically beside the captain, her face expressing no emotion.

Sarah wanted to rush to Cata, to embrace her, hold her tightly. Instead, Sarah turned to the captain and said, "Thank you, Captain Green."

"Do you need to call a taxi or a friend?" he responded.

"No, thank you. I drove."

"Then I will walk you to your car. Tonight is not a night to be on the streets." He led the way up the flight of stairs to the first floor, holding the door open for them to exit. As the captain guided them toward the main entrance of the station, the officer at the front counter called out, "Captain Green!"

"One moment, please," the captain said to Sarah and Cata. "What is it, Officer Burrows?"

"Mayor Lea is on the phone. Says it's urgent."

"I'm sorry, Miss Delaney, Miss Vasquez, but I will have to take that call."

"Of course," Sarah responded. "Thank you, again."

Captain Green held up his hand, signaling for them to wait. He strode quickly to the front desk to accept the phone from Officer Burrows, who sneered at them.

"Let's go," Sarah said, taking Cata's arm. "I don't want to remain in this building a moment longer."

They exited into the cold night air. Immediately, they heard angry shouts, pained cries, and breaking glass from a crowd out of control. "Let's hurry," Sarah urged. "I'm parked on the next block." As they rushed down the street, sounds of unrest grew closer. When they reached the corner to turn toward the automobile, Sarah spied three men entering the street from the opposite end of the block. One of them carried what appeared to be an ax handle, and he raised it, pointing the wooden club toward Sarah and Cata.

"Run," Cata urged. They raced the few yards to the parked car, Cata commanding, "Get in. I'll crank it."

Sarah opened the door and entered the cab. "Hurry, Cata, hurry," Sarah said under her breath, almost as a prayer, but the January cold slowed the car's start, and it took three turns for the engine to rumble to life. Sarah saw the men round the corner; she called, "Get into the car, Cata."

The first man reached Cata just as she stepped onto the car's running board. He grabbed her arm, pulling her from the vehicle, his hand fumbling to squeeze her breast. Cata regained her footing, whirling to smash her elbow into the man's throat. He released her to grab his throat with both hands, doubling over, coughing and gasping for air. Cata dove into the car. "Drive," she called to Sarah while she righted herself onto the seat.

Sarah saw the second man step behind the vehicle. She stomped the reverse pedal, backing into the man, the flared fender catching him in the groin, before the back tire thumped over his foot. Sarah shifted into low, throttling the vehicle forward. The third man stepped forward, swinging the ax handle, smashing a headlight as the vehicle departed the scene.

Sarah looked in her sideview mirror to see a river of rioters spilling onto the street behind them. She opened the throttle. "Are you all right, Cata?" she asked without looking from the road in front of her.

"Yes," Cata replied breathless from the exertion and excitement. "Are you?"

"Yes," Sarah answered, hearing the quiver in her voice.

Sarah drove a winding route home, trying to avoid packs of rioters who moved toward South El Paso and Segundo Barrio. Sarah prayed silently for Paola and her family, hoping they remained safe.

When Sarah neared the studio, she felt relieved to see a lone pedestrian on their street. Both Cata and she remained alert exiting the car and entering the studio. Once inside the apartment, they reached for each other, holding tight.

Cata said, "I am so tired."

Sarah knew Cata's weariness was more than physical. Sarah guided Cata to the bedroom, where they exchanged their clothes for nightgowns. They lay beneath the covers, Cata's head resting on Sarah's shoulder. After a long period of silence, Sarah said, "You have to go before a judge at nine thirty tomorrow morning."

"I know," Cata replied, "but let's not talk about it. Let's not talk."

Neither one slept much. When Cata rose before dawn, Sarah said, "I'll make a pot of coffee."

By the time Cata joined Sarah in the kitchen, the coffee had brewed. Sarah carried two cups to the kitchen table. She sat beside Cata, rubbing her thumb across the knuckles of Cata's hand.

"What if I am deported?" Cata asked.

"We'll hire a lawyer to fight the charges," Sarah answered.

"But what if I am deported?" Cata repeated.

"Then we'll escape to another city, to another state, to another country, if necessary. We won't be separated, Cata."

They drank their coffee in silence. Then Sarah stood. "We need to eat a little something." She bent to light the oven, then cut two slices of bread and several thin pieces of cheese. After arranging the cheese on the bread and the bread on a baking sheet, Sarah placed the food into the oven to warm. In a few minutes, she removed the tray from the oven and deposited each slice of cheese bread onto a plate that she carried to the table.

Neither of them had much appetite, but Sarah forced herself to eat the slice though it had the consistency of sawdust in her mouth. It took them a long time to finish their food. Then Cata said, "I should get dressed."

Sarah took both plates to the sink and washed the few dishes. While she dried the final plate, the phone rang. Sarah hurried to the sitting room, lifting the phone. "Hello."

"Sarah, it's Timothy." Without waiting for her reply, he continued. "I was working on a story about last night's riot, and I heard the police arrested Cata for vagrancy."

"Yes, Timothy. It's just awful. The police took her from work."

"Her arraignment is this morning, correct?" he asked.

"Yes. Nine thirty."

"I'll be there. I think she's going before Judge Bud Wilkins. I know him, frequently play cards with him. He's tough, but he's generally fair-minded, though I fear he's been doing the mayor's bidding with regard to Villa's officers."

"Oh no, Timothy."

"I don't have to tell you, it's a crazy time in El Paso. General Victoriano Huerta died last night, and his death is small potatoes compared to yesterday's riot. Sarah, fifteen hundred people stormed the streets last night. It took the entire police force, a company of the national guard, and Pershing's troops to prevent rioters from marching into South El Paso to 'clean them out,' which the rioters chanted, beating any Mexican in their path. Luckily, Pershing's troops stopped rioters from entering Mexican communities."

"Was anyone killed?"

"No. Folks on both sides ended up in the hospital. Police arrested about nineteen people." Timothy paused before asking, "How is Cata?"

"She feels betrayed. And she's nervous about the outcome of today's arraignment, as am I."

"I'll see you both at the courthouse," Timothy responded with a tone of closure.

"Okay, Timothy," Sarah answered, pleased by his decision to join them. Sarah returned the phone to the table.

She walked to the bathroom, pausing to peer into the bedroom. Cata sat on the bed, staring into space. Sarah entered the bathroom to prepare for the day. When she returned to the bedroom and found it empty, Sarah hurried into the kitchen, relieved to find Cata dressed and seated at the table, waiting.

"I'll be ready shortly," Sarah called to her, not wanting to expose her worry. Sarah returned to the bedroom and dressed quickly.

Though it was only eight thirty when Sarah reentered the kitchen, she suggested to Cata that they leave for the courthouse since they didn't know what roadblocks and detours they might encounter.

When Cata stood from her chair, Sarah noticed the gold heart hanging at Cata's breasts. Sarah reached to hold Cata, whispering, "I love you. Whatever the outcome, we'll be together." They kissed, then gathered their things.

Once downstairs, Sarah posted a sign on the front door of the studio announcing it would be closed for business today. Sarah wondered if other downtown businesses had chosen to do the same after last night's riot.

Outside, Sarah noticed the headlight dangling from the front of the automobile. She shuddered at the reminder of their near escape.

As they drove the short distance to the courthouse, Sarah noted that police and troop presence remained heavy, especially near South El Paso. Sarah parked in front of the courthouse.

Once inside the ornate three-story building, they located a clerk, who directed them up one flight to wait outside the room where the arraignment would take place. They stood at a window, engrossed in their thoughts when Timothy arrived, stating, "You should be called in shortly." He kissed the women on their cheeks.

Timothy turned to Sarah. "You made quite an impression on Officer Burrows last night." Timothy smiled. I found out about Cata's arrest from him. He was more incensed by your 'finagling' Captain Green's intervention than by any of the other crazy events that occurred yesterday."

At that, a door opened behind them. A man gripping a clipboard called out "Miss Catalina Vasquez."

"Yes," Cata responded and walked past the official into the courtroom. Sarah and Timothy followed close behind. The bailiff directed Cata to a table on the far side of the wooden railing that separated her from the seats he then directed Sarah and Timothy to take.

After a brief wait, the bailiff announced loudly, "Please rise for the Honorable Judge Bud Wilkins."

The black-robed man entered the courtroom and assumed his seat behind the elevated judge's bench. Court proceedings began quickly, with the judge calling for Cata to raise her right hand to confirm her identification. He then read the charge: Class A misdemeanor of vagrancy for the violation of the United States' neutrality laws.

A tingling rushed through Sarah when the judge informed Cata that if found guilty of the charge, she would be extradited to Mexico. He asked Cata how she pled, "Guilty or not guilty."

Cata announced firmly, "Not guilty."

"Are you or were you ever an officer in General Francisco Villa's army?"

"I was, but I am no longer."

Timothy stood, raising a hand to catch the judge's attention. "May I speak on behalf of Miss Vasquez."

"Are you now practicing law, Mr. Tompkins?" the judge replied, obviously irritated by the interruption in the proceedings.

"No, Judge Wilkins, but if I may approach the bench, I will share relevant information about the accused."

The judge paused to consider the request. "This is highly irregular. This is an arraignment, not a trial." Then he added, "But I will allow you to approach the bench with the proviso that I will stop you the moment your comments seem irrelevant or inappropriate."

"I understand, your honor. Thank you."

"Please take your seat, Miss Vasquez," the judge directed. The bailiff held open the railing gate for Timothy to pass through. Timothy stood next to Cata. "Judge Wilkins, I first met Miss Catalina Vasquez in April 1915 in the Mexican town of Irapuato. At that time, she served as a colonel in General Villa's army."

Sarah studied the judge when Timothy began to relay how Cata had rescued him from execution. She hoped Timothy's story would sway the judge's ruling in Cata's favor, but Wilkins's face remained inscrutable.

Timothy extended his hand in Cata's direction. "Had Miss Vasquez not intervened on my behalf, I would be dead, hanged as a scapegoat for actions taken by my government." He paused briefly before continuing to address the judge. "With all due respect to the court, what we are doing by charging Miss Vasquez with vagrancy is scapegoating her for the murders of the Americans at Santa Ysabel. Such action is unfair and should be considered un-American. Judge Wilkins, I vouch for Miss Vasquez. I am standing here today because she risked her life to save mine."

At the conclusion of Timothy's statement, the judge asked, "Is that it? Are you finished addressing the court?"

"Yes, your honor."

"Then you may return to your seat, Mr. Tompkins."

The judge remained silent until Timothy resumed his seat beside Sarah.

The judge then directed, "Miss Vasquez, please rise." He waited for Cata to stand before continuing. "Miss Vasquez, in light of the information imparted by Mr. Tompkins, I'm going to order adjournment in contemplation of dismissal. What that means is if you avoid arrest during the next six months, I will dismiss this charge of vagrancy."

Sarah shut her eyes in relief.

"If, however, you are arrested again within the designated six-month period, you will have to stand trial for this vagrancy charge as well as any new charge brought against you. Understood?"

"Yes, your honor," Cata responded.

"You may retrieve any money deposited for bail. Miss Vasquez, you are free to go."

The bailiff announced, "All rise."

Sarah could hardly contain her excitement at the outcome of the arraignment. As soon as the judge left the court, Sarah hugged Timothy, saying, "Thank you!"

Cata rejoined them, and the bailiff directed all three from the courtroom. Once outside the room, Cata took Timothy's hands in hers. "Thank you, Timothy. You have repaid any debt you felt you owed me."

Timothy responded by leaning forward to kiss Cata on the cheek. Sarah hugged Cata to her. "Let's go home."

S E P T E M B E R   2 2 ,   1 9 8 3

Kayla

"The family of the youngest ASARCO employee killed in the train massacre, published a letter in the *El Paso Herald* calling for calm to return to the city. They reminded El Pasoans that many 'Mexican friends' living among them had suffered loss and abuse of their own families during the years of revolution." Sarah rubbed the palm of her hand over the leather arm of her chair before adding, "Calm did return, but tensions and resentments remained high in El Paso."

"I think this is a good place to conclude today," Kayla suggested, noting a weariness to Sarah's voice. "We've gone longer than usual, and I don't want to overly tire you, Sarah." Kayla motioned for Abel to stop filming.

"Yes," the old woman agreed, "so much past to remember."

"But thank God," Abel interjected, "that Timothy convinced the judge of Cata's true character."

"Yes," Sarah agreed. Then chuckling, added, "Apparently, learning of Timothy's near demise gave the judge quite a fright. Judge Wilkins later told Timothy that his death would have cost the judge the supplemental income Timothy's bad poker play provided. The judge said he had to reward Cata for saving his additional source of income."

"And Cata?" Kayla asked. "How did she respond to the manner in which the charges were dismissed? After all, the judge essentially saddled Cata with six months' probation for an offense leveled against her out of prejudice."

Sarah's smile disappeared, and she glanced away before answering. "I think Cata began to believe that if she stayed in this country long enough, its beauty would rub off on her hands."

PART
FIVE

O C T O B E R   1 2 ,   1 9 8 3

Kayla

Kayla expressed gleeful surprise when Sarah answered the door cradling a large bouquet of crepe-paper flowers in the crook of each arm.

"Welcome," Sarah cheerfully greeted Kayla, handing her one of the bouquets. Sarah deposited a kiss on Kayla's cheek.

"Welcome, Abel," Sarah greeted. She started to hand a bouquet to Abel, but the equipment he carried in both hands prevented her from following through. "This bouquet is for you, but I'll place these flowers aside."

"I still want my kiss," Abel insisted, so Sarah leaned past the camera and lights he carried to plant a kiss on his cheek.

"Come in," Sarah encouraged. Sarah directed their attention to a tray of refreshments and announced, "Oatmeal raisin cookies and agua fresca. Please, help yourselves."

"This is all very thoughtful of you, Sarah, very festive," Kayla said as she admired the brightly colored flowers. Placing the bouquet on the table beside her seat, she said, "I'll pour agua fresca for Abel and me while he sets up. May I serve you as well?"

"No thank you, Kayla."

Kayla poured two glasses of the fruit-flavored drink. She carried the refreshments to Abel first, then returned for her glass. She took a sip. "Delicious," she said, taking her seat before placing the tumbler on a coaster.

Kayla studied Sarah, who watched Abel positioning the lights and adjusting the camera. Sarah looked cool and comfortable, Kayla thought, in the khaki pants and silky green blouse she wore in her usual style. "Sarah," Kayla prompted, "we appreciate your allowing us again into your home." She thought of how Sarah always pushed to schedule their next interview and how graciously she welcomed them, which was so contrary to her reputation for shunning company. Still, Kayla worried about the aftermath of their visits, so she asked Sarah, "Does reliving your past with us bring you pleasure or pain?"

Kayla felt fixed by Sarah's blue eyes. "Both." Sarah paused, then added, "And the pain isn't always from what happened; it is also from what didn't."

Kayla nodded, relieved when Abel declared, "When you two ladies are ready to start, I'm ready."

"Sarah?" Kayla asked.

"I'm ready."

Kayla signaled for Abel to begin filming. "Sarah Delaney interview, number five, El Paso, Texas, 10:14 a.m., October 12, 1983." Having completed that formality, Kayla reminded Sarah, "We concluded our last session with the discussion of El Paso's race riot and Cata's arraignment in January 1916."

"Yes," Sarah acknowledged, beginning anew. "After the race riot and the call for calm issued by the family of the youngest victim of the Santa Ysabel massacre, El Paso settled into an uneasy rhythm of business as usual. But several events quickly shattered any attempt at normalcy.

"The first week of March, El Paso experienced another tragedy, this one resulting from the city's fear of a typhus outbreak blamed, in large part, on what Mayor Lea described in a telegram to the US

Surgeon General as the arrival in El Paso of hundreds of 'dirty,' 'destitute,' louse-ridden Mexicans." Sarah shook her head sadly. "Not one to be dissuaded by facts, Mayor Lea, held this belief even though in February, the El Paso County Medical Society reported finding only two cases of typhus in the more than five thousand rooms health inspectors visited in what they described as the 'worst part of Chihuahuita,' a neighborhood housing some of the city's poorest Mexican refugees.

"So, as part of the campaign to save El Paso from typhus, the city's health department decided to delouse prisoners in the city jail. Health department officials oversaw the preparation of two tubs: one for washing prisoners' clothes and one for bathing prisoners. The tub for the clothes held a mixture of gasoline and disinfectant. The tub for the prisoners' bath contained a blend of kerosene and vinegar." Sarah paused as if steeling herself. "During the delousing process, someone lit a match."

Kayla gasped, covering her mouth with her hand at the envisioned horror.

"According to witnesses, gas vapors exploded, and flames instantly engulfed the entire jail. Approximately thirty-five prisoners caught fire." Sarah squeezed her eyes tightly shut while she described the aftermath. "Burned prisoners littered the alley alongside the jail, many shrieking their agony. The stench of scorched flesh permeated the smoky haze shrouding downtown." Sarah reopened her eyes. "Twenty-seven prisoners died as a result of that blaze." She paused, then added, "Nineteen of the dead were Mexican; several were being held on charges of vagrancy.

"The city called for a grand jury investigation to determine the possibility of criminal negligence. The mayor quickly released a statement supporting the health department and the physician overseeing the delousing of prisoners. He dismissed the notion of negligence or intentionality as cause for the blaze, stating instead, sometimes 'the unexpected happens.' After convening for several weeks, the grand jury concluded its investigation into the 'city jail holocaust' without issuing any indictments or reporting any findings." Sarah paused thoughtfully before she continued. "But El Pasoans had already lost interest in the horror at the jail because a new scare captured the city's attention. Three days after the jail fire, General Pancho Villa attacked the United States at Columbus, New Mexico."

MARCH 1916

Sarah

"**Oh** my God, Timothy!" Sarah exclaimed in disbelief. "Yes, I'll pick you up in half an hour." Sarah returned the phone to the table. She stood stunned, trying to make sense of the news Timothy had just shared. She didn't notice Cata until she asked, "What's wrong, Sarah?"

"Timothy just called. Villa attacked the United States around four this morning at Columbus, New Mexico."

Cata didn't respond immediately, seeming to consider the weight of the news. Then she asked, "Does the battle continue?"

"No. Apparently, after the initial surprise, troopers at Camp Furlong and citizens of the town mounted a successful defense."

"And you are going with Timothy to Columbus?" Cata asked in a tone suggesting she already knew the answer.

"Yes. I said I'd pick him up in half an hour, so I need to get ready." Sarah started for the bedroom.

"Why are you going, Sarah?" Cata followed her.

The question surprised Sarah. "To take photographs of what happened in Columbus."

Cata responded, "Your photographs will show the death and destruction of battle, which will help convince Americans who need little convincing that they should seek revenge against all Mexicans. The pictures won't show why Villa attacked."

"No, my photographs won't show why Villa attacked Columbus." Sarah added more emphatically, "attacked the United States." She paused in front of the chifforobe, fighting her irritation at having to justify her work. "I'm a photographer, Cata. I take photographs for newspapers; I take photographs for postcards; I take photographs for families; and if I'm lucky, I take photographs for history." Sarah removed a dress from the chifforobe. "Let's not argue. Let's not allow emotions of the day to affect us."

Cata nodded, stating simply, "I'll leave you to get ready."

Sarah tried not to think of Cata's comments regarding her photography. She knew the day's news heightened feelings in each of them.

Sarah dressed quickly, stepping into her undergarments, then pulling a gray woolen dress over her head. Sitting on the bed, she used a small hook to button her shoes. Sarah finished by positioning a black woolen hat on her head, securing it with a hat pin.

When she entered the kitchen, she saw Cata placing a thermos into a basket.

"I packed sandwiches and a thermos of coffee for Timothy and you."

Sarah crossed the room to hug Cata. "Thank you," she said, adding, "Cata, passions will be raw for many El Pasoans. Can you remain in the apartment today, call in sick?"

Cata shook her head. "I just started working at the cigar factory. I can't call in sick. Besides, I won't live afraid."

"It's not living afraid; it's being cautious," Sarah countered.

"I will work my shift at the factory today," Cata responded, concluding the conversation.

Sarah nodded.

"I'll carry the basket downstairs," Cata said, opening the apartment door for Sarah to exit.

In the studio, Sarah stopped to collect additional rolls of film. She remembered, then, that she had not put a handkerchief in her pocket.

When she mentioned she needed to return to the apartment to correct the oversight, Cata offered, "I'll go."

"They're in the top drawer of the chifforobe," Sarah called as Cata darted up the stairs.

By the time Sarah finished taping a sign to the door announcing the studio's closure for the day, Cata had returned with two handkerchiefs.

"Thank you, Cata," Sarah said, reaching for the cloths.

Cata nodded distractedly.

"Is everything all right?"

"Yes," Cata responded unconvincingly.

Knowing Cata must feel conflicted about today's news, Sarah chose not to further question the change in Cata. After slipping on her coat, Sarah grasped the basket and her camera. When Cata opened the studio door for her, Sarah urged, "Stay safe. I'll see you tonight." Sarah exited into the cool morning air to pick up Timothy.

After a brief greeting, Timothy provided directions for their seventy-five-mile drive to Columbus.

Turning westward, as Timothy directed, Sarah commented, "I've never been to Columbus."

"Well," Timothy pushed the fedora from his forehead, "you haven't missed much. It's a small whistle stop about three miles from the border. Camp Furlong, home to the Thirteenth Cavalry, is on the edge of town. If Camp Furlong were at full strength, Columbus would have a population of about thirteen hundred. But prior to Villa's attack, Camp Furlong's commander, Colonel Herbert J. Slocum, stationed some of the troops along the border. According to this morning's wire, only about 350 soldiers were in Columbus at the time of the raid, and about eighty of those were noncombatants, you know, medical personnel, cooks, and the like."

"And Villa's force?" Sarah asked without taking her eyes from the rough stretch of road.

"Slocum reports approximately five hundred Villistas attacked Columbus." Timothy cupped his hands around a match to light his cigarette. He took a deep drag. "What's amazing is how few Americans were killed. So far, the count is seventeen—eight soldiers and nine civilians."

"Thank God more weren't killed."

"Yes," Timothy agreed. "Apparently, the Villistas didn't fare as well. According to the report, dead and wounded Villistas litter the town's streets, thanks in large measure to the Thirteenth's machine-gun unit. Apparently, the Villistas blundered by torching several buildings, which illuminated what otherwise would have been dark streets."

Sarah imagined the horrifying scene. "Why do you think Villa attacked Columbus?"

"Who knows?" Timothy placed the cigarette to his lips and inhaled deeply. "Maybe Villa attacked out of revenge for American support of Carranza." Timothy pinched a flake of tobacco from the tip of his tongue before continuing. "Or perhaps Villa planned the attack in order to place Carranza in a politically awkward position by drawing the United States into Mexico."

"How would that place Carranza in an awkward position?"

"Well, think about it," Timothy replied. "In 1914, Carranza, like many Mexican citizens, deeply opposed the US invasion of Veracruz. Now that Carranza has President Wilson's backing, will Carranza risk alienating the Americans by opposing our pursuit of Villa into Mexico? Then again, will Carranza risk losing support of the Mexican people by allowing an incursion into their country?" Timothy took another pull from the cigarette before flicking it out the window.

"Do you think the US will invade Mexico?" Sarah asked, dreading even the thought of such action.

"I don't think US citizens will continue to tolerate President Wilson's approach of 'watchful waiting.' I think he's going to have to act; after all, Villa attacked Americans on American soil."

Sarah squeezed the steering wheel at the suggestion of a possible conflict with Mexico. She thought of Cata.

As if Timothy read her mind, he asked, "Does Cata know about Villa's attack on Columbus?"

"Yes. I told her what you shared this morning."

"What was her response?" Timothy asked.

"I think Cata is justifiably worried about how the US will react."

"After getting entangled in El Paso's lunatic reaction to the Santa Ysabel massacre, Cata must be concerned about the city's response to the Columbus attack."

"I think she's more concerned for Mexico." Sarah turned the steering wheel slightly to avoid a rut in the road. "I can't imagine the apprehension she must feel for her country and her people." Sarah spoke a truth she only now realized.

"I hope she will be careful," Timothy added.

"Cata insisted on going to work today. She is not one to cower in fear."

"And how is she liking her job at La Internacional Cigar Factory?" Timothy inquired. "Boxing cigars seems such a contrast to working as a nurse's aide at Hotel Dieu."

"Cata couldn't remain at Hotel Dieu Hospital working alongside someone who betrayed her. While the cigar factory may not challenge her talents, she is working among women she trusts." Sarah hoped her response brought finality to their discussion of Cata because this talk renewed Sarah's worry for her.

They drove in silence for another hour, each deep in thought until Sarah suddenly saw smoke rising in the distance. She asked, "Is that Columbus up ahead?"

"Yes, I think it must be."

Timothy's response concluded their exchange for the remainder of the drive to Columbus. Sarah suspected they both dreaded the nightmarish scenes and tales of terror and grief awaiting them.

Entering the town, they were immediately confronted with crews loading Villista corpses onto wagons and teams preparing to remove bodies of horses sprawled lifeless in the streets.

"Let's park," Timothy directed. "I want to walk the town, get a feel for what happened."

Stepping amid glass from shattered windows, Sarah noted the splintered clapboard and pockmarked adobe of buildings so recently scarred by the smack of bullets. She placed a handkerchief to her nose and mouth in an unsuccessful attempt to filter the cloying smell of kerosene and burning flesh.

"I think the army is burning Villista corpses," Timothy stated, his face screwing up involuntarily at the awful odor.

When Sarah and Timothy reached the charred, smoldering field of collapsed buildings, Timothy asked one of the troopers about the blackened ruins.

Pointing south, the soldier identified, "That large area there was the Commercial Hotel. Villistas murdered two men inside the hotel and another two men who attempted to escape from the building. Several women and children survived. The area next to it," the trooper shifted his extended arm to direct their look, "that was the Lemmon and Romney Mercantile."

Sarah informed Timothy that she wished to cross the street to take photos of the burned rubble of buildings and suggested they separate to make the best use of their time. Timothy voiced his concern for her safety, but Sarah called his attention to the troopers patrolling on horseback, soldiers working to clear the dead from the streets, and citizens gathering in small clusters. Timothy agreed to rendezvous at the car in three hours.

Once Timothy departed, Sarah photographed the smoldering ruins. She photographed the burned hull of a car parked near one of the destroyed structures, captured photos of mounted troops patrolling the streets and of soldiers standing guard near businesses with shattered windows, broken doors, and bullet-scarred facades.

Sarah crossed the railroad tracks to the two-story wooden train depot, where a group of townspeople, largely women and children, waiting anxiously on the platform for a train to take them to safety. They whispered their fears of Villa's return. Sarah photographed the crowd's collective stare down the distance of empty tracks.

From the depot, Sarah looked at Camp Furlong's rows of wooden buildings a few hundred meters away. She photographed the bustling camp before crossing the tracks into town to walk a street she hadn't traveled. She spied a small gathering of people in the distance and headed in their direction. Sarah was upon the group before realizing what she was seeing. Seven troopers and three young women posed beside an extinguished funeral pyre of dead Villistas. One soldier had retrieved a blackened corpse that still retained its human shape; he raised the charred figure to a semi-sitting position and pointed a pistol at the corpse's featureless face. The soldiers and their female companions grinned for an amused comrade who snapped the photo. "Wait, wait," called one of the soldiers to the photographer. The trooper removed his web ammo belt with scabbard, wrapping it around the waist of his girlfriend. Handing her the pistol to point in the direction of the raised corpse, he called, "Now, take another photograph."

Sarah walked quickly from the ghastly scene. She traveled a road cleared of human remains; the lone carcass of a horse still lay in the sand. Sarah entered a residential area, walking past scattered homes, many with broken windows, and some with doors hanging at odd angles from their wooden frames. At one house, a young couple worked to board up shattered windows while two toddlers played in the yard. They startled at Sarah's passing, watching her with haunted eyes. Sarah dipped her head in acknowledgement, not knowing what to say since "good afternoon" certainly didn't fit the day.

Stopping in front of a neat clapboard home, Sarah looked about, attempting to determine the best route back toward her automobile; it would soon be time to meet Timothy. Distracted, she stood unaware that a woman approached from the house. "May I help you?" the woman asked curtly. Adding, "If you're looking for Mrs. Maud Hawks Wright, she's resting from her ordeal and unable to see anyone." The buxom middle-aged woman appeared formidable, blocking the gate leading into her yard.

"I'm not looking for anyone," Sarah stammered. "I'm just getting my bearings."

The woman stared at Sarah's camera when she spoke, clearly doubting Sarah's explanation. "I am Mrs. Herbert Slocum, wife of Colonel Slocum. I will not permit any photographs to be taken of Mrs. Wright at this time." She continued speaking as though Sarah had raised an objection. "As a woman, please respect Mrs. Wright's need for privacy and rest. Just imagine how she must feel after being kidnapped from her ranch by Villa and his brutes, her husband taken at gunpoint and her baby boy wrenched from her arms before she was forced to endure nine days of riding with those animals only to watch them attack and murder her fellow Americans in Columbus."

"Mrs. Slocum, I am a photographer." Sarah raised her camera in acknowledgement. "And I do work for El Paso newspapers." Sarah lowered the camera to her side. "But I assure you, my stopping in front of your home was purely a coincidence. I didn't know you lived here or that Mrs. Wright rested with you." Sarah continued, anxious to clear any suspicions. "As a woman, I *am* sympathetic to Mrs. Wright's ordeal and cannot begin to imagine how she must feel. Please convey my well-wishes for a quick and safe reunion with her husband and child."

Sarah noted the softening of Mrs. Wright's stern expression. "I apologize for any rudeness born from misunderstanding your intent." The colonel's wife spoke without the previous sharpness to her voice. "As you might imagine, we are all on edge, Mrs.?"

"Miss Sarah Delaney, and no apology is needed, Mrs. Slocum."
Preparing to depart, Sarah added, "I wish you and all in this community
a return to peace and safety."

"Thank you, Miss Delaney." Mrs. Slocum turned to retrace the steps
to her house. Sarah continued her journey, which she hoped would return
her to the car.

Sarah walked along a road that skirted the edge of town when a woeful
commotion caught her attention. Against her better judgment, she turned
toward the wailing and protestations emanating from a small home. When
Sarah reached the front of the house, she saw three troopers forcing a young
Mexican man forward at gunpoint. The prisoner walked, his hands raised
above his head in surrender, followed by a woman with a baby on her hip and
two other small children tugging the folds of her skirt, all wailing in unison.

While the young Mexican protested his innocence, one trooper dangled a pair of field glasses from his raised fist as proof of the man's guilt.
The soldier taunted, "Go ahead and run for it, you Villa-loving bastard."
He added, "I'd like nothing better than to toss another dead Villista on
the funeral fire."

Sarah watched helplessly as the soldiers forced their prisoner onto a
wagon bed. She stood frozen when the troopers drove past, respectfully
tipping their hats to her while the prisoner exchanged a mournful, knowing look with his family.

The family's soul-wrenching wails unnerved Sarah. She turned south,
hurrying down another street of this deeply wounded town, anxious to
locate her automobile and Timothy, anxious to leave Columbus and its
pain. She spied her car in the distance and hurried toward it, observing
as she did so that the street had been cleared of its dead, leaving only
blood-darkened sand where bodies had lain.

Sarah rested against the automobile and saw Timothy walking briskly
toward her. When he reached the car, he said simply, "I'll crank her. Go
ahead and get in."

As soon as Timothy scooted into the vehicle, Sarah turned the steering wheel to U-turn, then opened the throttle, shifting into high gear.
Neither of them spoke.

Timothy removed a flask from his jacket and uncapped it. After Sarah
refused his offer of a drink, Timothy took a deep draught of the alcohol, coughed, wiped the back of his hand against his mouth, then took

a second drink before capping and pocketing the flask. He lit a cigarette, smoking it quickly down to a nub, then used it to light a second cigarette.

They drove thirty minutes before Sarah interrupted the silence. "I'm going to stop the car for a break. Cata packed some coffee and sandwiches for us. We should probably try to eat something."

"Coffee sounds good," Timothy replied.

Sarah guided the automobile from the road, careful to avoid soft sand. They stepped out of the vehicle to retrieve a basket from the rumble seat. While Sarah removed the wrapped sandwiches, Timothy poured two cups of coffee. Though lukewarm, the coffee provided a jolt each of them needed, and they drained their cups quickly.

Timothy took a bite of the sandwich thick with ham and cheese. Then took a second bite before speaking. "I think I'm losing my objective nerve." He paused before continuing. "I think my adventure in Mexico has made all this death and suffering very real." Timothy studied the sandwich rather than making eye contact with Sarah. "I'm not able to maintain a journalistic distance when I hear how a young wife had to be dragged from the edge of a balcony to stop her from jumping to her husband's body below. I'm not able to closet my emotions when I see the sprawled body of a Villista, who can't be older than fourteen, gut shot, lying in a pool of blood and urine." Timothy lowered the sandwich.

Sarah didn't know what words she could say to lessen Timothy's ache, so she remained quiet and let him talk.

"Those poor Mexicans who live in Columbus. Colonel Slocum has already decided they were accomplices in the Villista attack, and the white townspeople are quick to agree. Slocum has his soldiers searching homes and businesses of all Mexicans and Mexican Americans for even the flimsiest of evidence to arrest and run them out of town, or worse. And the fact that the Villistas left the Mexicans of Columbus largely unscathed only adds to suspicions of their complicity." He shook his head. "The soldiers and townspeople want revenge, and I'm afraid they will destroy their Mexican neighbors to get it."

Sarah thought sadly of the young man she saw arrested and wondered about the fate of his family.

"Did you learn more about why Villa attacked Columbus?" Sarah asked, resting her hip against the car while she nibbled at the edge of her sandwich.

"Well, there is no shortage of explanations for Villa's attack. In addition to Villa's anger at President Wilson's recognition of Carranza, Mrs. Wright, the American woman Villa held captive, said Villa spoke angrily about the Mexicans who burned in the El Paso jail fire. He swore he would 'make torches' of every American man, woman, and child in Columbus, except for the Mexican townspeople, who were not to be harmed." Timothy paused to take another bite of his sandwich. After swallowing, Timothy added, "I'm sure other reasons for his attack will come to light." Timothy placed the remainder of the sandwich into his mouth.

"And why was Camp Furlong, or Colonel Slocum," Sarah corrected, "caught off guard? I know the *Times* has printed numerous articles about sightings of Villa in the region and concerns about a potential attack?"

"Well, that's a question being asked by many. And it's not just Slocum caught off guard. Warnings of the attack ran through the chain of command from the State Department down. The current explanation is that there were so many conflicting sightings of Villa, no one could know with any certainty that Villa would attack Columbus." Timothy retrieved the thermos, offering it to Sarah, who shook her head no. Timothy drained the remainder of the coffee into his cup. "Frankly, I think that Slocum and others ignored warnings of Villa's attack on Columbus largely out of hubris. They simply couldn't believe a lowly Mexican bandit would attack the US Army on US soil."

The conversation concluded, Sarah wrapped the remainder of her sandwich and placed it along with her cup in the basket, positioning the basket again on the rumble seat. She scooted into the car while Timothy cranked-started the vehicle. Sarah steered the auto back onto the road leading to El Paso.

It was a little past 7:00 p.m. when Sarah dropped off Timothy at his *Times* office. She drove the short distance to the studio, parking in front. When she entered the darkened foyer, she heard Cata open the apartment door and saw her waiting at the top of the stairs.

"It's good to be home," Sarah said, climbing the steps. She kissed Cata before entering the apartment.

"I'm glad you are home," Cata responded. "It will be a while before supper is ready; you have time to bathe and change clothes."

"Thank you, Cata. I'd love a bath. We can talk over supper."

"Yes," Cata agreed.

Sarah still felt a stiffness in Cata's demeanor though Cata seemed struggling to overcome or at least mask it. Sarah hoped they would not have tension tonight. Entering the bathroom, she turned on the faucets for the water to run while she undressed in the bedroom. She walked naked from bedroom to bathroom, carrying her nightgown and robe with her. She stepped into the bathtub, allowing the hot water to envelope her tired body. Sarah rested the back of her head against the tub's cool porcelain rim and closed her eyes. When Cata entered the bathroom, offering, "here," and extending a glass of wine, Sarah realized she had slipped into sleep. She sat up to accept the proffered glass. "Thank you." She took a sip.

Cata sat on the edge of the tub. She picked up a sponge, soaked it in the water before soaping it, then began washing Sarah's back.

"Mmm," Sarah said, "that feels good." She closed her eyes and enjoyed the soothing motion along her back, neck, and shoulders.

Cata then used the sponge to rinse the soap from Sarah. She kissed the top of Sarah's head and said, "When you finish bathing, the food will be ready." Cata stood from the tub's edge and departed the room.

Sarah washed the rest of her body and then her hair. She took another sip of wine before stepping from the tub to dry off. She dressed in her nightgown and bathrobe, and carried the unfinished glass of wine into the kitchen.

"Sit," Cata directed. "I'll bring your plate."

"Smells good."

Cata carried two steaming plates of beans covered in a soupy green chile with onion and cubed beef. After setting their two plates on the table, she retrieved a warmer with freshly made flour tortillas. Before sitting, Cata poured herself a glass of wine and refreshed Sarah's glass.

They ate using pieces of tortilla to scoop bite-size measures of beans, meat, and chile. When they had eaten their fill, Sarah carried their plates to the sink and returned to the table with the open bottle of wine.

"Did you get the photographs you wanted?" Cata asked as Sarah refilled Cata's glass.

"I took a few photos for the newspaper," Sarah replied, pouring wine into her own glass before sitting.

"Do you have to develop prints tonight?"

"No, thank goodness." Sarah wearily wiped each eye. "I told Timothy I'd get the prints to him tomorrow."

"What did you learn about the battle?"

Sarah relayed the information Timothy shared with her about the disregarded warnings of attack, the initial unpreparedness, the machine guns, the burning buildings, the retreat and pursuit. Cata listened intently. Sarah chose not to share the suspicions of complicity and assumptions of guilt white soldiers and citizens held against Mexican residents of Columbus. And she didn't tell about the soldiers' use of Villista dead as props for their own staged photos. Though this information would not surprise Cata, Sarah felt unsettled by such thoughts.

"What about El Paso?" Sarah asked. "Any problems?"

"More police on patrol. More street corner talk of attacking Mexico."

"But you didn't have problems, did you?"

"Besides angry looks, no. No one arrested me; no one assaulted me," Cata responded with disgust. "But police are again arresting former Villista officers."

Sarah reached to take Cata's hand. "We'll have to be careful for the next few days. The anger seems to run its course in a week's time."

Cata nodded then stood to carry the wine glasses to the sink.

"Cata, I'll clean the kitchen; you cooked."

"I need to be busy," Cata replied.

They worked side by side, saying little. When they completed their work, Sarah could no longer refrain from yawning. "I'm going to bed."

"I'm not ready to sleep."

"Goodnight, then." Sarah kissed Cata and headed to the bathroom to prepare for the night. Once in bed, Sarah cradled her pillow and, within minutes, fell into a sound sleep.

In the early morning hours, Sarah dreamed she stood beside a funeral pyre, her camera gripped in one hand. When she squatted to photograph the gray ash and blackened bone, a charred figure rose faceless from the gruesome mound. Its hand encircled her wrist with fingers crusted from fire. Sarah pulled free of the scorched grip. Then the figure called her name, and its voice was Cata's. Sarah grasped frantically to pull Cata from the pyre, but she had disappeared into the ashpit. Sarah released a mournful wail.

"Sarah!" Cata called, "Sarah, wake up; you're having a nightmare."

Sarah woke with a start. It took a moment for her to become oriented. "Oh, Cata," she moaned, "what a horrible dream."

"It wasn't real," Cata whispered, soothingly.

"It seemed so real," Sarah said.

"What did you dream?"

"I don't want to say; I don't want to think about it."

"Here," Cata said, pulling Sarah to her, "put your head on my shoulder."

Sarah held tightly to Cata, who whispered reassuringly, "Go back to sleep. It was only a dream."

❋❋❋

"Two of those photographs are not mine," Sarah said quickly when Cata looked at the front page of the newspaper that lay open on the kitchen table. "My photo is the one of the burned buildings," Sarah said defensively, pointing to the bottom picture before Cata picked up the paper to study the grainy shots, one of Mrs. Maud Hawks Wright; the other, a photo of burning Villista bodies. Cata tossed the newspaper back onto the table.

"Is the US sending troops into Mexico?" Cata asked.

"Yes."

"Your troops will never catch General Villa," Cata responded confidently.

Sarah didn't know exactly why, but Cata's pronouncement made Sarah bristle. "What makes you say that, Cata?"

"Villa knows northern Mexico, knows the land, knows the people; the US generals don't. And," Cata added, "even Mexicans who hate Villa will hate US soldiers in Mexico more. Mexicans will not help them catch Villa, and the soldiers can't catch Villa without the Mexicans' help. American soldiers do not belong in Mexico," Cata stated with finality, then turned to walk from the discussion.

"How should the US respond to Villa's attacking and killing Americans on American soil?" Sarah challenged, knowing she waded deeper into an emotional quagmire she should avoid.

Cata whirled to face Sarah. "You talk as if General Villa struck the first blow. You forget how the US has played puppet master through selective arms embargos and permission for Carranza's troops to cross your

'American soil.' If the US wants Villa defeated, then continue to support Carranza and Obregón so they can defeat him."

Sarah sought to halt this discussion, urging, "Let's not fight over something for which neither of us has any control."

Cata presented her final volley. "Villa embarrassed the United States and its army; that is the reason for US troops to march into Mexico." Cata strode to the apartment door, calling back, "I'm going to work."

Sarah sat in the now-quiet apartment wishing she could start the day anew. She had wanted to urge Cata to be careful, to remain alert. She had wanted to warn her about the newspaper's announcement of arrests in El Paso of fifteen former Villista officers. Instead, she sat alone, regretting the morning's interaction.

❁❁❁

When the bell over the studio door jangled, Sarah stepped from behind the curtains to see a young soldier standing stiffly, his campaign hat underneath his arm.

"Good morning," Sarah greeted.

"Miss Sarah Delaney?" the young man questioned.

"Yes," Sarah responded, unsettled by the soldier's presence. "What can I do for you?"

The young trooper walked forward and extended a small envelope to her. "Mrs. Slocum asked me to deliver this message."

Sarah looked at the neat handwriting on the envelope.

"Ma'am, Mrs. Slocum asked me to wait for your response."

Sarah retrieved a letter opener from a cup on the counter. She opened the top flap and removed the folded note to read the precise handwriting.

> *Dear Miss Delaney,*
> *I am currently in El Paso with Mrs. Maud Hawks Wright; we are staying at the Hotel Paso del Norte. I write to invite you to join us for Sunday tea tomorrow at 4:00 p.m. in the hotel dining room. I would very much like you to be my guest so I might make amends for my rudeness when we*

met in Columbus earlier this week.

Please let Corporal Simon know if you are available to join us so that I may make the appropriate arrangements.

Sincerely,

Mrs. Herbert J. Slocum

P.S. Mrs. Wright is amenable to your photographing her.

Sarah read the note a second time. "Yes, Corporal Simon, please tell Mrs. Slocum I would be delighted to join Mrs. Wright and her for tea."

"Thank you, ma'am. I will inform her." He removed his hat from under his arm. "Good day," he wished with a formal military bearing.

As soon as the bell jangled his departure, Sarah began to question her acceptance of the invitation. She would have to arrange with A. J. to return him to the sanitorium earlier than usual. While Sarah knew A. J. would understand, she worried how Cata would react to Sarah's tea with the wife of the now infamous Colonel Slocum.

Sarah picked up the phone to call A. J. first. She waited while an attendant retrieved him. When A. J. finally answered the phone, the raspiness of his voice startled Sarah.

"Are you all right?" Sarah asked.

"Yes, just a bit of a cold," A. J. responded in a tone intended to dismiss her worry. "What do you need?"

Sarah explained about the invitation from Mrs. Slocum. Before she could suggest an earlier time for his work at the studio, A. J. responded, "I'll skip the studio tomorrow. It's better if I rest to see if I can kick this cold and cough."

"Are you sure, A. J.?"

"Yes, of course," he replied with his usual gruffness. "Hey," he said to stop her from hanging up the phone, "photograph Mrs. Wright. Her name is all over the news."

"I will, A. J. You take care, and let me know if you need anything."

"Will do, but I won't need anything."

Before Sarah could say goodbye, A. J. hung up.

Sarah entered the bustling lobby of the Hotel Paso del Norte. She glanced at the colorful stained-glass dome as she made her way to the large dining room. Sarah hoped she would recognize Mrs. Slocum since they had met only briefly in Columbus.

A black-suited host greeted her at the entrance to the dining area. When she mentioned whom she was meeting, he led her to a table near an arched window where two women sat. Mrs. Slocum smiled broadly when Sarah approached. As the host pulled out the chair for Sarah, Mrs. Slocum said with genuine warmth, "I am so glad you could join us, Miss Delaney."

Mrs. Slocum informed the host they were ready for their tea. Then she returned her attention to Sarah. "Miss Delaney, I wish to introduce you to Mrs. Maud Hawks Wright."

"I'm very pleased to meet you, Mrs. Wright," Sarah said, adding a brief nod of greeting.

"As I am you," the comely young woman responded. Mrs. Slocum quickly took the lead in the conversation, relating the story, with great chagrin, of her rudeness when she met Sarah in Columbus.

"Well, you were protecting me," Mrs. Wright defended, clearly having heard the tale previously.

"Yes," Sarah agreed. "Given the circumstances, yours was a completely understandable response to finding a stranger at your gate."

"Can you imagine," Mrs. Slocum spoke, "that was just last Thursday?"

Mrs. Wright replied quietly, "It seems a lifetime ago."

"Yes," Mrs. Slocum agreed somberly. "In many ways, it was."

Two suited waiters arrived to pause the conversation. One placed a porcelain tea set on the table then served each of them while the other positioned a three-tiered stand at the table's center.

"Thank you," Mrs. Slocum acknowledged. The waiters bowed before departing. Mrs. Slocum identified the food placed before the women. "The bottom plate has finger sandwiches," she identified, "egg salad, salmon and capers, and coronation chicken." She elevated the palm of her hand to the second tier, announcing, "Scones with strawberry and apricot preserves." Raising her hand to the top tier, she listed, "Petit fours and miniature cherry tarts. Enjoy," she encouraged.

"Please, you first, Mrs. Wright," Sarah insisted. Once the young woman had placed two finger sandwiches on her plate, Sarah took one slender egg salad and one chicken sandwich. While Mrs. Slocum selected her sandwiches, Sarah accepted the creamer and sugar bowl from Mrs. Wright.

Once they all had prepared their tea, Mrs. Slocum raised her teacup and toasted, "To new friendships and to the quick and just success of our country's Punitive Expedition."

Sarah thought of Cata as she swallowed the briefest sip of tea.

Each woman took a bite of a sandwich, and each remarked on its tastiness.

When Mrs. Slocum finished chewing, she dabbed her napkin to her mouth, then directed, "Mrs. Wright, tell Miss Delaney your most excellent news."

Mrs. Wright lowered her sandwich to her plate, smiling broadly. "They've found my Johnnie, my little boy. I'm going to be reunited with my baby."

"That's wonderful news," Sarah responded, genuinely excited for the young woman.

"Yes, he is safe. He is with a Mexican family in Pearson, Mexico."

Sarah studied the sun-browned face of the young mother whose eyes teared with emotion as she told the good news.

"I said I could walk to Pearson in three days to get my Johnnie, but Carranza insisted he will have Johnnie returned safely to me. My baby is supposed to arrive in Juárez in the next day or so."

"How old is Johnnie?" Sarah asked.

"He's two, but he's big for his age," the young woman stated proudly. When she added, "He looks just like his daddy," a sadness washed over her face. She touched a handkerchief to each eye. "You know," she said to Sarah, "I didn't cry when the Villistas came to our ranch in Mexico, stealing our animals and supplies, or when they took my husband, my Ed, or when they forced me to leave my Johnnie with the wife of a hired hand, not even when they forced me to ride with them for nine days, or made me watch while they attacked Americans in Columbus. I didn't cry until I learned my little Johnnie was still alive and my Ed was not."

"There, there," Mrs. Slocum soothed, "I didn't mean to upset you, Maud. I just wanted you to share the wonderful news about Johnnie."

She added encouragingly, "Our troops will soon march into Mexico to make that bandit Villa regret he ever had the audacity to attack Americans." She directed, "So, let's enjoy our tea and talk about pleasant things."

Sarah became acutely aware that both women had recently endured a terrifying ordeal, and both showed tremendous strength through their attempts to regain normalcy in their lives and continue forward with hope and talk of "pleasant things."

As they worked their way through the food on each tier of the stand, they attempted to avoid talk of Villa, Columbus, and the Mexican Revolution, but it seemed that every story returned to one of those subjects. Mrs. Slocum told of Colonel Slocum's transfer from Fort Leavenworth, Kansas, to Columbus to assume command of the Thirteenth Cavalry and patrol the border because of the unrest in Mexico. Mrs. Wright related living happily with her husband for six years on their ranch in Mexico, often interacting with various military factions of the Mexican Revolution without incident until March 1, 1916. In response to Mrs. Slocum's query regarding Sarah's career as a photographer, Sarah related stumbling into photography through a birthday gift and a visit to the Madero Camp in Juárez. As much as they attempted to avoid returning to talk of the Mexican Revolution, they couldn't. It was a permanent part of their lives, a formative part of each of their histories.

When they had drained the teapot and eaten their fill, their conversation lagged. Sarah noted how weary Mrs. Wright appeared and how the cheery graciousness of Mrs. Slocum waned. Sarah, too, was ready to bring closure to the tea. She thanked both women for their hospitality and for sharing a very pleasant afternoon. While she gathered her things to depart, Mrs. Wright acknowledged Sarah's camera and asked, "Would you like to take a photograph of me? I know I'm of great curiosity to many—I'm the woman who survived capture by the famous Pancho Villa."

Though Sarah had brought her camera for that very reason, she now felt ashamed, so she replied, "I will photograph you once Johnnie is returned, and you're holding him, again, in your arms. Then you will have a photograph to cherish."

The young mother smiled.

They stood from the table and started toward the door to the lobby, with Mrs. Slocum in the lead. Once outside the dining room, they hugged and said their goodbyes. Sarah turned to make her way to the hotel exit while Mrs. Slocum and Mrs. Wright waited at the elevator to return to their rooms.

When Sarah neared the stained-glass dome, she spied Cata sitting, waiting smilingly for her. Sarah warmed at her beauty. Sarah smiled her surprised excitement at seeing Cata stand to greet her. Then, a man's voice called urgently, "Miss Delaney!" Sarah turned in the direction of the voice to see General Pershing striding across the lobby toward her.

"Miss Delaney," the general greeted her. "I saw you having tea with Mrs. Slocum and Mrs. Wright. I didn't want to interrupt, but I can't let you leave without thanking you for your kindest of notes regarding the loss of my wife and daughters."

Sarah studied the tanned face and the eyes weighed heavy with sadness.

The newspapers had announced the selection of Pershing to lead the Punitive Expedition into Mexico to pursue Villa, so Sarah wasn't surprised when the general said, "I will be leaving El Paso very soon and don't know when or if I will return, so I couldn't allow this opportunity to escape without sharing how meaningfully your thoughtful words spoke to me at my time of great loss."

Sarah blushed.

"I won't delay you longer, Miss Delaney, but I wanted you to know how much your generosity of heart meant to me. I will not forget your kindness."

"Thank you for stopping me, General Pershing. I wish you all the best."

"I wish the same for you, Miss Delaney."

When Sarah turned from the general, she saw Cata no longer stood beside the chair. Sarah looked about the lobby, searching. When she didn't see Cata, Sarah circled the area, hoping to find her among the people milling about. Still unable to see her, she hurried from the hotel, pausing on the sidewalk, hoping to catch a glimpse of Cata. She was not there. Sarah started back toward the studio and the apartment, detouring to comb the plaza for Cata before returning home.

Opening the door to the studio, Sarah called out, "Cata!" She hurried up the stairs, entering the apartment, calling "Cata!" and searching each room, to no avail.

For the next hour, Sarah paced the apartment, unable to relax or to focus her thoughts on anything but Cata. When she heard the faint jangle of the bell below, Sarah hurried to open the apartment door. She breathed her relief to see Cata at the foot of the stairs. She waited until Cata reached the apartment door to speak. "Where did you go? I've been so worried."

"I walked. I had to think." Cata entered the room and removed her hat.

"I was so happy to see you at the hotel. It was such a nice surprise, but then you just disappeared."

"I had to think," Cata repeated.

"Think about what?" Sarah asked, standing before Cata.

"That was Pershing who called to you," Cata said more as a statement than a question. "He's the general leading America's invasion of Mexico," she added, again as a statement.

"He's leading the Punitive Expedition into Mexico," Sarah responded, both verifying and correcting.

"'Punitive,' what does that word mean?"

Sarah hesitated, then answered, "punishing." She felt uncomfortable with the sound of the synonym; it seemed more menacing, more vindictive than the official sounding "Punitive Expedition."

Cata replied, "Pershing is the general leading American soldiers to punish Mexico."

"To punish Villa," Sarah corrected. She explained, "General Pershing wanted to thank me for a note I wrote to express my condolences when his wife and daughters died in a fire. I didn't arrange to meet him. I didn't know he was at the hotel."

"I know," Cata said. "I had to walk. I had to calm my heart. I had to think about us."

"Cata," Sarah pleaded, "let's not allow the craziness around us to come between us. We can't control what others do. We can only control what we do."

Cata nodded her agreement. She extended her hand to Sarah, pulling her into an embrace. "You are my love," Cata whispered, "mi corazón."

"Mi amor," Sarah replied, pressing her lips to Cata's neck. She moved back to face Cata and speak her heart. "I love you, Cata" Sarah said. "I won't ever betray you," Sarah promised.

❁❁❁

"No, Timothy, I'm sorry, but I can't join you," Sarah spoke her insistence into the phone.

"Sarah," Timothy implored, "this is historical. I can't believe you're willing to miss the Punitive Expedition's march from Columbus into Mexico."

"I'm sorry, Timothy, but I can't leave the studio today."

"Sure I can't change your mind?" he pleaded.

"I'm sure." Sarah added, "You be careful."

"All right," Timothy answered resignedly.

Sarah replaced the receiver, aware that Cata stood in the doorway. "That was Timothy," Sarah explained.

"You aren't going with him to watch America invade Mexico?" Cata asked, wording her question to leave no doubt how she viewed the Punitive Expedition.

"No. I told Timothy I wouldn't join him."

"Thank you, Sarah. My heart would wither knowing you cheered an expedition marching to punish Mexico, to punish my people."

Sarah went to Cata, cradled her face with both hands, and looked into her eyes. "I promise I'm not going to Columbus, Cata. I told Timothy 'no.'"

Cata studied Sarah for a moment before nodding her satisfaction with Sarah's response. "Thank you," Cata said softly.

Sarah responded, "Now, we both need to get ready for work."

Cata was the first to leave the apartment. Sarah followed her downstairs. Opening the studio door for Cata, Sarah said, "Be safe. I will be here when you return." Sarah watched until Cata rounded the corner, disappearing from Sarah's view.

Sarah busied herself with getting the studio ready for the day's business. She removed the till from the safe, counted the money she'd need for daily transactions, then slid the till into the drawer of the register. As Sarah prepared to unlock the front door and reverse the status sign to "OPEN," the phone rang.

"Otis Photo Studio," Sarah answered.

"Miss Delaney?" a familiar voice asked.

"This is she," Sarah answered, trying to place the woman's voice.

"This is Nurse Buckley, one of Mr. Otis's nurses."

"Yes?" Suddenly connecting the voice with the name, Sarah asked, "Is A. J. all right?"

"That's why I'm calling. I'm afraid Mr. Otis has been transported to Providence Hospital. He has pneumonia and is in critical condition."

"Oh, no!" Sarah replied, sitting hard onto the wooden stool behind her.

"He didn't want me to phone anyone, but I knew you would want to know."

"Of course, Nurse Buckley. Thank you for calling. I'll go to the hospital at once. Thank you, again."

Sarah hurried up the stairs, stumbling clumsily in her worried rush. She gathered her hat, coat, and purse and started out the door when she thought twice and paused to hurriedly write a short note for Cata: *A. J. in hospital. Gone there.* She placed the note on the kitchen table, then swung her coat over her shoulders on her way out of the apartment.

Before Sarah reached the foot of the stairs, she heard banging on the studio door. She entered the front of the studio to see Timothy smiling through the glass, pointing to his watch, and motioning for her to unlock the door.

When Sarah opened the door, Timothy, noting her hat and coat, cheerfully asked, "Change your mind? You joining me?"

"Timothy," Sarah replied, breathless in her anxiousness, "A. J. is in the hospital with pneumonia. He's in critical condition."

"I'm coming with you," Timothy responded.

Sarah paused at the counter to pen a "Closed for the Day" sign, which she taped to the glass before locking the studio door. Sarah climbed behind the steering wheel. As soon as Timothy joined her in the car's cab, she pulled into traffic, heading to the hospital and A. J.

Catalina

Catalina placed the full-length cloth apron over her head, tying it in the back, before sliding an oversleeve onto each arm. After greeting two women who just arrived, she departed the cloakroom. At her workstation, she placed a stack of boxes to the side in preparation for her day's work of filling them with the factory's signature La Internacional cigars. As she scooted her stiff wooden chair out from under her station table, she heard her name called and turned to see the shift leader standing at the door of the long, narrow packaging room.

"The manager wants to speak with you in his office." He added, "Gather all your things and come with me."

Catalina felt staggered by a request thick with threat. She pushed her chair back under her station table, then returned to the narrow cloakroom to collect her coat, hat, and bag and remove her apron and oversleeves. When she stepped from the cloakroom, the shift leader directed, "Follow me."

The women in the room avoided meeting Catalina's eyes as if her fate might be contagious. She followed the shift leader, chasing his back as he led her through a labyrinth of hallways, depositing her in front of a man who looked too boyish to be seated behind a desk equipped with a phone, typewriter, and adding machine. "Tolbert," the shift leader commanded, "inform the boss that the employee he wishes to see is here."

"Will do," the young clerk responded, springing from his chair to tap on a wooden door before opening it sufficiently to insert his head through the narrow space.

The shift leader left the room without additional comment to Catalina.

Opening the door wider, the boy-man announced, "Mr. Levy will see you now."

Catalina entered a large, cluttered office to face a man she had never met.

The disheveled-looking individual with a red, bloated face neither stood from his chair nor invited Catalina to sit, so she remained standing.

"Habla usted inglés? You speak English?"

"Yes," Cata replied.

"Good," he said. "My español is not so bueno," he grinned. "You Catalina Vasquez?"

"Yes," she verified.

"The police have been by asking if you work here and for how long."

Catalina listened, staring blankly at the rumpled manager, forcing herself to mask any emotion.

"They tell me you were a colonel in Villa's army."

Catalina did not reply since he voiced the information as a statement rather than a question.

"Don't that beat all," he laughed, "a female colonel."

Refusing to show any emotion, Catalina continued to stare at the man's bulging red cheeks.

"Well, I hear you're a good, dependable employee, but given the bloody mess in Columbus and all the ruckus Villa is causing with us Americans, I'm going to have to let you go. I can't risk the company's reputation if word got out that we have a Villista officer working for us, even if that officer is a girl." Again he chuckled, shaking his head with disbelief. "You got your paycheck on Saturday. We don't owe you anything more." He stood as he spoke, then walked to open the office door. "So if you'll leave the building at once." He stuck he head through the doorway, ordering, "Tolbert, escort this señorita to the exit."

Catalina left the office without saying a word or waiting for Tolbert to guide her from the building. The young man chased after her, anxious to fulfill his boss's bidding. "This way," he called, directing her to an exit.

Outside, Catalina began walking before realizing she headed south toward Juárez rather than east toward Sarah and the studio. She corrected her path. Deep in a fog of thought, she stepped into the street without looking; the honk of a horn startled her to awareness. She returned to stand on the corner and gather her emotional strength. Waiting for a lull in traffic, Catalina breathed deeply. She thought about the last few weeks she had worked at the cigar factory and admitted to herself that she would not miss the mindless, soul-sucking job of filling shallow boxes with cheap smelly cigars. At that moment, she made her decision: she would accept Sarah's previous offer to work with her in the studio. She would learn Sarah's craft and work alongside her. Catalina crossed the street, surprisingly relieved, anxious to tell Sarah her news.

When Catalina reached her street corner, she stopped to monitor traffic, determined not to make another careless mistake. From the corner of her eye, she glimpsed a familiar figure in front of the studio. She turned to see Timothy cranking Sarah's car, then joining Sarah on the front seat. Catalina watched the car speed recklessly from the curb into traffic.

Catalina remained frozen, staring at the space vacated by Sarah. Finally, Catalina stepped from the curb into the street. At the studio door, she stared at the "Closed for the Day" sign. Then she unlocked the door to let herself into the dark, empty storefront. Catalina went immediately up the stairs to the apartment. She called for Sarah in a vain hope that her eyes had betrayed her.

Placing her coat, hat, and bag on Sarah's chair at the kitchen table, Catalina slumped into her usual seat. She remained there, silent and still, for over an hour, stranded deep in a well of dark thoughts. Finally, she stood and entered the bedroom, determined to examine what she had only glanced at last week when she retrieved Sarah's requested handkerchiefs. Last week, Catalina looked quickly away, not wanting to confirm what she knew she saw. Now, she needed to know. Catalina pulled out the top drawer of the chifforobe. She fished beneath the folded handkerchiefs and lingerie, lifting the stack of postcards from the drawer. Catalina stared at the photo of herself dressed for duty. She shuffled through the stack, seeing her image repeated on each picture postcard. Catalina imagined grimy white hands clutching her photo, a man grinning at his newly purchased souvenir of the Mexican Revolution.

Catalina removed her valise from the closet and packed all her things she could carry. Returning to the kitchen, Catalina set the satchel on the floor and placed the stack of postcards at the center of the table. She went into the sitting room to remove a sheet of paper and pen from the secretary drawer. On the unlined paper, she wrote, *¡Me traicionaste!* Catalina returned to the kitchen to place the note alongside the postcards. Then, she unclasped the heart-shaped pendant from around her neck and lay it across the stack of postcards. Catalina picked up her valise, draped her coat over one arm, and left the apartment and Sarah.

Sarah

Sarah entered the studio exhausted but relieved. A. J. seemed to be responding positively to the anti-pneumococcal serum therapy initiated by the physicians at the hospital, and though A. J. protested that he wasn't a child, he did allow Sarah to feed him a cup of broth. When A. J. slept with less strained breathing, Timothy and she left the hospital after securing a promise from one of A. J.'s nurses to call Sarah if his condition worsened.

Crumpling the "Closed for the Day" sign, Sarah climbed the stairs to the apartment. She looked forward to a quiet evening with Cata. Sarah decided to change clothes and begin preparing one of Cata's favorite meals, knowing that today's start of the Punitive Expedition would weigh heavily on Cata's heart. Entering the kitchen, she noticed the small pile at the center of the table and thought Cata must be home. She called, "Cata!" When she heard no response, she walked over to the table to examine the items. She froze at the sight of the postcards and necklace. Then she read the note written in Spanish: *You betrayed me!* Sarah screamed, "No, no!" She dashed into the bedroom to open drawers and doors of the chifforobe only to find them empty of Cata's belongings. Sarah shouted, "Cata, no!" She raced from the bedroom, out the apartment door, down the stairs, and outside the studio in a frantic search for Cata, who she knew did not want to be found.

OCTOBER 12, 1983

Kayla

"The next morning," the elderly woman said softly, "I found my note telling Cata I'd gone to the hospital to be with A. J. It lay on the floor beneath a chair. The note must have blown from the kitchen table. Cata never saw it."

"Let's stop here," Kayla announced, concerned to see Sarah physically sag with sadness. "Are you all right, Sarah?"

Sarah cleared her throat. "Yes. Please excuse me for a moment."

"Yes, of course," Kayla replied as Sarah stood from her chair, placing her hand briefly on the side table for balance before departing the room. Kayla and Abel exchanged uneasy looks. "I'm afraid these interviews are increasingly wearing for Sarah." Kayla quietly spoke her concern to Abel, who nodded in agreement, his brow furrowed with worry.

Kayla walked to the photograph she had examined on their first visit to Sarah's home. Kayla studied the image of the young soldadera, who returned her gaze with a bold, confident stare. "This must be Cata,"

Kayla said over her shoulder to Abel.

Abel moved behind Kayla to look at the framed black-and-white picture hanging on the wall. "Beautiful," he uttered.

"She was extraordinary," the old woman announced, reentering the room.

Surprised by Sarah's return, Kayla stammered, "This is Cata?"

"Yes, she is Cata."

"She is striking," Abel said.

"Yes, truly wonderful," Sarah added.

Kayla flinched when Abel asked Sarah, "Did you find her? Did you ever see Cata again?"

"Let me sit," Sarah said, sounding weary with emotion.

Kayla returned to her seat across from Sarah while Abel continued examining the photograph.

"I looked everywhere I knew to search." Sarah studied the backs of her hands as she spoke. "I looked every day for weeks, for months. Timothy and Paola searched, too, asking acquaintances if they had seen her, engaging sources to search for her in El Paso and Juárez. But Cata had vanished." Sarah folded her hands on her lap. "She may have left the border to try to reunite with her brothers, or she may have rejoined Villa and the revolution. I don't know." Sarah shut her eyes tightly. "She simply vanished."

Kayla and Abel remained silent, allowing the old woman space to tell her pain.

Sarah opened her eyes. "I never stopped looking for Cata. Never." The old woman smiled sadly. "Life has a sense of humor."

Kayla tilted her head questioningly.

"I found Cata a few months ago."

"Cata's alive!" Abel blurted.

"Yes," Sarah assured him. "Cata is an old woman, as am I, but she is alive. She lives in Juárez with a son she took in as a boy. He's in his fifties now, stronger in body than in mind."

"How did you find her?" Kayla asked.

"I saw her one day outside of a Juárez mercado. I was with my housekeeper. We followed Cata home."

"Did you try to speak with her?" Abel asked, entranced by the story.

"No," Sarah looked away. "After so many years of searching, I couldn't bear to lose her again if she learned I found her."

"So you know where she lives?" Kayla asked.

"Yes," Sarah answered. "Ironically, she has an apartment not far from the hills where the insurrectos camped before the first Battle of Juárez."

"And you're sure it's Cata?" Kayla asked. "I mean, it's been, what, almost seventy years, Sarah." She gently added, "People change."

Sarah chuckled. "Yes, we do," and she traced her fingers across wrinkles on her face. She grew serious again. "She is Cata. I'm sure."

"I wonder if she lived in Juárez all those years," Abel said.

"No," Sarah responded. "Her son, Chuy, said she returned to the city in the sixties."

"You've talked to her son?" Kayla asked incredulously.

"Yes." She explained further. "He doesn't know who I am. He only knows I'm a lady who buys the crepe-paper flowers he sells, the flowers his mother creates."

Kayla and Abel both looked at the bouquets of flowers Sarah had given them upon their arrival.

"Cata made our flowers?" Abel asked with astonishment.

"Yes."

OCTOBER 17, 1983

Kayla

Kayla depressed a nonexistent brake pedal on the passenger side of the car as Abel steered, one hand on the wheel, through downtown Juárez. She gripped her armrest at the stop and start of cars, bumper to bumper, changing lanes with only inches and car horns separating them from disaster.

"You know where you're going?" Kayla asked, needing reassurance.

"I'm pretty sure," Abel replied.

Kayla looked out the side window while they drove west from downtown. "You know that Sarah has manipulated us masterfully into doing her bidding?"

"Yes," Abel replied, without looking away from traffic. "But I don't mind."

"Nor I. I just hope we can deliver. I don't think I could bear to see Sarah's pain if Cata isn't Cata."

"Or if Cata refuses to speak with us," Abel added.

They entered neighborhoods of cinderblock and adobe homes, many built along the arch of hills that rose from the river. Cyan, lavender, lime, and pink gave a colorful richness to many of the houses, even a few that looked one door slam away from collapse.

When Abel turned onto a narrow road knifing steeply toward the river, Kayla expressed surprise that they now drove almost directly across from The University of Texas at El Paso, which rose from foothills on the American side of the border. Nestled against a mountainous backdrop, the university's Bhutanese architecture of thick sloping walls, recessed windows, red brick trim punctuated with colorful mandalas gave the campus a Shangri La-like quality. Kayla wondered how residents of this Juárez neighborhood felt viewing the conspicuous wealth across the thin thread of river separating Mexico from the United States.

The drop from paved to dirt road brought Kayla back to the mission at hand.

Abel soon slowed to park in front of a one-story cinderblock structure with three scarred doors facing the street. Looking up from a folded piece of paper he slid out of his jeans' pocket, Abel pointed to the first door. "According to this address, Cata lives in that apartment."

Kayla sat momentarily motionless, her pulse racing. It felt as though they were preparing to meet a ghost. She took a deep breath to settle her nerves before signaling to Abel. "Let's go introduce ourselves to Coronela Catalina Vasquez."

At Abel's knock, a woman's voice called out, "Un momento." Kayla and Abel glanced at each other in nervous anticipation.

The door opened sufficiently to reveal an elderly woman.

Abel greeted her, "Buenas tardes, Señora Vasquez."

"Buenas tardes," the old woman replied, shielding her eyes with one hand to better see the person addressing her.

Kayla allowed Abel to take the lead since his fluency in Spanish surpassed hers. He introduced himself and Kayla, identifying that they worked at The University of Texas at El Paso, UTEP, and he pointed toward the university across the river. They both extended their business cards to the old woman, who placed them in her apron pocket without a look. When Abel explained they would like to interview her about her life during the Mexican Revolution, the old woman stepped outside the apartment, closing the door behind her.

"That was a lifetime ago. What is it you want to know and why?" she challenged.

"You were a coronela in Villa's División del Norte, verdad, true?"

"Sí," she replied, offering no additional information.

Abel explained that, as part of their Institute of Oral History at UTEP, Kayla and he were interviewing individuals who lived during the Mexican Revolution. He told her that through interviews, they are working to preserve the experiences and knowledge of people such as herself for the education of future generations. While Abel spoke, Kayla studied the elderly woman, trying to see the Cata of Sarah's youth. Though slight, Señora Vasquez still stood without an aged stoop to her shoulders. Her white hair, secured with a decorative clip in the back, curled freely. A lifetime of labor lined Señora Vasquez's still handsome face; her eyes retained a fierceness.

"What do you want from me?"

"Señora Vasquez, we would like to film an interview with you in your home," Abel explained.

The sudden opening of a door at the neighboring apartment caused all of them to turn. A man in his twenties stepped outside to look at Abel, then Sarah. He asked in Spanish, "Is everything all right, Señora Vasquez?"

"Yes, thank you, Paco. All is okay." She added, chuckling, "They want me to star in their film about the Mexican Revolution."

He smiled, responding, "You are a star, Señora Vasquez. I'm right here if you need anything," he concluded protectively before reentering his apartment.

"So may we interview you, Señora Vasquez?" Abel asked.

The old woman shook her head, looking first at Abel then at Kayla. "You Americans think everything in Mexico is for the taking, even our memories."

"Señora Vasquez," Able calmly responded, "My full name is Abel Humberto Castellano Vega. I live in El Paso because my grandparents fled the violence of the revolution. Your history *is* part of my history and the history of millions of people who live along the border. Please allow us to honor your memories by recording them so others will know of your life, your struggles, and your joys."

The old woman paused, clearly reconsidering the request. She released a deep breath before responding resignedly, "Por qué no? Why not?" Adding quickly, "Not today. Mañana. One hour. No camera."

Abel looked to Kayla. "Sí," Kayla agreed, trying to mask her excitement. "Gracias, Señora Vasquez."

OCTOBER 18, 1983

Kayla

Kayla recognized the road that began the steep descent to Cata's apartment.

"How are you going to broach the subject of Sarah?" Abel asked.

"I don't know."

Kayla chewed the inside of her cheek as Abel brought the car to a halt in front of the cinderblock building. They exchanged encouraging looks before exiting the vehicle, Kayla gripping her notepad and pen, Abel carrying the satchel with two tape recorders.

Cata answered their knock, opening the door to invite them into the apartment. As Kayla entered, she reintroduced herself, extending her hand, and was surprised by the size and strength of the hand that filled hers.

"Por favor siéntate," the old woman directed them to a wooden table with three chairs.

Though the room darkened noticeably when the señora closed the door behind them, Kayla managed a quick inventory of the small, neat apartment as she took her seat. She glimpsed two bedrooms behind this front room, which appeared to be the main living area. A small refrigerator hummed noisily against the back wall between doorways exiting to the bedrooms. In this larger living area, an old narrow gas stove occupied one corner opposite a metal sink at the other end. Across the room, resting atop an upturned wooden crate, a small TV faced a blanket-draped love seat. Along the wall, between the love seat and TV, a garden of crepe-paper flowers sprouted from cardboard boxes.

Kayla took the seat Cata designated for her; the old woman then sat across from Kayla, facing the front door. Cata sat stiffly, her hands resting in fists on the wooden table.

To relax the tension, Abel attempted to exchange pleasantries with the señora, but she replied, "Una hora, no más," holding up a single finger to remind them of the agreed upon time limit.

"Sí, señora," Abel acknowledged. He opened the satchel to reveal two tape recorders. "May we tape the interview?" Abel asked.

"I don't know why anyone would want to hear more than once what I have to say, but you may record the interview if you desire."

While Abel removed the two tape recorders, positioning them at the center of the table, Kayla asked, "Do you speak English, Señora Vasquez?"

Cata turned from Abel to Kayla. The old woman's face remained impassive. "I prefer Spanish."

"I'm not as fluent in Spanish as Abel, so I may have to ask him for assistance."

Cata nodded.

"Testing one, two," Abel spoke into each recorder, playing back the message to ensure the recorders worked properly. "We're good to go."

Kayla took a moment to explain to Cata how the interview would work, that she would ask a question to start the session and that she may ask additional questions for clarification or to redirect the conversation.

"Profesora," Cata responded, her tone not unfriendly but direct, "you may ask what questions you wish. I will choose what questions I answer."

"Fair enough," Kayla replied, choking back a startled laugh. Regaining her composure, she said, "Let's begin, then."

Kayla signaled Abel to start recording. "Señora Catalina Vasquez Interview, Ciudad Juárez, 1:14 p.m., October 18, 1983."

In the shortness of an hour, Cata shared the story of her family's flight from the hacienda and told her memories of the revolution and her time in El Paso. She mentioned names familiar to Kayla and Abel through Sarah's interviews, but Cata referred to Sarah only briefly and only as the photographer. The old woman ended the interview abruptly, stating, "When people ask how I became involved in the Mexican Revolution, I tell them it's like asking how does a person become involved in an eclipse? I lived. That's how I became involved." She folded her hands in front of her on the table. "I've given you an hour," Cata concluded.

Kayla glanced at her watch and concurred. "You have, Señora Vasquez, and we appreciate your time and willingness to share your memories."

"I shared more than memories. I shared my life," the old woman corrected.

"Yes," Kayla agreed. "We thank you for your generosity. Your interview along with others we have collected will help historians and students better understand experiences of people during the Mexican Revolution."

"There can't be many of us still living. So many died in the revolution and so many more have died in the years since." Cata paused, looking briefly away. "I'm alive only because my heart lacks the wisdom to stop beating. I have lived a lifetime beyond most of my family, most of those I love," she added.

"We've interviewed someone you know." Kayla spoke before she fully formed what she wanted to say. "Someone who knew you during the revolution and remembers you fondly."

The old woman turned, pinning Kayla with her eyes.

"Sarah Delaney," Kayla said softly.

Cata's eyes filled with tears; she turned her head away from Kayla and Abel.

"Sarah would like to see you," Kayla added.

"You need to leave," Cata replied, regaining her composure.

"I've upset you. I'm sorry." Kayla reached across the table to take the old woman's hand.

Cata removed her hand from Kayla's. "The hour is over." She stood.

"Yes," Kayla agreed, pushing back from the table to stand.

Abel retrieved the two recorders, securing them in the satchel.

"Ready," he announced to Kayla.

The old woman followed behind, ushering them toward the door. Kayla paused with her hand on the knob and said, "Thank you for your time, Señora Vasquez. You have been most generous."

"De nada," Cata replied dismissively.

Kayla stopped just outside the apartment when she heard Abel say, "Señora Vasquez, here is my phone number." She saw Abel press a card into Cata's hand. "I know you can't change the past," he said, "but you can change how you remember it. Call me if you wish to see Sarah."

OCTOBER 21, 1983

Sarah

"Here they are, Sarah," Kayla said, waving through the driver's side window of their parked car.

Sarah caught a glimpse of Abel behind the wheel of a blue Toyota Celica as he drove slowly past before U-turning to park behind them. Sarah tried to calm her racing heart and slow her breathing.

"Ready?" Kayla asked, placing her hand on Sarah's shoulder.

"Yes," Sarah answered, leaning forward to exit without first releasing her seatbelt. She laughed nervously at her mistake as Kayla lifted the latch to free her.

"Let me help you get out of the car," Kayla said, then hurried to the passenger side.

But Sarah couldn't wait. Pushing open the car door, she scooted from her seat to stand and face Cata, who walked toward her. "I would recognize you anywhere," Sarah said as Cata neared, Abel at her elbow.

"We've grown old," Cata replied.

"Yes," Sarah agreed, "we've grown old."

"Why don't the two of you sit on the bench under the tree," Kayla suggested, taking Sarah's arm.

Sarah sat first. When Cata joined Sarah on the bench, Kayla said, "Abel and I will sit a couple of benches over. Stay as long as you like. When you're ready to leave, just let us know."

Sarah nodded, remaining silent until she saw Kayla and Abel seated. Then she began to speak. "I have so much to tell you, Cata, so much I want to say."

"Then tell me, Sarah. We don't have time not to say what needs to be said."

"I never betrayed you."

Cata waved her hand as though shooing a fly.

"Just listen, Cata. I did not betray you." Sarah met Cata's cold stare. Sarah told of A. J.'s pneumonia, the rushed drive with Timothy to the hospital, the note explaining her absence blown from the table, the postcards A. J. mistakenly printed that were never sold. As she explained the events of that day, Sarah saw Cata's hard look soften and her eyes tear. "I searched for you every day, Cata. I never stopped looking."

Cata reached across the bench and placed her hand briefly to Sarah's face.

Sarah wiped her eyes with the knuckle of a forefinger. "Our lives could have been so different."

"Our lives are what they are," Cata answered.

Sarah reached into the pocket of her blouse and removed the heart pendant, which she dangled from its chain, placing the gold heart on the palm of her outstretched hand. "This necklace is yours. It's always been yours." She extended her hand. "Will you take it?"

Cata looked at the necklace, then lifted it from Sarah's hand. She studied the heart before placing it to her lips. She fastened the chain around her neck, then touched her fingertips to the pendant that hung gracefully between her breasts. She sighed and said, "I should return to my apartment, Sarah. My son will be home soon. He will worry if I'm not there."

Sarah nodded she understood.

Cata pressed her hands against the seat of the bench to stand.

Sarah followed, standing beside her. Cata stepped forward, wrapping

Sarah in an embrace, kissing her gently on the cheek. "I never stopped loving you," Cata whispered before releasing Sarah.

Sarah watched Cata walk toward the blue car, watched as Abel trotted to meet and assist her onto the front seat. He gave a quick wave, throwing a kiss to Sarah before jogging to the driver's side.

Kayla joined Sarah, who said softly, "Let's wait until they drive away."

Sarah and Kayla exchanged brief waves with Cata when the car pulled from the curb. They continued watching until Abel turned right at the corner, disappearing into traffic.

"Ready to go?" Kayla asked, placing an arm around Sarah's waist.

"Yes."

Walking to the car, Kayla asked, "Will Cata and you meet again?"

"I don't know. I hope so," Sarah answered, then added, "but if not, we said what needed saying."

Kayla opened the car door and assisted Sarah onto the seat.

They drove to Sarah's house without speaking. When Kayla pulled to the curb, Sarah turned to her and said, "Thank you, Kayla. And please thank Abel for me. The two of you have allowed me to rewrite the history of my life."

"You're very welcome, Sarah. Wait," she encouraged, "let me walk you to your door."

At the front door, Sarah inserted her key into the lock, then turned to hug Kayla goodbye.

"May I call you in a day or so to check on you?"

"Yes," Sarah answered, "I would like that." She entered the house. Holding the door ajar, Sarah added, "Give me a couple of weeks before scheduling our next interview."

Kayla expressed her surprise. "You're willing to continue with the interviews?"

"The Mexican Revolution didn't end until 1920." Sarah smiled, adding, "as Timothy would say, 'I'm here to tell the tales I heard told.' I still have stories to share."

The End

ACKNOWLEDGEMENTS

Light, Which Impresses is historical fiction. All of the novel's major characters are fictional; however, real people or combinations of people who lived in the El Paso/Juárez area during the Mexican Revolution inspired two of the book's major characters: Captain Samuel Clendenin and Timothy Tompkins.

Oscar G. Creighton (aka Oscar Merrit Wheelock, aka James T. Hazzard) served as a model, in part, for the character Captain Samuel Clendenin. Creighton was a captain in Francisco Madero's army, earning the nickname "Dynamite Devil" for his prowess at destroying rail lines and bridges. Though his history prior to joining the revolution is murky, he is rumored to have engaged in various criminal endeavors. After he was killed in battle on April 15, 1911 (weeks prior to the Battle of Juárez depicted in part one of *Light, Which Impresses*), his body was exhumed from its battlefield grave and returned with honors to El Paso. Creighton is discussed in several books written about the Mexican Revolution, including *The Secret War in El Paso: Mexican Revolution Intrigue, 1906–1920*, by Charles H. Harris III and Louis R. Sadler.

Ivor Thord-Gray, who served as an officer with Pancho Villa, loosely informed Clendenin's Arizona gun-running episode. Thord-Gray provided a brief description of this gun-smuggling experience in his book *Gringo Rebel (Mexico 1913–1914)*.

The journalist Timothy Turner inspired the character Timothy Tompkins. In his book *Bullets, Bottles and Gardenias*, Turner detailed his experiences writing for an El Paso newspaper, especially during the Mexican Revolution. His descriptions of Ciudad Juárez after the 1911 battle provided some of the visual specifics included in *Light, Which Impresses*. Additionally, as a reporter, Turner traveled into Mexico aboard a press car attached to one of Villa's trains. Turner's journey to the interior of Mexico informed, in part, Tompkins's ill-fated trip in the novel.

Otis A. Aultman was a prolific photographer who lived in El Paso during the Mexican Revolution. His work instructed several of the scenes and photos described in *Light, Which Impresses*. Mary A. Sarber and Charles H. Binion provide a sampling of Aultman's work in *Photographs from the Border: The Otis A. Aultman Collection*.

Many books and articles furnished historical background for the novel. In addition to books identified above, the following sources proved most beneficial to me: *Ringside Seat to a Revolution: An Underground Cultural History of El Paso and Juárez, 1893–1923*, by David Dorado Romo; *The Life and Times of Pancho Villa*, by Friedrich Katz; and *The General and the Jaguar: Pershing's Hunt for Pancho Villa*, by Eileen Welsome. Additionally, newspaper archives—especially the *El Paso Morning Times* and the *El Paso Herald*—made available electronically through *The Portal to Texas History* at the University of North Texas afforded an invaluable window into events of the period and attitudes of El Pasoans during the Mexican Revolution.

Thanks to Sandra Blystone, Kathleen Condon, Sharon Owen, and Connie Wasem Scott for providing comment and encouragement during the earliest partial draft of the manuscript. Many thanks to Lupe Lopez and Valeria Delmar for assisting with the Spanish in the novel. My appreciation to Dr. Ann Gabbert for discussions about typhoid and tuberculosis in El Paso during the early twentieth century.

I would especially like to thank Connie Gamboa for her multiple close readings of the novel and for her constant, unwavering encouragement and support.

Finally, I would like to recognize my father, Col. (ret.) James W. Ward, a dedicated photographer of the border, for instilling in me a love for El Paso and the history of the region.

ABOUT THE AUTHOR

Dorothy P. Ward earned a PhD in English and American literature from the University of North Texas. For more than thirty years, she served as an administrator and faculty member at The University of Texas at El Paso. Currently, she lives on the outskirts of El Paso, Texas, with two unruly German shepherds, a blue-eyed horse, and a rescue donkey.

www.ingramcontent.com/pod-product-compliance
Lightning Source LLC
Chambersburg PA
CBHW020837020726
47497CB00005B/1138